C000140672

FINDING REDEMPTION

THE ROLLIN ON SERIES, #5

EMILIA FINN

bee*lieve*
PUBLISHING, Pty Ltd.

FINDING REDEMPTION

By: Emilia Finn

Copyright 2018. Emilia Finn

Publisher: Beelieve Publishing, Pty Ltd.

Cover Design: Amy Queue

Editing: Brandi Bumstead

ISBN: 9781792702303

This Book is licensed for your personal enjoyment only. This Book may not be re-sold or given away to other people. If you would like to share this book with another person, please purchase an additional copy for each person. If you're reading this book and did not purchase it, or it was not purchased for your use only, then please return and purchase your own copy.

To obtain permission to excerpt portions of the text, please contact the author at **info@emiliafinn.com**

This book is a work of fiction. The names, characters, places, and incidents are products of Emilia Finn's imagination or have been used fictitiously and are not to be construed as real. Any resemblance to persons, living or dead, actual events, locale, or organizations is entirely coincidental.

www.emiliafinn.com

The best way to stay in touch is to subscribe to Emilia's newsletter: Emiliafinn.com/signup

If you don't hear from her regularly, please check your junk/spam folder and set her emails to safe/not spam, that way, you won't miss new books, chances to win amazing prizes, or possible appearances in your area.

Kindle readers: follow Emilia on **Amazon** to be notified of new releases as they become available.

Bookbub readers: follow Emilia on **Bookbub** to be notified of new releases as they become available.

For Arelis.
Because the love you and M share is the kind we all wait and hope and wish for.
Tink's just for you, and I hope she's as awesome as you are.
xxx

ALSO BY EMILIA FINN

Full House

No Limits

Bluff

Seven Card Stud

Crazy Eights

Eleusis

Dynamite

Busted

Gilded Knights (Rosa Brothers)

Redeeming The Rose

Chasing Fire

Animal Instincts

Inamorata

The Fiera Princess

The Fiera Ruins

The Fiera Reign

Rollin On Novellas

(Do not read before finishing the Rollin On Series)

Begin Again – A Short Story

Written in the Stars – A Short Story

Full Circle – A Short Story

Worth Fighting For – A Bobby & Kit Novella

LOOKING TO CONNECT?

Website
Facebook
Newsletter
Email
The Crew

Did you know you can get a FREE book? Go to emiliafinn.com/signup to get your free copy sent direct to your inbox.

FINDING REDEMPTION

THE ROLLIN ON SERIES, #5

Emilia Finn

PROLOGUE
PRESENT TIME - TINK

*D*ancing elephants pound inside my head. Cymbals, the kind kids use to annoy their folks, clang against my brain and set every nerve ending in my body on fire. What tastes like vomit and mud sticks like a thick paste on my tongue, so thick, so gross, I have to work hard not to heave as the taste hits my senses.

I'm hot, overheated and sweaty, and I can barely breathe as a boulder pins me down.

I groan and try to roll, but my body aches like a train hit me and squished me dead.

Probably not the most tasteful analogy to use anymore, but whatever. I'm hungover and sick. I'm dying.

And I can't breathe.

Pulling my arm free with a jerk, I attempt to roll to escape this sweaty, hot bed of death, but a large hand latches onto my hip and hot breath bathes the back of my neck. "Not time to get up yet, Sunshine."

I freeze at the mumbled words.

No.

No!

This can't be happening again.

Opening a single gritty eye, I look down my body to the muscled forearm pinning me down, the tattoos I know by heart, the large hand that walks along my ribs and cups my boob even as its owner sleeps.

I painfully close my eye again, like closing a rusty shutter over a dirty window and scraping along the tracks the whole way down.

I'm pissed at myself for falling back into bed with him.

Again.

Why do I keep falling into *his* bed? Why him? Why can't I stop?

I don't want what he's offering. Not anymore. It almost always hurts. And not the good hurt. The hurt that squeezes your heart and makes your soul bleed.

I don't even remember our night together, which is the bitch of the situation. If I'm going to sleep with Jon Hart, at least the universe should let me remember it.

It was probably good, too.

The bastard knows how to rock my world.

Flashes of Tina's quickie wedding, Korean Elvis, casino bells and lights whir through my brain. Shot races with Jon. Glass after glass after glass of tequila lined up on the bar, and my stubborn ass trying to keep up despite the fact I'm literally half his size.

I should've gone to bed. Alone.

I shouldn't have stepped up to the challenge when he said I was done, that I should stop dancing, that I was going to kill myself with alcohol poisoning.

Fuck that. He should've known I wouldn't walk away all meek and shit.

I'm not a meek girl!

No doubt, he laid down the challenge on purpose. He knows me. He knows I'd never walk away. And he *knows* tequila means blowjob.

Every damn time.

Fuck that asshole.

I bring my left hand up to brush dirty hair out of my eyes – I'm ready to get this asshole off me and get lost – but let out an involuntary "Ow" when I whack the side of my face with something metal.

Slow, uncoordinated, lethargic and dizzy, I bring my hand up into the space above my face as the weight on my finger makes itself known. Slitting my eyes open and weeping at the feel of rusty shutters, I squint at the silver band, the cheap red gem and the circular face.

An engraved line circles the center of the thick band, and indented dots follow it around.

Is that… R2-D2? Star Wars?

When reality fights its way through the fog and realization hits me like that fucking train, I whip my head around and come nose to nose with a still sleeping, still heavy, still beautiful asshole as he pins me down.

My stomach drops.

This can't be real.

We didn't…

We couldn't…

No! We definitely wouldn't have…

No way would *he* have! No matter how drunk I get, he could never be *that* drunk.

Flying out of the king-sized bed with fresh energy, silky sheets whip away from my naked body as I race around and grab my crap.

My skirt. My sparkly top. My heels that even in this moment, I can admit are hot as shit. I throw them on, then freeze as my heart and brain explode at the sight of our marriage certificate.

Our marriage certificate.

What the ever-loving fuck!

Jon's signature sits right next to mine in a deep black ink.

Snatching the paper up and holding my breath so I don't hurl all over the fancy room, I fold it into a tiny square and shove it inside my purse. Grabbing my phone and whatever other shit I see floating around, with one last glimpse toward the man still asleep on the bed in the middle of the room, I race out the door and into the hall.

I need to get out of here.

Now.

I need to get a divorce, preferably before he wakes up.

I can't do this again.

I can't ride this train to hell again.

I barely survived the last round.

PART I

THE BEGINNING

1

JON

WAY BACK

Seven years old.
The last day before Summer break.

a hard knock to the back of my head has me spinning with raised fists, but before I can hit him back, he's bouncing on his toes and grinning like a dick.

"You're an asshole! Give my hat back!"

Dropping it onto his moppy hair, he bounces and brings his fists up. "Nah. I like it, so now it's mine." He skips to the side with a loud giggle when I surge forward. Parrying my arms to the side, he ducks to my left and dances like he's Apollo Creed. "And asshole's a naughty word. I'm gonna tell my mom."

"I don't give a shit about your mom! Just give me my hat and piss off."

He skips around without a care in the world. "I don't wanna give it back. I like it, so I'm gonna keep it."

He's such a loudmouth, show off asshole. He likes to dance. He likes it when the girls stop to watch. He reminds me of the peacocks I sometimes see on our shitty TV. But only when the picture's okay.

And only when my folks aren't home.

He's the popular kid who walks around school with a stupid grin and fancy shoes. He *loves* the attention. He loves it the same way my mom loves it.

Other moms don't dress the way she does; with her smelly perfume, her short skirts. Her *click-clack-clack* shoes, and her jiggly boobs.

My mom likes when people look at her. She loves it.

"Come and get it, Jon *Fart*."

Turning to keep him in view as he bounces around me, I narrow my eyes and think of ways I can beat his ass. "That's not my name, asshole. Give me my hat!"

"You're gonna have to take it, *Fart*."

"C'mon, Bobby." Aiden Kincaid steps up and has me moving back to keep them both in sight. "Just give his hat back. I wanna go home."

Aiden Kincaid's not a loudmouth like his big brother, but blood runs thicker than water. He'll hold me down so Bobby can kick my ass.

Again.

"I don't wanna give it back." He bounces on the balls of his feet, ducking and swaying the way Ali does.

Kids laugh and crowd us. They point and pick sides.

Bobby.

They're *all* on Bobby's side.

I don't want to give up on my hat. Besides ratty sneakers, and my too-small shirt and jeans, it's the only thing I own. I really want it back.

But I have to go…

The bell already rang. I have to get home. My baby sister's there, and she needs protection from them.

I can't let them keep her. Hurt her. *Taint* her.

"Bobby." Aiden's drawl sounds almost grown up, though we're still in elementary school. "Just give it back. Stop being a jerk."

"Make me–"

"I'll make you."

I jump back so fast, I almost fall on my ass. A huge man picks Bobby up by the scruff of his collar and shakes until Bobby's face turns white like Casper.

I want to smile. I want to shout *'that's karma for you, bitch!'* but I don't. Instead, with sick whooshing in my belly and the knowledge that if he catches me, I won't ever get home to Sissy, I turn on my feet.

Screw the hat, he can keep it.

"Dad–"

"Boy!" The man's commanding voice has my body locking up in terror. My chest thumps hard, and my hands sweat. "Stop for a sec. Is this your hat?"

If I run while he's holding Bobby, I could probably make it to the parking lot before he catches me. I run fast. I do it every day. I could hide between the cars, lay under one until this dude leaves.

"Seriously kid, don't run." The man sighs. "Bobby, what's his name?"

"I'm sorry Da–"

"Don't tell me you're sorry. You're only sorry you got caught. Answer my question."

"Jon. His name's Jon."

"Right." He puts Bobby down onto brand-new high-top sneakers that take his weight easily. "Give Jon his hat back." He turns to all the kids watching and jabs a finger into the distance. "Clear off. It's summer break, go home!"

Taking my hat off his head and stepping forward, Bobby's hands shake and have me taking a second look at the big man.

Is he scared of him?

Bobby's an asshole, but if he's scared, I can help.

Probably.

Maybe.

"Here ya go. Sorry."

"Bobby."

He jumps like the man's word is a gunshot. "Yeah, Dad?"

"What are bullies?"

His eyes drop to my feet and have me nervously shuffling them. My shoes aren't like his. Mine are torn and crappy. Mine came from a dumpster.

His sadness should make me happy. I should be cheering that someone bigger and badder than Bobby has shut him down, but I'm not.

I've never seen him sad before. Peacocks don't get sad.

"Bullies are cowards, Dad."

"So why are you bullying Jon?"

My name coming from this man's mouth has me taking another step back. Not a single man in this world is good. They hurt. They hit and grab, they shove and they control.

When you're someone's punching bag, you learn to run fast.

When they're faster, you learn not to cry.

"I was just trying to have fun, Dad."

"Did it look like Jon was having fun?"

Bobby's eyes stay low. "No sir, it didn't."

"I don't raise bullies, Robert. Real men don't bully. Real men help others. We extend a hand and help them up. If we pick on them, then we're just assholes."

Aiden's eyes snap wide. "Dad!"

Grinning, the man turns to his second son. "Don't tell your mother I said asshole."

Aiden giggles and throws his head back. His backpack covers most of his body from head to toe as he shakes from silly laughter. "You just said it again!"

The man's lip curls up at the side. "Don't tell her I said it twice and I'll buy you ice-cream."

Bobby's sad eyes light and snap up. "Can I have ice-cream too, Dad?"

"Yeah, you want some? What's your favorite flavor, B?"

Bobby grins and licks his lips like a dumbass. "Salted caramel. That's my favorite."

The man turns to me with a kind smile. "Jon?" I don't answer him, I just swallow my spit and take another step back. "Jon, do you like salted caramel ice-cream?" I take another step back. Adults don't do nice things for boys like me. This is a trick. "Well, kid? Do you like it?"

I nod softly. I'll say anything he wants, but I wouldn't actually know. I've never had salted caramel. I've never had ice-cream at all.

He smiles, and when he claps his hands together, I jump. "Good. You get Bobby's today."

"Dad!"

"Bullies are cowards, son. Bullies are assholes. I don't buy ice-cream for assholes."

"But–"

"So next time, you'll think about today and you'll remember to be a friend. Then maybe you'll get ice-cream."

"But–"

The man's dark eyes turn angry and have Bobby swallowing. "Do. You. Understand?"

Sad again, Bobby nods toward the ground. "Yes, sir."

"Good. Now hug it out."

"Dad!" Looking around the playground, though all the other kids already left, he turns back and hisses, "I'll hug you when we get home."

Smiling, he shakes his head. "I love you, son, but I didn't mean me. Hug *him*. Hug it out."

"Dad!"

As soon as the man's dark brown eyes flash the way a General might when his cadet disobeys a direct order, Bobby shrinks back. Resigned, he steps toward me and sends my face white with dread. "Just do it, man, or neither of us will ever get ice-cream again."

I shrug. "Fine with me." *Can't miss something you've never had.*

Even though I don't want it, Bobby takes the remaining steps forward and throws his long monkey arms over my shoulders. I tense up. I know he's not trying to hurt me, but my ribs smart anyway.

They've hurt since last weekend when my dad was pissed.

"I'm only hugging you because I want ice-cream," he whispers in my ear. He squeezes my shoulder tight. Too tight. And leaves me breathless.

In defense, I bring my fist up and tag him in the ribs. "And you're still an asshole. I hate you, Kincaid."

"Good job." The man rests a hand on our shoulders and pulls us apart. "Now let's get some ice-cream. Except Bobby, he just gets to watch."

"Aww, Dad!"

2

JON

A LITTLE LESS WAY BACK

Nine years old.
It's my birthday.

"Alright, Sissy. Put your shoes on." I scrub a hand over my face to wipe away the exhaustion and stress that sits heavy on my shoulders. Stuffing my backpack with clothes, a blanket, and my stashed jar of peanut butter, I tear the zipper closed, then reach under my bed and grab a couple books, shoving them in the front pocket.

One book is new; my birthday gift to myself. I stole it from the school library last week, put it down my pants, and walked right out. I know stealing is bad, but I did it anyway. The other is forever old, with faded and frayed pages from overuse.

I stole that one, too.

"Come on, Iz. We gotta go."

"Where's soos?" Her voice slurs, because her pacifier's too big and gives her a lisp. That's okay; I speak fluent toddler.

"Under my bed. Quick Sissy, put your boots on."

My baby sister turns excitedly, bouncing on her tiptoes like we're going for an adventure at the park. She's always happy, even in this shithole. She never cries. She never whines. She sleeps all night cradled in the hollow my knees and chest make, sucking her pacifier and snoring lightly.

I'll never let that light dim from her eyes if I can help it.

That means we have to get out of this house.

Now.

My folks ran into some extra cash today, so Dad got extra booze. When he gets drunk, he gets mean. Then my mom gets meaner, because she doesn't like it when he's a dick to her.

When he starts hitting her – his *preferred* punching bag – she takes her licks, then when he passes out, she comes looking for me like it's my fault.

And I can't even hate when she's around, because when she's not, he cuts out the middle man and comes looking for me instead.

This place is my own personal hell.

"Done." Iz jumps up with so much momentum, her soggy diaper sags between her legs. It's *only* wet, it doesn't stink, and I don't have any spares, so it stays.

"Come on." I fling my bag over my back and hiss at the sharp sting that burns through my body. Holding my breath and clenching all my muscles, I take her hand and hold in the scream I so wish I could release.

"Where going?"

I let it out on a silent gasp. "Fort."

Her eyes light up. "Beebee?"

"Not today, Sissy." I look at the clock on my wall and count out the numbers… almost ten. I'm not waking my best friend tonight. I'm not taking my shit to him this late at night. "No B. Not tonight. He's already asleep, but maybe tomorrow."

"Okay!"

"Shhh." I bring her toward the bedroom door, and silently inch it open. Peeking into the hallway, the sounds of a droning TV and loud snoring float in the air along with the smell of nicotine and bourbon. Slowly, we step into the hall, and for the only time ever, I thank the universe for my shitty sneakers.

They're so old, they don't squeak.

Creeping along the hall with my sister's tiny hand clasped in mine, we stop at the entrance to the living room, and when my eyes latch onto the two outstretched recliners, and my folks both laying back with their eyes closed and their mouths open, I swing Iz onto my hip and make a break for it.

We hit the front door at a run, and when a car turns in to our lane and lights up the whole trailer park, we tear down the front steps and move into the trees at a sprint.

My body zings with pain, but there's no pain compared to what's arriving in that crappy sedan.

Our trailer park sits on the very edge of this two-bit piece of shit town, and luckily, the forest butts up against the side of our place in rebellion against the shitty trailers everyone has parked here.

With my two-year-old baby sister in my arms, her tiny legs wrapped around my waist, her still chubby arms wrapped around my neck, and her hair in my face, I sprint into the forest and dodge low lying branches and sneaky rocks.

We've run this track most days since she was born, and I was doing it for years before that. If anyone cared to look, they'd probably find the trail I've worn into the dirt, but usually, as far as Sissy and I are concerned, if we aren't around, if we aren't seen, we're left alone.

"Soos!" Iz fights my hold and throws her weight around. "Soos!"

Slowing my run, since we're far enough into the trees, I pull back to look into her dark eyes. "What's the matter?"

"Soos!"

"What about your shoes?" I look down at her dangling feet, then with a bitten off curse, turn back to collect the tiny pink boot twenty feet back.

Bending low to pick it up, I hiss at the throbbing ache that radiates up through my ribs and into my chest. Now that we're not sprinting, now that we're safe – safer in the cold forest in the middle of the night, than we are at home with our parents – my aches make themselves known again, and my body threatens to shut down.

Picking up the boot, I shove it back on her tiny foot and turn back to keep moving into the trees.

I walk for a little more than fifteen minutes, the same track, the same fifteen minutes we do every night, and I let the moon light our way. We've done this so many times before, Izzy falls heavily against my chest and snoozes as the lulling rhythm of my limp relaxes her.

Reaching the fort that the guys helped me build last year, I walk through the shitty towel curtain door and toss my backpack to the floor. With Iz still in my arms, I drop into the old, worn beanbag I was gifted from the Kincaids last Christmas.

It started out yellow, like my own ray of sunshine, but now it's infested and chewed away in spots.

I don't even care.

It's the first gift I ever received, and it brings me comfort every single day while Iz sleeps in my arms. I pray she doesn't wet through her already soaked diaper.

Digging my butt deep into the beans to get comfortable, I let out a heavy breath as Iz readjusts on my chest and lets out her own sleepy sigh. Tucking her head under my chin and pushing my head up at a weird angle, her tummy touches mine, and her arms and legs dangle lazily over my sides.

"Go to sleep, Sissy." I lean toward my discarded backpack and drag it across the dirty six foot by six foot floor. Digging in the pockets, I pull out a flashlight and my tattered copy of *The Famous Five*.

I've read this book a gazillion times, but it still makes me happy when Dick saves the guys on Treasure Island. I always wanted a dog like Timmy and a brother like Julian.

I want to be the hero one day.

I want to go on regular kid adventures and have fun. I want an Aunt Fanny who thinks I'm cute and sneaks me snacks.

But, no.

Instead I get Shirley and Wayne.

But I also get Sissy, and that's a good trade.

I move my book aside, the yellowed pages folded and worn, and press a kiss to her shiny hair.

I love my Sissy.

Tomorrow, we'll walk over to Bobby's after Mr. Kincaid goes to work. Bobby will sneak us some breakfast, and we'll survive another day of hell.

3

JON

GETTING CLOSER

Twelve years old.
Saturday, Thanksgiving weekend.

I tap on Bobby's bedroom window as quietly as I can. Holding Sissy's hand tight in mine, I bring her close and rub my other hand over her shoulder to keep her warm.

It's cold as fuck out here. She needs to get inside before she gets sick.

Used to this routine now, Bobby silently slides his window open and takes Izzy's shivering hands. "Hey, Sissy." Gently pulling her through, he uses his training and strength to lift her effortlessly.

We're twelve, but Mr. Kincaid has been training him to fight since he was a toddler. Broad chest and strong arms, lifting my forty-pound sister through a bottom story window is easy.

Gingerly climbing in behind them, the central heating smacks me in the face in the best possible way. Sliding the window closed and stopping against the wall, I shiver and wait for the heat to warm my bones.

Sleeping in the fort in three sweaters, your big brother's baggy sweats and too-big socks while sleeping *on* your big brother, is fine. It's enough that she won't get sick.

But then that big brother is left with a ratty shirt, shoes, but no socks, and his little sister draped over his chest as his *only* warmth.

We have blankets in there now, even a little fire pit on the dirt outside, but it's not much when the November chill eats at your bones.

Bobby stands by his bed and studies my face; my split lip, my bruised eyes, the scrapes along my jaw. But he can't yet see the cracked rib or the bruised kidney.

He shoots his chin up in greeting. "What happened?"

I nod – just like he does – to convey what I can't say out loud. "Same as usual." He knows what I tell him, but really, he knows nothing. "Is Jim here?"

"Yeah." He climbs onto his bed and bangs a fist against the wall in a light tap-tap-tap. Jimmy's room is next door, and *he* knows this routine, too. Jim will take Iz to hang out and eat, and I'll collapse onto Bobby's *not* old and faded beanbag and nap until I don't wanna puke anymore.

Bobby Kincaid is my best friend.

The world's most arrogant peacock is the best friend any guy could ever ask for. He feeds me, he keeps my sister safe, and he provides a quiet hour for me to nap and rest while he keeps lookout.

It's the only hour a day that I can close my eyes and not wonder what I might open them to. He's the only person in the world who isn't looking to fuck me over for a quick buck.

"Just wait here." He climbs off the bed. "I'll be back in a sec."

I pause midway through kicking my shitty shoes off. "Where you going?"

"Gonna get you some food. There's heaps left, since Mom went crazy with the turkey and fixings this year. I'll get you some dessert, too. Fatten you up."

I nod.

Nelly Kincaid is the best cook and the sweetest mother I've ever known. She's the *only* real mother I've known.

I know Shirley, the bitch who gave birth to me, but she's no mother. She's a two-bit whore who *likes* to sell herself for enough cash to buy her next hit. And my sperm donor, Wayne, lets her, because he's hanging out for a hit, too.

I nod again, because Bobby's still waiting for my answer. "Okay, I'm gonna sit. I'm beat."

"Yeah." He turns and casually points toward his closet. He'd never make a big deal about it. We don't make big deals, we just *do*. "Grab a sweater or somethin'. I'll be right back."

"Make sure Sissy has food, too."

Her eyes narrow at my worrying tone. She's five, but she's got the attitude of a sixteen-year-old. She's so independent, so smart, and I already worry about her not needing me anymore.

Only five, but capable of applying bandages and butterfly stitches when I need it, and she can cook baked beans and feed us both when I can't do it.

"I can look after myself."

Ignoring her sass, Bobby nods and turns back to the door. He looks after her as much as I do. She's his baby sister now, too, so he's used to ignoring her sass. I wouldn't share her with anyone else in this world, but Bobby and Aiden and Jimmy; I trust them with my life.

"Yeah, I'll get it."

At the knock on the bedroom door, I look up as Jim lets himself in. Wild moppy hair and a silly grin, he has her forgetting her attitude in an instant as she darts across the room and twines her fingers with his.

Turning without a word for me or Bobby, they head back into the hall and discuss chicken, biscuits, and soda.

Jim will feed her. I never have to worry about a thing so long as I'm on Kincaid property.

"Alright." Bobby steps into the hall after them. "I'll be back. Chill out for a sec."

Standing alone in his small bedroom, I finish toeing off my shoes and kick them out of the way. Rubbing a still shaking hand over my face, I stumble toward the red beanbag in the corner and drop.

I need to sit down before I fall down.

I let out a grunt of pain as the impact reminds me I need an ice pack and Advil. My ribs crunch painfully together, like bone on bone, and dragging in a sickly breath, I work through the nausea that rolls around in my gut.

Fuck that asshole.

I'm gonna kill them one day. I'll kill every single person who's ever stepped inside my place, because to come to that house, makes you fucking slime.

Nobody goes to my place with pure intentions.

As soon as I'm old enough, as soon as I'm able, I'm taking my sister away and giving her the life she deserves.

She's not like them.

She's pure and innocent and perfect, and I'll die before I let them hurt her.

Relaxing into the beanbag and breathing through the pain in my ribs, I find my head dropping, my chin resting against my chest. My eyes flutter closed, though I try to fight it.

I'm so tired. So fucking exhausted.

But more than I'm tired, I'm hungry.

I need to eat first, or I might die.

Leaning across to Bobby's bed, I grab my tattered copy of *The King's Courtney* from under his mattress and open it to where I left off the other day. Breathing and waiting for my ribs to relax, I think of the story that I've read a million times before.

A secret kingdom, a king named Astrius, and a princess named Courtney. King Astrius opens tournaments each year for the townspeople to compete for the prize of a year of free rent. But Astrius is an asshole, and each year, he comes up with a reason why they still have to pay their rent.

Like most adults in this world, Astrius never intends to give anything away for free. He just wants to hold the tournaments to impress Courtney and show his... generosity.

Princess Courtney doesn't give a shit about him, though. She doesn't give a shit about his *peacocking* around.

She wants to compete, too.

She's cool like that.

I sink into Courtney's life for five minutes, blissfully leaving mine behind and joining her on a quest to learn how to shoot an arrow, when Bobby walks back into his room.

Silent, but with arms full of food and drink, my stomach rumbles noisily and sends my ribs aching with how much my gut begs for a meal.

I forgot I was hungry while I was buried deep in the *Uden* world. For as long as I have books, I forget that I'm sore, or hungry, or pissed. For as long as I steal, books are free. They help me escape, so bad karma or not, I'll never stop stealing them.

I'll never give them up.

It's the least the universe can do after giving me the folks I have.

"Here." Stopping beside me, Bobby passes down a loaded plate with turkey, beans, potatoes, biscuits, pasta salad, and stuffed mushrooms. Way too much, but really, not enough. As though he dumped an entire gravy bowl over top, my food swims enticingly, and my stomach attempts to jump outside my body in an effort to get to it sooner.

I haven't eaten since dinnertime Thursday night. School's out for Thanksgiving, and although I eat during the week because the state makes sure poor kids like me could eat at school, any other food we have – like peanut butter and bread – I try to save for Iz.

She needs it more than I do.

She doesn't understand the way I do.

She'll never *have* to understand.

It's not a big deal usually, since weekends are only two days, and we usually come to Bobby's at least one of those days, but we're on a long weekend now, and I'm fucking starving.

I mumble my thanks and stuff a dripping turkey leg in my mouth. My hunger and desperation reach a whole new level now that the food is right in front of my face. Manners forgotten, I eat and eat and eat, and even as my stomach expands, I still groan with pleasure and eat some more.

I try to slow down. I try to regulate my speed and savor my food, because I *know* from experience that slamming it down will give me a stomach ache.

But I just can't stop.

I watched Iz scrape the peanut butter jar and inhale the last of our bread last night. I almost wept, my heart shattered as I watched the last of our food go, but I didn't say a word.

My baby sister comes first every time. She needs it more than I do.

She doesn't understand the hunger pains.

And she'll never have to.

I'd cut my own arm off, grill it up, and smother it in ketchup before she ever felt true hunger.

But silent or not, I watched her lick her fingers clean, and inside, I cried like a little kid.

I was so hungry.

"Here." Sitting on the side of his bed and cracking open a can of soda, Bobby passes the drink without another word and watches me take it and chug half the can in one go. The cold liquid leaves goosebumps on my skin and a shiver in my bones, but it helps wash down the hard ball of food still sitting in my throat from lack of chewing.

Gas backs up in my stomach and threatens to push my food straight back out, so sitting tall, I let out a man sized belch and smile at the instant relief.

Bobby doesn't speak as I dive back into my meal. He doesn't disrupt or tell me to slow, he just sits close enough that his new jeans brush along my shoulder and he watches me mop up leftover gravy with slices of buttered bread.

I finish long before I feel full, but I know that in ten minutes, the hunger pains will be replaced by overfull pains.

The second kind are the best kind. I'll never complain about *that* kind of tummy ache.

And I find that, if I eat enough, fill myself to the point the food literally feels like it's in my chest, it'll usually carry me through a full day before the hunger pains start again.

Every time we come here, apart from my *now* meal, he'll also swipe stuff that'll stay in my bag. Bread. Peanut butter. Crackers.

Sometimes Mrs. Kincaid will even buy Pop-Tarts and Izzy and I will dine like royalty.

Nelly and Bryan Kincaid offer us a meal every time we're here. But not because they think we're hungry. As far as they know, we're here to play with the guys, and naturally, if the guys are eating, then Mrs. Kincaid will offer us a plate, too.

I'll never tell them that we're starving.

I'll never tell them anything, because if they know, they'll report my folks.

Shirley and Wayne are horrible people. They're junkies and whores, alcoholics and child abusers, but for as long as we stay with them, Iz and I stay out of the foster system.

The second we're removed from our home, they'll separate us.

I should let Sissy go.

I should let her find a new family.

A *better* family.

She's cute and smart and wonderful, and she'd have no trouble finding something amazing; but the people that would want her... well, they'd never want a potty mouthed boy with a bottomless stomach.

I'm not ready to let her go.

And even though I'm scared every day that she's hungry, or that she's cold, or that she'll get hurt, I'm selfish enough to keep her with me.

There's nothing I wouldn't do to keep her with me.

Bobby's foot gently taps my leg to pull me from my quiet thoughts. Looking down at me with kind eyes when I mop up the last of the gravy, he brings his calloused hands together and draws my eyes down.

He knows me.

He knows me better than anyone on this planet. "Talk to me, Jon. What happened?"

I shrug like my life is all roses. "Same, same. Did Sissy eat?"

"Yeah." He sits back on his bed until his back rests against the wall. "I made up two plates. Dropped the other one off in Jim's room. He's got her back."

"She's okay?"

"She's fine. Jimmy will take care of her. Tell me what happened."

I shrug again. "Shirley lost her job."

"She hit you?"

"Nah, Wayne did." I run my finger through a small drop of leftover gravy. "He's pissed she's broke. No money for booze. No money for crack."

Nodding in quiet understanding, he leans forward, bending at the hips, and reaches beneath his bed. Pulling out a little Lego case, he sits it on his lap and opens the lid.

We've done this enough, that I know there's no Lego in there. "He got you good, huh?"

I grunt in answer. The only answer he'll get. The only answer he ever gets. Knowing that, and okay with my lack of communication, he doesn't argue. He simply pokes through his case and pulls out the things we need; antiseptic, Band-Aids, Advil.

Nodding for me to hold out my hand, he drops two capsules in my palm and goes back to his work while I chug more soda and pretend my world isn't all sorts of fucked up.

He's sympathetic to my life. He helps me every single day and is possibly the only thing that stands between me and death. But he doesn't understand it.

To him, abusive parents just aren't a thing.

Mr. and Mrs. Kincaid are the dictionary meaning for perfect parents.

I don't mean perfect as in smartest, strictest, fanciest, or richest.

I just mean, they love their boys more than life. And luckily for me and Iz, we get some of the spillover.

Silently, he leans forward and starts working on my split lip. Wiping an alcohol wipe over the stinging cut, his eyes say sorry, but his strong hands say '*I've gotta do it.*'

"Whatcha reading?" He nods at the now closed paperback resting by my leg. Bobby doesn't read like I do. Not that he's dumb or anything. He's not, he does really good in school, seeing as his mom tutors them and accepts nothing less than A's, but he just doesn't have time for extra reading.

He's always riding bikes with his brothers, or training with his Dad. Bryan Kincaid is a fighter, not professional or anything, but he likes to go to the gym and train. He spars on the weekends, and sometimes, me and Iz get to go and watch.

Those are the best times.

We get to sit in the big chairs and watch the guys fight, then me and the boys get to practice and pretend, and we *always* get pizza when we're done.

Bobby's dad *never* says no if we want a snack.

I hiss when he rubs ointment over my lip. "King's Courtney."

"You crushing on an anime lookin' chick?" He smirks and chases a fresh dribble of blood that spills over my chin. "You're always reading that one. You got a cartoon fetish, *Fart?"*

"It's fun to read." I pick up the book and toss it under the bed. "She kicks his ass in the end. She's badass."

"You like tough girls? Want one that'll put you in your place when you get to be a jerk?"

I don't like wimpy chicks. That's for sure.

In answer, I just shrug.

"I got you a new one, by the way."

"A new one, what?"

"A book. It's over there." He nods toward his desk in the corner of his room.

Stuffed with textbooks and loose pieces of paper and pencils, his schoolbag sits precariously on top of the pile and sways despite the fact no one is even breathing on it.

In the corner of his desk, lined up perfectly as though Bobby nervously messed with it till it sat exactly right, sits a thick hardcover book with a purple jacket. "It's a new one I thought you might like. Garry Potter or some shit. It has dragons and stuff, so, I dunno…" He shrugs. "Figured you might like it."

Bobby doesn't have a job. He doesn't have money. He doesn't even get an allowance like most of the other kids we go to school with.

"Did you steal it?"

"Nah." He leans in to work on my jaw. "I asked Mom to take me to the bookstore. She's always reading." He rolls his eyes. "She was giddy when I asked to go. She would've bought the whole damn store if I asked for it."

Must be nice.

"Anyway, I hope you like it. I'll get you another one next month or somethin'."

I frown at his kindness. "You don't have to do that."

"It's okay. Just read them and give me the cliffnotes in case Mom asks," he chuckles. "There's a second one for that book, too. If you like the first, I'll get the second next time."

He's my best friend. "Thanks, B."

"It's cool, Jon Fart. That's what brothers are for."

I love my brother. "You're still an asshole."

His breath fans my face as he laughs and pushes my split lip back together. It hurts, but I don't let on. He's an asshole, but he'd feel bad for hurting me.

4

JON

LILIES IN THE DIRT

Thirteen years old.
Just a regular sunny weekend.

"*J*on!"

Popping up and peeking out the tiny fort window, I watch Bobby sprint through the trees, hurdle over fallen tree stumps, and duck under low lying branches as his awesome red Jordans flash in the sunlight.

I'm eternally jealous of my best friend's shoes. Not jealous, like I hate him, but jealous like I wish I could be him.

He got new Jordans because of his straight A's all year.

I get straight A's every year...

But I have no Jordans.

Heart pumping with adrenaline because of the terror in his voice, I toss my copy of *The Prisoner of Azkaban* down and jump up to search for Iz. I saw her only a minute ago playing in the dirt, but Bobby's screaming has me sick to my stomach.

Something's wrong. Something really bad.

"Sissy!" I step out of the fort and find her exactly where I thought she was. She's already paused in her play as she watches Bobby run.

He's got her spooked, too.

"Jon!" Bobby cries. He has actual tears streaming down his dirty face and has my heart lurching with pain. I sprint toward him, because, Bobby is... well, he's Bobby Kincaid.

He's almost fourteen, he's already kissed a girl, he's a peacock. He doesn't cry!

He crashes into me with a body slamming hug and knocks the breath from my lungs. Draping his heavy body over mine, he chokes on his sobs and collapses against me as though he simply can't stand on his own anymore.

Taking his weight the way he's done for me a million times since we became friends, I walk us toward a large rock half sunk into the dirt.

Pushing him to sit before he falls, I crouch in front of him. "Tell me, B. Say it quick."

"My dad!"

"What? What's the matter?"

"Beebee?"

Izzy stands from her play and wipes a skinny arm across her cheeks. She never cries. Never in all her life, but a lone tear sits on her cheekbone and glistens in the sun as Big-Bad-Bobby-Kincaid cries in her brother's arms.

I turn back to him. "Tell me, B. What happened?"

He heaves in an attempt to catch his breath. "My dad."

"What happened to him?"

"He had a car accident!" The sobs coming from his broad chest almost knock me on my ass each time he attempts to breathe in. He's a big guy, the biggest in our grade, and heavy. "Mom's crying."

"Is he okay?"

He shakes his head and slams the heel of his hands against his eyes like the sun's too bright. I don't know why he does that; I love the sunlight. Bad shit never happens when the sun's out.

"No." He hiccups. His pain filled words are like clouds sailing past and blocking the sun. "No. My dad... my dad... No. He's not okay."

I throw my arm over his shoulder and pull him in a tight hug. Tears sit in my lashes, and spill over only when Izzy walks up behind me and lays her face against my back. Her short arms come around my stomach, and her cheek rests between my shoulder blades and almost has me weeping.

This is bad.

This is really, really bad.

"Tell me, B. Please tell me."

"My dad." Drenched, chocolate brown eyes come up to mine and break my heart. "He's dead. He died."

It's as bad as it could ever be.

School's back in, the term's rolling ahead without us, the other kids' lives carry on like normal, but in the middle of the morning on what should be a regular Wednesday, I stand beside my best friend and watch Bryan Kincaid... the only man I ever considered a dad... being lowered into the ground.

I throw on my strongest armor, my thickest skin, my bravest face, and I try not to break down and roll into a ball of despair as soft music plays through the speakers and Mom sobs. The pulley system click-click-clicks and takes him from us, and each click, each fraction lower he moves, Mom gets that much closer to the ground.

Someone bought long stemmed white lilies to sit on top of his coffin, and though I know he'd laugh at them, he'd think them girly and silly, I also know he'd do anything, accept anything, *be* anything, to make this easier on his family.

Especially on Mom.

He cherished every hair on her head, every step she took, every smile she gave.

Bryan and Chantelle Kincaid made me believe true love existed.

I swallow and say my silent goodbyes as the box disappears below ground.

He was the best man I ever knew. The strongest, the bravest, the kindest, and fairest.

He bought me my first ever ice-cream cone, and he made his firstborn son watch me eat it. Because he was fair and kind, and he wanted Bobby to grow into a good man. He refused to raise a bully or a jerk, and Bobby learned his lesson that day.

Bobby's everything good that his dad was, and I hope to be even half that good one day.

That day at the ice-cream parlor, the day I ate the milky treat that I'd never experienced before in my life, I sat there with my baby sister in my arms – because no way was I not swinging by the trailer park to get her – a brain freeze tearing my skull apart, and nerves in my gut because I was terrified Bobby would be pissed and let me know about it the very next time we were alone...

Bryan also sat there, nibbled at his own treat, and within minutes of Bobby's contrite expression and lack of malice, he gave Bobby his ice-cream and set us on the path to where we are now.

Bobby had learned his lesson, and just like Bryan doesn't raise assholes, well, he's not an asshole, either. He's fair to a fault. And he gave me my best friend.

Bobby stands beside me in the sun. His mom to his right, and his hand clasped tightly in hers. Aiden stands on her other side, his arm wrapped around her stomach, his head almost higher than hers, even at eleven years old.

Izzy stands to my left and clutches to my hand as tight as her tiny six-year-old body can manage.

She's still so young, and though she might not understand it all – she doesn't understand it the way Jimmy does as he stands on her other side and clutches to her left hand – she knows it's bad.

This is a bad day.

This is probably the worst day of my whole life.

Taking a deep breath as my badass best friend cries, I slip my spare hand down to his and clasp it tight.

His drenched eyes come up to mine for the shortest beat. In thanks. In heartbreak.

We're teenagers now. Teenage guys don't hold hands, *especially* not Bobby Kincaid the peacock, but he doesn't tug his away.

He squeezes mine and goes back to watching his dad.

Bad stuff *does* happen in the sunlight.

My dad died in the sunlight, and now the shadows chase me every-where I go.

He took my sunshine to the grave with him.

5

JON

HP'S FINALE

Twenty-one years old.
It's my birthday.

"*I*t's finally here!" Bobby's big smiling face greets me as I walk into his bedroom.

With brand-new Jordans on my feet and my wallet fat with cash, I step in and hug my best friend and laugh when he squeezes the oxygen straight from my lungs.

"Hey, B."

Slapping my shoulder and stepping back, his big smile makes me smile like a fool. "Happy birthday, Jon Fart. I'm so happy you're finally here."

"You're still an asshole." I laugh and push his grinning face away. "My name ain't Fart."

"Who cares. You're finally twenty-one! Finally legal. I've waited *months* for this."

"I didn't make you wait for me!" I push him away, though inside, I kinda want another hug. "Nobody said you couldn't go out without me."

That's just a lie.

We do everything together.

We started our ink together. We got our licenses together. We bought our first cars at the same time.

He's my brother, and waiting six months for me to turn twenty-one would be cake for him.

It just wouldn't be fun for him to party without me.

He shrugs and turns away. He's practically jittery as he bops around his room. "You ready to find some pretty girls?"

Yeah, right. Like he needed to be twenty-one to chase tail.

Bobby Kincaid spends *all* of his time either fighting at the gym, or chasing girls.

He might be the only guy I know that won't ever settle down.

Well, and me. I'm never getting married, either.

There's not a single girl on this planet horrible enough to be saddled with my brand of messed up. No one deserves to be tied to an asshole.

I wouldn't do that to my worst enemy.

But Bobby's different; he's not messed up. He's not even an asshole – despite the fact I say he is seventy times a week.

No, he's just having too much fun chasing the girls around. He gets off on flirting with them, kissing them, then moving on to the next. And the girls don't even mind, since he does it so nicely when he pats their ass and sends them home.

"I got you something." Bobby's shy voice penetrates my mind, and when I look up, he stops at his old, still-littered desk. Grabbing a small rectangle parcel wrapped in navy blue paper, he steps toward me with his arm extended.

I already know what it is.

He gets me the same gift every year, and on the years there are no new releases – like last year, and two years before that – he buys me something from a different series.

My heart pounds with excitement as I rip open the packaging. Stopping on the seventh and final Harry Potter book, I look up and tell him I love him without saying the actual words out loud.

"I waited in line for that fucker last month."

I flip the book over as stupid giddiness fills my chest. My adult best friend gave his adult best friend a kid's book for his twenty-first birthday; and I couldn't be happier. I've been waiting two years for this, and though I'd been tempted to buy it myself, since it was released weeks ago, I knew my best friend would continue tradition.

Ever since that first time when I was twelve, every year for my birthday, Bobby adds the next installment to my collection. And he doesn't buy the shitty soft-cover books.

Nothing but the best for his best friend.

I haven't stolen a single book since that year, because just like promised, Bobby went back to the store with his mom and spent more of her money.

The month after I got book one, he came back with *Chamber of Secrets*. The month after that came my first *Lord of the Rings* book. Then the month after that, and every month after, Nelly took him to the store, and he came back with yet another book, yet another series.

After the sixth consecutive month of new books, I plucked up the courage to question his actions. I didn't want to question it, I didn't want to ruin my good fortune, but I had to.

Nothing free ever comes to guys like me, and the longer I rode that train, the longer I allowed myself to get used to it, the harder the crash would be when reality snapped back into focus.

I was right.

Nothing free ever came to guys like me.

But my payment was good grades. Good grades I'd already achieved.

When Bobby got A's in school, his folks bought him new shoes. When I got A's, Bobby got me new books.

I have walls full of novels now, but my Harry Potter collection sits front and center on a shelf that I walk by every single day.

And every single day, I tap the spines on my way to the kitchen for coffee, and every day I smile, because my best friend saved my life. He was the only person in this world who *knew* my birthday and cared enough to get me something other than a kick in the teeth.

I stroke the book jacket and look up. "Thanks, B. I love it."

"You don't have it yet, do you?"

"Nah, I'm still finishing up the last one." *Lie.* I finished *The Half Blood Prince* the same day he gave it to me two years ago. Swallowing away my girly emotion, I tap his shoulder with my book. "I really appreciate it."

He shrugs. "It's cool. You ready to go out?"

"Yeah, let's go find some pretty girls."

Turning as Aiden and Jimmy let themselves into Bobby's room, I throw the half-wrapped book down onto the desk, and smile when Jimmy grabs me tight. "Happy Birthday, Jon."

"Thanks, Jimmy. Only another…" I count the years in my head. "Five years before you can come out, too." I'm gloating, smug with my brand-new age. "We'll save some of the honeys for you."

"Yeah." Stepping away, he watches Aiden step in for a hug. "Too bad, really wish I could go." He turns and fingers through the paperwork on Bobby's desk. "Izzy at your place?"

"Nah, she's hanging at the fort for a bit, but she'll be home later."

"That's cool." He shrugs casually.

"Anyway." Bobby nods at the door. "Go away. We're heading out."

Aiden steps back to lean against the door. Thick arms folded across his chest, he frowns at Bobby's dismissal. And probably a premonition of his brother getting into trouble tonight. "Where're you goin'?"

"Rhinos," Bobby answers. "It's the only club within stumbling distance from my bed. I heard it's a shitty place, but I'm not driving into the city, so…" He shrugs.

"We should start our own club one day," Jimmy muses. "There's only that one place, and it's gross."

"Start our own club?" I push him back with a laugh. "We're not busy enough already? You got school, the gym, all of you suckers mow lawns on weekends. You think we have time for a club, too?"

"Well…"

"Exactly. It wasn't my big mouth that told people about our training. It was you. Then you told someone else. Then they told someone else, and now we have a garage full of bags and mats–"

"And a wallet fat with cash." Jim pushes me back. "Shut the hell up with your whining. That gym paid for your fancy shoes, so stop bitching."

"Not bitching, just saying, no new clubs."

Smiling, Bobby steps between me and his baby brother when Jim lopes forward to shove me again. "Rhinos will do for now." He pushes Jim back, then leans to the desk to collect his wallet and phone. "And when I become world champion, we'll get the rest."

"World champion?" Jim scoffs arrogantly. "You're just a whiny bitch. No way will they offer you a chance, dumbass."

Sneaking in a jab, Bobby has Jimmy folding over and wheezing out a laugh. "You owe me a hundred bucks the day I sign contracts. Now get out of my room."

6

JON

BOBBY, MEET YOUR MATCH

Twenty-six years old.

*N*ursing my beer at the bar, I watch my hands and mind my own business as clubbers party around me. My brothers are here, too. But they've already ditched me for girls.

It's what we do.

We *say* we're going to party together, but what we really do is walk in together, then we don't see each other again until tomorrow.

Today fucking sucks.

I'm tired, so I sit and sip and ignore my shitty life as memories from only hours ago flash in my mind. Like cockroaches, Wayne and Shirley just won't fucking die. They show up as soon as the lights are out. They ask for cash. They threaten to make trouble for me.

Or more accurately, they threaten to make trouble for Iz.

She's an adult now. She's nineteen and independent, but I'll always protect her, so when they threaten, I get mean.

I don't give my folks any cash. I never give them cash. I pump my shot gun and watch them walk their asses off my property, then I go into damage control to make sure Iz is okay.

But just like cockroaches, I know they'll be back. They always come back in the dark.

I wish I had a legitimate reason to slit their throats, to end their miserable lives, but unlike stealing books in my youth, killing in cold blood will land me in prison.

I refuse to go anywhere that'll keep me from protecting my baby sister. So I stay on the good side of the law, and I continue living with my pest problem.

Loud music pumps through the dark club around me. Deep bass you can feel in your chest thumps and has my heart bouncing. Lights flash across the room, colors, swirls, dots, move in a mesmerizing display and help lighten my mood.

Lights are good.

Pretty lights are even better.

Like the universe heard us bitching five years ago, a new club opened in town this year.

Some rich dude decided to throw a little money toward our little town, and unlike Rhinos, this place is rarely reduced to fights, and never once have I dodged needles in the bathroom.

A fresh beer slides across the bar and stops beside my hand, and when I look up with a frown, I stop on bright green eyes and an arrogant smirk. "Hey. You're Jon, right? I'm Casey."

She extends a dainty hand and raises her brow as if to say *'I ain't even insecure. I know you'll take my hand.'*

My lips twitch at her arrogant dare. Taking her hand in mine, I nod and catalogue her tiny features. Tiny hand enveloped in mine. Short woman. Short hair. Her attitude is bigger than her physical size.

"Yeah, I'm Jon. Hey, Casey."

I release her hand and look around the club. Stopping on Bobby standing beside a pretty girl in a black dress, I laugh under my breath and turn back to the tiny barmaid.

Good luck to Bobby's new friend.

She'll be in love by the morning, but by then, he'll be done and our asses will be parked in beanbags while we shout at the TV and PlayStation.

"So you're the brother from another mother?" Casey, christened only moments ago as *Tink*, blatantly looks me up and down. She's not shy, and she doesn't give a shit that I know she's checking me out.

That's alright. I'm checking her out, too.

She's hot.

A skintight tank top pushes up a set of luscious D's. A miniskirt shows off a set of strong legs each time she steps away to serve. And those amazing legs end in heels that are at least four inches tall and have me thinking filthy, body contorting thoughts.

Even with the heels, the top of her head would barely clear my armpits. She's tiny like a doll, though there's nothing childlike about her allure.

She's sexy like nothing I've ever seen before.

Bobby wasn't far off with the nickname; she's got this erotic cartoon fairy thing going on. Tiny, but with the sexy smoky eyes, and lips that are colored so deeply, I wonder if someone sucked on them recently.

Her hair's so short, it doesn't even touch her shoulders. It simply hangs and spikes out. She's edgy and full of attitude.

She's trouble.

But even knowing that, I continue to check her out, and I sit up tall and mentally gloat that I was working out all day today. If the sexy girl is gonna check me out, I'm glad I put in the extra reps today.

"Jon?"

"Yeah." Grudgingly dragging my eyes away from her tits, I refocus on her question. "Yeah, I'm the brother from another mother." Picking up my almost empty glass, I finish the last mouthful, place the glass down by her hand, and bring the fresh one closer. "Thanks for the beer, by the way."

She leans against the bar comfortably, and doesn't react whatsoever to the hundred thirsty guys shouting their orders around us. They call her by name. They call her by description. But it's like she's immune as her luscious lips turn up into a sassy grin.

"You looking for a new best friend, Jon?"

My brows pull in tight at her question. Turning toward Bobby and watching him lean in close to that chick, I shake my head. "No, I'm good. I've got a best friend."

She flashes a beautiful smile. "Not anymore. Looks to me like *your* best friend and *my* best friend just became best friends with each other. Looks like you and me are now in the market for an upgrade."

I laugh and spin my new beer. "Nah, mine'll be back. He'll be okay."

Her sparkling eyes turn flat. "Is he gonna hurt her?"

I bite my lip and think through my words. Bro code means I can't drop him in the shit... I'm fairly sure this chick is *the* shit. "Not like how you think. They'll have their fun, then he'll send her home tomorrow with a smile on her face."

"He's gonna use her, then she's doomed for the walk of shame?"

I shake my head and hide my smile. She's a chihuahua, but she thinks she's a bulldog. "Nah, he's not a complete asshole. No walk of shame. He'll drive her home. He respects women, Case. He respects the fuck out of them. He just doesn't do repeats."

Her eyes narrow to a glare. "She's not one of those girls, Jon. She doesn't just give it up to anyone."

"Are you sure?" Triumphantly, I turn and watch them stand hand in hand and walk to the middle of the dance floor. I spin on my stool and follow them with my eyes, then turning back, I wink arrogantly. "Looks to me like she has it covered. Then tomorrow, he'll get her home safe and I'll get my best friend back. It's a system. It works every time."

Her green eyes narrow to slits and have me swallowing nervously. I didn't think I'd ever see the day, but I think this girl could eat my bitter ass up and spit it out.

She's definitely trouble.

"What's your last name, Jon?"

Kincaid. "Hart. Why?"

She shrugs dainty shoulders and feigns nonchalance. "Just taking names. If my girl comes home with a broken heart tomorrow, you're dead." Her threat is said so innocently, so easily, it adds a layer of fear in my chest. "Then I'll get my best friend back, and you and yours won't break any more hearts. It's a system. It works every time."

"Me?!" I laugh, despite the truth in her words. "I didn't do anything! B can fight his own battles. Take this up with him."

"But if you knew he was a player, why didn't you stop him? Why'd you stand by and watch me give him the green light?"

"Are you insane?" I laugh, though I bring it to a choking stop when she leans closer and glares. "Ah, that is, we come out to see girls. Why would I stop him from approaching a girl?"

"Because she's different! She's special, and she's already hurt. I forced her to come out tonight, and now look what I did. Bobby breaking her heart is gonna be my fault."

I sigh at her defeated face. "He's not an asshole, Case. I promise. He'll be a perfect gentleman, he'll show her a good time, then he'll escort her home and leave her with a smile on her face. She won't be sad she spent the night with him, so don't sweat it."

Looking over my shoulder distractedly, her glare turns to a grin and has me spinning in my stool. Bobby and Kit slow-dance in a sea of boppers. They both wear smiles, and when I turn back to Casey, I smile at hers.

Four smilers.

I'll take it.

Her playful eyes flicker across my face, and before I get a chance to think up something witty, she leans in close and whispers, "You looking for a new best friend, Jon?"

I laugh and shake my head. "Do you get a break soon, or are you on all night?"

"I can take ten minutes." She throws down a dish rag and turns to another barmaid. "I'm taking my ten. I'll be back."

"No problem." As unruffled by the hordes of shouting orders as Casey is, her coworker grins easily and moves at her own pace.

They really just don't give a shit. You'll be served when these girls are good and ready.

Walking to the end of the bar and hitching herself up, Casey climbs over the top and doesn't give a damn that she flashes her panties as she plops down on my side.

"Follow me, Jon." She takes my hand as though we've been best friends for years. Leading me down the side of the club, we pass hot dancing bodies and slip into the fresh air outside.

A deep male rumble of laughter has me turning back to my old school friend as he stands at the entrance and checks ID's.

"I'm taking my ten, Mike."

"That's cool, doll." He looks to me with a smug grin. "These club girls, they make me feel like a big brother, ya know? Just like with Sissy. So I always worry. I always tell them to be careful when they walk out with a guy's hand in theirs and a smile on *his* face." He shakes his head. "Not this time. I know you, man, so I know my girl's in safe hands. But you, my friend, I'm compelled to tell you to stay safe. She's gonna win. Whatever this is..." He distractedly checks a girl's ID and waves a hand in my direction. "Whatever you intend to do out here, know she'll win."

Casey rolls her eyes and pulls me along. "Don't listen to him. He's cray." Leading me along like a lamb for slaughter, we stop at a short brick wall at the far end of the club. Sitting on the dirty bricks, she leans back and takes a deep breath as the soft breeze ruffles her hair. "You gonna sit down?" She pops a single eye open. "I've got eight minutes left till I have to go back in. We're on the clock."

Somehow, with barely a handful of words spoken between us, she constantly has me on the back foot. And now, here I am, standing in the dark at the back of Club 188 with a girl I met only an hour ago, and I'm watching her pretty hair flutter in the breeze.

Taking a deep breath, I sit on the wall and work to get my long legs comfortable. Hers are short enough even with heels, that her legs form a perfect ninety-degree angle. Mine peak sharply and have my knees almost as high as my chest.

Leaning forward and resting my elbows on my thighs, I turn and watch her as she taps my thigh. "Who are you, Jon? Tell me your story."

"My story?"

"Mmhmm. We're down to seven minutes. Tell me who you are." She angles her head so her forest green eyes twinkle in the street lights. "What do you do in your spare time? What's your job? Do you have siblings?" Her smug smile has my lips lifting. "Consider this a speed date. We have six and a half minutes till I have to go back in, then your boy's gonna break my girl's heart, then we'll probably never see each other again. But if we *do*, I'll be obligated under best friend law to run you down with my car."

She's bluffing. "Would you actually run me down?"

"Hell yes, I would!"

Oh my God, she totally would.

"I'd do anything for that girl. She's my best friend."

I believe her.

Pulling my bottom lip between my teeth, I consider my answer. "Alright, then. In my spare time, I fight."

Not impressed like I hoped she'd be, her brow lifts. "Like, you're a street brawler? Because I've spent plenty of time with guys who think they're gangster, but really, they're just annoying and loud."

"Not a street brawler," I laugh. "We train for real fighting. We compete. We even have trophies and shit." I feel like a thirteen-year-old punk trying to impress the pretty girl… and I used 'trophies'. Fuck. "Legit fighting, I promise."

"Trophies?" Gushing dramatically, she brings her hands to her chest and bats her lashes. "Oh my gosh, Jon Hart! Can I see your trophy case?"

"You're a smart ass." Laughing, I drop my eyes from hers and study my shoes instead.

She makes me shy.

She's the only woman in the world that's ever made me shy, so instead of looking into her beautiful eyes, I study my shoes.

I've moved on from my obsession with Jordans, but I haven't gotten over new shoes in general. I own more than any straight man should, but for a kid who never had any shoes that he didn't first scrounge from a dumpster, for a kid who had calloused feet because his dumpster shoes almost always had holes in the soles, I don't give a shit.

I have money now.

I have power.

I'm at no one's mercy, and if I find shoes that I like, I'm going to buy them.

"So just so we're clear, you're saying I *can't* see your trophies?" Snorting inelegantly, she bumps her shoulder against mine. "Figured you were probably lying. You haven't won any, have you?"

I'm tempted to shove her to the side just to watch her scramble. She doesn't come across like a prissy whiny chick. She'd play along.

Instead, I shrug. "You come to my house, I'll show you my trophies." *You come to my house, I'll fuck you in front of my trophy case.*

"Alright." Grinning like she knows what I'm thinking, she nods. "Siblings? You have five minutes."

I clear my throat and try to stop thinking dirty shit. "Ah, I have a sister. She's nineteen and the most amazing girl I've ever known. She's smart; books *and* streets." I knock my shoulder against hers. "She's a fighter, too."

"I bet she has more trophies than you, too."

She's savage. "You wear your smart ass streak like you wear your shoes. You know that?"

She laughs and stretches her leg out to point her toes. "I know. I've been working on it."

"You've been working on toning it down?"

"Hell no!" Her sexy eyes come back to pin mine. "I've been working on making it sharper. I pride myself on my wit and bullshit."

I never would have guessed.

"Quick, we're running out of time. Show me your hands." She snatches my hand from my knee, opens it palm side up, and studies it.

"What are you doing?

"I don't trust any man that doesn't have work roughened hands. If you're manicured and too smooth, I already hate your guts."

I laugh. "Are you kidding?" For the first time in my life, I might be happy for how hard I've had it. My hands are calloused. My knuckles conditioned and bruised.

No one can deny I've worked hard.

"Nuh-uh. Not kidding." Her soft breath feathers the tips of my fingers as she studies. "What's your job? I'm not interested in your money, I don't care if you have any or not, but I need you to have a job. Something to keep you busy and away from drugs and booze and too much spare time with other girls."

I know every word she just spoke comes from experience. Someone had her heart. Someone stomped on it. "Sounds to me like you know a guy who was unemployed and liked to drink and smoke and fuck other girls."

She looks up easily. "Uh-huh. He was my boyfriend at the same time he did those other things. Asshole."

"How'd he get out alive?" I don't take my hand from hers as she keeps her eyes on mine. The way she strokes my palm with the tips of her fingers feels nice. "You seem like the type of girl to cut a guy's dick off."

She shrugs. "I wanted to, but like I said, I'd do anything for Kit. She begged me not to go to prison and leave her here all alone, so I had to think of something less violent."

My lips tug up at the promise in her voice. "What did you do?"

"I swapped out all his shampoo for hair removal stuff, I sprinkled itching powder in all his clothes and sheets, and I keyed his car. Haven't heard from him since, and I didn't go to jail, so…" She lets the sentence hang and has me laughing nervously.

"You're a little scary, you know that?"

"I'm glad you noticed. It'll keep you on your toes and my heart intact."

Her heart? It's my heart that's doing weird somersaults every time she smiles.

"So you didn't actually answer. Job or no?"

I smile at her dogged attitude. "I've got a job. I already told you, I'm a fighter."

Her brows furrow. "Your job is to fight?"

"Uh-huh. I co-own a gym with my brothers. I'm there all day, all week. No time for bongs or girls."

She nods sharply, though her eyes continue to dance. "That's good. Means I didn't waste my ten minutes on an asshole. But, either way, time's up." Standing, she looks down and fixes her skirt. "Walk me back in?"

Standing, I stretch to my full height and smile down at her when her neck bends back.

"You're taller than I thought."

I cock my head to the side and study her heels. Her creamy legs. A tiny waist. Skimming past her chest before I stop and get in trouble, I grin when her playful eyes pin mine. "You're smaller than I thought."

She rolls her eyes and turns on her heels to leave. "Small like a little kid. Awesome. I can see how that's sexy for a guy."

"Wait, what are you talking about?"

"Nothin'." She takes my hand and drags me along. "Come on, I've gotta get back."

"No. Wait." I pull her to a stop twenty feet from Mike. I just want another second before we go back inside, back to the noise and the smell and the people. Back to my best friend breaking her best friend's heart. For the first time ever, I think Bobby's just about to unintentionally fuck something up for me. "Can I see you later?"

"Later?" She angles her chin up. "Tonight?"

"Yeah." I came here looking for a pretty girl to spend the night with. Casey's definitely a pretty girl, and her sense of humor has me more entertained than any plastic Barbie will ever achieve. "What time are you off?"

"Ah, no." She clears her throat. "I can't see you tonight."

"Why not?"

"Because I'm trying not to be a slut."

Stepping back like she slugged me, I blink in surprise. "Come again?"

She transfers her weight from one heeled foot to the other and considers her words.

Wrinkling her nose, she meets my gaze. "Since my ex-idiot, I was kinda in 'fuck it' mode, where I kind of just, well," she shrugs, "I wasn't too particular about the men I hung out with. Some shit's gone down in my world the last few months, it put life into perspective, so now, I'm turning over a new leaf."

"Okay..."

"So, if I see you later tonight after work..." She lays her small hand on my bicep and sends my muscles bunching. "If I come to your house, we both know what'll happen. You're looking for a fun time, and don't get me wrong, I love fun as much as the next girl, but... I just can't fuck you tonight, Jon. I wanna. But I can't."

My pulse jumps roughly in my throat. "You're not one to beat around the bush, huh?"

Removing her hand from my arm, her absence sends an instant bolt of cold through my blood. "No point bullshitting. I'm sure you're dynamite in the sack, Jon Hart, but I can't afford you."

She turns on her heel and grabs my hand. Leading us past a chuckling Mike, then back inside the too noisy club with the too smelly patrons – perfume, sweat, and beer – mingle and almost have me choking, though I've never felt that way when in here before.

Being alone in the fresh air with Casey's unique scent has spoiled me.

I follow her back to the bar, and when she steps onto the metal footrest at the bottom of a stool, I realize her intentions, stop her with a tug on her hand, and bring her confused body back to mine. Swinging her up into the cradle of my arms, I easily lift her across the bar and perch her ass on the far edge.

Sliding to her feet, she turns back and takes a fresh beer glass from beneath the bar. Sitting it beneath the tap, she starts pouring. "Thanks for the company, Jon. That was a well spent ten minutes, so," she finishes pouring and sets an overflowing beer in front of me, "on the house, as payment for the best date I've had in... well, ever." Shaking her head, she laughs. "And I didn't even have to put out. Bonus."

That was her best date ever?

Fuck.

Alone again, I sit at the bar for the next hour and watch her work. Customers, men *and* women flirt with her. She bats her lashes the way she did with me, and when men throw their heads back and laugh at her jokes, I frown that she so freely flirts back.

I remain in my seat when Bobby leads his girl off the floor, and I stay put when, as expected, he walks her out of the club without saying goodbye to the rest of us.

He's taking her home, which means he's ensuring a contract on my head in the form of a tiny best friend with a vengeance.

When I turn back to my would-be assassin, I can pinpoint the *exact* moment Kit and Bobby step out of the club. Pursed lips, narrowed eyes pointed right at Bobby's back, she barely notices the guy who gets up in her face and shouts for a drink.

Before I get a chance to smash his disrespectful mouth into the bar, she turns back to him, looks him up and down arrogantly, and verbally tears him apart until he's being escorted out under Mike's strong hold.

She's no one's damsel. She's not in distress.

Fifteen minutes later, a sharp tap on my shoulder has my eyes snapping away from Casey and stopping on Aiden. Glaring over my shoulder, I turn and follow his gaze and stop on Bobby as he furiously storms toward us.

Silently, I say goodbye to Casey.

It's done.

She's gone.

Then I move off my stool and meet him and Jimmy halfway across the dance floor.

"What's wrong?"

Bobby's dark brown eyes fire with rage. "Who the fuck is Jack?"

Not what I expected him to ask. When Jimmy, Aiden, and I look between each other the way we did when *someone* broke Mom's vase when we were kids, the look that says *we don't know,* or *we're not saying,* he pushes past me and storms to the bar.

Toward Casey.

Her eyes snap up as we approach. They flick to Bobby's, then mine, then back to Bobby. She sets a drink down in front of a customer and walks to us. "What's wrong? Where's Kit?"

"Who the fuck is Jack?" he spits out angrily.

I love my brother. I do. I'd let him get away with just about anything, but my hand still manages to slam down on his shoulder when my heart and brain register the disrespect in his voice. "Watch it, B. Find some fucking respect. Fast."

Uncaring for his rage, not scared at all, Casey simply clears her throat and leans on the bar. "Ah, Jack... How exactly do you know Jack?"

"Kit," he spits out angrily, "just left with three big ass guys."

Aiden steps back as though Bobby hit him. "What?!"

"Shit." She lets out a breathy sigh and leans heavier against the bar. "The three guys, one of them was Jack?" When Bobby nods, she lets out a low whistle. "Okay yeah, she's fine. She's safe. Jack on the other hand, is deep in the shit."

"Is Jack her ex?"

"Her ex?" She laughs. "Not even a little bit. But, like I said, she's safe. Just let it go."

"Let it go?" He leans closer. "Give me her number, T? You'd be doing me a huge favor–"

She smiles ruefully. "I'm sure I would, but no, I can't. I'm sorry. I'm sure you're a stand-up guy, but I just... can't."

He stands with his face half a foot from hers for a full minute, but when she doesn't crack, he turns on his heel and slams his shoulder against mine. "Fuck!"

"I think we had it wrong." Case taps her delicate fingers against mine when Bobby slams the club door open and it bounces against the wall. I turn back to find her victorious smile. "Kit's gonna be just fine. Your boy didn't break her heart, Jon. This round goes to the girls."

7

CASEY

THE HERNANDEZ FIGHT

I met a guy.

This isn't me. I don't *meet* guys.

I work at a club.

I meet people every day.

I meet *hot* guys every day.

I meet hot guys who like to flirt and buy me drinks every day.

Working at the club is a game, a game I play well, and when I count my tips at closing every morning, I smile with smug satisfaction when I remember who tipped better because I laughed at their shitty joke.

They pay better when you flutter your lashes and make them feel like big manly men.

I don't know why this *one* has stuck with me, but a month ago I met a guy named Jon Hart, and though he basically offered himself up on a delicious platter, though I'd be a lying whore if I said I wasn't tempted, it just didn't feel *right*.

Something's off about him.

There's vulnerability inside him.

Despite his almost six and a half feet of solid muscle, the dangerous look in his eyes, the sculpted jaw that I *know* has taken a few hits over the years; despite the dry humor and the fun we had together, there's a strange vulnerability in him that I'm not so sure I could disentangle.

Therefore, I didn't.

I would've enjoyed taking him to my bed, and I *know* he would have rocked my world, but I just couldn't bring myself to take the leap.

Somehow, I think Jon would've broken my heart before the sun rose the next morning.

Let's call a spade a spade; my rejection was purely a survival tactic.

I talk to my best friend every single day, so I know that she and Bobby have reconnected.

He was like a dog at a bone, and after a billion visits to the club asking for her number, after I had to tell him no a billion and one times, he found her anyway.

I know they're talking now, and I know he makes her skip and dance every damn day she sees him.

He looks at her the way *no* man has ever looked at me, so despite Jon's warnings that Bobby might have his fun and run, he seems to be sticking.

And they haven't even hooked up yet.

I've dated since before I was old enough to do so.

I dated Alan for two years; he took my virginity, he took my casserole dish, and two years after we began, he ditched and decided to spend his casserole cooking days with another chick.

My eighteen-year-old heart wept, but my best friend picked me up, dusted me off, and we moved on.

Then I dated Ty.

He was fun. He was good in bed. He *didn't* steal my kitchen supplies. But just like with Alan, two years later, our thing ran its course, and he ran away.

I guess my love life runs a certain holding pattern; good sex, fun times, two years, the guy finds his dick in someone else's panties.

My best friend picked me up again, and we kept on trucking along. Somewhere around my twenty second birthday, I met Todd.

I told Jon about him.

Two years after we officially hooked up, I realized his dopey ass was a waste of my time.

It turns out, I'm a serial monogamist.

I needed to spend some time single.

Single didn't mean *alone*, it just meant no commitment.

I was breaking my two-year curse by not entering a relationship at all.

Enter man number four and onwards.

I don't regret them.

None of them treated me badly.

Ironically, those one-night-stands treated me better than the men who claimed to be loyal to me. If you ignore the fact we slept together the same night we met, their behavior otherwise was perfectly chivalrous.

I'd found the elixir to life.

You don't need a boyfriend who'll treat you like shit, eat your cereal, steal your crockery, and bitch about everything. These other men treated me like a queen for the hour or two we spent together.

It was perfect.

But when, a few months ago, I stopped and realized I legitimately couldn't count them anymore, when the names and faces and the details were blurring together, I realized I'd dropped my serial monogamist label and picked up a whole new label.

It was time for me to just stop.

No dick for me.

No dirty kisses. No three a.m. fun.

Just no more.

I needed time to be me, *alone*, for a while.

Jon Hart almost made me forget the promise I'd made myself. He's someone I could easily fall into bed with, and I'd do it with a smile on my face. But when it's time for him to leave the next day... I don't know. He's just different, and I don't have it in me right now to figure out why.

But inevitably, if *my* best friend and *his* best friend start seeing each other, I can't avoid Jon forever.

Thank God I didn't sleep with him!

That could've made everything awkward.

I step around my couch and slump into the cushions with a beer in one hand and the TV remote in the other. It's fight night, and for the first time in forever, I'm watching alone.

Kit and I normally watch the fights together. We normally have a slumber party like the kind straight out of middle school with pizza and soda and giggles, but just like I need to stay away from boys, I also need to stop running to Kit when I'm sad and lonely.

I need to learn to cope on my own and stop relying on Kit to pick me up.

That's not to say I don't talk to her every single day. I do. But I'm not going to send her a whiny text when she's got so much else going on in her life.

Her dad died.

One of the best dads I've ever known, gone in his forties. Her brother moved into her home. She's dealing with lawyers, and injuries, and inse-curities...

My grief and longing for Mr. Reilly is nothing compared to hers.

But I considered him mine. I grew up in her house more often than my own, he treated me like a daughter, so when he passed, it hurt.

His absence will be felt for a long time.

But I'm determined to support Kit through this. I'll help her in every way I can, which includes *not* dragging her down with my totally non-important boy drama.

As though my thoughts have summoned her, I smile as my phone dings and her name flashes on screen.

Kit: *Hey! Whatchya doing right now?*

I laugh and dig my ass into the plush couch cushions.

Me: *Hey!! Just sitting down with a beer. What about you?*

I open my beer and wait for her reply, and within seconds, my cell dings.

Kit: *We're at the Kincaid gym. Watching the Hernandez fight.*

Damn her! I was over here being a big-girl-panties girl and not texting her that I was lonely, and she's off watching the fight anyway.

And she's with all the cute boys...

Me: *Bitch! I'm waiting for that fight to start, too. I didn't want to mention it because I know you've been stressed and busy.*

Kit: *It's cool. You should have! I totally forgot. The guys do a pizza fight night thing like we do, but at the gym. They invited us. You should come!*

My heart thumps nervously when I consider her invitation. Do I want to go? Hell yes! Should I go...? I'm not so sure.

Me: *Really? Now? Are you already there?*

Kit: *Yeah, Jack and I are here, and the guys. Pizza's here, and I brought some drinks. You should grab some ice cream and come over. Quick! Fight starts soon!*

Me: *Argh! But I'm in my pj's! It'll take forever to change and get there.*

Kit: *Wear them! It'll blow Jon's mind.*

Splat! Don't go there, Casey. Do. Not. Go. There.

Me: *Jon's there?!? Omg omg omg.*

Kit: *LOL, of course he's here. Who do you think asked me to text you? Seriously though, I'm wearing casual shorts and a messy pony. Just come, and hurry!*

If I wear my metal underwear and leave the key at home, everything should be fine. Right?

A bed partner, I don't need, but I could always do with more friends. And if Kit and Bobby are starting to see each other, then Jon and I will inevitably see more of each other.

I'm not actually a whore with no willpower.

I can be in the same room as a sexy man and not jump him.

Maybe.

Jumping up from the couch, I stub my toe as I run, but it doesn't slow me down as I blindly text and tear my pyjama pants off.

Me: *Okay, already running to my room. See you soon.*

My heart flips with happy butterflies when I climb out of my little old car and find Kit mounting a sexy man out in front of the gym. Her ex-boyfriend, Max, was a piece of shit, and never once did he kiss her the way Bobby kisses her now. He never looked at her, or held her, or crowded her the way Bobby does.

It does my heart good to see her smile so much.

To see her let go a little.

To see her live a little.

I approach the indecently-making-out couple as Bobby presses her against the wall and proves that there *is* someone in this world that can help her relax, even amidst the shit-show that is her life.

It's my job as her best friend to make her squirm. It's an honor bestowed upon a select few, and one I'd never be stupid enough to pass up, so I clear my throat with a girly, "Ahem."

Jumping away from Bobby as though he suddenly turned into an electric fence, she slams against the brick wall and knocks the air from her lungs.

I feel guilty – for two-point-three seconds – but her embarrassment makes me grin when her eyes come to mine. I step forward on a laugh and reach for her hand. "Shit, babe." I snort when her mortified eyes turn to fire. "Are you okay?"

"You asshole!" She snaps her hand out of my reach and has my laughter turning to tiny little piggy snorts when she peeks up at an amused Bobby. "Jesus, Case! What the hell are you doing sneaking around in the dark?"

I show her the bag of ice-cream bars in my left hand. "I'm here for pizza and sexy fighters. You knew I was coming."

She lets out a tiny mortified squeak and shoots a glance at Bobby. "Well... yeah. But did you sprint here? I only texted you a minute ago."

"No. You texted me ages ago, and now I'm here." I shake the bag. "See?"

Bobby looks down at her with a smug grin. "*This* is who you were texting when I came out?"

Her poor face looks like she might die of mortification. "Umm... yeah." When his laughter simply joins mine, she huffs angrily. "Whatever, I'm going inside. I'm hungry."

"Hold on a sec, babe." He turns to me. "Hey, Tink. Good to see ya. Now get lost."

Despite the annoying as hell nickname he *gifted* me with the night we met, I smile and step away without complaint. He can call me anything he wants, so long as he continues to grope my girl and make her feel pretty.

"Have fun, kids. Wear a condom."

I grab a package of drinks from Bobby's broad hands – since he needs those for groping – then I step into the gym and leave my girl standing in the dark with a sexy fighter.

I've never been inside this gym before. If I'm telling the truth, I've never been inside *any* gym before, and for good reason. It smells like dirty socks and ball sweat. With my nose scrunched with distaste, I stop at the front desk and turn around the small space to get my bearings.

Immediately, I peek past a small sectional divider and get a view of an open training room. Boxing ring. Boxing bags. More ball sweat.

My eyes stop on a familiar face; Jack – the little brother I've known since the day he was born. He's well over a foot taller than me, even at fifteen years old, and though he's been a real fucking jerk to Kit the last year or so, I feel like he's changing. He's growing.

Six months ago, he was the leading cause for Kit's stress, but the last little while, he seems to have realized he was a tool. He's not super obvious about it, he doesn't gush over her or kiss her feet, but I see the changes.

More studying after school, less backtalk, less disrespect.

Six months ago, he'd shout at Kit. He'd call her an uptight bitch. He'd scream his hatred for the only person in this world who truly has his best interests at heart.

He's still a smartass teenager, but he's trying to be kinder. He's trying to be a team member, rather than a spoiled prick.

He's still on my shit list, but he's working his way off.

"Hey there, Sunshine."

I spin in four-inch heels and manage not to drop the drinks or ice-creams. Coming eye to eye with the sexiest man I've met this year – or, you know, ever – I smile at Jon Hart as he stands by the door with thick arms folded across a thicker chest.

I let my eyes track his freshly showered body, over his chest, over a smug grin, stopping briefly on wet hair, then back down over a gray shirt that sticks to wet spots on his skin, and down thick thighs encased in sexy jeans.

I regret not buying *actual* steel undies.

I regret bypassing the metal fabrication warehouse.

I don't have the willpower!

I'm coming off a self-imposed dry spell, and Jon Hart looks like a tall glass of delicious water.

Dammit!

"Hey, stranger." Stepping to the desk six feet from where he stands, choosing to breathe sweaty balls over sexy post-workout, post-shower Jon, I place the drinks and ice-cream down, then turn back and casually lean against the desk like I'm not mind fucking him. "Good to see you again." *So* good to see him.

"Yeah." He grins like he knows a dirty secret, and has me thinking about our ten-minute date. I have to look away before I do something stupid; like blush. "And you didn't even have to run me down with your car."

I forgot about my threats that night. "*Your* best friend didn't break *my* best friend's heart. My shit-list remains free of *Rollers*. For now."

He laughs and looks down to shiny black and red high-top shoes. "That's a relief. I've seriously been looking over my shoulder every day for a month. You're a scary chick."

Even though it feels foolish to do so, I wink in an attempt to feign coolness. "Look at me keeping you on your toes. My powers are getting stronger. A whole month without even having to remind you." I make a 'sheesh' noise, like I'm a three-hundred-pound fighter that threatened him with a fist to the face. "Gotta say, I've impressed even myself."

Quietly breathing out on a laugh, the soft shake of his head has the soft hairs on the back of my neck standing on edge.

His eyes come up. "You been good, Case?"

I nod shyly and lean heavily against the desk. "Yeah, I've been good. Just working. What about you?"

He shrugs carelessly. "Just working. Tolerating Bobby's pouting ass, since *your* best friend broke *my* best friend's heart."

I smile triumphantly. "And you said she'd smile as he patted her on the ass and sent her home the next morning."

"Yeah, well…" He clears his throat nervously. "We won't repeat that too loud. I'm in uncharted territory here, but since they're getting along and neither of them have a broken heart right now, we won't let her know I said that. I'm pretty sure it's against bro code." Shrugging and pushing off the wall, he steps close and leans past me to throw the ice-cream in the mini fridge beside the desk. Picking up the drinks and pretending like he doesn't *know* I'm choking on the delicious scent of his aftershave, he nods toward the boxing ring. "Let's go get our spot. You're here for the fight?"

"Yeah." I frown thoughtfully. "You don't mind, do you? Kit invited me along. I swear I'm not stalking you."

He shrugs easily and waits for me to push away from the desk. "I don't mind. You can sit with me, I'll explain the fight to you."

"Yeah." I turn my eyes to the floor so he doesn't see my grin. He doesn't have to *explain* anything to me. Kit and I have been watching pay-per-view fights for years. I have money on tonight's fight. Wheaton, Hernandez's Irish competitor, has a wolfish grin, badass tattoos, and the skills to – hopefully – back up his arrogance.

I let Jon lead me toward the giant blue and black boxing ring in the center of a huge room.

He nods toward the group of men I've already met. "You remember Aiden?"

Reaching through the ropes, Aiden takes my hand in his. "Nice to see you again, Tink."

"And Jimmy."

"How you doin', Tink? It's good to see you again." He flashes a playful grin before dropping back to his ass and turning toward the screen.

"And you obviously already know Jack."

He holds out his fist to be bumped, and obliging, I tap his and lift a brow at the sight of pink, cracked knuckles…

Someone's been fighting.

Jon steps forward and climbs through the ropes, then planting one foot on the bottom two ropes, he pulls the top two up to create a huge gap for me to practically walk through.

Offering a chivalrous hand, I glance up into his dark eyes and allow him to help me onto the platform three or so feet off the blue mats on the gym floor.

As soon as I'm on his side of the ropes, he releases them so they snap back into place. Following him across the dark blue platform and stepping around still-wet patches of definitely-sweat and maybe-blood, I hide my expression when he looks over his shoulder to make sure I'm still nearby.

Slowly lowering onto my knees, I drop to my butt beside Jack, and when Jon slides in close beside me, he leans toward a stack of pizza boxes in the center of the ring.

His eyes come back to mine. "Loaded or girly?"

I frown. "What's girly?"

"Pizza. We get loaded for the men, and wussy chicken and cheese for Sissy."

I nervously glance around the gym. "Is your sister here?"

"Nah, she's not coming tonight. Loaded or girly?"

"Why'd you buy her *girly* pizza if she's not coming?"

He chuckles and lets out a playful huff. "We get the same all the time, it never goes to waste. Last chance, loaded or girly?"

"Loaded, please."

Impressed, he nods and sits back with a large box of steaming pizza. Setting it in the gap between our legs, he opens the box and indicates with his chin. "Eat up, short stuff. Knock yourself out."

The silly butterflies in my stomach turn to an instant ball of lead. "Two minutes? That's all it took to start picking on my height?"

His dark eyes search mine curiously. "I'm sorry. I didn't mean anything by it. I just meant... Eat up."

People commenting on my height, *or lack thereof*, is a daily occurrence for me. I'm firmly in the 'cute' category. At just over five feet, I'm tiny. My best friend is more than half a foot taller than me. Even when I'm in heels and she's in flats, she's still taller.

I'm always the shortest person in the room, always at the front of group photos, always at the brunt of the *cute* jokes. I can take most with good humor, I can laugh a lot of it away, but sometimes it hurts.

It's hard to feel like a woman, a *sexy* woman, when everyone makes me feel like I'm twelve years old. So when all six feet and four inches of

Jon Hart teases me, I'm just not sure if he's teasing for fun, or if he's putting me in the little kid category.

Am I a child to him? Or am I a woman?

Even if I'm buying my steel underwear as soon as I leave here tonight, even if I don't *intend* to sleep with him, I still want to be seen as a woman.

I want to be sexy.

Taking his apology with a huff of breath, I grab a slice of pizza and sit back against the bouncy ropes. Fixing the melted streams of cheese and sausage as they slide off my slice and threaten to burn my lap, I watch him watch me as he takes his own slice and sits back.

"Not working tonight?"

I shrug easily and plop a ball of cheese in my mouth. "No. Normally I would be, but I took tonight off. Usually we do something for the fights, dinner or whatever, but we forgot to make plans this time."

"Good thing *your* best friend met a fighter, huh?"

Shuddering dramatically, I laugh. "You're right. Without Bobby, I might be sitting at home all alone in my jammies. So lame."

He chuckles softly. "Tell me something…" He considers his words for a minute before meeting my eyes. "With *my* best friend and *your* best friend now practically best friends–"

I let my smug smile fly free. "You looking for a new best friend, Jon?"

He laughs and relaxes back until our shoulders touch. "Yeah, guess I am."

"Will you show me your trophy case? I told *all* my friends about it."

Please God, don't. I don't think even metal underwear would stop us if I go to his house.

Unaware of my thoughts, he laughs and takes a bite of pizza. "Anytime you wanna see it. I'd probably even dust them, first. You know, best foot forward and all that." When I snort and nibble at my pizza, his smile turns somewhat shy. "Actually, I kinda have a proposition for you."

"That sounds like it's gonna be illegal."

"No, you dumbass." He bumps my shoulder and has me bumping into Jack. "Legit. Nothing illegal."

"Alright." I'm *that* cat that will *always* die of curiosity. "Shoot."

"Wanna be my friend?"

I choke on my laugh. "Wow." I cough to get the ball of dough to move down my throat. "I feel like we're in kindergarten right now. You don't have to *ask* to be my friend. People do it every day without actually announcing it." His smile is breathtaking, even while shy. "Wait." I suspiciously search his eyes. "Is this one of those *friends with benefits* things? Because I'm still not looking for a man."

"No, I mean a legitimate friendship. No benefits. Kit and Bobby mean something to each other, so I'm gonna see you around. Bobby's ditching my ass for... well, ass." He grins again. "So I need a new bro."

My lips twitch. "You want me to be your *bro?*"

"Well, that's a weird way to say it," he laughs nervously. "But yeah, I wanna add you in my phone. I want to text you just to say hey, and I don't mean the three a.m. kind of texts. Just hey. I want us to be cool."

I consider his words with a narrowed gaze, and work to push aside the mental images of sex we'll never have. We're consciously friend-zoning each other... most people go the opposite way.

"Okay..." I extend a hand and wait for him to take it. "I'll be your new best friend."

He squeezes my hand and has my heart tripping in my chest. "Yeah?"

"Uh-huh." When he releases me, I sit back and lean against his shoulder. He's my friend. We can do this. He makes me smile, so we're off to a good start. "So my name's Casey Irvine. I'm a Taurus, and you're a...?"

His brows pinch. "Leo?"

"Are you not sure? Because this is important."

"Why's my star sign important?"

"Because it matters! If we aren't compatible, then we may as well not bother." I'm mostly joking, but his amused face makes it worth it. "Leo's are protective, right?"

He gives a single sharp nod. "You could say I'm protective."

"And loyal?"

Another nod. "And loyal."

"You're a show pony?"

His head tilts to the side. "A show pony?"

"Do you like being center of attention? Do you like people looking at you?"

"No." Just like his nod was sharp, his *no* is even more severe. "No show ponying for me. Definitely not. What's your star sign say about you?"

"My star sign animal is a bull."

He laughs at my proud announcement. "That doesn't surprise me one bit."

I glare playfully. "I'm a determined person. Stubborn's another word people like to throw around. I like to indulge; good food, good clothes, good shoes. Good times."

He knocks his knee into mine playfully. "You gonna send me broke, Casey?"

"Nah, I have a job. And my birthday was just last month. You're set for almost a whole year."

I scoot closer to Jon when, hand in hand, Kit and Bobby make their way inside and sit down beside me. As soon as they're comfortable and whispering between themselves, I turn back to find Jon's eager gaze waiting for my attention.

"What?"

"My birthday's coming up." When I stare in confusion, he continues, "In August. Just so you know."

I laugh. "Leo the Lion's birthday is in August. Makes sense. What do you like for gifts?"

"Cake."

I cock my head to the side. "Cake?"

"Yeah, I'd really like a chocolate cake."

I study his handsome face. *Cake. He just wants cake.* "Homemade or store bought? Because I'm not really a baker."

"A real best friend would bake it."

"Has Bobby ever baked you a cake?"

He barks out a laugh. "No, he hasn't. But it's already been established he doesn't love me like a best friend *should*. Pretty girl turns up and he drops me like last week's trash."

How could I say no to his humble request? "Alright, Jon. I'll bake you a cake. I promise."

8

JON

SUNSHINE

*T*he day after Wheaton smashed Hernandez in the octagon, taking the title belt back to Ireland and cementing my brand-new friendship with the beautiful Casey Irvine, I bring my phone to my ear and smile as I wait for her to answer.

I had a nice time last night.

Besides my sister, I've never really had female friends. I've had Bobby and the guys, and Sissy was always with us, but before Kit turned up, we never had pizza night with chicks before.

It feels weird.

But at the same time, it felt pretty cool.

She's comforting. She's half my size, but possesses this maternal comfort that I never got from my own mother. It's almost like an open invitation to lay my head on her chest and just… rest.

I just have to ignore my twitching dick.

I'm trying to make a go of this.

This new friendship I've fallen into. A *real* friend. No sex.

Bobby has no time for me anymore, especially now that he and Kit have an official date coming up. He's already sunk, and until they get their fill, I'm out in the cold and in need of a new friend.

With Kit comes Casey, so why the fuck not?

Friendship *without* the benefits is best case scenario for us. I *want* the benefits. Fuck yes, I do. But strangely, I'd rather the warm balm she unknowingly soothes me with each time she smiles.

Kicking my shoes off in my living room, the line connects and has me smiling. "Well, hey there, Leo the Lion. Whatcha up to?"

Just like that, she makes my day brighter.

Who the fuck am I?

"Hey, Sunshine." I throw my hat onto the side table and run a hand through my short hair. "I'm finished up at the gym for the day. Wanted to say hey."

"And it's not even three a.m." She tsks obnoxiously. "You really are a man of your word. That's such a rare quality in men nowadays."

"I'm definitely a man of my word." I chuckle. "So what're you doing?"

"I don't know if you heard, but there's a big date on tonight. Some playa' named Bobby thinks he can step up to the big leagues. Boy meets girl, girl says yes after the eleven billionth time he asked her out, and now here we are, at her house with hair rollers and lipstick while we pick out slutty underwear."

Can't say that's an unwelcome thought. "Do girls really pick each other's underwear before a date?"

"Just me and Kit. We're tight like that."

"Sounds like it," I rumble out. Stopping in my kitchen and simply staring at the wall, I imagine Casey... and underwear... and prettying herself up for a date.

"Not like that!" she rushes out. "We aren't tight like *that*. If you're thinking dirty thoughts about my best friend, I'll stab you."

Shaking my head and laughing, I step toward my fridge and take out a bottle of water. "Don't worry, Case. She's all Bobby's. I'm not thinking about her." *I'm thinking about you.*

"Well... Good then." She huffs. "So Kit's in the shower. Jim's downstairs with Jack–"

My eyes narrow. "Jim's there?"

"Yeah. He's a funny guy, you know that?"

I do know that. Usually, I'd agree, but now he's hanging out with *my* new best friend, he's being funny, as in, he's flirting, and suddenly, I want to dislocate his jaw.

Tomorrow.

"Yeah, he's alright. You're upstairs?"

"Yeah, I'm in Kit's room, waiting for her to get out. She won't be long. Bobby said he'd be here soon."

"What're you doing after Kit and B take off?" *She's not staying with Jim.*

"I was gonna go home. Maybe order some Chinese food."

Good idea. "I could order Chinese."

"Okay... well, don't call for at least an hour. I wanna get my order in first. I'm starving."

When I mention to my *other* best friend I'm ordering food, he simply drives over and parks his ass on my couch without a word being spoken. I guess girls don't work quite the same. Except Sissy. But she's one of us. She's not a *girl.*

"No, dummy. I can order, and we can eat together. You could come over and hang out. Best friends hang out over takeout all the time."

"Oh, right. Alright." She clears her throat. "I guess I could come over."

"I'll text you my address."

She hesitates with a string of 'Oh's' and 'Umm's' until finally settling on, "Alright."

Rejection stings, even when it isn't said outright. "You don't have to come over if you don't wanna. Forget I asked–"

"No. I do..." Again, she clears her throat. "It's just that... well..."

I blow out a breath of frustration. "Spit it out, Sunshine. My *other* best friend tells it straight. I never have to guess, so I'm gonna need you to get on board with saying it how it is."

"It's just..." She pauses. "No benefits, right?"

"Best friends. No benefits. Scouts honor."

She giggles softly. "Were you ever a Scout?"

"Nope." Laughing and finally relaxing back against the kitchen counter, I bring the bottle of water to my lips. "But I'm a man of my word. I've had your number for a whole day, and not a single three a.m. booty call."

"That's true. You're an honorable man, Jon Hart. Alright, text me your address. I'll come over when Kit's whisked away in her carriage."

"Not sure you could call Bobby's Rav a *carriage,* but it squeaks enough, if she closes her eyes, she could probably imagine it."

"Good enough!"

I laugh again. "Good enough."

"Okay, well, I have to go. Kit's out. But I'll see you in a bit."

"Bye, Case. I'll text you."

"Bye."

Taking the phone from my ear and ending the call, I flip to my text screen and send my address immediately. I don't even care if I look *too* keen. I'd never overthink inviting a guy over, so I'm going to treat this like that.

I open a text for Izzy, since she technically lives here; she technically lives everywhere; she has a bed and clothes in each of our houses, she's welcome in any of our houses, though she spends the majority of her time here.

Not tonight she's not.

Me: *Where are you? Can you bunk at Aiden's tonight?*

I don't suggest Bobby's, because it's not cool to be a cockblock. And not Jimmy's, because he spent the afternoon flirting with Casey and I'm pissed at him, plus, he's sleeping at Kit's tonight to hang with Jack.

Walking to my room and tossing my sweaty training clothes to the floor, I step into the shower and try not to touch my cock while thinking of Casey. We may be friends *without* benefits, but she's still hot, so I'm still going to shower and not stink like a pig around her.

Maybe she's not going to be treated *exactly* the way I'd treat B, because I don't give a shit if I smell around him, but not smelling around her just seems like the gentlemanly thing to do.

Stepping out five minutes later and wrapping the towel around my hips, I head into my bedroom and poke around in my drawers. If it were a regular night, if I was alone, or it was just Iz, I'd toss on sweats and a tank and figure that was good enough.

Tonight, I pull on a pair of jeans and a navy shirt. Running a hand through my hair and stopping in front of the mirror, I nod.

Good enough.

Walking back to the kitchen and picking up my phone, I frown at the absence of texts from Iz.

It's been ages.

She should've replied by now.

I dial her number and prepare to hunt her down. At the snap of fingers, my non-date with my new best friend is gone from my mind. Iz's sleeping arrangements, cockblocking, flirting brothers, it's all gone from my mind as my heart races and I wonder where she is.

I just need to know Sissy is safe.

My entire life has revolved around making sure my sister is safe. From the day she was born, nothing ever mattered as much as her, and that shit doesn't go away simply because I met a girl and asked her over for Chinese.

My heart almost seizes when the call rings out. My stomach drops, my hands ball into fists, and my imagination conjures all of the worst-case scenarios.

If Wayne and Shirley went looking for her, if they came within five-hundred feet of her, I'll kill them. I'll slit their fucking throats and pull their tongues out the bleeding wound.

Iz *knows* me; she never ignores my calls.

Never.

Just as I press my thumb down to call again, she blows through my front door all fluttering long chestnut hair, and an overweight book bag tugging her down on one side. "Relax! I'm here."

Tossing my phone aside and stepping toward her, I take her bag and drop it to the floor near the couch. Looking her up and down from top to toe, I stop on her hands. "You're not missing your arms. Your thumbs are perfectly intact, Iz. You got a reason why you didn't text? Where were you?"

"Relax." Stepping in, she wraps her arms around my waist and presses her face to my chest. "I was walking down from the bus stop. I was almost home, so figured I'd just wait to talk to you."

"Don't wait, Sissy."

"Sorry. I'm here now, and yes, I can sleep at Aiden's. Or maybe Jim's. I'll call him–"

"Jim's at Kit's house tonight."

Like I punched her in the face, her head snaps back so she can look up into my eyes. "Who's Kit?"

"Bobby's date… Why?"

"Ohhh, Kit! Yeah, she's cool. I saw her at the gym."

"Yeah, her."

"So why's Jim staying at hers?"

"Jack needs a babysitter."

"Jack, her brother?" Laughing, she wanders to her book bag and begins piling heavy textbooks on the coffee table. "Jack's no baby. He's a giant."

"Well, apparently he's a giant asshole and in need of supervision while B gets laid."

"Gross." Standing, she slams a heavy fist against my arm and has me stepping back and bringing a hand up to rub the injury. Just like the rest of us, Iz has been training and fighting since she was old enough to walk.

Bryan Kincaid was a fighter. He had three sons, and he taught them to fight, too. And as soon as Iz and I turned up and became their pseudo kids, we started training, too. No dollies and strollers for Iz. She was in the yard with the rest of us, and when we started training in an actual gym, she was right on our heels and keeping up.

"I *don't* need to know about Beebee's sex life," she snaps. "And while we're on the subject, I don't wanna know why *you're* kicking me out, either. Yes, it's fine, I'll stay at Aiden's. Nothing else needs to be said."

"No, Sissy. My thing… it's not like that."

She throws her hand up to silence me. "I *really* don't wanna know, but just so you're aware, this is inconvenient. The Outlander season finale is on tonight, and you *know* Aiden won't want to watch it."

"Of course he won't! Pretty boys in skirts, why the hell would he want to watch that shit?"

She rolls her eyes. "You should give it a go. There are loads of cool fight scenes and stuff."

"Is it romantic? Is it a love story, Sissy?" At her nod, I consider my point made. "I'm not watching a fairy romance."

Shaking her head, she walks toward the hallway. "You're missing out. Claire's hot, too. I'm getting changed, then I'll get out of your way."

"You wanna take my truck? Or call Aiden?"

She steps into the hall. "I'll just take a bus."

"Sissy!" I wait for her face to come back around the corner. "Truck or Aiden?"

She sighs with exasperation. "Call Aiden."

Opening the door to my glamorous Sunshine, I smile at her sexy skintight jeans and five-inch fuck-me heels. She *prettied* herself up, despite the fact we're just watching TV and eating Chinese – that I still haven't ordered.

Pretty damn glad I chose jeans instead of sweats.

"Hey."

Walking through the open door and catching me by surprise, she wraps her arms around my hips and rests her face on my chest. "Hey, Leo. I missed you since yesterday."

Instinctively, I bring my arms down and hold her delicate frame against mine. "Umm... Hey."

"Best friends hug, right? That's cool?"

Well, shit. Me and Bobby don't hug, and he's the only best friend I've ever had, but I'll start hugging him if I have to. "Best friends can hug. Definitely." Bending my neck and inhaling her scent, I declare this day *'always hug your best friend day.'*

She smells like a cinnamon donut.

"You going out later?" Stepping back, I pointedly look back down at her sexy jeans and floating top. "You look like you got somewhere to be."

"Nope." Walking into my living room and looking everywhere at once, she teasingly swipes a finger across the TV cabinet the way an old matron might do a white-glove test. "Not going anywhere."

"Why so dressed up?"

Turning back and looking down at her thighs, she frowns. "This is just me. These are my casual clothes."

"You wear heels around the house?"

"Not at home. But I'm not at home right now, am I?"

"You wanna take them off? Get comfortable? I could probably rip a pair of sweats in half. You could use one leg."

Flashing a dangerous glare, she has me biting my lip to stop from smiling. She has size issues; no teasing allowed. "No, I don't want your stinky sweats. This is fine."

"But won't you be uncomfortable?" I don't know why I'm arguing with her. She looks amazing, she literally *feels* good to look at, but I just hate the idea that she might be uncomfortable in my home.

She shrugs. "I'm comfortable when I feel like I look good. This is comfortable for me."

Well, she definitely looks good. *Do best friends touch each other's butts?*

"Fine, your decision. Want a beer?"

"Yeah." Turning a slow circle of my living room, she turns back and grins. "A beer would be great, thanks. Can I look around?"

Stepping toward my kitchen, but looking over my shoulder, I admire her delectable ass as she looks around. "Sure. Look at anything you want. I'll call in our order, then I'll give you a tour."

"Alright." Standing in front of my main bookshelf and looking up high, she strokes the spines of my beloved Harry Potter collection and smiles.

"Do you have any allergies? Dislikes?"

"Nah, I'm easy." Answering me with a distracted mumble, she busily pulls down a copy of the Lord of the Rings, flips it over and studies the back, then replaces it and continues her stroking journey.

Walking back into the living room a moment later with a beer in each hand, I stop close beside her, but besides distractedly accepting the drink, she ignores me and keeps studying my bookshelf.

I guess she likes books, too.

Alrighty.

Leaving her to it for a minute, I walk back to the kitchen and place our order. I ask for one of everything. Every chicken dish. Every beef dish. Everything with seafood in it. I order enough to feed a family of five, but I'll be damned if I get it wrong and she sits in my living room and picks at her food because she doesn't like what I ordered.

I want to give her variety, and I want to give her a reason to sit back and pop the button on her jeans.

I want her to be comfortable.

Nothing will go to waste, and finally, now, at twenty-six years old, I have the money and freedom to buy a pretty girl some dinner.

Eight-year-old me wouldn't even know this me.

Eight-year-old me didn't have enough food for himself, let alone extras *just because.*

Slumping onto my couch after I close the front door to the delivery guy, I place the bags of food onto the coffee table and start tearing the plastic bags open.

"Guest's choice; what do you wanna watch?"

She turns to me with a playful grin. "Do you watch Outlander? Season finale's on tonight."

"No." Shaking my head, I pass her a napkin to lay out on her fancy jeans. "I don't do romances, nor do I watch dudes prance around in skirts. Wanna watch Star Wars?"

"Star Wars?" Her lips twitch with secrets. This is a test, and if she answers wrong, this friendship is over. Doomed from the start. "Which one?"

"Episode one, of course."

"Of course," she laughs. "Alright, sure. We can watch Star Wars. You're lucky I'm recording Outlander at home."

I roll my eyes. "Wouldn't want to miss that."

"Don't judge me, Leo!"

"I wouldn't dare." Taking the container of piping hot chicken and ginger stuff, I peel the lid off and take a deep breath. "Mmm." I turn to her. "You like chicken?"

Shaking her head morosely, she sighs. "A *real* best friend would know the answer to that. Kit knows if I like chicken."

"We've only been best friends for twenty-three hours. Give me time, woman."

"Do you think we'll ever be such good besties that you'll buy me tampons if I need them?"

I laugh and knock her shoulder with mine. "I know you're testing me. I have a sister. Trust me, I've bought tampons before. You're gonna have to try harder if you wanna make this weird."

She tsks and lifts the chopsticks over the container of chicken. "Next time, Leo. I'll think of something better next time."

Grabbing the remote and flicking on the TV, I flip channels until I find the Blu-ray player. It just so happens the movie we need is already loaded, so I start it up, hit play, and lean back into the cushions and get comfortable when Casey leans back with her chicken and rests her shoulder against mine.

The soundtrack that is possibly the most relaxing sound in the whole world, thrums through my sound system, but for the first time ever, I find myself not watching the screen. Instead, I watch Casey as she hoovers the chicken.

Note to self: Casey likes chicken and ginger.

I watch the way she smiles when Anakin asks Padme if she's an angel, then as she bites her lip when they meet again ten years later.

Her lips turn up into a sexy smirk. "Quit watching me. You make me feel like I have chin hairs or something."

I laugh and turn back to the screen... for a second. "Sorry."

"You know this is a romance, right?"

"What's a romance?"

"Ani and Padme."

"No! Don't ruin this for me."

"Whatever," she laughs. Setting the empty containers on the table and grunting with comfort as she lays back against the cushions, she kicks her heels off and perches her tiny polished feet on the table.

There she is.

"Comfortable?"

"Mmhmm." Taking my arm and laying it across her lap, she studies my ink and forces me to work on my body's reactions to a woman's touch. Her fingers graze my forearm. They trace the patterns in my tanned skin and have goosebumps breaking out along my spine. "I like these."

"Yeah?"

"Mmhmm. They look good on you."

Inside, I contentedly sigh at her praise. I don't care what kind of benefits we did or did not agree to, I want her to like what she sees. "Do you have any?"

She shakes her head and traces a design that brings her fingers up to my bicep. "Nah. The idea of paying someone to stab me six billion times just seems so..." Her playful eyes come up to mine. "Dumb. I *want* some, but needles freak me out." She shrugs. "I'm too chicken. Kit has a few, she said it's not so bad. She said she'd hold my hand. But I haven't done it yet."

"I'll go with you." I flex my fingers and pray she doesn't notice how much I'd like to stroke her delicate flesh. "If you ever do it, call me. I'll hold your hand."

Her eyes come back to mine. "You would?"

"Sure. I'll distract you, and you'll hardly notice they're doing it... What would you get done?"

She shrugs and goes back to studying the script on my forearm. "I dunno, but it'd have to be pretty important. Something I'd want to keep forever."

I nod thoughtfully. "Good plan. Where would you get it?"

She shrugs again. "Maybe my ribs? Tattoos on ribs are sexy."

No arguments here. I think a tattoo on Casey's ribs would be sexy as hell. "We'll do it whenever you're ready, Sunshine. I'll make sure I'm there for you."

Her mischief filled eyes meet mine. "That's what best friends are for, right?"

I flex my hand discreetly. "Exactly. It's my duty to be there for you."

Despite the movie lasting well over two hours, it was never going to be long enough. By the one-hour mark, Casey's soft body turned to mush until we found ourselves cuddled up with my arm over her shoulder and hers over my hips. Then by the two-hour mark, cue the end credits rolling, her hair was in my face and her cinnamon scent in my lungs.

Fastest two hours of my life.

Not ready for her to go home, not ready to say goodnight, I jump up and put the next movie in.

If I don't give her a chance to run, I won't have to actually *ask* her to stay, but in the ten seconds I'm gone from the couch, she shuffles along to the end and has my heart shattering in my chest.

I wasn't done hugging her.

I sit back where I started and frown. "Do I smell?"

Shaking her head, she pats her lap. "No. Come here."

When I don't move, when I confusedly glance between her eyes and her lap, she takes my shirt in her hand and pulls me down until my head rests in her lap. "You don't smell. You can rest on me."

This is better.

This is so much better.

I rearrange my broad shoulders and make the awkward angle work. I don't give a damn that my shoulders bow in and will leave me with knotted muscles tomorrow. I don't care that my long legs hang three feet off the end of the couch. There's no way in hell I'm moving away.

Resisting the urge to press a kiss to her firm thigh, I bring my knees to my chest and tuck my hand between to keep it away from her. "Am I squishing you?"

She laughs softly. "You've got a big fat head, Jon Hart, especially with all those books you've read, but no, you aren't squishing me. I'm comfortable." Her hand comes down to my head, and her nails scratch gentle patterns into my hair and leave me practically purring. "Rest now, Leo. I've got your back."

Within minutes, my eyes drift closed and Scottish accents replace the whooshing sounds of lightsabers on the TV.

9

CASEY

JUST ONCE, PADME

"*H*ey." Letting myself through Jon's front door using the key he gave me a couple weeks ago, I wander into his living room to find him slumped on his couch while he channel surfs.

Throwing the remote down and standing as soon as I step into view, as has become tradition since the first time I came here, he takes me in his arms and holds me tight so my ear rests against his strong beating heart.

We both sigh. We let go of our day's worries and simply luxuriate in a hug that only a best friend can provide.

"Hey there, Sunshine."

I smile into his shirt. "Hey, Leo." Stepping back and dropping my bag to the floor, we slump onto the couch like a couple beached whales.

It's movie night – every night that I'm not working is movie night for us, and when I am at the club, Leo's sitting at the bar being my lion.

My tips haven't declined, but the number of men openly flirting with me has. I don't even mind. The number of times my skin crawls each worknight has decreased exponentially, *and* I get to hang out with my best friend while he sips on a soda and watches me work.

"You ready for Episode Two?"

"Definitely." I smile mischievously. "It's time for Ani and Padme to kiss."

"Stop trying to ruin this for me!" Groaning, he throws his arm over my shoulder and pulls me into his side. "This isn't a romance, Sunshine, so stop trying to make it one."

"It is what it is, Jon. Let me ogle Anakin, and you can gawk at Padme's sexy back. You just wait until we get to Leia and her sexy swimsuit. This is a mutually beneficial movie. Everyone's happy."

"Mmhmm." He rumbles unhappily and hits the play button.

This has steadily become our thing.

We eat, we watch movies, or we binge watch Game of Thrones and cheer when the next good guy loses his head.

He's remained stubborn on the whole Outlander thing, but that's fine, because each night after he passes out with his head in my lap, I switch over to the DVR and watch while I play with his hair.

Somehow, more often than not, I wake up in his bed with my legs tangled in his and a dribble line running from my mouth onto his sexy chest.

But it's all innocent.

We're just a couple friends that really enjoy each other's company.

I still feel that same vulnerability in him that I felt the first day we met. There's a boy inside this man's body, something happened to him, he's been hurt, and he's using me, *us*, as an opportunity to just... be.

I'm okay with that, because he helps me relax, too. I've been in this man's house and bed for the better part of a month, and we haven't had sex. He's been a perfect gentleman, and I've had neither a one-night-stand nor have I entered another two-year time bomb.

We're happy as best friends, just like he promised.

He leans into me comfortably. We're not shy anymore. There are no boundaries. "How was your day, Sunshine?"

"Shh, the music's starting."

He chuckles and squeezes my shoulder. "We've seen it a hundred times, you know what happens."

"Be quiet! You *never* talk during your scenes. Just when the love stuff happens."

He shrugs. "What can I say, the love stuff bores me. How was your day?"

I sigh. He's not going to let this go. "My day was fine. Hung out with Kit. Hung out with Izzy. Cleaned my apartment."

"You and Sissy hang out without me?"

I turn and look up at his furrowed brow. "Of course. She's cool. She's actually cooler than you."

He rolls his eyes and goes back to looking at the screen. "Whatever."

I let the silence hang for a minute. I let the familiar sounds of Star Wars soothe us, but I have to know. Shit went down at the gym recently, and tonight, Jon's hug is tighter... His adrenaline is still turned up high. I can *feel* it in the air. "Jon?"

He lifts his chin in silent acknowledgment.

I take his hand and twine our fingers together. "How are you feeling?"

Looking down at me, his lips stop barely half an inch from my forehead. *If I just leaned forward a tiny bit...* "Feeling about what?"

"About what happened with Timms and Kit." I was front row and center last week when a gym regular felt the need to ask Kit out on a date... more than once... with bad language when she said no.

I watched on as Jon physically held Kit behind his back when Timms had a toddler-like meltdown and started throwing mean words around. Then I watched on as Aiden – the sweet, mild tempered, quiet Aiden – hit Timms and knocked him on his ass when he crowded her against the wall and suggested she suck his cock. "And about your *other* best friend moving in with his girlfriend."

He shrugs easily. "Timms is a fucking tool, he won't be coming back to our gym again." His voice is harsh, and his heart races beneath my cheek. "He's lucky we didn't kill him. And the other thing..." He shrugs. "If B's happy, then I'm happy. Kit makes him happy." He smiles softly. "Yeah, I'm cool with it."

"And you say romance bores you," I scoff. "Your best friend is practically married."

He chuckles. "I honestly didn't think he'd ever settle down, but I knew that if he did, he'd fall hard. I'm not surprised; his mom and dad had the best love in the whole world. He's a lot like his dad; he finds what he wants, then it's all over. Nobody gets a choice. He'll romance the fuck out of her until she's stuck loving him for life. Just like Bryan."

I laugh. Such a romantic speech. "Bryan's his dad?"

"Yeah. He's gone now, but have you met Nell?"

"Nah." I finger the hem of his black shirt and bring my knees up to lean against his thighs. "Though Kit's going to meet her soon, I think."

He nods easily. "Yeah, we're having dinner soon."

"You'll be there, too?"

"Sure. Probably Sissy, too. You should come."

"Me?"

"Uh-huh. You're Kit's family. You're my family. You should come."

I look into his dark eyes as a mixture of shock and emotion course through my blood. "I'm your family?"

"Of course." He pulls me in until my arm wraps around his hips and my chest almost rests against his. "You're my best friend. You're family."

I bite my lip and consider my next words. I've been curious since the day I met him. Since the day he told me he doesn't do romance. "Jon?"

"Hmm?"

"Do you think you'll ever fall in love?"

He shakes his head. "Nah. That's not for me."

"Love's not for you?"

"No. I'm not made for it. That's for... other people. People like Bobby. People like you."

"But not for you?"

He grins. "Not me. You know how we're born with personality traits, genes, whatever? Some people are born like Bryan and Bobby. Some people are meant to have a grand love-of-their-life thing. But not me. I wasn't born with the love gene."

"But you love your family. You love your sister and your brothers."

"I love you, too. But that's a different kind of love."

My eyes snap up in shock at his easily thrown around words. "You love me?"

"Of course." He finally presses a gentle kiss to my forehead. "You're my best friend. I'm your Leo. I'm protective and loyal. I love you like I love Bobby."

"But you're not made for the other kind of love?"

"No. I'll be the best man at your wedding. I'll be your kid's uncle. But I won't be a dad myself. I won't get married. I'll just... be me."

"That sounds lonely." *That makes me sad.*

"But it's not, because I have all you guys. There'll be loads of nieces and nephews to love, too. But I won't be passing on my genes."

"But what about Izzy?"

His eyes narrow dangerously. "What about Izzy?"

"Don't you think she should get married someday? Have kids?"

His glare is bone chilling, and if I didn't know better, the danger in them might scare me. But I do know. He'd never hurt me. "Not until she's thirty. Maybe thirty-five."

I laugh and rest my face back on his strong chest. "Okay, but when she's thirty, she'll still have the same genes as you. Does that mean you think she doesn't deserve a husband and family?"

"No. Sissy… she's different. She's special. She's not like me."

"Sounds like a convenient excuse for the eternal bachelor life."

He shrugs carelessly. "Call it whatever you want."

"So no kids, no wife."

"Nope." He turns back to the movie. "That night we met, before I knew you, I was only offering the one night. We'd have had our fun, we'd have fucked like crazy until we walked away with chafing, but that's it. I couldn't offer you anything more."

"That's all a bit tragic, Jon. Everyone deserves happiness. Everyone deserves family and love."

He simply shrugs; he's done with this conversation.

We watch the movie in silence, but I struggle to focus, even when Ani steals a kiss from Padme; one of my favorite scenes of all time. Jon's words have ruined it for me.

Instead, I think about how sad he must be to think he doesn't *deserve* the things he does.

Jon's a good man.

He has a wonderful heart.

There's something fucked up in the universe if someone as sweet and kind as him can't find his happily ever after.

Turning to him, I hitch my knee up to get closer. "Jon?"

He sighs dramatically when I interrupt an on-screen fight scene. "Yes, Sunshine?"

"You're my best friend?"

His patronizing eyes turn soft. "Yeah."

"You love me?"

"Yeah. Like I love Bobby."

"Tell me something?"

He nods for me to continue.

"What happened to you?"

His eyes narrow menacingly, then he turns back to the movie. "Nothing special. Regular childhood."

"So why are you so bitter?"

"I'm not bitter," he argues. "I'm just a realist. Can we drop it?"

"Best friends don't let best friends drop it. I drag all the shit out of Kit."

"No, that's not a best friend thing, Sunshine, that's a chick thing. Keep your estrogen out of my house." He's only joking, his smirk eases the coil of tension that tightens in my stomach, but smirk or not, he's still dismissing me.

"Why do you call me Sunshine?"

He sighs. "You're a Chatty Cathy tonight, huh?"

I snuggle against his chest and hide my face in his shirt; I'm finding it difficult to hide my feelings, and right now, my face says *bullshit!* "You're being super evasive tonight, huh?"

He sighs. "I call you Sunshine because it fits. You're bright and warm and soothing. And when you go away, it's not so bright anymore and I'm a little lonely until you come back."

I scoff at the irony. "And you say you don't do romance."

Displeasure rumbles through his chest. "What are you talking about?"

"Nothing. Watch your movie, Jon."

He watches me a moment longer, but when I ignore him and pretend to watch the TV, he huffs. Digging his arms under my legs and picking me up easily, he deposits me on *my* cushion at the end of the couch. Settling me in comfortably and passing a throw cushion, he lies down, rests his head in my lap, and puts my hand on his head.

"You know…" I drag my nails over his scalp and smile when he buries his head and purrs. "I used to have a dog when I was a kid. A beautiful girl, though her name was Scooter."

"You named a female dog Scooter?"

"Yeah, well, I was a kid. Anyway, she used to walk up whenever I sat down, and she'd dig her snout under my hand. She'd bounce her face and shuffle my hand until it rested on her head."

I can *feel* his smile against my thigh. "What's your point?"

"She did it because she wanted a head scratch. She did it every day, and she was stubborn as hell. I'd push her away, but she'd come back and dig her snout in again. I'd tease her and stick my hands under my butt or behind my back. It didn't put her off. She'd dig her snout under my ass instead, or she'd walk around behind me."

"Maybe you shouldn't have pushed her away. Maybe you should've just scratched her damn head."

I laugh at his lack of subtlety and press my nails against his scalp. "I'll scratch your head, Jon. You can rest now."

"Thank you." He closes his eyes; not to sleep, just to relax. He does this. He says he wants to watch whatever's on TV, he argues over Outlander, but he almost always closes his eyes and just lies there.

I spend the next hour watching a movie I don't particularly want to watch, and when his breathing evens out, I wonder if he's awake or asleep.

But no matter what, I keep scratching. Because I like to make him happy. I like to be the reason his muscles relax.

I like that he trusts me to watch over him.

"Hey, Case..." His gruff voice rumbles along my thighs.

I look down and focus on his dark hair. "Hmm?"

"Ask you somethin'?"

I smile at his husky voice. "Shoot."

"Do you wish we had that one-night-stand? Do you wish we'd had that one time, then I'd left you alone?"

My hand stills when he turns in my lap to face me.

"What are you talking about?"

"I'm thinking about the night we met. We could've had our fun, then gone our separate ways. Then you wouldn't be stuck with a bitter ass like me for a friend."

"*Best* friend," I snap defensively. "And no, I'm not sad. I'm really happy to have you as a friend, Leo. You make me happy to hang out with."

"Do you wish we hooked up first? Do you mourn what could have been?"

Yes. Every time I look into your eyes, I mourn the opportunity I rejected. Instead of admitting this, though, I do what I do best. I deflect. "Do you?"

"I don't *mourn* it." He sits up beside me and has my neck arching back to keep our eyes connected. "I don't mourn, exactly. But I wonder what could've been."

I sigh. "I bet you would've rocked my world, Leo."

He chuckles shyly and has my anxiety easing for the briefest second, then his hand comes to the back of my neck and sends nerves skittering through my blood. Goosebumps cover every inch of my skin as his thick fingers stroke the top of my spine. "I think we might have killed each other, to be honest."

"Jon—"

"I know I promised no benefits—"

"Don't do this." My voice cracks with nerves and want. "You're gonna ruin our friendship."

"No." He licks his lips. "Nothing will ruin our friendship. You have my word. But I wonder..."

"Jon—"

"Could we try once? One kiss."

I bring my hand up to cup his jaw and stroke a gentle thumb over his bottom lip; I've been dying to do this since the first time he flashed his pretty smile.

Plump, cherry colored lips give way under my touch and move to the side as my thumb gently traces from left to right. On my second trip across, his tongue darts out and tags the tip of my finger daringly.

I swallow nervously. "Just one time? One kiss and nothing else?"

His pupils grow larger as they flick down to my lips. "Just one."

"Why?"

"Why what?"

"Why now?"

I'm stalling.

I want this.

I want to run away.

I *don't* want to ruin the relationship we've forged over TV repeats and takeout.

"Because I feel like if I don't try just once, I might regret it for the rest of my life. Because every time I see you, I stop myself from kissing you…" He pauses. "Because every time you hug me, I wonder if we can be friends with *some* benefits. Just one kiss."

"And we'll go back to normal after? You promise?"

He strokes the back of my neck. "I promise."

He's a liar. I know he is. Because this conversation alone has already altered our friendship. We can never go back to who we were five minutes ago. Everything's already changed. And yet… "Okay."

"You're sure?"

Nervously, I nod. Because if I don't try just once, I know I'll regret it for the rest of my life.

He smiles and slides his hand along my thigh. "May I?"

I angle my head in confusion, but he doesn't explain, he simply picks me up and places me on his lap so I straddle his tented jeans.

My head drops forward on a groan as his erection presses against my pulsing core. This is all about to go to shit, we're going to let sex ruin everything.

"Ignore that, Sunshine. Kiss me."

My eyes snap to his; ignoring his erection is about as easy as staying away from him, but winding his fingers in my hair and cupping the back of my head, he takes the decision out of my hands.

He pulls me forward and has me catching my weight against his strong chest, and though I try to push back, my weak arms are nothing on his strength. Sliding my hands along his pecs and over his shoulders, I find myself cupping the back of his neck and resting my forearms on his strong shoulders.

"Please don't let this ruin us."

"I won't let anything ruin us, Case. I promise." Done with talking it out, his lips come down on mine and have popping candy fizzing in my brain. He wastes no time, as though he thinks this is a once in a lifetime offer, when really, my willpower is nonexistent.

I want to kiss him every time I see him, too.

His teeth nip at my bottom lip and have me sighing, and when my lips open in invitation, his tongue darts in.

It's better than I ever dreamed.

And I've dreamed about it.

About him.

He pulls my bottom lip between his teeth, bites down, and swallows my gasp when the momentary sting registers in my mind.

"You taste better than I ever dreamed."

"Mmm." I rearrange myself on his lap, lift my torso, wrap my arms around his neck, angle my head, and take everything on offer before it's gone.

My tongue plays with his; his slow dips, his aggressive tasting, his thorough savoring. His left hand remains on the back of my head, holding me prisoner, even as his right hand traces my ass. He cups me, pulls me tight into his lap and pushes the breath from my body with the force of his hold.

Best friends or not, one time or not, I find myself grinding down against him. It's a natural instinct, and I can't stop the movement any more than I can stop the groan ripping along my throat.

Jon's hands hold me tight. His mouth devours mine as my nails dig into his scalp to keep him close. His left hand comes down to cup to my ass, then with a whimper from us both, he drags me over his pulsing cock and digs it in in the most delicious way.

Pulling away with a gasp, I clamor for oxygen and screw my eyes shut.

If he asked, I'd rip my jeans off and let him have me. In a heartbeat, we'd be naked and together, and I probably wouldn't even regret it.

Except I would.

"Okay." His breath bathes my face as he pulls back and lifts his hands in surrender. "Okay. I'm sorry."

"No. It's… fine. It's okay." My breath comes in fast and shallow pants. My chest rises and falls erratically, and my pulse throbs in my underwear. "We can't do that again."

"No. We can't." He picks me up and gently sets me on the couch beside him. "Are you okay?"

I drop my head into my hands and nod. I can still *feel* his hands holding me. I can still *taste* him in my mouth.

"Nothing changes, Case. Best friends forever."

I nod against my cupped hands. "Yeah."

"I gotta go take a piss."

I don't bother looking up. I have my own crisis to deal with.

Best friends or not, now I'll always know that, together, we explode.

Damn.

10

JON

CHOCOLATE BLOB

"*Happy* birthday, Leo."

I glance up from my phone, from Bobby's smartass text about not going out tonight, and smile as my tiny ray of Sunshine walks through the front door, drops her bag and keys at the table, and walks into the living room holding a giant platter.

She lets herself in like she lives here.

I love it.

I jump up to take the heavy platter, and when I look down, I try to control the expression on my face at what genuinely looks like... well... Scooter shit.

Balancing the platter in one hand, I take her in a hug with the other, and when she presses her face to my chest, I finally let out the day's tension. I breathe her in; she still smells like cinnamon.

Delicious and inviting.

Edible.

Exactly like we promised, we're still best friends.

After the kiss that might've changed my life, I ran my *un*happy ass to the bathroom and splashed cold water on my face in an attempt to calm the fuck down. When that didn't work, I tried counting to a thousand by threes. When *that* didn't help, I tried imagining Gandalf and Dumbledore in a three way with Doctor Who.

That didn't even help.

When my dick continued to throb and the pain in my jeans was too much, I decided to face reality and deal with it the way I knew would work.

I leaned against the cold bathroom tile, closed my eyes, and whacked off wishing the girl panting on my couch twenty feet away could be the one wrapped around my dick.

Those thoughts had me finishing in record time, then I was able to face her again.

It was awkward at first, but I forced her back to normalcy.

I sat down, she twitched.

I pulled her into my side, she twitched some more.

I kissed her brow, she sighed.

I restarted the movie, and this time, I pulled her head to my lap, then played with her silky hair until she fell asleep.

I wasn't ruining us because we kiss well together.

I *need* her. I need her friendship.

I can just keep whacking off. It wasn't so bad.

"Better take that to the fridge before the icing melts." She steps away and has me looking back down at the platter of shit. Leaning closer, I take a cursory sniff; it doesn't smell like shit. It smells like sugar, actually.

"What is it?"

She spins and slams her fist into my chest. "It's your birthday cake, asshole."

I bite my lips to stop the smile that'll end up with her hitting me again. I know beggars shouldn't be choosers, and I know this is the first birthday cake that was *ever* made specifically for me, but I mean… it looks awful.

"It's Chewbacca. See? He has brown fur, that's chocolate icing. I used a fork to make those lines. The tiny marshmallows are the studs on his belt, and the white chocolate buttons are his eyes. Can't you see it?"

Not even a little bit… "I'm sure it tastes nice."

"You're an asshole."

I laugh when she slams her fist against my arm. "You look pretty today, Sunshine. Super pretty. Are they new jeans? They make your ass look awesome."

"No. Shut up. Go and put the damn cake in the fridge."

"Why fridge? We can eat it now." Taking her hand, I lead her to the couch and push her down. Sliding the heavy platter onto the coffee table, I move into the kitchen and come back with a couple forks, a couple beers, and a bottle of scotch Bobby gave me for my birthday.

"Mixer or a beer?"

"Ugh, I hate scotch. I'll take the beer, thanks."

Smiling, I pass it and a fork, then I plant my ass so close to hers, I'm practically sitting on her. "Dig in."

"You're not going to have dinner first?"

I study the cake with a salivating mouth and a racing heart. *Where to start? Chewy's shit head? Or Chewy's shit belt?* "We can order whatever you want, Sunshine. But I'm eating my cake now."

She laughs. "You sound a little excited."

I turn to her with a goofy smile. "I am!" *This is the best birthday of my life.* "I've been waiting all month for this, since you *promised* a cake. Now it's here, but I had to wait all day."

"You're lucky I took off work, or you would've had to wait longer."

"That would've been a tragedy."

She leans in close and has me smiling when she wraps her arm around mine. She's still my best friend, and since getting to know her, I've realized something; we both have attachment issues.

We like to touch; always hugging, always leaning, always touching.

"Did you have a nice day, Leo?"

"Uh-huh. I rolled with B for like, three hours straight. He's been neglecting me since Kitten came along."

"God forbid you don't get to roll around on the floor like a couple stray dogs."

"You just don't get it." Leaning forward after deciding on the entire head section, I start spooning it into my mouth. It's delicious. Even the poo-brown icing. "Me and the guys have been training together since we were kids. If a day went by and we didn't roll, then something was wrong. Now B's doing a whole other kind of rolling with Kit, and he's left me in the cold."

"You're so dramatic," she laughs. Leaning toward the table, she takes a much smaller forkful of cake and brings it to her delicious lips. "Did you get nice presents?"

Nodding, I take a long pull of my beer to wash down the giant glob of cake threatening to choke me. "Uh-huh. B got me the bottle of scotch. Sissy got me a box of condoms and a pair of ugly as fuck socks; I think she's trying to find the crappiest gifts in the world. The other guys got me some shit, too."

She rolls her eyes. "Your day's just full of shit, huh?"

"Yeah. And now my mouth is, too."

As expected, she rears back and slams her fist into my shoulder. It kills me a little inside every time she does that, because her strikes are weak and sloppy. She's already told me she doesn't *do* gyms. She won't let me help her.

Leo the Lion can't stand the thought that she can't fight or defend herself. It just means I'll have to stay close and keep watch.

Not such a hardship.

I wasn't surprised when Bobby talked Kit into training. It's what we do. We equip those we love with skills to look after themselves. Even Nelly knows how to fight.

It's the world's best kept secret.

"You're such an asshole, Jonathon Hart." She massages her aching knuckles. "I don't even know why I hang out with you."

Because you love me. "Did I tell you you look pretty today?"

She snorts and turns back to the cake. She *thinks* she's mad, but it works every single time. She's a sucker for a well-placed compliment.

Sighing, she shakes her head. "What am I going to do with you, Leo?"

"Well, since it's my birthday, I want you to watch a movie, scratch my hair, and eat cake with me. Do what we do best."

"You're pretty easy to please."

Wicked thoughts race through my mind, but faster than they manifest in my brain, I lock them down. There's joking, then there's flirting with danger. Telling her the ways she could *satisfy* me could end up with us in the same position we were in last week, but with less clothes.

I wouldn't regret the amazing sex I *know* we'd have, but I'd for sure regret the damage to the foundations of our friends-without-benefits arrangement.

I can't risk her.

"I got you something."

Surprised, my eyes snap to hers. "Something, what?"

"Something for your birthday, like a gift."

"Why would you do that?"

Her brows pull low. "Why would I buy you a gift?"

Forgetting my delicious cake and the thoughts of eating it from her belly button, I nod.

"Because you're my best friend, dummy. Because it's your birthday."

"But you made me a cake."

"Yeah, well, I also bought you something. Stop being a baby. Hold on…" Standing from the couch with a grunt and needing me to push her jean clad ass forward, she laughs and moves toward her dumped handbag.

I can't explain the stupid giddiness that bounces around inside my gut. It washes away my dirty thoughts and replaces them with the excitement a kid might feel on Christmas morning.

I've never had this feeling, this carefree excitement.

Even when the Kincaids practically took Sissy and me in full time, and even more so after Bryan passed away, I was still underage, then when I wasn't, Izzy was.

Every day of my life, I worried my folks would swoop in and take her from me. I mean, if they *wanted* to, they could. They're her parents. They had the legal rights I never did.

She turned eighteen only last year, but even though I was finally free of the fear they would take her, I still worry even now that they're going to fuck something up for her.

No matter how long Nell had been cooking for us, no matter how many nights in a row I didn't have to go back to the trailer park, I never let my guard down.

When the guys were giggling like fools on Christmas morning, and Sissy was running around as carefree as I'd always hoped she'd feel, I was still on guard.

I was *never* a giggling kid.

But Casey's the first person that's ever made it so I can rest like this.

The tiny woman who can't fight makes me feel safe. She makes it so I can finally breathe.

Turning back from her bag, she steps forward and has me focusing on the small blue package in her hand. She wanders toward me slowly, almost shyly, and has me quirking my brow.

My Sunshine isn't shy.

She's crazy and outgoing, she's flirty and loud.

She's a smartass, and if she were a dude, we'd have already had a beat down. She's got a mouth on her that can cut the most badass guy down, and a dry wit that often makes you wonder if you're an idiot.

"So, I know this is something between you and Bobby. I don't mean to step on your bromance toes, but I got you something that I really hope you like." She stops between my open legs and has me looking up into her bright green eyes. The sparkle of her eyes is usual, but the color to her cheeks is new.

She's blushing.

She's nervous.

I reach out and wrap my hand around her thigh to keep her close. "What've got for me, Sunshine?"

Holding it between us, she grips it tight as I try to pry the package from between her fingers. Laughing when the gift finally snaps from her grasp, I don't let go of her thigh until she nervously pushes the cake aside and sits on the table.

Her bent knees sit between mine, and her thumbnail goes to her teeth and tempts me to pull her into my lap. I don't think I've ever seen her nervous like this…

Peeling open the dark wrapping paper, my hands shake with adrenaline. It's a book. I already know that. But why is she shy like this? Why do her nerves ping around the room and lodge themselves in my heart?

Opening the package and folding the tape over neatly, I refold the paper and smile at the sight of a cartoon train and a flying car staring back at me.

She awkwardly clears her throat. "It's a first edition."

I frown with disapproval. "First editions aren't cheap."

She shrugs it off easily. "Don't worry about that. Look inside."

Looking into her shy green eyes, studying the long lashes I *know* she painstakingly paints every morning before she comes out of the bathroom, I swallow down emotions that I refuse to feel.

Case doesn't do casual.

She does makeup and heels and iron flattened hair first thing each day. I don't know why she bothers; her done-up look is like a sexy fairy, but her freshly awake face is something else. All innocent and soft.

Stunning.

Sometimes she wakes up looking like a rooster, but that version of her is beautiful, too.

As nervous as she is, I open the cover and lovingly run my thumb along the deep indentations from a pen pressing hard against paper.

Jon. Life can be magical. Let it.

Well, shit.

"How'd you get this?"

"I flew to London, locked her in a basement, and broke her ankles?"

I look up and wait for her eyes to meet mine. "Casey... Your pants are on fire."

She giggles shakily. "Okay, I sent her an email. Or well, probably her PA, but whatever. Someone in another country replied to my email, took my credit card details, and sent me a book."

I laugh. "That's dangerous, Sunshine. Probably don't expect the same results if an Algerian prince takes your digits."

"Noted. And to think, I almost replied to that email. He said we'd share millions of dollars. I could've done with the cash." Her lips turn up at the side teasingly. She's good at deflection when she's nervous.

I take her right hand in mine. "This is the best gift anyone's ever bought me. Thank you."

She scoffs. "Well that's just not true. You got a box of condoms and socks today."

I ignore her sarcasm. We'd never get anywhere if I always indulged her every tangent. "Thank you, Case. I love it."

She sighs happily. "You're welcome. Happy Birthday, Jon."

"Wanna hug it out?"

She stands with a smile on her face. Kicking her heels off and toeing them under the table, she pushes my shoulder down so I lay along the couch and my head rests on the cushion on the end. Climbing over me and digging in elbows and knees, she lays in the gap between my side and the back of the couch and brings her leg up to rest across my hips. She throws her arm across my stomach and lays her cheek over my heart.

If you looked really close, you'd probably see a Casey-shaped indent in my body where I pull her close every night and refuse to let her go until the sun comes up.

We haven't *slept* together yet. We might never. But we *sleep* together most nights.

My life is perfect, the closest to happy I've ever been.

But five months is all the perfection we're gifted.

Five months, six days, and a few hours.

The universe is a cold hard bitch, and I was never supposed to have the happy ending.

PART II

THE ENDING

CASEY

KIT'S BIRTHDAY

"*H*ey, birthday girl! Are you excited for tonight?"

"Yes!" Applying my lipstick, I smile at Kit's excited voice screeching over the phone. I bet she's dancing on her tippy toes. "Oh my God, Case. I can't wait!"

My girl, my *other* best friend, turned twenty-five yesterday. So we're going out to party.

Just like the old days, it's the Kit and Casey show.

No boys allowed.

Bobby's big fight's coming up in just a few weeks, so he and the guys are training ridiculously long hours. Jon said he'd be at the gym as long as Bobby is, then he'll go home and chill. I'm under strict instructions to call him later for a ride. Aka: call him, so he can climb into my bed and snuggle.

I have the two *best* best friends in the whole world.

Kit's my sister, and I love her like I would if we were blood related. She's been by my side since grade school; she was the first to know about the first boy I kissed, she was my biggest ally when we had to deal with snooty bitches in the school cafeteria, and she was the first person I called after I lost my virginity.

I sat in the bleachers year after year and watched her run track – I honestly don't understand *why* she'd want to run for fun, but I don't judge her choices.

I was there to support her no matter what.

I was her loudest cheerer when she won, embarrassingly so, and I was the first to bring her ice-cream and hot guy pictures when she busted her knee.

She was there every time to pick me up and chew out my asshole exes, and she always encouraged my shoe obsession; never once nagging me about overspending.

I was happy.

I had a happy childhood with her by my side.

Jon doesn't replace her, he just fills a different need. And since his *other* best friend is Bobby, and Kit kinda loves Bobby, we get to hang out as a group of four all the time.

My life is good.

But it's her birthday and the guys are busy, so it's a girl's night out. The only downside to today is the fact Iz isn't old enough to come with us.

Not that Leo the Lion will ever willingly allow us to take his baby sister out to clubs. Wouldn't want to be a bad influence on his *seemingly* innocent sister.

"I finish work at five," Kit continues. "I've already picked my dress and shoes. Bobby and I tested the shoes out last night." Like a dirty uncle, she laughs. "He likes how they poked his lower back. Said the pain felt good."

I laugh and fan my face at the same time. "Swear to God, Kit, you're a freak. I had no clue you had it in you. Are you training tonight?"

"Yeah, I'm hitting up Jon's class, I think. Bobby's with Aiden, Jon's taking groups. I'll finish up about six, then I'm racing home to slut up."

"Meet me there, or do you want me to pick you up? Pre-drinks at your house?"

"Nah, I'll just meet you there, otherwise we'll never get out. If we're still at home when Bobby and the others roll in, we have no chance of getting out. The guys will do that pouty thing they do. You know the thing?"

I know the thing.

Jon will push his head under my hand, I'll scratch it like I was forced for years to scratch Scooter's, then we'll fall asleep watching long ass movies.

"Oh, Case, wanna get some dinner at the club?"

"Uh-huh." I poke my head into my closet in search of an outfit for tonight. "I'll let work know. They'll reserve us the best table."

"Awesome."

"Alright." I tug out a leather skirt and study the silver buckles. "I'll see you in a few hours. Be good. Go easy on Jon."

She laughs. "Maybe you should call him and tell him to go easy on me! I swear he likes to make me sweat. And not in the sexy way."

I roll my eyes and try to banish mental images of sweating with Jon Hart. "Okay, I'll see you in a few."

"Hey, Tink, before you go–"

I snort at my nickname.

It stuck. Because of Bobby and his stupid big mouth, it stuck.

"Yes, Kitten?"

"I miss you."

My playful smirk turns to a soft remembrance as I replay in my mind all of the good times we've had together. A lifetime of silly girl sleepovers and boy talks. "You miss me? I saw you yesterday, silly."

She sighs. "I know, but life is different now. With Bobby and Renee and Jack. I haven't been neglecting you, have I? I know I've been absent–"

"No, babe. You haven't. We've both been busy, but I miss you, too. We should organize a Mr. Darcy and ice-cream night. Just the two of us."

"Yeah, we should." Yawning through the phone, she has me frowning. It's the middle of the afternoon, but her extended family, legal troubles, wills and estates, everything that she pays all her hard earned money for her lawyers to fix, it all has her so tired.

Kit is the mother hen.

The fixer.

But who mothers her? Who fixes things for her?

"I have something special planned for us tonight, okay? Let me spoil you, then tomorrow, we can do Darcy and ice-cream while the guys serve our hungover asses."

She snickers. "That sounds amazing. Okay, I better go. My boss will get mad soon. I'll see you in a bit."

"Okay. Oh, hey, Kit?"

"Yeah?"

"I love you."

"I love you too, Case. So much."

"Sunshine—"

"Sorry, Leo." Smirking arrogantly, I sit at the bar and stir my drink. "It's girl's night. I don't have time to take your calls—"

"Sissy was attacked!" His panicked voice cuts through my heart and leaves me sitting tall and clutching at my chest.

I've been sitting here, sipping my cocktail and chatting with the bar staff while I wait for Kit to drag her ass in. She's never late anywhere, she should've been here an hour ago, but she was training tonight.

To me, that easily excuses a long shower.

Not everyone is as anally punctual as Kit, so an hour late is no big deal to me, but now I wish she was here. Now I wish we were all together, so I could hug Jon and take the panic from his voice, then Kit could hug me, because suddenly I need a damn hug.

"Izzy was attacked? Is she okay?"

"She's in the hospital," he rushes out. "We've been up here for a couple hours. Is Kit with you?"

"No. She's at home getting dress—"

"Casey, listen to me! Is Kit with you?"

My heart thumps painfully against the wall of my chest and threatens to rip its way through the skin that holds it in.

"Casey! Answer my fucking question."

"No, Jon! She's not with me."

"Fuck! I gotta go—"

"Wait. What the hell's going on?"

"Kit's missing. Sissy was hurt."

"Kit's missing? What the fuck do you mean she's missing? Kit doesn't just go missing!"

"Can you go to the hospital? Sit with Sissy."

"Jon! Where are you?" I stand from the stool, grab my purse, and swing out the front door past Mike. "What are you doing right now?"

"I'm going with Bobby."

"Where's Bobby going?"

"He's going to fucking find her!" Jon's harsh words barely register in my mind, since I'm still stuck on my best friend being *missing*.

Not even Bobby knows where she is.

I was sitting at a fucking bar, laughing at Derek's ridiculous shaker moves as he mixed cocktails, while Jon's sister was attacked, and now Kit's missing.

"Let me come with you. Let me find her. I need to find my best friend."

"I need you to go sit with Sissy. Please."

"You're making me choose between you and Kit."

"There's no fucking choice!" His breath races out as though he's running. "Sit with my sister, Casey. I *need* you to sit with Sissy. I'll find Kit."

"Are you alone? Jon, don't be dumb."

"I'm with Aiden. We're gonna find Bobby and Jack now. Sit with Sissy!"

I swing into my car as Jon hangs up on me.

As though the situation hasn't processed in my mind, as though for the first time ever, Jon is lying to me, I swipe screens on my phone and dial Kit's number.

She'll answer, even though she didn't answer the two calls I made in the last hour. I wasn't calling to nag, I was having fun with Derek, anyway.

I was just checking in.

When her phone goes to voicemail, my hands shake the way they never have before.

She's not missing.

He's messing with me.

This can't be real.

This is all Leo the Lion and a stupid fucking scheme to keep his girls at home and away from a silly night at the club.

Laying my hand on Bobby's shoulder, I don't react when even in his sleep, his muscles bunch and flex beneath my touch.

He lies with his face in Kit's open hand and his back bent at an unnatural angle. "Hey. Wake up, B."

"M'okay."

"Wake up, honey. Your mom's here."

Lifting his head with confusion, Bobby's eyes sluggishly track from my hand on his shoulder, to Kit, as a new day begins and she remains asleep. Sighing when she doesn't open her eyes for the ninth day in a row, he shakes his head and shakes my hand off.

The doctors stopped sedating her days ago. She should've woken.

Even battered and broken the way she is, she should've opened her eyes and bitched us out for keeping vigil and watching her sleep.

She wouldn't like this attention; this round the clock watch, the crying and sadness. She wouldn't like us standing around with broken hearts.

Especially not Bobby.

Or Jack.

"It's my shift, B. Your mom's gonna take you home for a shower."

"No. I'm staying." Despite the fact Bobby hasn't slept lying down in a week, despite his vending machine diet and lack of self-care, his voice is steely and hard.

None of us have slept in a week.

None of us are eating anything substantial.

The only sensible person here, the only person making sure we don't die from chips and soda overdose, is Nelly.

Her job first and foremost is to make sure her children are safe and well.

She lets him get his way most of the time, but today, she's making a stand. She's taking her baby home, to force him to eat something with less sodium, and to make him sleep.

No negotiations.

He runs his hands along the spiky stubble covering his jaw, and angling his head to the sides, cracks a stiff neck. "I'm staying, Tink. You can go home. I'm not moving."

"It's my turn, B." Reaching up and squeezing his shoulder, because I need the contact, I drop my bag on a spare visitor chair and study Kit. "I missed her all night, so now it's my turn. I wanna spend some time with my best friend. You're always monopolizing her time." I smirk as best I can, though joking is the last thing I feel like doing.

Mostly, I want to climb onto Kit's bed, straddle her hips, and rest my head between her breasts. I want to hug her. I want her to wake up and tell me she's okay.

To tell me she forgives me for not being there for her.

Instead, I was sitting at a bar and laughing, while horrible people hurt her, while she had to trudge through white snow made pink by her blood.

My best friend almost died; she could *still* die.

"Your mom's here to take you home for a bit. I want to spend some time with my best friend." When he shakes his stubborn head again, I pull out the big guns. I'm selfish like that. "She was mine first, B. She was *mine,* and you stole her. I want a few hours alone with her. You owe me that."

"Come on, baby." Entering the shadowed room, Nelly takes Bobby under his arm, though she couldn't actually move him if he didn't want to be moved.

On another sigh, he looks to his mom, then back to Kit.

Then to me.

"Don't leave her, Tink. Not even to piss. Don't you dare leave her side. If you do, I'll never forgive you."

"I've got her, I promise. I won't leave her for a single second."

"Let's go," Nelly murmurs with her best soothing mama voice. Unfortunately, the only voice that will truly ever soothe us again is deep asleep and refusing to wake up.

"Can you take Jack, too, Nell? He needs to rest."

"Yeah, sweetheart. I've already got him up and moving. We'll be back in a few."

"Alright." I sit in Bobby's still warm seat, and take the hand Bobby slept in. Her nails are broken, the skin on her fingers no longer torn and bloody, but raw and scabbed over.

IV lines hang off her every extremity. Her left arm is bandaged from shoulder to wrist. The bones are broken from the car, the bicep sliced open by her sadistic crazy bitch cousin strung out for her next hit and some financial relief.

Broken ribs. Bruised organs. Sliced open limbs.

Despite the horror her cousin put her through, the car accident caused her worst injuries.

Her head is what has us most worried.

The doctors considered more surgery; removing a section of her skull to allow room for her swollen brain, but every day, they send her for scans, and every day, the doctors swear she's improving.

The swelling's going down, she's doing better.

We just have to watch and see.

I brush a long lock of blonde hair off her shoulder and frown. As soon as I'm allowed, I'll wash it for her. Brush out the tangles, smooth it out. I think she'd like that.

"So, on a scale of one to we'll never be friends again, how mad are you at me?"

She doesn't answer, of course, but I imagine her words, the well-deserved vitriol that if she were awake, she'd spit on me without remorse.

I hate your guts, you self-centered bitch. We'll never be friends again. You left me alone, I needed you. I needed my best friend.

I highly doubt those are her actual words; she's too kind for that. But that's what she *should* be thinking.

I'm a horrible best friend.

I organized a birthday night, *her* birthday, and she got hurt instead.

I should've helped her.

"Knock, knock."

I turn in my seat and watch Izzy quietly let herself into the room. She looks just as beautiful as ever; long, shiny mahogany hair, a sporty body wrapped in yoga pants and a Rollin tank. It's freezing outside, but she wears so little, and simply carries a coat just in case she gets cold.

But beautiful or cold, I know she has a giant egg on the back of her head. Struck down by the same people that hurt Kit, she was left in the snow to be found... or not.

Jon's been a basket case since the first time he called me in the club. He's on her back about every little thing. He's reverted right back to caretaker mode, back to his childhood that I *know,* despite his silence on the matter, that he raised his baby sister.

He's become obnoxious about watching over her, as his anxiety seeps through his home and claws its filthy fingers beneath all of our skin.

Izzy escapes the house in the mornings and runs up here to see Kit, because she'd rather spend her time with an unconscious woman and live with Bobby's devastation, than see her brother and live with his.

I don't meet her gaze as Izzy sits in the chair opposite mine. I simply stroke Kit's hand and work around the needles and tubes. "Hey, Izzy."

She leans forward and drops a gentle kiss on Kit's forehead. Kit still doesn't wake up. "No change?"

"No. But I got Bobby out."

Nodding, Iz studies Kit's right hand like I do the left. "That's surprising. I didn't think he'd go."

"I used Nell, but he'll be back soon."

"Yeah."

"How you feeling, Sissy?"

She sighs sarcastically. "You sound like him, you know? You and Jon spend too much time together."

I swallow my guilt at the blood stains the nurses missed when they cleaned Kit up. "Sorry."

She smiles and traces circles in Kit's skin with her pointer finger.

"Don't be sorry. He's different now. Well, except this past week. He was kinda *always* like this before you came along, but now you're here, he's been different. You make him more bearable to be around."

She's joking.

She wouldn't leave her big brother for anything. But her attempt helps me smile, and it helps me volley the joke back to relieve tension.

"I don't know about that, Sissy. He's pretty unbearable to be around, even since I've known him. He's a pain in my damn ass."

"Yeah, well. You don't even know it, but you've been my shield. It's been wonderful. He's almost as obsessed with you as he is with me. Little longer, and I might be able to transfer that anxiety exclusively to you."

"Gee, thanks." I roll my eyes at her silly grin. "That sounds just peachy, but no thanks. He's already full on. I don't need your share, too."

She scoffs. "Welcome to my world, Tink. Where the men are obsessed with protecting you, and though they do it out of love, smothered is smothered, and them sitting on your chest to keep you still, still makes it hard to breathe."

My heavy eyelids droop with exhaustion.

Unlike Bobby, I *have* been sleeping in a bed. Jon's bed. And just like always, he pulls me over his chest like a human weighted blanket and helps me get comfortable, which is quite possibly *the* most comfortable way to sleep, *ever*. But when your mattress is a bundle of anxiety, and your skin is touching his, even comfortable mattresses suck when you wake up more anxious and more exhausted than when you began.

I already carry enough guilt.

I can't deal with his, too.

Jon has created a weakness within himself, this *need* for me to be in his bed so he can sleep, and though it's nice for now, we can't do this forever.

He's not interested in a relationship, and I'm not looking for a fuck buddy.

I wasn't looking for a relationship with a man, but I don't want to be alone forever, either. Eventually, I'll be looking for something more, something Jon has told me six billion times he can't give anyone.

Not even me.

So when it's time for me to quit this unhealthy friendship, when it's time for me to find the man I'll spend the rest of my life with, well, this mystery man isn't going to be okay with tag teaming me.

Like, he and I can be a couple Monday through Thursday during daylight hours, but I go *home* to Jon in the evenings and weekends…

No. That wouldn't work.

And if by crazy chance I end up with an anomaly, a man who doesn't give a shit if I sleep in Jon's bed – which is *not* the kind of man I want, anyway – I don't see Jon feeling that same charity.

Together or not, commitment or not, Leo the Lion will *not* be cool with me jumping beds like that.

Exhausted, and finally able to let go of some of the anxiety that sits in my stomach, I carefully lay my head against Kit's side and begin humming the song that's been in my head for months.

The tune to *You Are My Sunshine* vibrates past my lips, soothing me, and hopefully soothing Kit, too.

She always said my singing made her happy.

"I like that song."

"Mmm." A slight variation in my humming is the only answer Iz gets. Mirroring me, she lays her head on Kit's other side and snuggles in.

Kit is the heart of our group.

We don't eat without her.

We don't sleep.

We don't rest.

We need her back.

Walking in my front door and dropping my bag and keys to the floor, I stumble to my fridge on weak legs and swallow down the grief that threatens to choke me.

I need a drink. Preferably alcoholic.

Preferably enough to tranquilize and stop the guilt that stabs me from the inside out.

Another day down, another day Kit doesn't wake up.

Another day we tick off the calendar.

The doctors told us the longer she stays under, the more likely it is she sustained permanent damage.

Worse yet, the longer she stays under, the more likely she might *never* resurface.

She should've regained consciousness already. They stopped sedating her. It was an exciting day, we were smiling, Jimmy brought balloons. We stood around her room with smiles on our faces and our hearts in our throats, and... nothing.

She didn't wake. She didn't call us weirdos for watching her sleep.

A day passed us by.

Then another.

And another.

Now I find myself unable to sit with her a moment longer. I'm drowning in misplaced guilt and worry for everyone around me. Jon's a mess. Jack's a child missing his big sister. Izzy carries around her own guilt, because Kit was scared, she called Iz for help, but she was still hurt.

I'm not eating properly. I've lost weight.

Bobby's hardly eating at all.

He's dropped the most.

He was training for the heavyweight title. He was eating over eight thousand calories a day. He was bulking. He was training all day, every day.

Then he just stopped.

Weeks of no training and no eating, though his metabolism is still firing as though he's training, means he's lost a lot.

Taking the bottle of vodka from my freezer and slamming the door shut, I noisily slide a dining chair across the room, climb up with a huff, and pull down a set of shot glasses from above the fridge.

Kit put them up there. With her long arms and legs, she teased my lack of height and said I'd never need them without her. She said she'd always be here to get them down when *we* needed them.

Well she's fucking not!

She's not here, and I need them *because* she's not here.

"Fuck it." She's not waking up tonight. Jon can sleep on his own. It's Izzy's turn to shield me, because I'm getting drunk.

Jumping down from the chair – and landing it, even in heels – I push the chair back to my table and swipe away the first angry tear.

I'm not a crier.

I don't do that shit, and tonight won't be the start of a new bad habit.

Except the drinking. I'm starting that right now.

My ringing cell vibrates in my bag on the floor, and though I want to ignore it, I want to shut the world out and wallow in self-pity, I still scramble across the room and fish it from the side pocket.

It could be the hospital.

It could be Kit.

"Hello?" I turn it up the right way in shaking hands. "Hello?"

"Sunshine, hey." Jon's rumbling voice echoes through my brain. "Where are you?"

"Is Kit okay?"

He sighs. "She's fine. She's the same. Where are you?"

"So you're not calling about Kit?"

"No."

"Alright, well." With a noisy grunt, I climb to my feet and move back to the counter to pour my drink. "I gotta go, Jon. I'll catch you tomorrow."

Taking the phone from my ear, with my thumb poised over the red hang up button, I stop when he shouts, "Wait!"

I can't wait. I can't stop crying, because Kit's still *the same*, and the disappointment is crushing. I had a single second to wonder and hope, and now, his simple words weigh twice as much as I can handle.

I clumsily pour the shot, spilling the precious liquid over the lip of the glass, but picking it up anyway, I throw it back and savor the burn.

How many do I need to feel numb?

"Casey? Are you still there?"

I wipe an arm across my lip. "What?"

"You didn't say where you are. Are you coming home soon?"

His sad puppy voice hurts my heart.

Time to find a new coping mechanism, Jon. I'm tapping out for the night. "I am home. I need some alone time. See you tomorrow."

"Casey–"

I end the call and toss my phone onto the counter. Pouring a second shot, my single, traitorous tear turns to a devastated river that flows of heartbreak.

I want my best friend back. I want her to forgive me.

And I want Jon, even though I just rejected him.

I'll make it up to him tomorrow, I'll blame it on PMS.

He's spent enough time with me now to know I become a raging bitch for a few days a month. True to his word, he bought tampons when I asked, and from years of painful endometriosis causing cramping bad enough that I need to curl up on the couch with a heat pack, he caught on quick and started with the hot chocolate and massaging hands.

I don't know why he's so damn stubborn about his stance on love and relationships.

He's essentially already in a monogamous relationship with me –

minus the sex. He picks his shit up, he leaves the toilet seat down, he buys chocolate for no reason at all.

I pour a third glass, carry it across the room to my bag, and slide along the wall until I sit with my knees bent. With the glass resting on my kneecap and my face buried in my legs, I sob.

I sob because one of my best friends is in a coma. It's been three weeks, everyone's dead inside without her, and I'm terrified she might never wake.

But on top of that, I cry because I'm in love with my *other* best friend. Real, in-your-bones, your-heart-squeezes-when-he's-near love. It's different to how Bobby loves him, and it hurts like nothing I've ever felt before, because he'll never love me back.

Not the way I need.

I've spent almost every single day for six months in Jon's home. Every night he carries me to bed, every morning we wake up and chatter about nothing and everything, every time he lays his head in my lap and breathes against my thighs.

Every day, he does these things for me, and as a result, I've steadily fallen stupid in love with him.

My heart aches every night as we cuddle on the couch.

It breaks every time we go to bed together and I can't tell him how I feel.

I didn't want this. He didn't, either. He warned me he never would, and yet, my stupid ass still fell in love, and now he carelessly ping pongs my heart around and has no clue he's bruising me.

He'd never hurt me on purpose. If he knew, he'd probably run for the hills to *save* me from himself.

Which means I can never tell him.

I can't risk losing him.

So that leaves me in heartbreak lane, and there are no exits in sight.

JON

I'LL BE YOUR SPOON

Something's wrong.

Something more than this already horrible fucking month.

Something's wrong with Case. I *felt* her dim, even over the phone. Casey doesn't dim. She's sunshine, she's bright and beautiful and everything good in this world.

I don't give a damn that she asked for *alone time*. I've never given in to her shit before, and I'm not gonna start now. Not this month. Not right now when I need her the most.

Inserting my key in her apartment door, I push it open fast, but come to a thudding stop when it slams into something, *someone*, and a hiccupped yelp has my heart racing.

"Shit. Casey?" I push the door slowly forward when she doesn't answer, and sliding her along the floor out of the way, as soon as I can squeeze through, I race in, drop to the floor next to my sobbing best friend, and pull her into my arms.

This is bad.

I can't do this.

I can't take any more hurt. I can't take any more heartache.

She's not allowed to break, because I need her to hold me together. I'm the weak fuck that needs a one-hundred-pound fairy to hold me together, because I'm not strong enough to do it myself.

"Sunshine." I brush the hair from her face and stare into mascara smudged eyes. "Casey, are you hurt? What's the matter?"

She doesn't answer, instead, she throws her arms around my shoulders and stuffs her face in my neck.

Howling like her heart literally bleeds, her sobbing wracks her tiny frame and sends a bead of panicked sweat sliding down my spine the way it hasn't in so long.

"Tell me, Case. I'm begging you. Tell me what's wrong."

"I love you, Leo."

I push her hair aside again and press a kiss to her smudged cheek. "I love you too, Sunshine." *If I could love anyone the way a man should love a woman, it would be Casey.* "Why are you crying? Are you hurt?"

"My heart hurts."

Anxiety and relief wage war within me. "Are you physically hurt, though? Any broken bones?"

She shakes her head and buries her face in my shirt. "No broken bones. Just my heart."

"I know you're scared, Case, but Kit'll be okay. I promise."

I have no fucking clue if Kit will be okay, but for my two best friends' mental wellbeing, I need her to be.

If she goes, she takes Bobby and Case with her.

They need her.

And I need them.

Standing and lifting her light frame in my arms, I stop at the liquid mess on the tile floor.

She's not drunk.

But she's hurting bad.

Taking her to the couch, I sit and rock her in the cradle of my arms. "Talk to me, Case." I press her hand to my heart. "You're breaking me. Please tell me what's wrong. I'll fix it, I promise."

Scrunching my shirt in her fist, she simply shakes her head and hiccups on her tears. "I don't want to talk today. Don't make me talk."

"Want me to hold you?"

"I want to be alone."

"No. I'm not leaving you, Sunshine. Tell me what you need."

Her cries dig deeper and louder, and the pain in the sound send my eyes scrunching shut in self-defense.

This isn't her.

She's always bright and happy.

Her sadness cuts me like a million papercuts all over my body; they hurt, they sting, but they're not enough to allow me to bleed out and escape.

"Jon…" She shakes her head. "I need something you can never give."

"I have money. I have things. I have power. I can give you anything you want, Case. Just name it. Anything. Anything in the whole world." *There's nothing I wouldn't give her.*

Shaking her head, she refuses to answer, and instead, reburies her face in my neck. Bringing my hand up, I create space between us and thumb the tears from beneath her smudged eyes.

"Please don't cry, Casey." My gruff voice crackles over the tears I feel in my throat. "You're tearing my heart out, Sunshine." I lean forward and press a kiss to her closed eyes. Her soft lashes flutter against my lips and take another chunk of my heart, but I keep going, because I'm powerless to stop my movements. I press a kiss to the wet flesh beneath her eyes, and take away the tears that continue to fall.

She's hurting for her best friend.

I can relate. I feel a similar devastation right now as I cradle Casey's sobbing body in my arms.

I know *why* she's sad and hurting, I don't know how to fix it, but I can make her feel loved today. I can take away her pain and give her something else to focus on for a little while.

She deserves it. She deserves the world.

Which is exactly why I can't give her forever.

But we can have right now.

"I've got you, Sunshine. Lean on me." I press a kiss to her other eye, and when her hiccups turn to a sigh and her lashes kiss my lips, I smile. Pulling back so her bright eyes meet my brown, I study her running mascara, her quivering lips.

I didn't come here to kiss her. I didn't intend to touch her.

I've held off for months. I promised it was just that one time, that one kiss, and even with itching hands and a stirring heart, I've kept my promise. But sleeping with her every night has weakened my resolve. Sleeping with her *on* me has made me a slave to her every whim.

I didn't come here with sex on my mind, but my hands roam her ribs, anyway. I pepper kisses along her jaw and swallow her gasp when my fingertips brush the side of her breast.

"Jon." She shakes her head and tries to turn her beautiful face away from mine. "No, I can't–"

I take her chin in my hand. "Just one time, Case? Just once?"

She lets out a strangled sob. "You're going to break my heart, Jon. I can't afford you."

"I'll never hurt you, Sunshine. I'll protect you for the rest of my life, you have my word." I lean forward when her eyes flicker between mine and my lips.

She's as powerless as I am.

But I don't close the gap.

I'm weak. I'm powerless. But I'll never force her.

I watch the indecision in her eyes. The heartbreak. The want.

"One time."

And the decision.

When her plump lips gently press against mine, unlike the explosion from last time, the salty tears on her lips have us moving slower. Her gentle sigh fills my lungs, and her long lashes tickle the tops of my cheeks as she leans in impossibly close and tightens her arms around my neck.

Finally.

Snaking my tongue out hesitantly, I will myself to stay in control and not spook her. Last time, we had a flashfire, but that's not what she needs tonight. She's soft and sad and vulnerable. She's devastated and worried for her best friend.

She needs love and a distraction.

I can give her both.

It's easy.

Letting my tongue explore her soft mouth, I pull her juicy lip between my teeth and frame her face between my hands.

She's so delicate.

So soft.

So small.

Releasing her mouth and waiting for her eyes to reopen, I stroke her jaw and savor the way her breath races for me. Her forest green eyes flutter open in question, almost rejection, because I stopped. I shake my head. "Let me help you, Sunshine. Let me soothe your aching heart."

Indecision, terror, and want all shine in her eyes, mixing together, fighting for dominance, so I don't know what she'll choose. She's so scared for Kit. I'm scared for her. I need her.

"Please, Sunshine. I want to make you feel better. I want to be with you."

She swipes a shaking hand along her cheek and pushes the mascara smudge back. "Okay."

My heart skips a beat; exhilaration and fear in one. "Back to us tomorrow?"

She nods. "Okay."

"Promise me, Case. Back to us tomorrow?" I can't lose her over this. I'll never lay with another woman again if it means I get to keep her.

The tradeoff is no tradeoff at all.

Bringing her shaking hand up to my face, she strokes the soft pad of her pointer finger over the bridge of my nose and lets out a weary sigh. "Okay. I promise."

"Thank God." Shuffling her in my lap and bringing her legs around to straddle me, I stand and move toward the back of the apartment. We spend most of our time at my place, since I would never ditch Sissy, but I've been here enough to know where her room is.

Her strong arms hold me close, and her jean clad ass fills my hands in the most delicious way. Laying her in the center of her bed, I crawl over top and settle my legs between hers and my weight on my elbows on either side of her face.

Fingering her hair aside, I uncover bright green eyes. "You're my beautiful sunshine, you know that?"

My words make her sad and have her turning away. "Don't be too kind to me, Jon."

"I'll always be kind." With a finger beneath her chin, I bring her eyes back to mine. "You *are* beautiful, Casey. The most beautiful woman I know." Slowly running my hand along her leg, I lift it, find her ankle, and hitch her firm thigh over my hip to anchor my cock against her core.

She cradles my body perfectly, despite our size difference, and her breasts cushion my chest softly.

She's perfect.

I bring my lips down to hers and slowly, hesitantly, let my tongue play with hers. When she lets out a sweet little sigh and brings her hands up to cradle my head, I smile triumphantly and press closer.

Her legs draw tighter around my waist, and her arms pull me in closer. Despite her hesitance, she doesn't want me to escape.

My fucking pleasure.

I pull her plump lip between my teeth, and lifting to my knees and putting space between our torsos, I slide her silky top up over delicate ribs and lace covered breasts.

No regular everyday sports bra for my Sunshine. She told me a long time ago that she likes to indulge. Matching panties and bras are an indulgence I've long ago noticed and enjoyed.

We may have not hooked up in the past, but I see her every night at bedtime, I see the laundry hamper; I see the beautiful lingerie she owns.

Pausing with the fabric touching the bottom of her chin, I groan and suckle on her tongue as she pushes it past my lips and finally takes control. Darting my tongue out to duel with hers, I press my hips down against hers until the breath rushes from her lungs and into mine.

Pressing up for the smallest second, I pull her shirt over her head and toss it across the room with no care for where it lands.

I let my hands surf her skin, and dive back in to take her mouth. Cinnamon, strawberries, and maybe just a little chocolate. My hips jut forward without my permission, and each time I do, she pushes up and half levitates off the bed.

It's a natural instinct, one neither of us have a chance of stopping.

The universe wants this for us.

"Jon..."

"Mmm." I let my lips cruise along her jaw, tasting her, nibbling on the sweet perfumed skin, and nuzzling the warm spots of her neck. Like burying my face in a bag of cinnamon sugar, I breathe in the warm scent that pulses around her neck and breathe it in like a drowning man.

Hungry hands slide along my back, down to my ass, and cup as she pulls me against her. I grind my hardened cock against her warm core, and groan when her hands slide beneath my shirt, teasing my bare skin.

"Jon, take it off."

Lifting away from her, I breathe heavily as she fumbles with my shirt and works to push it up my long torso. Bringing my hands over the back of my head, I fist the fabric at my shoulder blades and drag it off. Laying back over her, she sighs when our bellies touch and our warm skin slides together.

Leaning up onto her elbows to reach me easier, she takes my lips with hers and hungrily suckles until I'm breathless and ready to pass out.

Breaking free of her mouth, I nibble along her jaw, to her neck, then to the warmth just behind her ear.

"Jon..."

"Mmm." I pepper kisses along her flesh, stop on her collarbone and bite down on the delicate flesh until she pants and angles her hips up to meet mine. I suck on her skin, *suck, suck, suck,* and when I pull away, I grin at the mark I left behind.

Flicking open the front clasp on her bra and revealing something I've been coveting for months, I take her pebbled nipple between my teeth and groan at her explosion of breath.

"Jon!" Her hands shoot into my hair and hold me close. Her unique flavor drugs me, she's a nirvana that I'd willingly drown in.

I switch breasts, take the other in my mouth, and tease the first between my calloused fingers.

Her hot skin scorches, but it's a good hurt.

For the first time in my life, it's a good pain.

Her back arches and lifts from the soft bed, and as she pushes against my mouth, she cries out with pleasure when I bite down on the hardened pink flesh.

Letting her nipple go with a soft pop, I trail my lips over the valley of her stomach, toy with her belly button for a moment, then pop the button on her jeans and slowly lower the zipper.

Matching panties – black silk and lace – exactly what I knew I'd find.

"So beautiful." I peek up the valley between her breasts until I meet green eyes. "Can I?" I place my hands in the back pockets of her jeans, and when she nods, drag them down over perfect globes and sensual hips.

I pull the denim along creamy thighs, and stopping at the strappy black heels, shake my head. "Swear to God, I love the shoes you wear, Sunshine. You send me crazy every single day strutting around the house in these." I study bare thighs. The heels. "You have no clue how many times I've thought about this. Exactly this. Naked, but for the shoes." Lifting her leg and pulling the denim away, I press a gentle kiss to her ankle. "You're my best friend, but I notice how sexy you are. So fuckin' sexy, Case."

"Jon." Her painful sigh squeezes my heart. I don't want her to feel pain. I just want her to feel loved, to feel cherished.

I want to make her feel *good.*

"Rest with me, Case. Just this one time, don't overthink it."

I press a second kiss to the delicate skin over her ankle, then pinching the sweet ribbon that fastens her sexy heels to her feet, I unravel the knot and let the heel fall to the floor.

When the second is gone, I finish peeling her jeans away, then throw them to the floor along with her shirt and shoes.

Kissing my way up the inside of her thighs, I savor the sounds of her breath catching and releasing as I near her pulsing heat.

Pausing at the top of her thigh, I look up at her face expecting to find heat, or at least a smile, but instead, I find a tortured expression right before she slams her hands over her eyes.

Scrambling up her body, I rest my belly against hers and press a gentle kiss to her lips. "Hey. Look at me."

She shakes her head stubbornly. Grabbing her hands, I peel them away and wait for her eyes to clear. "Talk to me. What's going on in your pretty head?"

"I'm scared."

I sigh. "I know, Sunshine. I'm scared for Kit, too, but we can take a few hours to just be us. Let's be Leo and his Sunshine. Let's leave the world behind for a little while and just be together."

Her breath comes out on a broken shudder. "Kit. Yeah..." She takes a deep breath. "Hey, Leo?"

Sliding her panties away, I barely notice the tremor in her voice. "Mmm?"

"Make love to me? Just one time."

"Yeah, Sunshine. That's exactly what I'm gonna do."

Sitting back on my haunches, I pop the button on my jeans, shuck them down, and kick them off. Lining myself up and finding her wet and waiting, I slide inside her body smoothly.

We don't need all the fanfare. We don't need wild and reckless and fun. We just need us, soft and quiet and soothing.

I let out a grunt of pure, pleasure-filled satisfaction, and when she sighs and wraps her legs around my hips, I lean forward and press a gentle kiss to her lips.

She's perfect for me. The perfect fit. The perfect feel.

She's just... perfect.

Rocking against her slowly, I time the smooth strokes and bury my face against her neck. There's no rush today, no wildfire, no frantic pace. There's just us and the silence in my mind I haven't experienced since... ever.

Her nails dig into my shoulder blades and drag along the muscle, and her strong legs cinch around my hips and anchor my body to hers.

"Jon." Her breaths come out in soft pants over my ear.

Nodding in silent agreement, I slide my tongue along her neck and take the delicate flesh between my lips.

I've spent six months wanting this woman. Coveting her. Holding her at night, but unable to truly touch.

If this is a one-time thing, then I'll savor her. Then when it's all done and I never get this chance again, I'll have the memory tucked away, and I'll be able to revisit the only woman I ever truly loved.

"You feel so good, Case." Gently swaying, I drive us both up a slow and tender crest, stand on the edge, and sway some more.

A small part of my brain remembers I'm inside her without protection. I didn't mean to do this without a condom, but I know I'm clean. Casey takes a little pill every single day. We're safe, and I trust her.

She's my best friend.

"Jon." Her walls flutter and squeeze around me. The heels of her feet dig into my lower back, and each time I rock closer, she lifts her hips and meets me.

"Yeah, Case." Standing on the very edge of the cliff of pleasure, I wait for her fluttering to turn to crushing pressure, and when her quiet sighs turn to cries of pleasure, I bury my face in her neck, step off the ledge, and come deep inside her. "Casey…" Her name drags its way up my throat and begs me to declare my love for her. My heart demands I give her the world and all its treasures within.

But I can't.

My heart wants one thing, but my head knows the truth. She deserves so much more than I can give. I can't claim her when all she'd get is a quarter of a broken heart and a whole shell of a broken man.

When my hips still and our panting breath is the only sound in the dark room, I pepper kisses along her delicate shoulder and memorize everything about this moment. I tuck it away for the lonely days when I won't have her anymore.

"I love you, Case." *I do. I really do.*

If I could love her more, if I could love her the way a man should, then I would.

She'd be my choice.

But my choice was taken from me long ago.

Her breath hitches against my shoulder.

I'm too weak to lift my head, too weak to notice the glistening tears in her eyes. "Yeah, Jon." She swallows and runs her nails through the hair on the back of my neck. "I love you, too."

Slipping out of her and rolling to my back, I pull her on top of my chest so her face rests over my heart and her hair bathes my nose. I cradle her body and hold her tight. "Sleep, Sunshine. Rest with me."

I hum her song and stroke her back.

It takes only minutes for her breathing to even out and her body to fall heavy against mine.

I love you, Sunshine. Maybe even more than I love Bobby.

13

CASEY

HART'S HEART

Late January

*K*it's awake!

Five weeks and three days ago, she opened her eyes and scared the shit out of all of us. Three weeks after that, she was released from the hospital and sent home on a strict rest and physical therapy regime.

She struggles to do just about anything for herself; she's weak, she's lethargic, and she's still working to replace a lot of the blood she lost. She was given transfusion after transfusion just to make surgery safe. So that, along with her new screws and casts and crutches and stitches, she's at least eighty-percent machine.

But we love her, anyway.

She attends physical therapy sessions every single day, and Bobby carries her just about everywhere he can.

Much to Kit's disgust.

She's the strong, independent woman that takes no one's shit, and though she loves her big, strong overprotective man, she *hates* being treated like a child.

Her insistence to prove the guys wrong only sets her recovery back, but she's stubborn as an ox, and despite her physical ailments, her bad attitude soothes my heart more than anything else ever could.

She's awake.

She's safe.

And she still loves me.

The morning after the night I spent with Jon was... normal.

Surprisingly, blissfully, normal.

He didn't make it weird.

He didn't make me regret it.

He simply pressed a kiss to my brow and made a cup of tea before he ran out to check on his sister and *other* best friend.

We haven't had sex again since, and just as promised, we're back to normal. He's my best friend, he holds me most nights, and we laugh and watch movies on the nights I don't have to work at the club.

I don't know how we've managed it, but we kissed, we had sex, we've experienced two separate, potentially explosive friendship-ending occasions, and both times we've come out the other end and kept our promises.

We went back to being best friends the next day.

I still love him.

Like, really, truly, monogamous relationship love, but the ache in my heart has eased.

It's a nice love.

I smile when he's around, I flirt with him during the day, and sleep with him at night. If I ignore the fact that he doesn't know my true feelings, nor does he reciprocate them, then I'm okay.

Denial is my *other* other best friend.

It's working out well so far.

Jon's anxiety seems to have eased since that night, too. Like our being together soothed him, and with his sister safe, Kit waking up, Bobby's life back on kilter, and my life no longer attached to tubes and wires in the hospital, Jon was happy simply because the rest of us were happy.

His life is back to perfect; *except* for the stomach flu that just won't leave me alone.

Now he's become my caretaker, fetching cups of tea, making soup, warming blankets, and rubbing my feet while I lie on his couch and eat nothing.

I've lost weight. I'm not hungry. I've been vomiting. And no matter what I do, no amount of NyQuil is fixing it, so resting at Jon's insistence,

I've called out sick from work and set up camp in Jon and Izzy's living room.

"I'm going out for a bit." Izzy breezes past my mostly dead form and zooms through the tissues and ginger-ale littered living room. Stopping at the top end of my temporary bed, she lays her cool palm on my forehead and clucks the way Jon does.

They're as bad as each other.

"You're warm, T. You need some more Advil?"

I shake my head slowly, and groan when the movement sets off a nasty twinge in my stomach. I've been vomiting so much, my throat burns and my head aches. "Nah, I'm good." My voice is a pathetic croak. "Already took some. Going back to bed soon." I turn over slowly and groan into the back cushions. "Miss Kit. But don't wanna make her sick."

Iz tuts and brushes the hair from my brow. "She knows you're sick. She understands." Standing, Iz leans to the side like that'll help Jon hear clearer from the kitchen. "I'll be back later."

He pokes his head into the living room and scowls. "Where're you going?"

"Just out," she answers. "I'll be back late, so don't wait up."

"Sissy…" His brows pull in tight and add a decade to his face. He's not dealing so well with the fact she's not a baby anymore.

The idea of her dating gives him a coronary.

God help us all when she loses her virginity. If she hasn't already…

"See ya." She snags her bag and slings it over her shoulder. "I'll be back later. Take care of Tink."

His eyes snap down to mine and switch from mother of Iz, to mother of the sick.

The evening passes by in a blur.

I'm vaguely aware of the chicken soup Jon spoon feeds me, but within a single minute of the tasty broth hitting my stomach, I bring it up and cry tears of frustration and pain into my bucket of spew.

I doze as Jon rubs my feet, and I dream of making love to him again.

Though of course, we don't.

The next morning when I wake no better, I finally swallow my pride and call my doctor. My period has arrived with a vengeance, and the vomiting just won't go away.

My cramps have taken on a whole new level of painful, which is a bitch, since the nausea seems to have high-fived the cramps and now they both laugh maniacally and kill me from within.

"Are you sure I can't come with you?"

"It's fine, Leo." I scrunch my eyes closed to ward off the nausea and the cramps. "Lacey's coming to get me. You need to go to the gym. Bobby's out, so you need to pick up the slack."

"But the guys won't mind if I'm late. I want to come with you."

"Seriously." I blindly reach out for his hand. "I'm fine. I've already called Lace, she's on her way. I'll grab some antibiotics or something, then I'll be back to normal and not stinking up your house."

His large hand presses gently against my warm forehead. "I'm worried about you, Case. Your cramps are giving me cramps."

The doorbell rings and has my stomach vibrating. "See." I let him help me sit up. "That's her now. I'll be gone an hour, then I'll come back and sleep until you get home."

He slowly helps me to my feet. "What do you want me to bring home? Ice-cream? More soup?"

My head swims and his voice echoes in my brain.

"Hey, Case. You here?"

"Yeah, hold on," Jon snaps. Gently lifting me off my feet, he carries me through his home and almost lulls me back to sleep with the rhythm of his steps.

"Thank you, Leo. Love you."

His strong hands squeeze me close. "I love you too, Case."

"And ice-cream. That might be nice."

"Alright." He presses a gentle kiss to my forehead before we round the last turn and come into view of the front door. "Text me after you finish at the doctors. I wanna know what's up."

Nodding lethargically, I grin as the pink-haired and blue-eyed Lacey steps into the hall and takes my hand when Jon sets me on my feet.

They're acting like I'm an invalid, and though my attitude demands I snap at them for it, my nausea won't let me. "Alright, guys, I'm okay." I clutch at Lacey's hand when waves roar in my head. "Thanks for coming, Lace. I'll see you after, Leo."

Jon stands at the door in navy sweatpants that ride low on trim hips, a Rollin tank that clings to his broad chest, and dark eyes that track my every move. He blows a tiny air kiss, invisible to anyone else, but I see it, and I smile.

"Bye, Sunshine."

Lacey helps me walk down the path to her parked car, and though my brain demands I'm fine and able to get there myself, my stomach reminds me I haven't eaten a whole meal in a week, and I'm exhausted from broken sleep.

I'm stubborn as a mule, but if I fall on my face in Jon's driveway, he'll never stop mothering me.

"So…" Lacey laughs softly. "You and Jon had sex lately?"

"Ha." I roll my eyes. "No. Not recently."

She knows about the first and only time Jon and I were together. We were working at the club together, she asked about him, and voila, I spilled my guts.

Well, not *all* my guts.

She has no clue I love him, but she knows we hooked up.

That's normally something I'd share with Kit, but flashing my jazz hands and announcing I'd had sex with her boyfriend's best friend just as she woke from a coma felt inappropriate.

"Mmm." She hums under her breath as we reach the car. "But he's so fine. How are you in his house every damn day and not dropping to your knees?"

"It was a once in a lifetime deal, Lace." I close my mouth and hold my breath as nausea whooshes and threatens. "One time." Black dots swim in my vision as she helps me into the passenger seat of her tiny Mazda. "One time only." I close my eyes and lay my head back as she runs around the hood and jumps into her side.

"So if it was a once in a lifetime thing and you're *just* friends, does that mean he's available?"

Fuck no! "Yeah," I sigh. "I guess."

She laughs under her breath and pulls away from the curb. "I heard that sigh, girl. You want him, so why not claim him?"

"It's not like that." A new wave of nausea rolls in my stomach and has me wishing I brought my spew bucket. "Can you drive smooth, Lace? Don't stop and start too hard, I feel sick."

"Yeah, hon, we'll be there in two minutes. Lock it up."

"Mmm." I recline in the chair and close my eyes.

―――――

"How long have you been feeling like this, Casey?" Dr. Storan removes the thermometer from my ear, reads the screen, and jots the numbers on a pad of paper.

"Um… all week, I guess."

"Have you had a fever the whole time?" He presses his stethoscope to my back, and has goosebumps breaking out along my skin from the cold metal touching my hot flesh.

"No. Just a couple days."

"And you've been vomiting?" He writes more notes, then threads my arm through a blood pressure cuff.

"Uh-huh. I've been vomiting for the whole week. Nothing will stay down. But I'm not hungry, anyway."

"Any other symptoms?" Ripping the Velcro open on the cuff, he slides it away and turns the noisy machine off.

I flex my arm to get the blood flowing. "I've been cramping, but that's normal." Dr. Storan knows about my years of endometriosis. He's been my doctor since I was twelve and came to him with tears in my eyes and clawing cramps turning me inside out.

He nods and makes notes. "What date was the first day of your last menstrual period?"

"Today. It started overnight."

"Alright..." Taking a pen light, he points it into my mouth and distractedly checks my throat. My eyes flash to Lacey as she sits in the corner and watches. "So apart from an inflamed throat," he continues, "which we'll assume is from your vomiting, you don't have any other symptoms of a cold or flu. No runny nose. Your eyes and ears are fine. Your chest is clear."

"So what's wrong with me?"

"I actually don't know," he chuckles softly. When a new cramp rolls through my uterus and has me folding in half, he frowns and taps a pen on his desk. "Are your cramps worse than usual this month?"

"Dunno, I guess." I groan and hold my breath. "I've been sick, so all my problems have kind of melded together into one giant pain in my ass."

His lips twitch playfully. "Alright, well I think we'll have to run a few blood tests."

I whimper with dread. "Needles?"

"Just one needle, Case. I'm sorry." He reaches into a drawer beside his leg and pulls out a yellow-lidded cup. "I need a urine sample. We need to check for a kidney infection, possibly urinary tract. Take this into the bathroom and fill it up."

"Umm." My face burns hot as I take the specimen cup. "I have my period, so..."

"That's alright, I've seen blood before. Just pee and we'll do our best, but don't sweat it, because we'll also test your blood samples."

"Alright." Standing shakily, I hobble across the office and into the attached bathroom. Sitting on the toilet, I pee and catch it in the cup. I've done this so often in the last decade, I've basically mastered the art of not peeing on my hand.

It's a skill I wish I could list on my resume.

I'd hire me.

Finishing up and capping the jar, I wash my hands and blush at the rose-pink urine. Gross.

Stepping back into his office and placing the jar on a stack of paper towels on the corner of his desk, I sit back in my chair and breathe like I've just run a marathon. "Here you go."

Pulling on a set of rubber gloves, Doctor Storan leans over my sample like a scientist ready to create the next Frankenstein. He takes three-inch strips of cardboard from the desk drawer, dips them in the pee, then lays them out on the paper towel.

Flicking his gloves into the trash can, he studies the strips and frowns.

"Casey..." With pinched brows, his gaze travels to Lace in the corner. "Maybe you'd like to ask your friend to step out for a few minutes?"

"Oh!" Standing abruptly, Lacey grabs her bag and shoves her phone in. "Yeah, no worries, I can g–"

"No." I throw my hand out to stop her from leaving. "It's okay, she can stay. I don't mind."

"I really don't mind leaving."

"No, it's fine." I turn back to Storan. "What's up, Doc?"

"Ah, well..." He picks up one of the three strips. "So, I don't think you have any infections; in your bladder, urinary tract, or kidney... though we'll rule that out for sure with blood tests."

"Okay..."

"But, this strip right here." He lifts another and studies it closely. "Well... This one says you're pregnant."

The cramping that had me bending only a moment ago now vanishes from my mind. "Pr–" I think I might be experiencing my first ever mini stroke. "Pregnant? No." I wave him away like the words are simply pesky bugs in the air. "No. That's not right."

"I know this might come as a shock to you–"

"*Might* be a shock?!" Lacey jumps in my peripherals, but Storan continues neutrally staring into my eyes. "It's *definitely* a shock! You told me it's unlikely I'll *ever* get pregnant. You said I'd need to have surgery for my endo scarring. You said–"

"I didn't say it was impossible, Case. I said you might have trouble. You still need to have protected intercourse."

"I did! I've been on the pill for a decade. I haven't missed a single day. I've had sex only *once* in more than a year! This can't happen to me."

"I think we need to get you in for scans, Casey. You're cramping and bleeding, and while both aren't uncommon during pregnancy–"

"I'm not pregnant!" Tears burn the backs of my eyes, but at least the nausea is forgotten. "I can't be!"

"While both are not uncommon," he continues patiently, "with your history, your scarring, the pain you're in…" He sighs. "We need to get this checked as soon as possible."

"I'm not preg–"

"Then there's the fever you've been nursing."

"I've got the flu!"

"Your fever has me worried, Casey. I'm concerned this may be ectopic. You're bleeding heavily, you're in pain, you have a fever… we can't ignore this."

"I have the flu!"

"We're stepping into another room." He stands and slides a cellphone into his back pocket. "Come with me. We need a scan today, Casey. If it's all good, then I'll help you manage your fever and vomiting and we'll figure out why you're having them. But if it's not good, then we need to deal with it before it gets worse."

No.

I try to ignore the sharp cramping that stabs me from within. Storan can't be right. He's definitely wrong. He's never been wrong before, but today, he is.

Today he's an incompetent idiot that knows nothing.

I've spent the last five years knowing that, if I ever wanted kids, it would be a battle that my hypothetical husband and I would have to fight at the time. That I'd have to have surgery, because of the scarring on my fallopian tubes. I was told that I rarely ovulate, because the scarring blocks everything up.

I've been on the pill since I was fifteen years old, not because I was scared of getting pregnant, but in an attempt to regulate my body and try to control out of control periods.

I've taken my little cream-colored pill every morning for a decade, and

I've never once stopped and considered babies. That was something for later, something for when I had a man... that wanted babies.

I can't accidentally get pregnant.

I *especially* can't fall pregnant with Jon Hart's baby.

He doesn't want babies. He's told me a million times since we met. He'll never marry. He'll never have children.

"Come on," Lacey murmurs in my ear. She helps pull me from my chair. I let her do all the work, because inside, I'm mourning the loss of the most important man in my life.

He won't like this.

He'll hate me.

He'll hate the baby.

Holding my weight against her not-much-larger-than-me frame, she helps me hobble along the hall behind my doctor and into a different room, a bigger room with a big bed, a bigger machine, and an even bigger screen on the wall.

"I need you to remove your pants and underwear–"

"But my period–"

"It's fine, Casey." Storan moves around the room and powers up computers and machines. "Just take them off, lay down on the bed, and put this towel over yourself. I'll come back in a minute so we can get started. It's totally your decision if your friend stays or not."

"I'll just–"

I snag Lacey's hand before she escapes. "Please stay with me, Lace. Don't leave me."

"I think I should call Jon." She looks up when the door closes with a soft snick. "He's your best friend, he's involved in this. He should be here."

"No! Absolutely not. Jon can't know about this, not today."

"But if he's the father–"

"He might not be!" *Lie.* "We're just friends, and we're definitely not exclusive." *Lie, lie, lie.*

"Oh." Her eyes flare with realization. "Oh! Right, okay. I didn't realize you'd been with other guys." I haven't. I even shouted that at Storan barely two minutes ago.

"Yeah." I wave her off and die a little inside. "Jon and I are just friends. I still date." Unbuttoning my jeans, I walk into the attached bathroom. "I've just gotta…"

Lacey nods in unspoken understanding. Tampons are gross. Periods are gross. This whole fucking week is gross.

"Please don't leave, Lace."

She sighs. "Okay, I won't. I promise."

Sitting and peeing a second time, I work to clean myself as best I can, then waddle back to the main room and climb onto the bed and fix the towel.

Walking in moments later, Storan fiddles with the machine, and just minutes after that, I catch a glimpse of Jon's baby's heartbeat on the giant screen on the wall.

Devastation.

Pure, unbroken devastation floods my body, because I know Jon doesn't want this.

Yet, a tiny glimmer of hope wages a battle.

I know this wasn't in our plan, this wasn't what he wanted.

Hell, it wasn't what I wanted, either. But Jon's created this heartbeat within me, and no matter how scared I am of his reaction, no matter how unprepared we are for this, I find my hand stroking my flat stomach, and my own heart growing and enveloping the tiny flickering beat.

He's already mine.

Jon might not want him, but that's just because he's scared. I can help him accept this. We can do it together.

This wasn't my plan, but plans change. Rules can be broken. Hearts can grow, and Hart's can learn.

I can give our baby life. I can make this okay.

"I'm sorry, Casey." Storan's deep voice rumbles through my consciousness. "This is what I thought it would be. Your fetus isn't viable. It's attached outside the uterine wall, this is what we call an ectopic pregnancy. Your baby won't survive, Casey. We need surgery today to remove it."

Devastation reigns supreme. "Remove it?"

"Yes. I'm sorry. It's dangerous for you if we leave it there." Standing from his position between my legs, he removes the probe from within me and snaps his used gloves into the trash can. "We need to remove it immediately. This is considered a medical emergency, Casey. We have to do this today."

"Today?" My lip quivers on the word, but he doesn't wait for me to breathe, or grieve, or argue. He simply takes out his cell and makes plans for my body and baby while Lacey steps closer and blocks my view.

She takes my shaking hand in hers. "It'll be okay, Case. I'll stay with you."

I nod at her words, but in my mind, I see Jon. I want Jon. I want him to hold me. I want him to want our baby, and I want him to want me.

But he doesn't.

An hour after Storan's words batter at me like gunshots, he wheels me into an operating room, and I fall asleep all alone with my non-viable baby and tears in my eyes.

A little while after that, I wake to a dark room, those same tears in my eyes, and Doctor Storan standing by to explain that it was a *success*. My baby is gone, as is my right fallopian tube.

I have one left.

One scarred tube for my hypothetical husband and I to work with in the hypothetical future.

I'm minus one baby and one tube, and in exchange, I gained two new scars and a broken heart.

I turn away from my doctor, away from my friend, away from reality, and I weep and apologize to the baby I got to love for only a few minutes.

I'm so sorry, baby. I'm sorry I couldn't care for you the way I was supposed to.

14

JON

GLANDULAR FEVER

*S*he didn't come home today.

It's almost the middle of the fucking night, and she didn't come home.

Knocking on her front door, I don't give a damn if I'm being loud, I don't give a shit if I wake the neighbors, I don't even care if I wake my Sunshine.

She didn't come home, she's not answering her phone, and she hasn't been back to my place to collect her car.

That shit's not on.

I don't know where the fuck she is, I don't know what the hell happened with her doctor, and she never texted like she said she would.

She should be home with me!

If she has a cold and wants to be in her own bed, that's fine. But she still needs to send me a damn text and let me know. That way, I can make sure my sister is safe, then I can bring my ass over here and be with her.

She doesn't *have* to be at my place, but she doesn't get to drop off the side of the planet and expect me to be okay with it.

The door swings wide just as I bring my fist up to knock a second time, but Casey's eyes aren't the eyes I'm met with. Lacey with the weird hair pins me with a dangerous glare and blocks the doorway. "Can you stop? She's sleeping."

"Suns–" I cough away the name I rarely use around company. "Casey's sleeping?"

"Yes, dummy, so be quiet. I'm staying with her tonight, so you can just go–"

"Nope." I push past her and into the tiny apartment that the tiny girl lives in. "I'm staying with her, so *you* can go."

"She doesn't want–"

I spin when I arrive in the empty kitchen. "What happened today? What did the doctor say?"

"I… um." She fusses with her nails and avoids my eyes. "That's probably something between her and her healthcare provider."

I stop searching the kitchen and pin her with a glare more severe than anything she'll ever be able to conjure. "What. Happened. Today?"

"Look," she sighs, "she knew you'd probably turn up at some point." *Yeah, no fucking kidding she knew. I'm her Leo, and we had an ice-cream date.* "She told me to tell you the surgery was routine and it went fine."

"Surgery?" I rush forward and stop inches from Lacey's face. "What fucking surgery? She wasn't having surgery today!"

"No, she did. Um, her doctor said she had fibroids or something, had to take them out. That's what was causing her cramping, no big deal. It was an hour tops, she was sedated–"

"She was sedated?" I want to shake this bitch. *This is a big fucking deal!* "Casey was sedated, as in she was *asleep*, and they operated on her? What the actual fuck?"

"It was keyhole surgery," she hisses. "She's fine, so can you please stop shouting! She's tired and needs rest, and you need to leave. She wants me here tonight."

"No." I stalk toward the hallway. "But you can fuck right off. I've got her now."

"Jon!"

I turn back and stop at the plastic bag on the counter. "What do I need to know? Medication? Is she in pain?"

She sighs with frustration. If she could, she would've already kicked my ass. "She's on some pretty strong drugs. She's actually pretty high right now, so don't talk to her. If you do, don't listen to anything she says. She's loopy, so whatever she says can't be held against her. Just let her sleep."

"Does she need pain relief in the night?"

"Yeah." On a defeated sigh, Lacey plucks packages from the plastic bag. Passing a small bottle of pills with shaking hands, she looks up into my eyes. "Set your alarm, give these to her at two a.m. She'll be awake for her next lot at eight, so she'll be able to do those herself."

"Okay, you can let yourself out. See ya."

I turn and fill a tall glass with tap water. Pocketing the pills, I walk down the hall and let myself into her room. Kicking my shoes off and pushing my jeans down, I place the water and pills on the bedside table, lift the covers, and climb in, resting my chest against her back.

I'd normally pull her over my body so she can sleep on my chest, almost like a weighted security blanket that I didn't realize I needed until I met her, but I have no clue what happened today, and I don't want to hurt her.

Instead, I bury my face in the back of her hair and breathe her in until I doze off.

She's safe and fine.

We're fine.

"Wake up, Sunshine." I press a gentle kiss to her lips, her cheek, her chin. I literally don't know where she hurts, so I can't shake her shoulder to bring her awake. I don't even know what a fucking fibroid is; is that in your neck?

"Sunshine, honey, wake up."

Her lashes flutter open, and as she surfaces from unconsciousness, her face screws up in pain. "Jon?"

"Yeah, Sunshine. It's just me. Here you go." I wrap her fingers around the water glass. "Take some pills, then we can go back to sleep."

"Okay." Her hands shake, and her word is a slur, but I help her sit up and drink, then I lower her again, and bring her head to my chest.

"Rest now, Sunshine. I've got you."

"Okay." She snuggles against me and attempts to lift her thigh over mine, but with a pained groan, stops and whimpers in her sleep. Shuffling closer, I fold my body around hers until she stops moving.

"Love you, Jon."

I press a kiss to her brow. "I love you too, Sunshine." *Definitely more than I love B.*

I wake up with a vise squeezing my heart, because Casey squirms in her sleep and groans in pain. Bending at the waist, she clutches at her stomach and whimpers.

Her pain hurts me.

"Wake up, Sunshine." I blink to clear the sleep from my eyes. Looking at the clock, I blink some more at the flashing 08:21. I'm late for the gym, *and* late on medication for Case. "Shit. Time for some medicine. Time to wake up."

"Jon?" Her voice croaks painfully, but she clutches to my shoulders as I try to move back.

"Yeah, Sunshine, I'm here." I push dark hair out of her eyes. "How are you feeling?"

She burrows back in closer and tucks her face into my neck. "Sore. My tummy hurts."

"Gotta wake up, Case." I push her back again. "You need more medicine, then you can go back to sleep."

Like an ant bit her ass, her eyes pop open, her face drains of color, and her expression has my stomach dropping. "What the f–" She skitters back in a panic, but stops again and clutches to the sheets as though to cover herself up. "What are you doing here, Jon?"

"Be careful." I move closer to pull her off the edge of the bed, but she slaps my hand away.

"No! What are you doing here? Where's Lacey?"

Her harsh dismissal does things to my heart. "I sent her home last night."

"You stayed here all night?"

"Yeah. You didn't come home last night, so I came looking for you."

"Jon." Her voice breaks with emotion. "I *am* home. This is my bed. This is where I live."

"Okay…" I want to scream at her. *Her home is wherever the hell I am!* But I don't. She's in pain, and I refuse to upset her. "Take some medicine, Sunshine." I lean toward the bedside table and grab the bottle of pills. Flipping two into my palm, I gently press them into hers and close her fingers around them to stop the shaking. "Take these, then you can tell me why the fuck you ignored my calls and didn't tell me you had surgery."

So much for not upsetting her.

Her white face turns corpse-ish. "What did Lacey tell you?"

"She said you had surgery. Case, why didn't you tell me? Why wouldn't you let me be there for you? What the hell is the matter with you that you don't tell me that stuff?"

"What *exactly* did she tell you?" She leans up onto her elbow. "What were her words?"

"She said you had fibroids or some shit." With fingers under her jaw, I push her face up and look at her neck. There's no swelling, no stitches, no bruising or neon signs that say *'this is where I had surgery!'* "Are your fibroids swollen because of the flu?"

She tilts her head to the side and does her *'inquisitive fairy'* thing. "Swollen fibroids?"

"Yeah, like…" I press my fingers to the sides of my neck. "You know."

Her lips twitch just the tiniest amount. "I think you have your anatomy lesson messed up, Leo. I think you mean glands. Fibroids are a chick thing."

"How chick?"

"Umm, fibroids are like a mass on the walls of your uterus. Like a non-cancerous–"

"You have cancer?" *What the actual fuck!*

"No! Jesus, calm down. *Non*-cancerous! But don't worry about it. I'm fine. It's, umm…" She takes a deep breath. "They're all cleared out now. Problem solved." She turns and studies the clock. "You should probably get going. The guys will be waiting for you."

No. "So where're your scars?"

Her scared eyes come up to mine. "Huh?"

"How exactly did they take these things out of you?"

"Umm, through my belly. Tiny keyhole surgery."

My head swims in a red haze of worry and anger. "They had your stomach open yesterday? They cut your belly open, and you didn't think it was something you should tell me?"

"No, it…" She clears her throat nervously and avoids my eyes. "It just kinda happened. They found out why I was cramping, so they sent me for a quick scan. It was like a five-minute thing. *Surgery's* not even the right word for it. It was like getting a filling at the dentist. Not a big deal."

"I don't remember ever leaving the dentist with scars or narcotics, Casey."

"I'm fine! Can you go to work now?" She throws the sheet away. "I need to have a shower, then I'm going back to sleep." She attempts to push her legs over the side of the bed, but her breath races out on a whimper as her body jams up in pain.

I stand and move around to her side of the bed. "Can you stand by yourself, Sunshine?"

"Yeah." She breathes through her nose. Lifting her hands, she stares at my feet and breathes through the pain. "Just pull me up?"

Rage courses through my blood as I gingerly pull her to her feet. She can't get out of bed on her own. *And she wants me to leave?*

"Thanks, you can go." Sliding her feet two inches to the left, she works on shuffling away. "I'll see you tonight. Or maybe tomorrow. I'll text you, in case I'm too sleepy."

"Fuck no."

With tears in her eyes, she looks up at me. "What?"

"Fuck no, I'm not going to the gym." I take my phone from the bedside table. "I'm calling Bobby. They'll figure it out for me."

"Jon, no."

"I'm not leaving you, Casey!"

"Don't tell Bobby I'm not well." She clutches onto my arm, and I suspect it's just as much needing me to hold her up, as it is her trying to make me listen. "Don't tell him. He'll tell Kit, and she's too sick for this. She can't take on more worry."

"You bet your ass I'm telling Bobby–"

"Jon…"

"It's alright, he'll only tell her what he thinks is right. He won't hurt her, but I'm telling him where I am, Casey, and I'm staying right here with you."

"I really don't want you here right now." Tears gracefully slide along her cheek. "I need to be alone."

"I'm not leaving." I take her hand and help her sit before she falls. "A *real* best friend wouldn't leave. Sit down and rest. Let me take care of you. We'll make those fibroids regret ever touching you."

I go to work doping Casey up, making her tea, helping her in the shower, and tucking her into bed, then I call Bobby and tell him what's up.

It doesn't matter that the gym is down to a skeleton crew. It doesn't matter that he's run off his feet, too. He takes my call, we take care of business, then I spend the next six days in bed with Case while she cries and recovers.

I ask questions about her procedure, but she doesn't want to talk about it. I Google the procedure, but she won't answer my follow up questions.

She just watches movies, or sleeps, or cries.

Sometimes all three at once.

She stopped taking her pain meds three days after her *minor surgery* that was definitely *not* in her neck. She was up and walking without pain in five days.

She never vomited again, but she took antibiotics for almost two whole weeks.

Even when she told me to drop it, I researched the shit out of fibroids. I educated myself as best I could manage, and I tried to help her as intuitively as I could; considering she refused to ask for anything.

In fact, she just didn't talk at all.

Casey locked me out emotionally, but I was still in her home, I was still in her bed.

On the seventh night, she slept on my chest again.

But on the eighth night, we slept in separate homes.

Somehow, for some reason, our relationship had changed. *She'd* changed, and I had no clue what happened or how to fix it.

The sun wasn't so bright anymore.

Casey and I became best friends exactly one month after we met.

We kissed for the first time around the two-month mark, and we made love for the first and only time four months after that.

And now, almost eight months after the first flirty wink she threw my way at Club 188, my Sunshine has abandoned me. I was desolate and alone, even when we were in the same room together.

It would be more than five months before she willingly spoke to me again beyond a cold *'hello Jon', 'goodbye Jon.'*

I was Jon, not Leo. And not her best friend.

I didn't know it yet, but my Sunshine was gone, and the world was darker than ever.

15

CASEY

LOVING YOU HAD CONSEQUENCES

February

*B*obby's name flashes across my screen as the phone rings. Snatching it up with shaking hands, the cold sweat sliding down my spine almost makes me sick.

I spoke to Kit only an hour ago, but my obsession with making sure she's okay and comfortable helps me cope with the rest of my shitty life.

An idle mind is my worst enemy.

I haven't seen, nor spoken to Jon in an entire week. I haven't answered his calls. I haven't opened the front door to his incessant banging. I've closed all my curtains, and I've spent my time mourning him, our broken friendship, and the child we'll never know.

I didn't even *want* a child two weeks ago, but that two minutes I was carrying *his* child, I fell in love.

I was terrified, but I was in love.

And now because of that tiny flickering heartbeat, I'm a changed person.

I can't see Jon right now.

I can't see his face or hear his deep gruff voice.

I can't look into his dark eyes, because I wonder; what color eyes would our baby have had? Jon's beautiful brown, or my bright green?

I can't bear to be in the same room as Jon right now, because my heart is torn completely in half.

My body couldn't grow his baby.

My faulty body killed it before it even had a chance.

But I was in love, and Jon was always so damn vocal about *never* having children.

The two minutes I had with my baby, the two minutes I had to hope and plan and dream, those one-hundred and twenty seconds were tainted with fear.

Fear of Jon.

Fear *for* Jon.

I was terrified of going home and telling him what we'd made, and his bitterness and the fear he'd put into my heart changed me.

I knew his feelings on the topic, but he didn't have to bring it up six hundred fucking times in the six months we'd known each other.

I got it; no kids, no marriage, no forever.

Not ever.

I just... can't. I can't focus on him or his baby anymore.

I've lost *more* weight. I have no appetite. I barely sleep, and when I do, I dream of Jon.

I just can't.

Bringing the phone to my ear, I clear my throat and pretend my heart isn't irreparable. "Hey Bobby, what's up?"

"Hey there Tink, how are you?"

Mostly dead inside, thanks for asking. "I'm good. Kit okay?"

"Yeah." He sighs dramatically. "She's fine. She's a stubborn ass, and she's copping an attitude when Jack and I try to help her."

I laugh softly, and the unfamiliar feeling has my face crinkling like an old book being opened for the first time in years. The fact I notice that it's unfamiliar, hurts. "That's my girl. What do you need?"

"I can't just call because I miss you? I feel like I never see my tiny fairy anymore."

"Ha." I roll my eyes. "Hilari-Ass. What do you want, B?"

Like a verbal eye-roll, he sighs. "You're all business, Tink. You need to lighten up."

"Mmhmm." He's probably right. It's like I'm not even trying to be the real – funny, smartass – me anymore.

"Alright, Captain. I need a list."

I purse my lips and try to find the old sass that used to keep me company. "What kind of list, B? Best street walkers in town? Best places to buy weed? Kincaid brothers in order of hot to fugly?"

"I'm not even surprised you have a street walker and weed dealer list—"

I shrug. "What can I say? I know all."

"Wait! Which Kincaid is the hottest? And which one of us is fugly?"

I laugh. Bobby might be a pain in my ass, *and* he stole Kit from me, but he's making me smile today. Score one for the not-fugly Kincaid. "Aww, B, did I offend your pretty sensibilities?"

"Which one of us is the hottest, Tink?"

I'm pretty damn sure he's serious. And I know when he gets his answer, he'll either go home and gloat, or he'll beat up the *winner.* "Can't tell you, big boy. It's girl business. But seriously, I've got shit to do." I don't. I just can't keep up my happy charade for much longer. "What list do you need?"

"I need a list of every person my girl loves."

I narrow my eyes and bring a cup of tea to my lips. "Why?"

"Because Lila Royale's gonna help me propose to her."

"You're... what?" I choke on the tea and slam the delicate cup to the table. Pressing my free hand to my chest, I work on bringing the liquid up from my lungs. "What the hell, Bobby?"

"Royale concert is up next week. I want you to make a huge girly deal about *not* being able to go. As far as she knows, I only have two tickets, and she'd feel awful if she didn't give me her spare. But I have as many tickets as I want. So, who would she want there?"

"You're proposing to Kit. In a week?"

"Yeah."

"To get married?"

"Yeah, dumbass. C'mon, I got my pen and paper ready. Hit me."

"My girl Kit is going to be engaged? To marry a man that she'll have to be with for the rest of her life?"

It's just... woah. *When did we stop being kids and become old enough to get married?*

"I fucking hope so, but you're letting the team down, Tink. Names. I need names."

A week later, I find myself standing with Iz behind overflowing racks of sparkling clothes while Lila Royale sings about Romeo and Juliet.

"I've missed you, Tink." I look up from the sleeve of a white captain's coat that I secretly wish I could steal, and my heart lurches when I look into familiar, beautiful brown eyes. "You just kind of disappeared on us. You were sick, I went out for the night, then you disappear. You haven't been back in weeks. Did Jon do something stupid?" She smiles playfully. "Because he does that a lot, but you shouldn't hold it against him."

"No." I reach out and take her hand in mine.

Jon *does* often do stupid shit, but this time is different, and what's worse, he doesn't even know what's going on.

Logically, he's done nothing wrong.

I shouldn't even be mad at him, but I'm just not ready to go back to Leo and Sunshine yet. I'm not ready to pretend that tiny baby never existed. "I'm just busy at work, Iz. I took almost two weeks off when I was sick. I need to pick up extra shifts to make rent."

"Well, without you around, Jon's on me like white on rice. You're not blocking for me anymore, which means he's up *my* ass."

I shrug. "Sorry." *Not really.* "I'll be back when work calms down." *Not true.*

"Speak of the annoying devil." She glances over my shoulder and has my heart seizing up. He's right there. I can *feel* him. "I swear," she murmurs, "up my ass. All. The. Time."

"Sissy."

Iz sighs dramatically. "Jon. I'm right here. I'm alive. No one has punched me in the head today."

He lets out an unimpressed grunt. "I wasn't sure where you were."

She rolls her eyes. "I'm right here with the shiny sequins and Tink. You can go."

"Yeah." His hot chest almost touches my back. He's *that* close. "Sissy, could you give us a minute?"

"Actually, no." I step forward and force the distance between us before I simply step back and lean on him. "I've gotta go, anyway. Bobby has me on a schedule tonight, and *Strong Love's* just about to start."

"Casey."

I turn and allow a single moment of weakness. I look into his eyes, and if they had words like a book, his would say *hurt*. Plain and simple. I've hurt him. "I'm sorry, Jon." *For more things than you'll ever know.* "I'll call you later." *Lie.*

I run away from that backstage, and I don't call him again.

Months pass before we speak again, and that's only because I *have* to, to keep the peace in our family.

I've become so skilled in ducking, not even Chuck Norris in his prime could find me.

I spend the next four months working hard and taking as many shifts as the club will throw my way. I hang out with Kit and Iz as often as I can when the other guys aren't around. And when we *must* hang out as a group, I arrive late, leave early, and stay busy making drinks or cleaning away bottles and pizza box messes.

I'll do anything to avoid having to sit and talk to him.

I see Jon in the club a lot. He doesn't dance. He doesn't even drink. He just sits at the bar and watches me work. And though my heart aches each time he walks through the doors, though seeing him reminds me of things I'd rather forget, a small pocket of my bleeding heart still smiles that he's my protective Leo.

He never tries to speak to me.

He doesn't try to force his company on me or demand I serve him.

He just sits, watches, protects.

CASEY

PERFECT FOR EACH OTHER

June

*I*t's time for a girl's night in.
        Mr. Darcy.
Ice-cream.
Fake flower arrangements.
And no boys.

Kit and Iz are coming over so we can prepare wedding bouquets for the engagement Kit said *hell yes* to. My best friend is getting married, and despite the fact I'm sick as a dog – regular sick, not ectopic pregnancy sick – I didn't tell her I was feeling like crap, because I didn't want them to cancel and cut me out.

I miss my girls.

I miss my group.

"Honey!" The door swings open noisily. "We're home."

I scrunch my eyes and bury my face in the blankets in defense against Kit's loud shouting. Throwing back my blanket, I work to sit up.

Too hard. Too tired.

I slump back and groan. "Stop yelling. I'm in here."

Iz and Kit move through my kitchen and stop in the living room. Kit was sick and sore not so long ago, but in an instant, she switches on her maternal bossiness and storms toward the couch.

"Hey, what's the matter?" She sits on the couch and presses her hand to my brow. "Are you sick? I only saw you yesterday. What gives?"

I groan and scrunch my eyes closed. "Someone gave me germs. Cold is killing me."

Her eyes narrow. "*Just* a cold?"

I reach out and fist a bunch of tissues. "Just a cold. Promise." *Not a lie.*

"Let me make you some soup. We can watch a movie and chill."

"No, it's okay. I took Advil ten minutes ago. As soon as it kicks in, we can do your thing."

I woke up this morning with a raging headache and a queasy stomach. It felt like déjà vu, and though it's ridiculous, though it's impossible, I freaked that history was somehow repeating itself. I dragged my ass to the drug store and bought pregnancy tests.

I needed to know.

The test came up negative, *obviously.* I knew it would, but the pain still came. I saw the missing blue line, dropped onto my couch, and with my tissues and ginger ale, I've done nothing but wallow all day.

I haven't been with a man since Jon, so obviously the test would be negative, but when I got my answer, I was both sad and relieved.

January still haunts me, and no matter what I do, no matter how much I work, how much or how little I see Jon, I just can't move on.

I'd be more than six months pregnant by now if my body had done its job.

Who knows where Jon and I would be, but it couldn't be any worse than where we are now.

I haven't felt him in months.

I haven't heard his laugh in months.

I've slept alone, and though I silently admonished him for creating a safety blanket weakness within himself, I never realized I'd developed the same dependency of my own.

It took weeks before I slept well without him. It would take hours before I could fall asleep each night, and then when I did, I dreamt of him.

I still dream of him.

"We don't have to, Case." Kit takes my germy hand in hers. "We can just relax. Izzy's having a shitty day, too, so why don't we just order some takeout and chill?"

My aching eyes narrow to slits as Iz sits on the single recliner and pretends to not notice me here. I shoot up with newfound energy. "What's the matter, Iz? Why are you crying?"

"Not crying." She studies her nails and pretends her eyes aren't as pink as mine.

"Okay, nitpicker, why *were* you crying? Don't lie to me, baby sister. That's twice in a week, and that's *not* you."

"Nothing has happened." She rolls her eyes and slumps back onto the couch. "Like, Jim still hates me, Ben's still a prick, and life is still kinda shit. But nothing actually *happened*." Her lips turn up into a grimace. "And I think I'm catching whatever you have. I told you it was a bad idea to kiss yesterday."

I pop an attitude-filled brow. "I think you forget how smart I am. I haven't been around much lately, but my memory isn't that bad. Talk to us and stop trying to deflect. We didn't kiss this week, but nice try."

With sad eyes, she smiles softly. "I've missed you, Case."

I've missed her, too. More than she'll ever know. Leaning forward, I snag her hand and pull her onto the couch beside me and Kit, and when I simply stare, she huffs out a breath and throws her head back against the cushions. "Fine. I don't know what's wrong. Maybe I'm menopausal or something."

Nope. "You're twenty, dummy. Try again."

Iz laughs softly. "Now I remember why I didn't miss you so much. I dunno, guys, I just feel... flat." She rolls her head to look at us. "Honest. I just feel crap. Broken. I'm so tired. Sometimes dizzy. All the time defeated. I feel like I have a cold, but Advil isn't helping. And then there's Jimmy... And since you both think you're so smart, it won't surprise you that he breaks my fucking heart every single day that he ignores me." Her beautiful eyes turn misty. "I think I ruined us. He's never been mean to me, not in all these years we've been friends. But he's mean, now."

"Izzy..." Hesitantly, Kit takes her hand. "You said he was the first boy in your bed. Did you..."

I sit up so fast, I swear the bones in my back snap. "What! Izzy, what? How did I not know this? Jim's a dead man. D. E. A. D."

"No, stop. We haven't. It's not like that. Sure, he's been in my bed a million times. But not like that. God, can you imagine if the other guys knew?" She laughs bitterly. "My dad was an asshole. Like, really bad. One time he beat Jon so bad that Jon took me out of the house, walked us across town with his busted ribs and smashed up face, and as soon as we climbed through Bobby's bedroom window, he passed out. Flat out." She claps her hands together and breaks my heart. "He got me to safety, fell to Bobby's floor, and was out for the next ten hours or so."

"How old were you?"

She shrugs. "Four? Maybe five. We lived this same scenario a million times over the years. He got me out, got me to safety, passed out to cope with the pain. Bobby was always busy with Jon, and Jim was my friend, so he'd come into Bobby's room like it was totally normal that a couple kids snuck into his house. He would take my hand, and we'd go back to bed. Bobby was busy, and Jon was unconscious, so as long as I was warm and safe, no one asked where I was. We were never caught." She shrugs. "That's how it started, and after a while, it became habit. If I wanted a hug, I'd sneak into Jimmy's window. If he wanted company, he'd sneak into mine. It's just been that way for as long as I remember." Her eyes meet mine. "He's snuck into my room at Jon's place a million times." Then Kit's eyes. "And your house, too. It doesn't even feel like we're being sneaky. Breaking into someone's house doesn't count for us, because it's just what we know. It's like saying it's wrong to go upstairs to bed. That's where you go to sleep. Well, we go to each other to sleep."

Jon's going to have a damn conniption. And Jim's a dead man.

I reach up and swipe a tear from beneath Iz's eye. "You love each other... I don't understand the problem. Why don't you choose happiness? Why don't you choose to be together?"

"I do choose him!" she snaps. "He won't choose me. He's a damn coward. He doesn't believe in himself, or us, or... I don't even know! He knows what I want. If you guys know, then he knows, too. It's not like I've been hiding my feelings. I don't understand why he's not jumping in with me, and I don't know why I'm crying so fucking much." She angrily swipes away a tear. "I've never cried so much in my damn life."

"Iz, honey..." I reach across and take her hand. "You didn't sleep with Jimmy. But what about Ben?"

"Yeah. We were together for months before I... He was my... We..." She nods pathetically. "I just wanted to be treated like a woman, you know? Jimmy refuses to let me grow up. My brothers refuse to let me grow up. Ben treated me like a woman."

I bet he did.

"I just wanted to be held," she pleads. "I wanted it to be Jim, but he wouldn't even let me say the words."

"I'm not judging, Iz. We all do stupid shit sometimes. Trust me, I get it. I just meant..." I trail off and meet Kit's eyes. With a devastated breath,

I bring my hands up to my face. "I can't even…" *Please God, let me be wrong about this. Please don't do this to Iz. Please don't do this to Jon.*

Removing my hands, I noisily climb to my feet and turn back to grab Iz. "Come with me. Do me a favor? I don't want you to ask questions right now. I just want you to trust me to take care of you." I turn back and grab Kit's hand. "Come on. You, too." I let out a deep sigh. "I'm not doing this shit alone." With my heart in my throat and dread sitting right about where my baby once did, I drag the girls through my kitchen, into the hallway, then into my room. Stopping at my bed, I release their hands and walk into the attached bathroom.

My hands shake as I open and close drawers.

Please don't let it be true. Please let this be a figment of my heartbreak and flu.

With a single foil packet fisted in my palm, I pause at the door and take a cleansing breath. Who do I pray to, to get this right?

Iz's heart is just about to break.

And Jon's world is going to tip and fall into the ocean like a painful landslide. He hasn't told me much of anything, but I know he raised her, and I know her being so young and single and having a baby is going to kill him.

How ironic that I worried about telling him about his own baby.

This is much, much worse.

Another breath, I step back into the room and extend my hand. "Don't think about it, don't freak out. Just set my mind at ease and do a wee. We'll be right here waiting, and when you're done, come out and we'll look at the results together."

Izzy's chocolate eyes wheel around in panic. "Are– What– Umm…" She studies the pee stick and lets out a sigh. "Fuck. Okay."

As soon as she steps into the bathroom, Kit spins on me. "Casey! What the fuck? Why do you even have those?"

"I have tests because I'm a grown ass woman who has sex sometimes. I was feeling shitty with this cold, so I peed on a stick. It was negative, so cool your jets. And I asked Izzy to take a test because she's also a grown ass woman who has sex sometimes. She's emotional and feels weird. It's a logical step to pee on a stick, just in case. It's not a big deal, Kit." *Big fat lie. It's a huge fucking deal.* "Once she does, we can rule it out and maybe get her some multivitamins to help her feel less *flat.*"

"I can hear you two. The door is literally still open. Stop talking about me like I'm not here, you jerks."

I turn to the door. "Did you pee? Just pee on the end, it's pretty foolproof."

"Yeah, I peed…"

"Well…? Come out."

"No, you come in." She noisily pulls her pants up and flushes the toilet. Looking at each other one last time, Kit and I link hands and scramble into the bathroom together.

Kit stops and stares at the test lying on the counter – face-down. "How long do we have to wait?"

"Two minutes," I answer. I've done this before. "The brand is literally 'two-minute tests.'"

"Doesn't matter." Iz washes shaking hands at the sink.

Kit frowns. "What doesn't matter? You peed on it, right? You didn't miss?"

"Yes, I peed. No, I didn't miss. I mean, it doesn't matter, we don't have to wait." Finally, she turns and faces us. "It came up instantly." She gulps noisily. "Two lines means positive, right? Two lines came up before I even finished peeing." Her eyes spill over. "Oh my God. It came up instantly. It's *super* positive."

Oh.

Fuck.

Poor Jon.

Kit and I rush forward and take her shaking body in a group hug.

We make our way to my bed, and we all cry.

Iz cries because her whole world just blew up in her face.

But I cry because I know this will hurt Jon.

No matter what becomes of us, no matter how much time passes between seeing each other, I love him.

I care that he's happy, and this is going to rip his heart out.

But there's also a small sliver of my heart, a horrible vicious part of me that's bitter and angry that Iz is pregnant. I'm not. I couldn't carry my baby, and I might never be able to.

Jon needn't worry.

He doesn't *want* kids.

I can't *have* kids.

Ironically, we're perfect for each other.

17

JON

A MAN DESERVES TO KNOW

*H*olding my cell to my ear and switching the ignition off in my truck, I swing my legs out onto my concrete driveway.

It's been a long day.

Jesus, it's been a long fucking year.

Casey's gone.

Izzy's never home.

I train all day surrounded with my brothers and noise, but I always end up in an empty home at night.

The shadows follow me everywhere.

Night after lonely night, everywhere I look, the shadows peek around corners and taunt me. They claw sharp fingers into my skin, ruffle my hair in the invisible breeze, and tickle the soles of my feet and send me mad.

I've been seeing Sonia for a few weeks; she helps a little. She's not like my real Sunshine, but she helps a little. I guess. She says how I don't need Casey to see the sunlight.

I've just gotta open my eyes.

She's wrong.

But she's not making it worse, so I'll keep seeing her.

The line connects and Bobby speaks immediately. "Hey, Fart. What's going on?"

"Just got home. What's up?"

He ignores my original question. "Where'd you go this afternoon? You took off early."

I was with Sonia. "Nowhere. What's up?"

"Ah. We're having dinner at ours tonight, you should come over."

"Yeah?" I pause at my front door and slip the key into the lock. "Who's going?"

Please God, don't say Casey. Please God, do say Casey.

"All of us."

"All?" *Fuck. That means Casey.*

"Yeah. Listen." The stress in his voice has my eyes narrowing and my door slamming harder than necessary. "Something's up."

"Kitten okay?"

"Yeah. No. I dunno. The girls are being weird."

"Which girl?"

He pauses for a long beat. "All of them."

Fuck this vague shit. "Which one, B?"

"Well, Izzy mostly." He clears his throat. "But the others are being weird, too. Like they're all keeping secrets."

I turn on my heel and head back toward the front of the house. "What's wrong with my sister, B?" Picking up my keys, I swing the door open.

"Nothing, Jon. Relax."

"Relax? Fuck you, Bobby! I'm on my way."

"No! Just cool it for a sec. Jesus, Fart. Just breathe for a sec. Don't come yet or you'll spook them."

Red tinges my vision and almost knocks me on my ass. "What the fuck is wrong with my baby sister, B? How would me visiting *spook* them?"

"Ugh!" It's like I can literally *feel* him scrubbing a hand through his hair in frustration. "Nothing's wrong with her! Fuck, Jon. I saw her literally twenty minutes ago. She was whole and safe and with the other two. She's fine."

"She was with the other two? Kit and Casey?"

"Yeah, she was with them both. We're catching up for pizza in a bit. I'm not saying something is wrong, just that they've been weird. I was gonna start asking questions, but Iz came to the gym just now, said she wanted to hang out for dinner. She told me to call you, too."

"Why didn't she call me herself?"

"Gee, I don't know, Jon Fart! Probably because you're an overreacting psycho."

"I'm on my way, asshole."

"No!" I swear, the panic in his voice almost has me spewing as I storm down the path back to my truck. "No, seriously, don't come yet. Come in an hour. Stick to the plan. Don't spook her, Jon. I didn't sleep last night because I was worrying. Don't spook her off."

I stop at the side of my truck and rest my arms against the door. "Bobby. You're hurting my chest."

"Just give them the hour. I know she's yours, Jon, but she's mine, too. Kit's keeping secrets, and Sissy's walking around with a bad case of the sads. Don't scare her off now."

I close my eyes to fight off the heartache. "She's sad?"

"Yeah. She's a little down. Just take a breath, then lose your psycho pants. We can't help if we don't know what's wrong. They won't tell us if they're scared. You need to cool your shit, Fart."

"Yeah." I take a deep breath. "Okay, B. One hour. Not a minute more."

"Alright. Sit down for a sec. Put your head between your knees. She's safe and in my home. That's all that matters. It'll be okay."

Yeah, easy for him to say.

Fifty-nine and a half minutes later, I pull up at Bobby's house, pick up my cell, and dial. Sonia's soft voice answers immediately.

She was expecting my call. She's worried about me. "Jon?"

"Yeah." Nerves batter at my heart. "I just got here."

"Alright," she murmurs kindly. "It'll be okay. Take a deep breath and hear them out. I know you're worried, but let her talk."

"Yeah." I'm trying. I'm really fucking trying to breathe through this shit, but every breath I take pumps me up for war.

"Call me after, if you want," she finishes quietly.

Closing my eyes, I lean against the steering wheel and try to let her silky voice soothe me. It's helped before, but right now, no.

"Yeah. I'll call you after. I dunno what time."

"It's alright. Call me whenever you like. I'll take the call." When I say nothing more, she adds, "Bye, Jon."

Climbing out of my truck on weak legs, I head toward the front door just as Aiden pulls up behind my truck.

Breathe. Breathe. Breathe through it.

Fuck that.

I swing the door wide, but like he sprinted across the yard, Aiden's strong hand comes down on my shoulder. "Jon. Think it through. What-ever you're gonna do right now, think it through."

I shrug him off like he never spoke, then move through Kit's house and stop at the doorway to the kitchen. Iz sits at the head of the dining table with pink eyes and shaking hands, and Kit and Casey sit on her sides and guard her.

From me.

They're guarding her from me.

Izzy's eyes turn to her hands, but that only draws my gaze to three cups of steaming tea on the table.

My mouth goes dry.

I know who made those cups of tea. I know who tied the strings around the mug handles to stop the teabag from falling into the boiling water.

My eyes turn to Casey, to my Sunshine, and when hers meet mine for the first time in too long, my heart simply stops.

It's not a good 'my heart skipped a beat', but a bad 'the pain is unbearable'.

I've *needed* her, but for no reason at all, like she decided one day she was over it, she fucking dumped me. She left me like ten-day-old garbage without so much as a goodbye.

I want to be mad at her. I fucking hate that she left me so easily, but her beautiful eyes captivate me. Like a spider in a web, she draws me in, spins me up, and when I'm well and truly fucking stuck on her, she eats my head off and leaves me to die.

Alone.

I never deserved her. I knew that, and I knew our time was limited. I knew she'd figure it out eventually, but I didn't think it'd hurt so fucking much when I sat alone in the dark every day after that.

The dark now is darker than it ever was before her.

I tear my eyes away before I drop to my knees and beg for one more chance, then I look to Bobby. Standing behind the girls with his hand on Kit's shoulder, he shakes his head slowly.

It's girls against boys. Or maybe just girls against me.

But he's on their side.

He chose the girls. He chose Kit.

Not surprising, but the ache in my chest doesn't care that I should've expected it.

I don't bother speaking; Bobby's silent *no* is enough. They're not talking yet, so I pull out the dining chair at the bottom end of the table and drop down.

I'm so fucking exhausted.

Walking in noisily, the final piece to our puzzle, Jimmy has my sister's lips turning white. "What's going on?"

When her moist eyes come up to meet his, my knee bounces beneath the table. "Sissy?" My voice shakes. My whole fucking body shakes. I've looked after my sister since the day she was born. I know her, and I know she never cries. Never fucking ever. "You need to talk to us, baby. I can't fix it till I know."

Stepping forward, Jimmy moves past me. "Bubs? Say it. Say whatever you've gotta say." Walking around the table and cutting through the girls, he takes Izzy in his arms and holds her when she buries her face in his chest and howls.

The hairs on the back of my neck stand tall. Goosebumps skitter along my skin as he holds her close and strokes her hair.

What the actual fuck?

"Izzy?" He presses his lips to the top of her head. "Talk to me."

"Jimmy." Iz clears her croaky voice and clutches to his shirt. "Jimmy."

"Bubs? I'm begging you to talk to me."

Who the fuck is Bubs?

"Talk to me. Please."

Pulling back, Izzy holds his hands to her face in a caress that doesn't sit right in my gut. "I need you to promise me something."

"Anything." His eyes flash with secrets. "Absolutely anything. Forever."

"Promise me, someday, probably not today…" She swallows back fresh tears. "Someday… promise that you'll forgive me."

"What are you talking about, Bubs? What. Has. Happened?" He squeezes her face and has her lips puckering. "Just tell me. There's nothing to forgive. There's never anything to forgive… I just need you to tell me what's hurting you."

"Just promise you'll try to forgive me? I didn't mean to hurt you."

"Bubs…" He looks up to meet the girls' blotchy faces and red eyes. They know what's happening. It's bad. Whatever it is, it's bad enough that Casey's eyes spill over and flicker to me.

"I need the words, Jimmy!"

I can literally feel a pain in my chest.

This hurts.

Whatever this is, this hurts so fucking bad.

"Fine!" He looks back to her. "I promise to forgive you. Whatever happened, whatever happens, I promise to forgive you." He lowers his forehead until they're almost touching. "I'll always forgive you, Bubs… because I'll always love you."

That sheen of red dashes across my vision again. Standing tall as Iz slides out of my brother's arms, she swipes away her tears and turns to face the rest of us.

She meets my gaze first. She knows this is going to hurt me.

This is bad. This is probably the day I die.

Standing and taking a white envelope in her hand, Casey moves to Iz's side, then Kit follows. Turning as one, a single wall, they stop and meet my eyes.

This is for me. This whole show is for me.

The three girls join hands and my heart gives a single final thump in my chest.

This is going to hurt.

"Umm." Clearing her throat, Iz's eyes wheel around in fear. "Okay, I need you all to hear me out. Don't freak out. Please."

I can't handle this anymore. I can't handle the drama. I can't handle the heartbreak or the anxious silences. "Get to the fucking point, Isabelle."

"Leo." Casey's voice, her single word, possibly the only thing that could break through my anxiety in this moment, has my eyes snapping to hers.

She addresses me directly for the first time in almost six months. She breaks my heart by leaving. She breaks my heart by looking into my eyes with hers full of tears. Why didn't she want me? Why'd she leave me?

"Listen." Her sweet voice rumbles sadly. "Don't react."

"Sissy?" Bobby's much gentler voice pulls our attention. "Band-Aid. Do it now. Put us out of our misery."

"Okay, fine." She exhales and fusses with the envelope. "Umm…" She shoots one last broken glance at Jim, then to me.

Hers beg my forgiveness. They sparkle with a deep sorrow that I've never known before.

"I'm pregnant… I'm having a baby."

Red fills my vision. My body floods with adrenaline. I'm tempted to pick the kitchen table up and smash it down on whoever did this to her. I want to pick this whole fucking *house* up and smash it down on whoever did this to her.

I storm toward my sister, en-fucking-raged at this bullshit. "What the fuck are you thinking, Iz? What the hell is the matter with you?"

"I didn't–"

"How stupid could you be? You're a child!"

"I'm not a–"

"Jon!"

"You're nineteen!" Spit flies from my mouth as I rage at my crying sister.

How could she? After everything I've done for her?

I took the beatings for her. I took so much worse, and I did it to shield her. I did it because I refused to ever see her tainted. She's a fucking baby! I held her on my chest every night for years. I slept with her as my little spoon for years after she was too big for my chest.

I fucking starved so she could eat.

I shielded her from their poison. I took Wayne and Shirley's poison. I took my share, and I took hers, too.

Why? Why bother, if she's just going to repeat the cycle? She'll become a teen mother, too, then she'll breed feral kids that'll have to learn how to dodge a fist, too.

What the fuck was it all for?

"Jon!" Kit fights to pass Bobby, but he won't let her out from his arms.

I relive a million memories. A million nightmares.

A million pairs of disgusting old man hands as they grab at me, as they hold me down and shove my face into a pillow.

I couldn't breathe with my mouth and nose pressed into the bedding, but I still felt the pain. I still felt it all.

Why would she do this to me?

Why doesn't she care what I sacrificed for her?

"Jon." Casey slips around Kit and Bobby and presses her soft body against my chest. "Jon. Stop." She presses her hands to my chest and waits for my eyes to come down to hers. "Please just stop."

I can't stop! These things I endured, the things I shielded Izzy from, they're the *exact* reasons why I can't have someone as good and pure as Case. My life was ruined, I purposely stepped into the line of fire to shield my baby sister, and now it's all for naught!

"Can we sit and talk?" Iz murmurs.

My eyes snap away from Casey's, stop on Kit's, then come back to the pair I dream of every night. "Did you girls know about this?" I look to Kit. "Did you fucking know?"

Bobby pins me with a glare. "Watch it, Jon. You don't speak to her that way."

"Shut the fuck up, Peacock!"

"We found out last night," Kit interrupts calmly. *How the fuck is she calm right now?* "We *all* found out last night."

I look back to Iz, then I replace her devastated face with that of Sonia's. *Breathe through it. Fuckin' breathe, asshole!*

Letting out a painful breath, I look to Kit and shake my head. Turning on my heels, I slam back into the chair before I lose my *other* best friend because I swore at his soon-to-be-wife.

I need to breathe. I need to stop and think before I spill my guts about my whole fucking life all over this room.

I watch on as Kit pulls Iz back to her chair. As Casey steps away from where we stood chest to chest only a moment ago. Bobby takes up position behind the girls. Jack watches on in horrified entertainment. And Jim... I look around the room... Jim is gone.

I don't even fucking care, but tomorrow, I will.

Tomorrow, he and I have business to discuss.

No one speaks. No one is brave enough to broach the fucking grenade my sister just plucked the pin from.

I need answers.

I need answers before my pained heart gives out completely.

My whole life can't have been for nothing. Iz was worth it. Iz *has* to have been worth it. Worth the pain.

Worth Casey.

I look up and meet her tear-filled eyes. "What happened, Sissy? How the fuck did this happen?"

"It just..." She shrugs. "It was an accident."

"You're pregnant?" I think I'm gonna be sick. "You're really pregnant? Like, expecting an actual baby?"

"Yeah, Jon. An actual baby. An *actual* baby will be here around Christmas."

"Christmas?" I mentally attempt the math. "So you're..."

"Nine weeks." She exhales tiredly. "Thirty-one to go, according to the ultrasound lady."

"Ultrasound? You've already seen..." *The vermin. The thing that's half Hart inside her. My parents' bloodline on repeat.* "... it?"

"Yes." She watches her hands. "I've seen it. I made an appointment this morning, the girls drove me there, then we came home. I'm telling you now, because I didn't wanna keep the secrets."

Anger courses beneath my skin like electricity. "Whose is it?" I can't help the growled words that tear up my throat. Who fucking dared touch my baby sister? He won't have hands tomorrow. "Ben." When I remember the girls mentioning she was dating a dude, his name flashes in my brain like a neon sign. "I'm going to kill that f–"

"Yes," she cuts me off. "The baby is Ben's."

"Does he know?"

"No."

"What are you going to do about..." *the half Hart, half Ben,* "...it?"

"I'll be keeping it." Her shoulders come up stubbornly. "I'm not aborting."

"Sissy, it's not too late. This can be fixed... Your life doesn't have to change." Surprising even myself, that actually hurt to say. She's just a baby, she doesn't need this, but the thought of killing that baby hurts me already. It's like giving permission for someone to hurt Iz.

How the fuck did I get so attached so quick?

"My life has already changed, Jon. I'll be keeping my baby. This isn't your responsibility, and it's not your fault. I can do this. I can do it on my own."

I choke on the tears that almost spill over. Shaking my head, my voice cracks at the very thought of my baby sister ever being truly alone. "No, Sissy. Not alone. I'm not walking away now."

Casey knuckles a stray tear from her cheek and looks away when I look up. I frown. I don't like seeing her tears. Even after six months of nothing, I still love her. I still care if she hurts, I'll still fix it for her.

"Can we see?" Jack pushes away from a tall stack of unopened pizza boxes. "The scan," he clarifies with an embarrassed tinge to his cheeks.

I look back to Iz and the envelope on the table. "Yeah. Is that a picture of..." *My niece or nephew. My family.* "... the baby?"

"Umm, yeah. Here." Iz shakily passes the envelope.

Slowly, carefully, I peel the white stock paper open and blink past the tears in my eyes. Taking out the small image as Aiden and Jack step closer to my back, I stare at the grainy picture of... well, nothing.

It's just black and white dots, and possibly a jelly bean if you squint the right way.

"Nope." Jack tilts his head to the side. "I don't see it."

"Yeah." Sissy lets out a watery laugh. "It's kind of just a blob. But the lady showed us his tiny arms and legs on the screen.

"He?" Aiden's eyes snap up to hers. "It's a he?"

"No. I don't know." She shrugs. "It's too soon to find out."

I hope it's not a boy; he could be too similar to me. Or my parents.

If there's anything good and pure that came from my blood, it's Iz. Let her little baby be a girl, perfect and sweet just like Izzy was.

"When can you find out?" Jack asks and tilts his head the other way.

She shrugs. "I don't know, maybe another seven or eight weeks? Don't know if I'll find out."

"Izzy, honey." Bobby pulls Kit from her chair, sits in it himself, then pulls her back into his lap. When they're comfortable, his eyes come back to Iz's. "When will you tell Ben?"

"Dunno." She leans into Case and sniffles. "Do I have to?"

"Yes, Sissy, you do." I frown. "Of course you do."

I might want to kill him.

Hell, I might *still* kill him, but if he's the daddy, then he deserves to know.

That's his baby.

"A man deserves to know, no matter what."

18

CASEY

WASH AWAY YOUR TROUBLES

*W*alking along Jon's front path, my heart booms in my chest and nervous sweat slides along my spine. I stop at the front door and argue with myself; *use the key I still have, or knock?*

I doubt he'd mind, but it doesn't feel right to just let myself in. Things are different now. He's not my Leo anymore, and I'm not his Sunshine.

A *real* best friend wouldn't have deserted him the way I did, no matter the circumstances that led to it. Sure, I was hurt with everything that went down, but he never even had a chance to understand.

I blamed him for something he never knew he did.

Bringing my hand up to knock, knowing that he needs me tonight – or maybe it's that I need him – I pray he doesn't have someone else inside. I pray that he doesn't throw me out on my ass. I pray that he doesn't tell me he hates me.

If I know anything about Jon, it's that with his sister at Bobby's tonight, her big news will have knocked him on his ass.

He'll be looking for a little light while she's not right under his nose.

I can help him, and I can securely lock my heart behind a brick wall that I won't let him scale.

I know better this time.

"Yeah, hold on. There's someone knocking." Jon's deep voice rumbles through the heavy front door and sends my heart skittering. Swinging the door wide with one hand, and holding his cell to his ear with the other, his eyes lock onto mine and his body stills.

His deep, dark brown eyes almost spill over as he studies me from my feet to my hair.

I swallow hard. I've missed him so much.

"Sonia." He coughs to clear his throat. "I gotta go. I'll call you tomorrow." He ends the call and shoves his phone into his back pocket, then he simply stands in the doorway, folds his arms across his chest, and stares.

It's my turn to speak.

My turn to explain.

He sure as shit isn't going first.

For the first time in my life, I'm nervous around him. "Hey, Jon."

His brows furrow in silent judgement. Flicking a glance across my face, along my body, then back to my face, his arms tighten. "Casey."

He's so cold.

I want to step in and hug him. I've done it since the beginning, but today, I can't. I don't have that freedom anymore. "Are you okay?"

"Where'd you go?"

My stomach flips. I know what he's really asking, but I try to deflect, anyway. "I was just at home, but I wanted to see–"

Cutting through my bullshit, his eyes flash. "No! Where'd you go six months ago?"

"Jon." I sigh. I'm an awful friend. It all just hurt too much. "I'm sorry. I just… needed space."

"You needed space?" His chocolate eyes slice right through me, nick my heart, and let me bleed. "You needed space from *me?*"

"I'm sorry."

"Did I do something wrong?"

You impregnated me and didn't even know it. And worst of all, I never told him.

A man deserves to know.

"No. I just got caught up with work. Kit was hurt, then she got engag–" Pathetic lies. I'm a pathetic person. "No. You did nothing, Jon. I'm sorry. I'm really, really sorry."

"Are you back?"

I swallow hard. "Do you want me back?"

His eyes shutter like he's fighting an invisible pain. "I never wanted you to go, Sunshine. I haven't slept in six months."

He wounds me so deeply. "I'm sorry."

"Were you seeing someone else?"

"Someone else? You and I weren't–"

"No." He sighs. "We weren't. But have you been seeing someone? Is that why you left?"

My poor sweet Jon thinks I left him to be with another man. "No, Jon. I haven't been dating. I'm really sorry you thought that. I've just been working, I promise."

His eyes follow my every tiny move for a full minute. He's having a whole conversation in his head. His heart is reminding him of how good his security blanket feels, but then his brain steps in and reminds him how horrible I am.

I don't even have the right to explain myself. I don't have the right to try to convince him otherwise.

I'm simply at the mercy of whatever decision he makes, then I have to live with it.

He stares… and stares… and stares…

Then his lips turn up into a playful smirk and has my heart seizing. "You looking for a new best friend, Casey?"

I smile for the first time in what feels like a decade. "I guess I am."

As though he was in the octagon facing a three-hundred-pound meat-head, he rushes forward and wraps his arms around my hips. I squeal and kick my legs out as he picks me up and throws me over his shoulder, and I laugh and pound on his back with closed fists when he kicks the door shut behind us.

He carries me through the living room that I've missed dearly, then through the kitchen that I've eaten in a million times. "Where are you taking me, you big dummy?"

"We're going to bed." He slaps my ass and has my stomach flipping. "I haven't slept in six months."

"To bed?"

He chuckles and has deep vibrations rumbling through his chest and into my belly. "It's okay, Sunshine. The old rules apply. Friends, no benefits. Though you can give me benefits anytime you want." He slaps my ass a second time and has me squeaking in pleasure and pain. "It's late, and I've gotta work tomorrow. Bobby's starting to think he's hot shit, since I've been off my game. A good night's rest will fix me up." Stopping in his bedroom, he flips me off his shoulder and onto the bed. "Go pee, brush your teeth, do your girly shit, then come back to me."

He steps away and begins unbuckling his belt. My mouth waters with the knowledge that he's right here. I could be with him, truly *with* him, if I just said the words.

I jump up from the bed in an attempt to escape him and my dirty thoughts, and as I pass on the way to the bathroom, he slaps my ass a third time.

I'm disgusted in myself that my underwear slick with want.

Apart from one single time with Jon, I haven't slept with a man in something like eighteen months. Before that, I had a new man in my bed every weekend.

Hell, I had a man in my bed most weeknights, too.

I had an itch, and a constant stream of men that were happy to scratch it.

I was a sexually open person, I wasn't shy about it. I knew my needs, and because I wasn't shy, they were usually met. But it's been such a long time, my body thrums with need and the knowledge that a very capable set of hands are nearby and willing to help.

I enter the familiar bathroom and smile. It feels like I've finally come home. Nothing has changed; the same ugly brown towels still hang on the rack, the cinnamon candle I left in here so long ago remains unused. The wick is still white. Jon never lit it, and he never moved it.

My toothbrush literally still sits in the frosted glass beside his, and my bobby-pins – now a rusty orange – stain the white counter.

I look under the sink and find my hair straightener, the prized GHD that I had to replace at home, because I was too scared to ask for mine back.

He didn't throw any of my stuff away, he simply existed around it.

Instead of only washing my face and brushing my teeth like I'd first planned, I push my pants down and start the shower. Pulling my top over my head and tossing the fabric to the floor, I refuse to turn to the mirror and study the tiny scars still on my belly.

It's been a long day. I need a shower. I need to relax.

Yesterday was huge, huger than huge. Izzy's world changed. Then today, Jon's world changed, too.

Remembering the exact nuances of Jon's shower, I turn the cold tap far enough that I don't burn to death, but not so far that I freeze.

Everything is still the same.

But nothing is the same at all.

Ignore it. Ignore it all.

Stepping into the shower, I smile at the soap holder and pick up the two bottles of body wash. One is Jon's; sexy and masculine. The other is mine; pomegranate and cinnamon.

I flip the cap open on my three-quarters empty bottle and take a deep breath, then I puff Jon's so the masculine scent wafts in the steam and fills my lungs.

This is his smell, his brand, the scent he leaves in every room long after he's already left it.

My house smelled like him in January, *especially* the bed we shared every night for a week. I didn't wash the sheets for as long as I could get away with it, then I didn't wash his pillowcase for even longer after that.

I spent weeks hugging that damn thing and crying my heart out. Eventually, the pillow came to smell like me and not Jon. That was the day he was truly gone; even as he continued to knock on my front door and call out for me to let him in.

I used to know his scent so well, I'd stopped noticing it. I'd become desensitized to it, but after months of not being in this home, of not being near him, I've forgotten again.

It hits me like a bus as I stand in his steaming shower with my eyes closed and the bottle of wash beneath my nose.

With shaking hands, I blindly replace his soap in the holder and turn to breathe something else. Anything else.

I need to pull my shit together.

I need to figure out how to be with him, *without* getting my heart cut out, ripped up, and lit on fire.

I have to tell him about January.

I know I do.

A man deserves to know, and Jon definitely deserves to know.

"Hey, Sunshine?"

My eyes snap open and my hands come up to cover my boobs. Squinting through the frosted glass, I watch his large silhouette move around the bathroom.

"Ah... yeah?"

"Relax, I can't see you."

"Okay..." I hesitantly release my breasts and begin washing – using *my* soap. I'm too vulnerable. Naked. Alone. In the shower. "What's up, Leo?"

He chuckles loud enough, neither the shower, nor the exhaust fan can stop the taunting sound from reaching my ears. *"Leo."* He makes the click noise he does with his tongue when he's feeling contemplative. "I haven't heard that in a long time." He pauses for a long beat. "I didn't realize you were gonna have a shower."

I frown and frantically scrub shampoo through my hair. "Okay…?"

"I missed you," he murmurs almost silently. "I thought you'd be right back, then the water started. I realized you could be gone for hours."

I smile at his words; I can *feel* the smirk in his voice. "I'll be out in a minute, Leo. Never fear, I won't drown."

His dark silhouette moves around the bathroom, then with a grunt, he leans against the counter and crosses his arms.

"Hey, Jon?"

"Yes, Sunshine?"

I can't take another minute of not seeing his eyes, so I wash the soap out of my hair, then open the shower door an inch and peek out. "Do you wanna talk about Izzy?"

His humor-filled eyes turn stormy in an instant. "No, I definitely don't."

"But–"

"No." He shakes his head with finality. "I don't want to talk about that right now. I need time. I just…" He shakes his head a second time. "I can't think about Iz right now."

I watch him for a long minute, but he's made up his mind. Nodding softly, I pull back inside the shower and close the door.

I won't force him. Hell, I have no right to force him into anything. I've been missing for months. I'm lucky he even let me in his front door. "Alright Leo. Your house, your rules."

He lets out a bitter laugh and has my lips twitching. I've missed this. I've missed chatting with him. "What's so funny?"

"Rules, Sunshine. So many fuckin' rules." I frown when he doesn't elaborate. He's silent long enough that I have time to rinse and repeat with the conditioner. "Maybe if we didn't have so many rules," he finally presses on, "maybe then, we wouldn't be able to *break* them. Maybe then, you wouldn't leave me for a rule I may or may not have broken."

My head drops back with defeat. "Jon?"

"Mm?"

I want to tell him about January. I fully intend to tell him soon, but not right now. Not tonight. Not while I'm naked in his shower and his warm body stands only inches from mine.

"You didn't break any rules. I never stopped caring about you, okay?

I've been gone, but I *never* stopped thinking about you." *I never stopped loving you.*

The shower door swings open and has me jumping back against the tile. My hands come up to cover my breasts, but his eyes don't stray from mine. He doesn't look down at my wet and naked body. His watery eyes simply bore into mine. "Are you really back?" he murmurs intensely. "Truly back?"

I nod and consider my words. "I'm back. I want Leo and Sunshine back. I've missed us, Jon."

Like that was invitation, his eyes leave mine and have me holding my breath. His intense eyes pin me to the wall, and his warm gaze slides along my body and down my legs. He frowns when he passes over my stomach, then he stops frowning when his eyes move over my chest.

Stopping on my lips, the intensity in his glare almost has me cowering in fear. "I've dreamt about you, Casey."

I've dreamt about you, too.

"I've missed you," he continues, "but more than just your ass sitting on my couch every night. I want *that* back, but I've missed you in my bed, too. I've missed your hair in my face while we sleep. I got to taste you, Case. I got to *really* touch you only that one time, and though I never had a chance to get used to it, I've craved it." His eyes finally leave my lips and come to mine. "I've wanted *more* for so long. But I feel like wanting more, even if I never said it out loud, I feel like you leaving was punishment for not being happy with what I had. I was always happy with what I had, Case, but I wanted more, too."

My stomach flips with happy nerves, even as my heart screams *no! I can't do this again.* "But you said–" *No commitment. No forever.* "You didn't want that."

"I don't want *marriage*," he clarifies. "I don't want a family. But I want you." He steps into the shower fully clothed, and his gray shirt turns black instantly from the water. His broad chest blocks the rest of the world from view, and his large hands frame my face, catching tears camouflaged as shower spray. "Can I have more, Case? Can we be together? I won't tie you down. When it's time for you to go, you can go." He swallows heavily. "When it's time for you to go, I won't stop you. But can I have you *for now?*"

My mind screams *fuck no!* My mind screams that he can't have my body if he never intends to take responsibility for my heart, too, but his lips are on mine before I get the chance. As soon as his plump lips touch mine, my mind deserts and my body is the only thing left to think with.

His rough jeans press against my warmed and sensitized skin. His lips play with mine and swallow my sighs. An equal in want, my hands explore his broad muscles. I reacquaint myself with his delicious body, a body I knew despite our relationship *without* benefits. My tongue darts against his with a desperation that speaks of being separated from the man you love for half a year.

His knees are bent, his neck is bent. He's doing his best to compact his large body and be on my level, but he's a big man and I'm a small girl. He knows this, and within minutes, his hands cup my ass and pull me up to pin me against the wall.

His impressive frame unfolds and opens up to all his glory, and my legs wrap around his hips, though I needn't use my strength to stay up.

Jon has more than enough for both of us.

"Make love to me, Sunshine?" He buzzes his stubble covered jaw along mine. "Give me what's mine. You know you're mine."

"Yeah." The breath races from my lungs when he pulls the sensitive flesh of my throat between his teeth. My hips move against his, and my hands frantically claw at his shirt. "Take it off."

His mouth leaves my skin for only half a second as he reaches over his head and tugs at the wet fabric. He pulls it over his head and carelessly tosses it to the floor, then his lips find mine, and his hands roam my flesh and set my body alight from the inside.

I can do this.

I want this.

I slide my hands away from his shoulders and stop at the button on his jeans. Fumbling nervously, I rush to get them undone. The last time we did this, the *only* time, it was quieter, softer, slower. But today's different. Today we're desperate to reclaim something we'd lost for half a year.

I'm not even sorry this is happening.

I'm exhilarated.

I'm turned on.

I'm in the moment.

The consequences can wait for when the sun rises tomorrow.

Pulling back just a fraction to help, Jon's hand moves between us, and though he's only trying to undo his jeans, his knuckles move over my throbbing clit and have me gasping.

He slams his lips over mine and swallows my cries. Clumsily, but strong as a bull, he works on his jeans and pushes them down over strong thighs. He kisses my jaw, and bites along the bone as I pant in his ear.

"You still on the pill, Sunshine?"

"Yes." I moan with anticipation, but he catches me by surprise when he lines up and pushes inside. "No!" Panic sends my heart skittering as his bare skin moves inside me. "No. Jon." I try to move away, but I'm stuck between him and the wall. I wriggle my hips in an attempt to dislodge him, but all it does is pleasure us both. "Condom! Jon, you need a condom."

His hands keep me up, but like my vagina just grew teeth, he pulls out of me like he was going to lose his dick. "You're *not* on the pill?"

"I forgot to take one the other day." *Lie.* "It's not safe without a condom until I regulate again. I just wanna be careful."

"Okay." He's so averse to having babies, so against *that much* commitment, he sets me on my feet and turns away. "Alright. Just hold on a sec." He darts out of the shower stall, then darts back in so fast, I swear he should've slipped in the wet.

He rips open the small silver packet with his teeth, tosses the trash to the shower floor, sheaths himself in half a beat, then picks me up and slams me against the wall in one smooth, tear-inducing move.

My forehead comes down to his shoulder and a groan rolls up my throat as both pleasure and pain slash across my heart. "Jon…" He pushes into me fluidly. Strong thighs hold us both up and move him inside me easily. We can be so good together. We *feel* so good together.

"Casey." His strong hands squeeze my hips and have my tailbone bouncing off the tiles. I wrap my arms around his thick neck and hold him close. His right hand slides up my body, threads through my hair, and tugs back painfully to expose my neck. "You feel so good, Case. So fuckin' good."

"Mmm."

"I've missed you."

Fire pools low in my belly as my legs shake and struggle to hold on to his momentum. "I've missed you, too, Leo. I've missed you so much."

"I'm not going to last." He grunts in my ear and slams me against the wall. "It's been too long, Sunshine. I've waited too long for this."

His hand leaves my hair and snakes down between us. Though I know what he intends to do, though I expect it, the second his fingertips touch my throbbing clit, I explode and squeeze him with my legs, my arms, my pulsing pussy.

He cries out as soon as my orgasm takes me under. His hips jut and slam me against the tiles as his orgasm rolls on for an eternity. He pushes into me and builds me up to come undone all over again.

For the first time in my life, I come twice in a row, and of course it's with *this* man.

Of course it's *Jon Hart the eternal bachelor.*

Breathing heavily, I bury my face against his shoulder and count the thudding beats of his heart against mine. My head swims in the choking steam of the almost-boiling shower. As though he can hear my thoughts, Jon's hand swings to the taps and shuts them both off.

Bringing it back, he cups my cheek and brings me back to look into his eyes. "Hey."

I might've just set myself up in Heartbreak lane. I'm willingly walking into oncoming traffic, and it already hurts so much. "Hey."

His soft lips press against mine. "You okay?"

Don't cry, Casey! Don't you do it. "Uh-huh."

"Did I hurt you?"

I shake my head and bite my shaking lip . "No."

Unknowing that I'm on the verge of an emotional breakdown, his lips turn up into an arrogant smirk. "Did you just come twice?"

The tears that almost choke me release on a stupid laugh. I slap his shoulder. "Put me down you big ape."

"No." He leans forward and presses a soft kiss to my lips.

"No?"

"Not till you admit that I made you come twice." He bites my bottom lip and has me sighing.

"You think you're hot shit?"

"I know I'm hot shit." His strong body squeezes me against the warm tiles. "I just fucked you, Sunshine. You came *twice.* I've been waiting a long ass time for this."

I shiver in his arms, not because I'm cold, but thankfully, he mistakes it for cold, sets me on my feet, and reaches out of the shower for an ugly poo-brown towel.

Wrapping it around my shoulders and patting me dry, he does what he does best. He takes care of me. Pressing a kiss to my lips, he steps out of the stall and peels the condom off.

Tossing it in the tiny trash can and washing his hands, he comes back and picks me up the way a child might move a favored toy from one activity to the next.

I punch his shoulder in defense against his caveman behavior – I don't need to be carried around, my legs work just fine – but it's who he is. He touches. We touch. We always sat with each other, *on* each other, touching each other. I always slept *on* him or wrapped *around* him like a vine.

But the ass slapping and *carrying* me like this is different.

"Where are we going?"

He chuckles. "We're going exactly where I put you last time."

The blood rushes to my head as I hang upside down. "I still didn't brush my teeth!"

"You had your chance, woman. Now it's bedtime."

He throws me against the soft blankets and has me laughing as the down comforter puffs up around me. He tears my towel away like it's totally normal we see each other naked, then he struts across his room, flicks off the lights, and walks back to me in the dark.

His weight comes down on the bed, then as though I truly was a ragdoll that weighs nothing, he wraps his arm around my waist, picks me up, pulls back the covers, and *puts* me in bed.

He climbs in next to me, and as our naked flesh slides together, I let out a content sigh.

We've done this a million times before, but always with clothes. This new feel, this skin on skin adds a brand-new element of intimacy that I can't find in my heart to regret.

He turns to his back, then as smooth as though our time apart never happened, he pulls me on top so our chests rest together and my face rests above his heart.

He presses a gentle kiss onto the top of my hair. "Go to sleep, Sunshine. Welcome home."

Letting out a deep sigh, I press a kiss to his chest and lie back down. I never would have done that six months ago, but everything's different now. We're not the same people we used to be.

It terrifies me.

"I'm so tired," he murmurs.

I know.

He hasn't slept in six months, either.

"Rest now, Leo. I'm here."

19

JON

I KICKED THE PUPP(IES)

July 4 – Kit's Wedding Day

*C*asey walks along my mom's garden path with a small bouquet of lilies in her hands and a smile on her face, and she matches her steps to the soft music playing over the speakers.

Her beautiful gown sways in the perfect summer breeze, and her eyes, they're all for me.

When it's time for you to move on, I'll let you go. When it's time, I won't stop you.

I was *trying* to tell the truth. I feel like it was as close to true as I could be, but damn, why can't she settle on me? Why can't I give her what she wants?

Because she's going to want a family one day, that's why. I can't give her what she deserves.

Case stops beside Izzy on the opposite side of the flower lined aisle, then the music changes and Kit enters the yard through large French doors in a beautiful ivory gown.

Like an excited puppy, Bobby pushes off to get to her.

Like the stern dog walker, my hand snaps down to his belt to keep him here. It all happens right in front of me; Bobby's belt straining, Kit running. Bobby catching her. Casey laughing.

I know it all happens around me. I know people laugh. I know this is a happy day, I *know* all this, but I can't take my eyes off Case.

I'm in love with my best friend.

Deep, pains in the chest, probably going to die if she ever leaves me again, *deep* in love. And though I want to be happy, I know we're on the clock. We've always been on the clock.

She's not mine to keep, because she's entirely too good for me. I can't taint her, but damn, I want to.

I want to hold her here with me in the fiery pits of hell, but real, true, deep, pain in the chest love means selflessness.

I can't hold her down, because she was always meant to fly.

But I'll look at her, I'll cherish her, I'll make love to her for as long as I can.

I've had her back for seven nights. She's been in my bed, in my home, in my skin every night for seven amazing nights.

She's given her body to me.

She's given me her laughter.

Her love.

Her everything.

She might not be mine forever, but for right now, she's completely mine. And when it's time for her to go, I just hope that I can still find life in her friendship. I just hope I can find life, full stop.

A couple hours after the backyard ceremony, after posing for a trillion pictures, after Kit and Bobby conspicuously sneak away for a wedding day quickie, Mike, acting as emcee for the night, calls upon the bride and groom for their first dance.

Two minutes after that, it's my turn to stand and take Casey's hand. Her uncertain eyes meet mine, a shy smile crosses her lips, but I need this today. I need to dance with her, to feel her against me. I need to lay some kind of claim in public, even if it's quiet and goes unnoticed by everyone except me.

"Dance with me, Sunshine?"

Looking up through long lashes, she grins and allows me to pull her to her heeled-feet. Holding her hand in mine, I steer her to the middle of the floor and pull her close.

"So…" Laughing softly, she lays her face against my chest and snuggles in.

I smile. "So, what?"

"Your boy got hitched. You jealous?"

I breathe her cinnamon scent in. "Jealous of what?"

"Your best friend's officially off the market. Are you jealous that there'll be no more 188 nights for you two to meet girls?" Smiling, she pulls back to meet my eyes. "It's the end of an era."

I laugh and pull her back in close. "Not a whole lot's changing, Sunshine. He's been practically married for months. They just have a contract now."

"A contract." She snorts inelegantly and slaps my arm. "You're such a romantic, Jon." We sway together and move around the dance floor. "I wonder when he's gonna be a daddy?" she murmurs against my chest. "I bet they'll try soon."

"Well, there's no rush." I frown. "We're still so young. They have years to do that crap."

"No," she ponders softly. "I don't think they'll wait. Look at them." She nods toward the loved-up couple as they dance and whisper. "I bet there'll be babies everywhere soon. Starting with Bean."

I flinch and hold her closer than I should. I'm not ready to face my sister's new reality.

"Look at her, Jon." She nods toward the almost empty table where my sister sits with her eyes on the floor. "She needs your support."

"I am supporting her! I'm offering her a home. An education. I'll put her kid through school when it's time." *Anything to ensure an educated child, instead of a mongrel heathen set on repeating history.*

Casey's angry eyes come back to mine. "I don't mean financially, Jon. She doesn't want your money, you jackass. She wants a damn hug. She wants you to tell her it's okay. She *needs* you to forgive her."

"It's not that easy, Case. I'll always love her, I'll always support her. But what she's done is *not* okay." *I sacrificed everything.* "I don't forgive her right now. I can't."

"I get that you're upset. I do. But she's not a baby anymore. She's a woman, and she's having a baby. You need to–"

Taking a step back, I put space between her body and mine. Memories assault me and send the waves whooshing in my ears. "You can't possibly think this is okay. She's a kid!"

"She's a woman, Jon. Shit happens, but she needs you to support her. Your disappointment hurts her."

How am I the bad guy here?

"Yeah, well, her having sex and making a baby hurts me. I can't believe she'd be so fucking stupid!" Casey's eyes drop to the space between us. Her brows furrow, and her soft body turns hard. "Babies don't come out of nowhere, Sunshine. She had unsafe sex. She's smarter than that!"

"Sometimes even smart people make mistakes, Jon. It only takes one time to create that heartbeat."

"She knows better!" I snap between clenched teeth. "She knows what runs in our veins. She's creating another one of *us*, when she should've let our bloodline die with us."

Casey's body snaps back as though I hit her.

This wasn't supposed to happen. We're not supposed to be arguing right now. I just wanted to fucking dance!

"You want it to die with you?"

"Bet your ass," I seethe. "We've already discussed this, Case. I won't be passing this poison on. I can't in good conscience pass this shit on."

Her warm body, the pliant and loving limbs I've known all week, has turned cold and hard.

She simply nods. "Yeah. I see."

"Bobby. Look."

Kit's soft voice cuts through the blood roaring in my ears. I follow her gaze, and in my distraction, I don't notice the tears in Casey's eyes.

I watch in the way someone might watch a car crash. You shouldn't look, but you just can't turn away. I watch Jimmy stiffly approach my sister. I watch them talk. I watch them come to the dance floor.

Every second that the four of us pretend to dance, we watch my baby sister's heart break with every blowing word Jimmy throws at her.

Like that crash I knew was coming, I watch my sister pull away from him, then I watch big fat tears escape her stubborn eyes as she races off the dance floor.

Kit works to step away from Bobby. "I'll go."

But Casey detaches herself from me, similarly to how Iz escaped Jim. "No, you stay here."

Fuck.

20

CASEY

RINSE AND REPEAT

*T*he next year or so of my life passes much the same way the previous one did.

Jon and I were Leo and Sunshine. He was my best friend. He was my closest confidant. He was my constant lover.

Except when he wasn't.

I was a twenty-seven-year-old miniature barmaid with no college education and no actual future with a man or a family planned.

I had a twenty-eight-year-old emotionally stunted, commitment-phobe, though gentle and thoroughly loving, sometimes-boyfriend who doesn't actually use the word *boyfriend*, because that borders on commitment.

I was in love with a man that never had a chance to be a boy, so now he uses me for that security blanket, the pacifier, the maternal touch.

Except when he doesn't.

Sometimes he's with other women.

We're not exclusive. We never said we were. But after the first month of Jon and I being 'back together,' the *shininess* of what we rediscovered wore off and his attention began wandering.

He'd get home late so often, I stopped even worrying his truck was somewhere in a ditch. He never explained his whereabouts, he simply walked in each time and expected everything was cool.

Those nights resulted in us having an epic fight the way only best friends could. I'd storm out, I'd go back to my *real* home, I'd pout for a day, a week, a month at a time.

He *always* came looking for me. He'd throw me over his shoulder the way only he does, he'd drag me back to his place, and the cycle would start again.

Other times, he'd take calls from girls.

He *never* spoke to them in front of me, he just gave a canned *'I can't talk right now.'* He'd hang up, sit down, and put his head in my lap like a not so well-trained Scooter.

That would result in another epic fight, and around and around we go.

He doesn't want me, he just doesn't want to share me, either.

Surprisingly, I'm coping with this ridiculously dysfunctional relationship better than I ever expected. I did it; I've numbed my heart to his hurtful ways, and now I'm essentially living in a purely friends-with-benefits relationship.

This was never the plan I had for my life, but it's what I got anyway. Sadly, my *friend* is a douche a lot of the time.

A couple months after Iz's baby announcement, just like I'd numbed my heart to Jon, I was able to numb it to my baby, too. I was finally in an emotional place that I was able to suggest and help host a baby shower for Iz. Despite Jon's *the world is ending* attitude, that baby was a miracle, and I'd be damned if I let him tarnish that for her.

By the time Iz officially moved out of Jon's house and into her new home, he was coming around. He was a damn mess. He was worried sick about her. But despite his insistence that nothing good could come of it all, he was beginning to accept it was happening.

He *tried* to set up a nursery for his niece, and even if he messed it up and came to the rest of us for help, my heart both swelled and broke to see Jon in a baby goods store as he compared cribs and bought cute outfits.

He was accepting his niece.

He was already in love with her.... he told me so.

That should've been our baby!

By the time the nursery was set up and ready for the reveal, I faked a work shift and got the hell out of dodge. I was willing to snap my leg just to have an excuse not to watch him fawn all over Izzy's eight months pregnant belly.

I was happy for her.

I loved her, and I loved Bean, too. I even really loved that Iz and Jim would eventually get together and create their perfect family.

But love and envy aren't mutually exclusive.

I could feel both.

I *did* feel both.

My heart was hardening, and I was becoming a bitter bitch.

When Bean was finally born and Jon rushed to be by their side in the hospital, I couldn't be there. I couldn't watch him hold a baby that shared his blood.

The times he declared her as *'his'* sliced me open.

The times he fawned over that tiny baby, which was *always*, hurt me in ways that would never truly heal. Every day that passed and I was exposed to Jon, I was turning more and more bitter, though of course, I put on a good show.

I love Iz and Jim and Bean, I really do, but I was jealous. So fucking jealous, because not only had I lost mine, but it was never going to happen for me.

I had one single scarred tube left.

Even if I had a man who actually wanted to marry and make babies with me, it still wasn't going to happen.

I was broken in more ways than anyone would ever know.

Time passed and our group grew.

Bobby married Kit. They were trying for a baby.

Jimmy finally got his girl; they married, they already had their baby.

Aiden met his girl; Tina Cooper waltzed into town and instantly became one of us. She brought her sweet baby girl with her, and voila, Aiden got his girl and a baby, too.

Even Jack has a girlfriend.

I now had three sisters whose eggs were under siege by their husband's invaders, and two adorable nieces who helped soften my bitter heart.

Everyone had a future. Everyone had their family.

And then there was me, sitting on the edges while Jon visited other women, took their calls, then had the balls to get mad when I got mad.

He's never going to change, and though I love him, I really, *really* love him, I'll never be enough for him.

There's nothing I can offer that would make him stop and consider something a little more. I was his non-exclusive fuck-buddy, and he was my annoying as hell, almost-always housemate.

And now I find myself sitting in Aiden and Tina's beautiful bathroom, half drunk, half devastated at the memory of Jon's pure revulsion from an hour ago as he glared and asked me if I was pregnant.

"Did you pee too?" he spat out angrily.

He's *never* spoken to me with such venom before, but that single moment stole what little relationship we had left.

He took our friendship, or more accurately, he took what tiny sliver of a functional heart I had left, and he crushed it between strong fingers.

He broke it.

"We talked about this, Casey!"

He has nothing to worry about.

We've used condoms every single time since the first. I'm not pregnant. My numb heart won't let me make the same mistake twice.

There was no way in hell I could allow him inside me without that barrier. No way I could allow that kind of intimacy.

But despite it all, despite my numbed heart, despite all the work I've put into numbing myself, the look he gave me tonight while I sat alone in a prison cell cemented exactly what I've known all along.

It's over between us.

He doesn't want me, and I can't keep giving myself to him.

It's time for me to cut the cord and move on.

Even if I die in the process.

"Oh my God."

I look up at Izzy's shaking hands. With a white face and wide eyes, she stares at her test. "I got one of them." She looks to me. "One of the positives is mine."

Tina pulls Izzy to her feet. "Are you okay with this? It's okay, right?"

Of course it's alright. She married her Prince Charming. She's happy. He *wants* babies with her.

Bitterly, I look down at my test and study the missing line.

Mine's negative.

Just like I knew it would be.

"Yeah. I mean. Shit. You know?" Pink colors her cheeks. "Jim... Shit." She laughs. "He's gonna be over the moon."

Kit stands and places her test face-down on the sink. "What about you, though? Are *you* over the moon?"

"Well..." Iz considers. "Yeah, I can be okay with this."

Tina's eyes grow frustrated. "You're killing me Iz! *But?* You can be okay with this, *but?"*

Iz laughs softly. *"But,* my vagina still doesn't look right since the last time. I'm going to kill Jim for mutilating my poor vag with a big fat fighter head."

Laughing, Tina pulls her in for a gentle hug. "You'll be okay."

I swallow the emotion from my throat and let the bitterness out on a deep breath. "Tina? You're up. Positive or negative?"

Her kind eyes flip to mine. "Negative. You?"

"Negative."

Tina, Izzy, and I turn to Kit and wait. Her eyes are terrified, and her body literally shakes.

Standing, I pull her tall body into my arms and press my face against her chest. Even in heels, I'm still *that* short. "Flip your test, honey. It's your turn. Show me your baby."

"What if it's not positive?" Her blue eyes spill over. "What if–"

"Well, *not* turning it won't change a thing. Whatever's gonna happen, it's already decided. Turn the test over. Show us. We'll deal with it together."

Her hands shake. "I'm scared."

I'm scared, too. "It'll be okay." I reach up and swipe a tear from beneath her eye. "No matter what, I promise it'll be okay."

"It's positive," Iz murmurs distractedly. Her hand hovers over the now flipped test on the sink. "I wanted to put you out of your misery. It's positive. You're having a baby."

Kit's eyes snap between Izzy's face and hand. "Are you sure?"

She nods nervously. "That's what it says. I promise."

"I'm having a baby?"

A goofy smile spreads across Iz's face. "You're having a baby."

Kit grabs her chest. "I think I'm going to have a heart attack." She breathes dramatically. "Oh my God. This must be how Bobby feels most of the time."

"Stop." Hugging her tight, I laugh and hold on for a minute longer than I should. "Congratulations, Mommy. I'm so unbelievably happy for you."

Her face comes back until our eyes meet. She saw Jon's venom an hour ago as clearly as I did. "Are you okay?"

"Yeah." *No.* I take her face in my hands and squeeze. "I want you to know I'm really, *really* happy for you, okay? I'm so happy for you, and I'm so proud of you, and I love you so much. You're my sister, and I'll love you for the rest of my life."

Her bottom lip wobbles. "But?"

"I have to go home right now." Before she explodes, I shake my head. "I wanna celebrate with you. I do. I will. But I have to leave right now."

"Jon's such an asshole," Iz spits angrily.

Shaking my head, I take her hand and pull her closer. "No, he's not. We're just not compatible. We're just not right for each other. I don't want to ruin your celebrations tonight, so I have to leave."

"Tink–"

"I swear, I'm not going home to mope. I'm not upset. I just need to put some space between me and Jon before something explodes. You guys celebrate tonight, then I'll call you tomorrow."

Izzy squeezes my hand. "Please stay. I don't want you to leave, Case. It doesn't feel right to let you go."

"I can't stay, but I swear I'll see you guys tomorrow."

"Get Jon to drive you home."

I scoff. "Yeah, no. I'm ordering a cab. I'll be fine."

Kit's eyes flare. "It's not safe–"

"Don't worry, mama bear." I take my cell out and start dialing. "I've been playing *loads* of Mortal Kombat lately. My muscles are pumped, I'm all set." I'm still a master deflector.

When I finally get a text that my cab's only a block away, I hug Kit one last time and press a gentle kiss to her soft cheek, then I hug Izzy and Tina, too.

I pick up my test and glance at the negative one last time.

I let the hurt fuel me, I let it coat my heart and protect me, then I storm out of the bathroom and toss it at his chest.

It's over. We're done.

I'm done.

I allow myself one moment of weakness, one single second of looking into his beautiful eyes, then I break my own heart. "It's negative, dick. Just like I said it would be." I snatch up my purse and move toward the front door. "Go fuck yourself, Jon. I'm done."

He lets out a roaring *"Fuck!"* as I run out the door and into a heavy dump of summer rain, but I don't stop.

Instead, I sprint to the gates.

He'll be behind me in a matter of minutes.

That's just who he is; Leo the Lion, controller of the universe, micromanager as far as his Sunshine is concerned.

I need to get away, and I need to *not* go home.

He'll follow me there, and I don't want to be found.

"Main Street, please." I slam the cab door and close out the downpour, and as the car pulls away from the curb, I sit back and hold in my tears.

No more tears. Not for Jon.

I can't allow him to control me anymore.

I literally won't survive him.

I've been holding on for so long, accepting whatever scraps he'd *generously* throw my way, and ignoring his bad behavior.

Because I loved him.

But I deserve more.

The cab slows in front of Club 188, and though I know it's almost time for close, I pay for my ride and dart through the rain and across the lot.

I need to get drunk. I need a numb brain to go with my numb heart.

"You're back, Doll."

I look up and paste on a fake smile for Mike as he stands under the eave of the door and avoids the rain. Club patrons trickle out, drunk people hang off other drunk people, others practically dry hump against the brick exterior of the building.

This is my life. This is my job.

"Yeah." I clear my throat and squeeze under the doorframe. "I decided to come for another drink. I'm not done for the night."

"Where're the guys? They found you, I guess."

"Yeah, everyone went home." I don't mention that we were all arrested only a couple hours ago. "Don't worry, Mike. You're off duty now. The Kincaids have their girls in bed already." I pat his shoulder. "Stand down, boy."

"What about Jon?"

My chest tightens. "Jon's home, too. Everyone's tucked away for the night."

He's like a dog at a damn bone. "So why are you out?"

I squeeze through the door and shrug. "Wasn't ready for bed yet."

Walking inside and away from the too-protective bouncer, I walk against the tide of drunk leavers and emerge into the main area of the club.

"Well, hey there, pretty girl."

I turn and force a smile when Scotch, band front-man and house hottie, flashes a grin. He and his friends finally broke into the live music scene, so now they regularly play sets at Club 188.

Scotch, Angelo, Marcus, and Luca are here most weekends, but though the other guys seem cool, Scotch is the only one I've actually really talked to.

From the very first night these guys approached our girl group to hang out and shoot the shit, Scotch has always been cool. He's sexy as hell and his nice smile is a bonus. He's sweet and charming and funny as hell, but best of all, when I told him I was emotionally unavailable, it's like he completely *got* it.

I've been in love with someone else for years, so, sexy or not, funny or not, I had nothing to offer Scotch except the regular – non-benefits – kind of friendship, and a smartass workmate who would pour his drinks with a heavy hand.

I turn and try harder with my fake smile. "Hey there, Wine Spritzer. How you doing?"

He rolls his eyes and jumps down from the stage. "I'm good, T. We had a good set."

I walk to the bar and take a seat. We might be closing to the public, but I'm gonna get my drink on. "I heard you earlier. You guys almost sound good enough to get paid."

"Hey."

I jump at the voice so near my ear, then aftershave mixed with a light tang of sweat invades my senses and almost has me groaning in defense. I don't have it in me for small chat. I just wanna drink!

His thick brows furrow. "Are you okay?"

"Yeah, I'm fine, Mojito. Just trying to have a drink."

"Wanna talk about it?"

Deflect. Deflect. Deflect. "Wanna fetch me a glass of vodka?"

Chuckling under his breath, he swipes a long finger across his jaw, then thoughtfully, he taps my temple. "I see you in there, Tink. I see you hiding. What's troubling you? Maybe I could help."

I refuse to get into this. I refuse to spill my guts. And when I clamp my lips shut, he smiles and pulls out a stool.

"Alright. Want a drinking buddy instead?"

I perk up. A drinking buddy, I could do with. "Sure, take a seat, Lemon Drop. Why don't you tell me your troubles?"

Sighing as he gets comfortable on the stool, his thick thigh brushes against mine. I *want* to feel something. A tingle. A flutter. A pitter-fuck-ing-patter. But I get nothing.

I *should* be attracted to his plump lips. I should be half in love with his ocean blue eyes. Objectively, any girl would fall over herself to own his lips… Or at the very least, taste them.

The same way a woman would kill to have Jon's thick lashes. No mascara needed.

But I feel nothing. I'm officially numb.

Maybe I've not only numbed myself to Jon, but perhaps, to everything. Everyone.

It's best this way.

"Hey, Cosmo? Tell me your real name?"

He rolls his eyes playfully. "You can just call me Scotch."

"Right. But I know your mama didn't write Scotch on your birth certificate."

Laughing softly, he shakes his head at the same moment Lacey *finally* slides a drink along the bar. She walks away without a word and leaves me alone with the alcohol.

Both kinds.

"No. My mama didn't write Scotch on my birth certificate. In fact," his eyes come up to mine, "my mama wouldn't believe you if you said you were referring to me. As far as she knows, I'm an angel."

I roll my eyes. "I bet."

His hand comes up to gently rest on my shoulder. "I don't like seeing you sad, Tink. Since you and your girls forced us into this big-brother-little-sister bullshit... well, I'm feeling a little protective of the usually sunny girl looking sad."

I squeeze my eyes shut against the thump-thump of my heart. "Don't call me that."

"Call you what?"

"Sunny. Sunshine. Any of that shit." I pick up my drink and begin chugging. The numb is going away. I need it back. I desperately need to *not* feel.

"Alright." His singer's voice slides along my skin. "I won't call you that. What do you wanna talk about?"

"You have a girlfriend yet, Scotch?"

He forces a chuckle and turns back to the bar. "Not exactly. I'm not quite in the right headspace for that right now."

I look over and pin him with my eyes. *"Not in the right headspace. Sounds awfully fucking convenient, Sambuca. Why do guys insist on never getting serious? What's the allure to the eternal single life? Doesn't it get tiring?"*

He shrugs carelessly and watches the bar staff. "I'm not tired of it yet."

"Figures." I throw back the last swallow of liquor and bite my tongue to stop the tears. Lacey watches me from the end of the bar. She's watching me because she's worried, because she knows every last tiny, dirty detail of my life, but I pretend she doesn't, and nod instead.

Another drink, please.

I hate that she knows everything. She knows it all. She knows every tiny pathetic detail, and though she's sensitive enough to keep it to herself, I know she's thinking about it. Especially now.

"I don't get how it could be so satisfying to chase a new girl every night. Why not just love the one you already know? Why not be happy with the good girl who bakes a cake?"

Scotch's eyes search mine curiously. "I was following you all the way up to the cake thing, Tink. I was even on your side. But you don't strike me as a baker."

I scoff and turn to wipe a tear away with my shoulder. "I'm not. The times I've tried, they turned out shit. Maybe that's why he won't commit," I ponder quietly. I'm only joking. Cake won't make or break Jon.

He's already broken.

I shake my shit off and refocus on light and easy. "What are your hobbies, Strawberry Daiquiri? What do you like to do in your spare time?"

"Mine? Well, I like to jam with my brothers." He shrugs, not knowing that I've been flung back in time to this very club two years ago.

Brothers? Or Brutha's?

"I like to go to the movies. I like to hang with my brother and sister. I like to write songs." He winks. "I especially like talking to pretty girls."

"Ha."

Lacey sets another drink in front of me with a stern glare. This is all she's bringing me tonight. That's alright. I have enough cash for another cab fare. I can drink at Rhinos; they serve alcohol, and they don't even pretend to serve responsibly. "What do you like to watch at the movies, Gin and Tonic? What's the last thing you watched?"

"Ah…" He frowns as he thinks. "Oh! The new Hunger Games. And the new Star Wars before that."

"Yeah?" I turn to him and smile. "I watched that, too." Jon and I had gold class seats, hot wings on the leather chairs, and cold beers in our hands as we snuggled together. No cheapie popcorn and soda for Jon.

"Small world." Scotch chuckles.

"Yeah."

"Hey, you wanna know what's cool about being in a band?" He watches over my shoulder and has me spinning in my seat.

Luca stands at the edge of the stage and sucks face with some chick. Marcus and Ang pack away their instruments and tidy cords, and at the very opposite end of the platform stands a group of girls who watch the guys with hearts in their eyes.

"Some girls really don't give a shit if you're ugly as shit or dumb as a bag of rocks," Scotch continues. "Some chicks just wanna bag a rocker."

"It's just their luck that you're neither ugly nor dumb."

He laughs and bumps his shoulder into mine. "What can I say? I'm blessed."

"Yeah." I try my best to study him with a woman's appreciative eye. I want to *see* his broad chest, but it's not as broad as Jon's. I want to see his impressive height, though he's not as tall as Jon. He has the pretty blue eyes, which are objectively prettier than Jon's brown, but I can't be objective, because nothing is as pretty as Jon's eyes.

At least Scotch has the nose ring and shaggy hair. Jon doesn't have those.

Another stray tear slides down my cheek, but I don't get a chance to swipe it away before Scotch's large hand comes up. He slides a thumb along my cheek and watches me with sad eyes. "Casey..." He sighs. "Life is too short not to be with him. He's right here. Barely five miles away. Why don't you go home? Go find him."

One second, Scotch is in my face whispering things that are impossible for me to do. His words push painful splinters through my heart, but then he's gone, and a lion-like roar rips through the mostly empty club.

Jon picks him up like he weighs less than me, and he literally *throws* Scotch at least twenty feet across the room.

"Get the fuck off her!"

21

JON

THE TRUTH SHALL SET YOU FREE

*I*t's time to sort my shit out.

It's time I'm honest with her, and with myself. Then it's time to let her go like I'd always said I would.

Every single day that I keep her, I hurt her.

She deserves more than me, so it's time I let go.

What happened tonight only cements that fact.

We've been doing okay, just the usual Jon and Casey, Leo and Sunshine shit. We've been existing, we're happy enough. I was even hopeful of lulling her into a sense of *this is us, this is what you get.*

I wouldn't force her to stay, I wouldn't even ask, but if she just so happened to not leave, I would happily keep her forever.

But as soon as those pregnancy tests surfaced tonight, my stomach cramped, the sweat broke out on my forehead, and I was flung right back to five-years-old in the trailer park.

I've tried.

I've tried for years to talk through my shit, to try to process and understand it.

I was trying for Casey, but the progress I *thought* I was making was all for naught when I imagined my sweet Sunshine growing a poisonous Hart inside her body.

Sonia gets mad when I refer to it as poison.

She says it's no such thing, that I'm *not* my folks, and that I'm special and worthy. But her words don't mean shit in the face of me hurting Casey.

It's time for me to let her go.

It's too hot down here in Hell, and she deserves to fly.

I saw the hurt in her eyes tonight. Everyone is partnered off and happy, and I'm holding her down. She can't move on and start a relationship with someone else, because I won't let her sleep in her own home, and she sure as shit won't be bringing a man back to my place; which is exactly why I don't let her go home.

I was coming here to be noble. I would be the martyr. I would fall on my sword and set her free... That was, until I step into Club 188 and find a punk ass prick leaning in to kiss her.

Nope. Not on my watch.

I grab him by the scruff of his neck and throw him as hard as I can. With adrenaline firing through my body, it's easy to send him flying. His hundred and eighty pounds aren't shit for my broken heart to handle.

"Get the fuck off her!"

He takes out tables as he slides along the floor. Chairs ping into the air, and half empty drinks splash and shatter over top of him. Broken glass rains down and stains his shirt.

But worst of all, perhaps the most painful thing I've ever experienced in my life, is Casey running... to him.

She runs right past me and drops to her knees. "Oh my God, Scotch! Are you okay?"

Scotch. What kinda stupid ass name is that?

I can't be noble. I can't fall on my sword and give her up.

She's mine!

I step forward to tear her off him, to take back what's rightfully mine; to declare to the world who belongs to who, but my steps are halted when a beefy arm slides around my neck and yanks me to a stop. Mike pulls me back, then the rest of *Scotch's* band geeks help him pull me away from my Sunshine.

Adrenaline more potent than anything I've ever felt before floods my body as they drag me from her. I throw my elbow back and catch Mike's face, then I kick my legs out and nail the pussy blonde band guy.

Mike grunts in pain, but his arm doesn't let me free. We've trained together too long, he knows my shit, he knows my weaknesses, but he doesn't know Casey is mine.

He drags me backwards and digs his muscled arm into my windpipe.

He presses over the pressure point in my neck, which means I only have seconds before I'm unconscious and Casey is free.

She might run away.

She might run away with *Scotch.*

Throwing my head back, I nail Mike's nose and barely register the splatter of his blood on the back of my neck. His arm slips loose, so I duck out of his hold and turn back to Casey.

I expect to find her on the floor licking her boyfriend's wounds, but instead, she stands barely two feet in front of me with her hands on her hips and her eyes on fire.

Such pretty mossy green eyes.

"What. The actual. Fuck! Is your problem, Jon?" She tries to shove me back, but my adrenaline filled body isn't going anywhere. "What is your damn problem? What do you want?" She slams her fist against my chest. "Well?" She shoves me again. "What. Do. You. Want?"

I glare over her shoulder and watch the asshole shakily climb to his feet, then my jaw literally snaps closed as he steps up.

He grabs Casey and shoves her behind his back.

He's about to die.

It's done. This isn't a fucking game.

He's manning up. He's stepping up, and I'm not backing down.

"Woah!" Case jumps away from his hold and tries to step between us. "Nope. No way." She tries to push my chest, but I step toward him.

A small part of my brain knows I'm pinning her tiny body between us. She's so tiny, her face is nowhere near his, so I swing out and slam my fist down on his pussy jaw.

His head snaps around, and his body drops to the floor so suddenly, Casey falls, too. I pick her up and throw her over my shoulder. I hate myself for how rough I'm being, but I can't stop. I have no control over my shit. I've finally gone mad.

"Put me down!" She slams her closed fists over my back. "Jon! Put me down."

Nope.

I walk past a stunned and bleeding Mike. Then the wide-eyed groupies that watch from the corner and cower like I'm gonna whale on them as I pass. The rest of the Backstreet Boys stand by Marky Mark's unconscious body, but I don't spare them a second glance as I haul Casey toward the parking lot.

"Put me down!"

"No."

"Put me down! You can't just carry me around. I'm not a fucking doll."

"Yes. I can." *You're mine.*

"I hate you, Jon." The tears and truth in her voice have my steps faltering. "I fucking hate you. I wish I never met you."

She slays me.

I stop in the middle of the club parking lot under a heavy downpour, and slide her soft body off my shoulder. Bringing her to her feet, I stare at her soaked eyes. "You don't hate me. You don't mean that."

"I do." She swipes tears and raindrops away as they bead over her lips. "I really do. I'm done, Jon. I'm done with us."

I know that's exactly what I'd come here to do, but– "No you're not. We're just having a fight, then tomorrow we'll be back to normal."

"No! We're not just having a fight, Jon. I'm done. I'm tapping out." She shoves against my chest. "I don't want you anymore!"

That's not true. "But I love you, Sunshine."

"Well, I'm not Sunshine, and you're not Leo. I'm just Casey. I'm *just* Casey, and Casey isn't good enough for Jon."

My eyes flare wide at her stupidity. "Not good enough? You've always been *too* good."

"I can't be *too* good, Jon." She throws her arms out to the sides. "You've had me for two years! I see no commitment. I see no promises. I see nothing!"

"That's exactly it. You're *too* good for me. I've told you this!" *I'm so sick of repeating the same shit time and time again.* Rain drops fly from my lips as I shout. "I can't give you those things, because I don't have them to give!"

"Those are just words, Jon. Excuses! You *do* have those things to give. You have *you*, and you're all I wanted!" She slams her palm against my chest. "I played your part-time whore for two years, Jon. I did it in hopes you might toss me a little more, but nothing. You give me nothing!"

She turns on her heels and sets off into the street.

Nope. Not getting away.

I jump forward and grab her dripping arm, but she spins and looks at me in a way she never has before. "I saw your disgust, Jon. I saw the way you looked when you worried your precious freedom might end. You hurt me! You hurt me that after all this time, after our friendship, after everything we've been through, it hurts that you'd look at me like I was nothing more than a two-bit whore who might trick you into a family." She snaps her arm from my hand. "Don't worry. I won't be carrying your babies."

"Exactly!" I race through puddles in the street to catch up. "I won't put my poison in you! I won't do that to you, Case. I won't pass my shit on to a whole new generation of broken boys."

"Broken? Why are you broken, Jon? Because from what I see, you're a grown ass man that is choosing this life. You're choosing to be a lonely bitter man, and you're taking me down with you."

"Choosing?" My eyes fill with that familiar red haze. I take a step back before I do something stupid. I want to hit something. I want to smash something beneath my fists. I spin on the spot to escape her, then I spin back and face her. "You think I choose this?" My fists shake. My body sweats, even in the rain. "You think I *chose* to wake up to dirty old men helping themselves to my body for a whole decade? Do you think I chose to be raped? Do you think I *chose* to be sold?" Like a coward, I stand over Casey and shout in her face. "I was sold by my parents! I was five years old the first time I was torn open! *Five!"*

Her angry eyes turn sympathetic. "Jon…"

"My parents had to figure out ways to pay the rent, since their money went to their next hit. They sold my body to *any* filthy piece of shit that had the cash. They sold me for most of a decade. And when they couldn't sell me, they beat me. They beat me so fucking often, I didn't even know what it would feel like *not* to have broken ribs and blood in my piss."

I cover my face and scream into my hands. I scream like a little kid. I scream the way I did every time they did those things to me. I scream my frustration that I was strong enough to survive it then, to escape it, to protect my sister, but now that I'm grown and no longer under their power, I'm too weak to let it all go.

I scream until my voice is hoarse and my throat hurts, then I move my hands and stare at the most beautiful woman in the world. Dark hair sticks to her face, and her mascara runs with the rain.

She knows all of me now.

She wants to save me, but can't.

I can't have her, because I'm unsaveable.

"I'll spare you the details," I push out between clenched teeth, "but *that's* why I won't be perpetuating that cycle. Hart men will die out with me. *That's* why I'm broken, and worst of all, that's why I can't make babies with you."

She steps toward me. I expect sympathy, but instead, I get fire. "Jon, those things, when you were a boy, they weren't your fault. I'm really *fucking* sorry that happened to you. I wish you'd told me. You didn't have to live with that alone. I could've been your Leo for a while. I would've held you and scratched your hair, and I would've tried to make it better. But you didn't share. You didn't let me in. And now, you don't have to worry. I can't have your babies, anyway. Hart men *will* die out with your bitter ass."

She understands. She finally understands. And it hurts so fucking much I want to cry. "Exactly!"

"No." She shakes her head sadly. "Not that I won't. I *can't*. I can't have any babies."

"What are you–"

"I had yours once." Her eyes turn sad. "I had your baby in my belly for a little while. I had him inside me, and I loved him for as long as I had him."

My heart beats a dangerous tattoo inside my chest as pressure squeezes my skull. "What the fuck are you talking about?"

She nods like this conversation isn't nearly as important as it is. "I had your baby in my belly. I even saw his heartbeat on a screen. Do you wanna know why I've been so mad at you?" She shoves me back as her sadness turns to anger. "I lost our baby. I lost him in a very painful way, but in the short time I had him, I was terrified to tell you. I was terrified! I couldn't celebrate with you, and then I couldn't mourn with you. I couldn't do anything but go to surgery alone. They took my baby, and I never got to see him." Her eyes spill over with angry tears. "I came home, and what did you do? You took care of me! You were so fucking sweet, but you reminded me at least twice a week, every-fucking-week that you would *never* procreate. You would never marry."

I had a baby? She carried my baby? "You should've told me."

"How could I?" She shoves me so hard, my weakened body actually moves with her blow. "How could I, when you were so damn vocal about how *smart girls don't make stupid mistakes*? How could I tell you, and give you more reason to hate me? To hate you."

"Hate you? I would never–"

"You hated me tonight when you thought I might be pregnant. I saw your eyes. You hated the very thought of having something more with me."

"No! I hated the thought of my poison tainting you."

"Well, it already did. But it wasn't your child that tainted me. It was *you*. You and your poisonous attitude."

"Casey–"

"But don't worry." She steps back. "It's all done. It's all over. My baby's gone. I'm gone. I have nothing left for you, Jon. I'm officially out. Take your poison, take your good intentions, and take your bullshit. Give them to Sonia. Maybe she can save you."

I cringe from the blow. *Bullseye.* "How do you know about Sonia?"

Her sad eyes spill faster. "Because I'm a smart girl, remember? You live with a guy long enough, you learn shit. Even shit that you wish you could turn a blind eye to. I don't want to be your side piece, Jon. I don't want to tag team with Sonia." She stops backing up, takes a deep breath, and straightens her spine for the final blow. "If I can't be your everything, then I'll be your nothing. Goodbye, Jon."

PART III

THE REAL ENDING

JON

ANNIE

ack! Get out here!"

"Baby, relax."

"JACK!"

"Kit–"

"Bobby, swear to God, if you tell me to relax again, I'll kill you. I'll run you down with your own damn car, then I'll back it up and do it again."

Sitting on the couch in my living room, I lean my head back against the cushions and smile.

It feels like I'm back in the trailer park all over again.

"You just need to calm down, Kit. Take a deep breath. This isn't good for the baby."

"Jack! Get out here."

"Baby, you're acting crazy."

Oh, shit!

Springing to my feet, I sprint from my living room and race toward the front door to watch my domestically disputing trailer-trash neighbors argue in the street.

It was all fun and games until Bobby called her crazy.

"Crazy?"

"No. I didn't mean–"

"You think I'm crazy?" Kit's voice takes on a whole new epic level of screech.

"Kit. I'm sorry—"

I slide onto my front porch just as Jack steps into the yard with his hands held high, and a shaking body.

He's a dead man, and I *really* want to watch.

Skidding along the porch in training shorts and a tank, I stop and watch Kit walk laps into her front lawn. Strangely, she carries a yellow and white wedding bouquet in her left hand, and a book in the right.

I look toward Jim and Iz's porch, because my body's trained to always know where my sister is during a conflict, but she and Jim watch the show with grins on their faces. I turn to find Aiden and Tina doing the same from theirs.

In a cute little pink dress, Evie darts across her lawn toward the excitement unfolding with Uncle B and Aunty Kit, but I skip forward and grab her up before Kit accidentally tramples her.

"Stay with me, Bug."

"Kitkat has fowers."

"I'll buy you your own flowers if you stay with me."

"Kit." Jack steps forward warily, like she was a wild dog, and he's just about to lose his face. "I'm sorry, okay? I'll have them fixed."

"You can't fix them! They're ruined." Kit thrusts the bouquet toward Jack's face. "Where did you find it?"

"Baby." Bobby steps toward his wife as slow and warily as Jack did. He places his hand on Kit's forearm and pulls her back a step. "It's okay. You made them once, you can make them again."

Every time Kit stomps around, every time she thrusts her fist toward someone, a new flower falls from the mutilated bouquet. The ribbon hangs loose. Stems poke out, but the flower is missing completely.

She stabs the air with an equally mutilated paperback book in her right hand, and when I read the title, I squirm with discomfort. The spine hangs tattered, chunks of pages missing, the cover half torn.

If somebody ruined my book like that, there'd be hell to pay.

"Bring it out here. Now!"

Jack shakes his head. "You've scared her, Kit. She won't come out when you're screaming like this."

Her?

Jack's got a girl inside?

"Her? It's a her?" Lilies fall from the bouquet as Kit slams it against his chest. "Her? What the hell is *it?"*

He lifts his hands in surrender. "You just need to calm down for a sec. This isn't as big a deal as you think it is."

"No, I think it is!"

"Baby–"

"She ripped my bouquet, Jack! This was the *only* picture I had of Dad. The only one! This ribbon came from flowers he bought me before he died! This stuff isn't replaceable."

"Kit, I'm sorry–"

"What are they talking about?" Aiden's words float in the air behind me. I simply shrug.

I have no fucking idea.

"This is all I had of him, Jack! Now they're ruined. They're ruined, and I have nothing left."

"Baby–"

"You have me." At Jack's whispered words, Kit stops in front of her little brother with tear-soaked eyes. "I'm sorry she messed up your flowers, but it's not the end of the world. Dad's not here. I know that hurts, and I know your baby maker hormones make it hurt more, but I'm here. I mean, that's enough, right?"

"Jack–"

As though Evie knows exactly what's going on, she stills in my arms and watches the emotional breakdown between siblings.

On a wailing sob, Kit flings herself forward and throws her arms around Jack's shoulders. "I'm sorry!" His hands come up to hold her closer, and watching over her shoulder, his eyes meet a speechless Bobby's. Not much silences the peacock. "I'm sorry, Jack. You're enough. You're definitely enough."

Jimmy steps off his porch with Sissy's hand in his. "Whew, that shit was close. Now that Reilly disarmed that bomb, you idiots wanna tell us what the hell's going on?"

"I don't actually know," Bobby admits. "We just got home from a baby appointment. Our house looks like a bomb went off."

"I didn't hear any bombs, B."

He shrugs and watches Kit warily. "I dunno, Jim. The couch cushions have *exploded*. Fake flower carnage and book pages are everywhere. It's a damn mess in there."

"Puppy!" Evie bounces in my arms and points toward the house. "Puppy!"

Following her gaze, my eyes slide up the front of the house and stop on a bedroom window on the second story.

I burst out in the first laughter I've felt since Casey walked out of my life, when, with a juicy black nose pressed against the window, a giant dog wags its tail and its tongue lolls out to the side as she watches us.

Her breath steams up the glass, and big excited eyes follow every micro move Jack makes.

I don't think she's scared at all. I think that dog might just be dumber than a rock.

"Ah, Jack."

His eyes snap from Kit, to me, then to his window, and when their eyes lock, I swear, man and beast both smile.

Holding his gut, Jimmy laughs and bows my sister in half as he leans on her. "Jack! Where'd you get a dog?"

"A dog?" Kit's teary voice turns lethal in a heartbeat. "Why is there a dog in my house? That's not my dog!"

"She's mine."

"Where'd you get a dog?"

"I found her."

Jim laughs. "You can't just keep someone's dog, numb-nuts. You gotta get her scanned or something. The vet will find her real owners."

"No, I know." Jack turns away from his doting dog. "She was hurt, Kit. She was hit by a car. I found her."

I frown. "Jack, if she was hit by a car, she needs to go to the vet. You can't just hide a dying dog in your bedroom."

"Oh, nah." He shrugs. "I already took her to the vet. She's good now. Annie!" He whistles and has the dog's ears snapping to attention. One second, she's in the window, the next, she's gone.

She literally *thump-thump-thumps* and sprints down the stairs, then emerging through the still open front door, she bounces into the yard and circles Kit and Jack.

"Puppy!"

My eyes flare wide. "Jack! She's only got three legs."

"I just told you," he huffs. "She was hit by a car."

"What kinda dog is that?" Aiden steps closer. "Appalachian werewolf?"

Jack rolls his eyes. "She's a Labrador cross."

"Crossed with a giant black bear," I argue. *"And* she's missing a leg."

"She looks fine to me," Tina comments. "She's running around pretty happy for a dog who got hit by a car."

"Oh, yeah. She got hit ages ago. Like, two months, at least." He shrugs like everything is cool. "She had surgery and they had to take her leg, but she's mostly better now." Crouching down, he makes out with his dog.

Well, she makes out with him, he just hugs her. "You're all better now, aren't you, Annie girl? All better. Such a good girl."

"She was hit two months ago?" Kit's voice takes on that dangerous tone that means we're all about to die. "How long has she been in my home, Jack?"

Gulping, he detaches himself from the werewolf-bear hybrid and stands tall. "Like... six weeks, maybe."

"You've had a giant dog in my house for more than a month? How did you sneak her in? How have you fed her?" Her eyes flare. "How did you pay for her surgery?"

"With my money. It's cool, I've been saving, I have heaps leftover."

"Heaps leftover?" *We're in so much trouble.* "What money? You don't have any money!"

Oh shit.

"The guys pay me, Kit. Relax."

Jimmy grits his teeth dramatically. We're so dead.

Kit turns to Bobby. "You pay him? Since when?"

"Of course we pay him, baby. He's there as much as we are now."

"You never told me you pay my brother a living wage!"

"I didn't know it was something that had to be discussed," he bravely shoots back. "He works, he gets paid."

"Puppy!" Evie squirms in my arms when Annie wanders closer. "Put me down, Unca Jon."

Jim steps closer and shields us from the dog. "Is she safe?"

"Oh, yeah," Jack answers easily. Taking it for the lifeline it is, Jack steps away from his steaming sister and comes to his bear. "You could put Bean's skull in her mouth, she'd be totally fine."

"Um, I'd rather we didn't do that," Sissy murmurs. "Not that I don't trust your werewolf not to crush my child's skull between her teeth."

"Her name's Annie?" I squat down with Evie in my arms. Extending my hand cautiously, I wait for her to move closer and sniff.

Jack steps closer with a silly grin. "Yeah, her name's Annie. You can relax. I promise, she's a good girl. She's been sleeping in my bed for six weeks. She didn't eat me yet."

"When does she go back to her family?" Kit asks.

His head snaps around angrily. "She *is* home. She's mine."

"Jack–"

"She's mine, Kit. I'm not letting her go."

"But you didn't even ask, Jack! You can't just bring a horse into my home."

"I would've asked, Kit. But you would've said no. She's mine. I'll move out if you want, I'll take Lindsi's old place, but I'm not giving her up."

"We have a baby on the way!" She rubs circles into her still small stomach. "What if she hurts it? We don't know that dog."

Annie's tongue slides from the tips of Evie's fingers and doesn't stop until it wraps under her armpit. Flailing and giggling, Evie convulses in my arms. Having said hello, Annie turns and trots toward Bean and Sissy. Standing with Evie still in my arms, I step closer and get ready to snatch the girls away.

Annie simply sniffs, licks, and bounces to the next person.

"She's a good girl," Jack repeats. "I know her. I trust her."

"I guess we have a new dog then, huh?" Aiden pulls a smiling Tina into his side. "She's kinda cute, I guess. In a giant Killer Whale kind of way."

"Cute?" Bobby asks skeptically. "She only has three legs!"

"She was hurt real bad," Jack replies sadly. "I found her and fixed her up. She'll never turn on us. We're family."

"So Annie's what happened to your flowers and stuff?" Jim's eyes light up with trouble when he drops Jack right back into the shit and has Kit's eyes narrowing.

"I'll fix them, Kit. I swear. That's the first time she's gone silly. I don't know what happened, but she's a really good girl. We've been working on training. She knows your smells already. She already knows all of you." He stops and catches Kit's eye. "You just saw her with Bug. She knows us. I trust her."

Just as Jack's final words leave his mouth, a menacing growl rips from Annie's throat and has me swinging Bean, Izzy, and Evie away in one swoop.

Stepping in front of the growling dog, I prepare to kick the pretty thing in the face if she steps toward my girls.

But she doesn't.

She's not after me.

Turning on her three legs, she rips out a second ear-aching growl and stalks toward the estate gates.

As a group, we look toward the nosy older couple as they peer through the iron bars. The gates sit at the end of our driveway, about ninety feet from where we stand, and just like I can tell they're a man and a woman – older than us, maybe even a little older than Nell – just like I can know that about them, they can see us, too.

Cupping his mouth, the man shouts and has Tina's face paling. "Sarah!"

"Oh my God–"

"Peaches." Aiden's angry jaw clenches. "Who's that?"

Cuddling into Aiden's side, Tina's body trembles with fear. "That's my mom and dad."

My eyes snap to hers as memories batter over me. "They sold you?" My hands flex. "That's what you said. They sold you to Sean? They chose money over you?"

She swallows nervously. "Well–"

"Yes or no, Christina."

"Yeah." Shakily, she nods. "That's the gist of it."

"Right." I pass Evie to her mom, then pushing Sissy and Bean back to Jim, I take Annie's collar in my hands. "Let's go."

"Jon." Bobby steps in front of me. "No."

"Time to earn your place in our family, Tripod. I'm not letting this go, Peacock. Get outta my way, or I'll run you the hell down."

Annie's lips stay drawn over her lips. Her hackles, high on her back. Her large rib cage brushes against my thigh as we walk forward.

Bobby said no, but that doesn't mean he doesn't have my back.

Within a single beat, he falls into step beside me, then Aiden, Jimmy, and Jack follow as we stalk to the gates. Tina's parents watch us, and I can't even blame them for the several steps they take back at our approach.

I don't release the gates.

I don't trust myself to have that kind of access to these people. I'm not exactly in the best emotional space right now.

"Hi." With a shaking voice and a shaking chest, the man takes another step back. "We're here to see our daughter."

With teeth bared just like the dog, I snap, "No."

The woman's face blanches. "No?"

"No." Aiden stops beside me. "No, you're not going to see her."

The man's face burns red. "I don't know who you are, young m–"

Annie lets out a snapping growl and has the not-so-brave man skipping back in fear. His beady eyes flick between Annie's and mine. He's not sure who's more dangerous right now.

Moving back another step, the piece of shit actually angles his body behind his wife's. "We're here to see Sarah. We have no business with you."

"Correct, you have no business with us." Aiden steps closer to the gate like he has a secret to tell. "You have no business here at all. Sarah doesn't live here. Sarah doesn't exist. Leave before we open the gates."

"We saw her!" Braver than her husband, the woman steps forward. "We saw her, and our granddaughter, too. We have a right to see them."

"You have *zero* rights!" Aiden snaps. "Zero! You lost your rights when you sold them for a pretty house. Sarah and Katie no longer exist. Get the fuck off my property. Now. You have three seconds before I let the dog out."

Letting out a perfectly timed growl, Annie has the couple jumping with fright.

"We'll call animal control."

"You can try," Jack dares. "But I bet she rips your arms off before you get your phones out. I watched her rip Sean's face off only a few weeks ago."

Well that's not true at all…

"We'll call the police."

I smile like they just told an amazing joke. "Call them, lady. Ask for Alex. Tell him I sent you. In the meantime, get your raping, money hungry, piece of shit asses off our property before I take a stick and show you exactly how you fucked your daughter over. Bonus, motherfucker, I'll do it for free."

The man's eyes flare with indignation, but one more snapping growl from the bear has them turning on their heels and skittering back to their car.

"Jon." Turning angrily, Aiden slams his hands against my chest. "I get what you did, I get that you helped, but if you ever paint a picture like that again, with my girl and a stick, I'll kill you." He presses a hand to his stomach. "I think I'm gonna fuckin' vomit."

I let out a shaky breath and work through my own overwhelming nausea. Adrenaline slams around my body and has my hands shaking. "I'm sorry, Aido." I try to shake it off, but like a horror movie that just won't shut off, images flash through my brain and leave me weak. "I'm sorry."

As soon as the couple's taillights disappear around the corner, Annie's growls drop away and her tail thumps Jack's thigh excitedly.

"Annie." Her happy face pops up at my words, and when I crouch down and pat my leg, she waddles over. Falling flat to my ass, because I'm flat out of energy, I throw my arms around her neck and take a hug. "Welcome to the family, girl. You're the best thing Jack ever did wrong."

CASEY

KOREAN ELVIS

"*W*ith the power vested in me by this great state, I now pronounce you," *hip thrust, hip thrust,* "husband and wife. Aiden, buddy," Korean Elvis's luscious dark hair whips over his sweating forehead, "You may kiss your bride."

Aiden roughly smooshes Tina against his chest. He bends her almost upside down, then he kisses her indecently as Korean Elvis impregnates us all with his hip thrusting.

Despite the fact Jon stands beside me and tries to catch my pinky finger with his, despite his constant requests to talk, despite the fact I've seen him only a couple times in the last month and my heart still bleeds for him, I smile, because I'm so unbelievably happy for Tina and Aiden that I can forget the rest for a minute.

They've been through so much, but seeing them now, making out with a lot of tongue, though they hide it from their daughter as she stands just a few feet away with Gramma Nelly, I can *feel* their happiness.

I want to be that happy someday.

After our epic, friendship ending, heart shattering, almost bordering on illegal fight in the club parking lot, I simply went home and hid.

I sat in the dark and researched what I could, and when threat of eviction and starvation pushed me back into the real world, I worked, then I went home and sat alone some more.

Eventually, once Lacey got sick of my shit, she pulled me aside at work and metaphorically slapped my face. *"Stop moping. Stop thinking of the negatives, Case. Positive thinking brings positive results."*

Her backwards zen talk was more helpful than she'll ever know, because she was right; I'd spent the previous two years pining over someone I could never have.

I was pathetic, so I stopped obsessing about what I don't have, and instead, started thinking about what I *want*.

I want to be happy.

I want my forever.

And no matter how much he hurts me, I really, *really* want Jon to be happy, too.

In the last month of alone-ness, I've been working on me.

I need to find the old me again, the me *before* Jon. I think I'm on the right track. Maybe. Probably not, since I've spent the whole month researching child sexual abuse cases and earning my Google law degree as I try to understand the statute of limitations on such heinous crimes.

I have no clue if Jon wants justice for what happened to him, but I've compiled a folder full of old cases where the victim reported their abuse decades after it happened.

In our state, from what I've read, he can actually report up to thirty years after the fact. I've found cases where the victim was successful in having their attackers prosecuted and sent away.

I'll do this for Jon, because I love him.

Even if grown-up-Jon doesn't want to revisit this stuff, the young brutalized boy deserves justice.

I'll compile the information, but that's where I'm walking away. I won't push him to do anything with it if he doesn't want to, because I'm not his Sunshine anymore, and he's not my Leo. I'll give him the names of specializing lawyers, I'll give him case studies, and I'll give him a direction to walk in, but that's the end of it.

He can do with it what he wants.

I just want him to be happy. Whatever happiness means to him, whatever that picture looks like, I want to give it to him before I leave.

Annoyingly, his pinky finger hooks around mine and has me snatching my hand away. His lips – lips I so wish I could taste just one more time – come to my ear to whisper more *'we need to talk'* messages, but I step away.

I hook my arm in Kit's, and angle my body so Jon will get beat up by his *other* best friend if he leans that close to Kit to pass on a message.

I need distance, and I'm petty enough to let nature take its course; you would think a fight between a lion and a peacock would end with the peacock's feathers in the air, but *this* peacock might just slow the lion enough to give me a head start as I haul ass out of here.

Aiden *finally* releases his flushed bride and lets her stand on her own two feet, and like the group of squealing girls we are, we pile in for a group hug and congratulate the happy couple.

With Evie's hand in hers, and Bean's stroller beside her hip, Nelly steps up to Aiden and Tina last. "I'm so proud of you both." She kisses Tina's cheek. "I love you." She kisses Aiden. "I love you, too. I've got the babies. You guys have the entire night to party."

Aiden hugs his mom tight. "Thank you, Momma."

"You're so welcome, honey. You know which room we're in. My phone is on, so you can contact me any time, but I want you to not worry." Nelly takes Izzy's hand in her spare. "You, too. I've got the girls, you guys have fun."

"Thank you."

"You're welcome, sweetheart. I'd tell you all not to do anything I wouldn't do, but most of you are already married or pregnant, so I figure the damage is already done. Have fun, text me pictures of the really dumb stuff."

Jimmy laughs and steps in to hug his mom. "We're definitely *not* texting you anything, Mom. That's just weird." He pulls back and studies her face. "Take care of my girls, Momma. I hope they sleep for you."

Aiden pushes in and elbows Jim in the ribs. *"Your* girls? That's *my* girl."* He picks Evie up and nuzzles his spiky chin against her neck until she convulses and giggles. "I love you, Smalls."

"I wuv you, Biggie."

"You have fun with Gramma, okay?"

"Okay." She wiggles to be passed to Tina. Cupping her mom's face, she squeezes Tina's cheeks until she makes the duck lips. "I wuv you, Mommy."

"I love you too, baby. Sleep well. I'll see you at breakfast."

"We have pancakes?"

"We're at a buffet, baby. You can have a million pancakes."

"Okay! Let's go, Gramma."

We watch as the three pack up their overflowing diaper bag paraphernalia, then as Jack says his sulky goodbyes, since he's years away from being old enough to party. He grabs the heavy bag in one arm, and picks Evie up in the other, and they follow Nelly and the stroller out of the cheesy chapel toward the elevators.

Jim claps his hands gleefully. "Bubs, we're out of here!"

Sweeping her feet out beneath her, Aiden picks Tina up and catches her in his arms. "We're going to our room."

I roll my eyes, but then Bobby throws his arm over Kit's shoulder and turns her toward the door, too. "We're going to see how they make twins."

With Izzy still tucked under one arm, Jimmy kicks his leg out and slams it against Bobby's back. "That's not how that works, dumbass. You obviously didn't pay attention in Mrs. Burns' sex ed class."

"No shit I didn't pay attention! She was a seventy-year-old crotchety bitch with lipstick on her teeth and potpourri perfume."

Aiden laughs. "Did you ever stop to think she was purposely placed in that class as a birth control tactic? I mean, I sure as shit couldn't muster a boner on sex ed days."

"Can y'all stop?"

With a stupid grin, he looks down at Tina. "Don't be so cranky, Peaches. It's our wedding day. Let's go make triplets."

Laughing, she elbows Aiden. "Excuse me for not wanting to hear about crotchety old bitches and my new brothers' boners on my wedding day."

"Don't fret, Tina." Jimmy runs his tongue across his teeth. "I'll send you pics."

"Fuck you will!" Stepping forward, Aiden slams his foot against Jim's thigh, then he turns on his heel and takes his wife away to make triplets.

"Alright. They're out." I turn to Kit and Iz. "Come party with me?"

"I already have something planned." Bobby kisses Kit's brow. "Sorry, Tink."

"And I got a lovely delivery of photos this morning, which, by the way, I need to kiss my brand-new sister for that. She does amazing work."

Bobby's eyes snap to Jim's. "You got pics, too?"

"Yeah, I did." Jimmy's drawl makes me want to take a shower to get the cheap porn star smell off my skin. "I got pics. Now we gotta go recreate some of the poses."

"Dude!" Jon shoves Jimmy. "That's my baby sister."

"Lucky for me," Jim slaps Izzy's ass and has her skipping forward, "she ain't my baby sister. We're out."

"You're a fucking pig! Don't touch my sister, she's an angel."

When Korean Elvis leaves out a side door, Bobby leads Kit away, and Jimmy sweeps Izzy into his arms, my heart thunders in my chest when I realize Jon and I are alone in the cheesy chapel.

Shit! "Alright. Well…" *I'm out of here.*

He grabs my hand before I bolt. "I'll party with you, Sunshine."

"No. It's best if we don't." *No shit, it's best.* I'll end up back in his bed, back on the starting blocks, and I'll be bleeding all over again. I'm already woozy with blood loss. "I'm going to bed."

His brows pull tight when I tug my hand from his. "But it's only eight. You haven't been asleep by eight since you were three."

I haven't been asleep before midnight in about that much time. Perks of working in a club, my inner clock is a little skewed. It's practically still midday for me. "That's alright. I'm fairly tired." *I'm not. I'll probably just jump casinos and get drunk elsewhere.*

His lip twitches, but not in an amused way. Mostly, he looks fucking pissed. "So that's it, then. Not even friends? We're not even gonna be socially pleasant?"

"I am being pleasant. I haven't even asked about Sonia yet today."

Dammit!

I made a list of shit I wouldn't say to him; bitter, horrible things that I wanted to be a grown up about and not show how much of a bitch I truly am. Sonia was the very first thing on that list.

I don't know who the bitch is, but she's probably younger than me, probably taller, too. She probably has beautiful long hair like Kit, Iz and Tina. I can see how filling out the group with another like her would be aesthetically pleasing in holiday photos.

Most photos till now consists of all the tall girls standing with their tall boys, then little ol' me, usually sitting in Jon's lap to gain an extra couple inches of height.

Jon's hands come up to scratch at his face, a habit I've noticed in most of the guys. I wonder if Mr. Kincaid used to do that? "Listen Sunshine. We need to ta–"

"Casey."

His eyes peek out from behind his hands. Sighing, he drops his arms down by his sides. "What?"

"My name is Casey. Or Tink. You can call me Tink like everyone else, if you want."

His lip turns up in a sneer, and his words, pure revulsion. "I'm not gonna call you Tink."

I hate that I have to look up so high to meet his eyes. He stands close on purpose, like he needs to prove how big and strong he is. "Why not? It's my nickname. I think it's stuck."

He points toward the door. "I'm not them, okay? I'm not them. You and me... we have more. You're not Tink to me!"

"I'm not anything to you, Jon. Now we're just Kit's best friend, and Bobby's best friend. It's the way it was always supposed to be. I've gotta go, okay?" I turn on my heel and leave my beautiful, broken, former best friend behind, and I head through the chapel reception area past the bigger lady as she sits and files her nails.

I walk as fast as I can without attracting attention to myself – I'd hate for security to think I'm stealing their chips or something. I walk straight through the lobby and swing into one of the million bars this place has.

Slipping onto a stool and holding my breath to keep the tears locked up, I flag down the sexy bartender with the lip and nose rings.

He kind of reminds me of Scotch.

My stomach flips at the memory of Jon throwing Scotch. Then of him knocking Scotch out cold.

That poor, poor man.

He was only trying to protect me, and look what he got for his troubles. With guilt sitting low in my belly and dread causing my hands to shake, I went to find Scotch the day after Jon's ape attack. Turns out he lives in an upstairs apartment above a garage, and when I arrived, not only was he there with his giant split lip, cuts and bruises, and a tender body, but his bandmates were there, *and* his big brother.

Talk about walking into enemy territory.

They were fuming.

As in, vigilante-justice-with-pitchforks-and-steel-beams fuming, and though I know they're not fighters, not like Jon and the guys, they were still pissed enough that if that showdown came to be, people were going to get arrested.

Or worse yet, hurt.

Where the band was loudly planning their attack, Scotch's brother simply stood back and watched in that dangerous silence that promised *he's* the one I should truly be worried about.

Scotch's brother, Alex Turner, just so happens to be a cop in this town, which makes my life a hell of a lot stickier.

Jon was wrong to hurt Scotch, but the look in Alex's eyes had me pleading lenience.

I should've let him arrest Jon.

Jon doesn't deserve leniency for what he did.

Then I could've bailed his dumb ass out, but not before standing on the outside of the bars and taunting him about being a good boy and making smarter choices.

Any other time, any other part of our relationship, I would've done exactly that. It would have been a fun laugh, but we aren't those people, anymore.

I told him the night before that I'd lost his baby, and in exchange, he told me of his horrific childhood.

I don't see how we could ever find us again. Nor do I don't think I want to.

"What can I getcha, cutie?"

Groaning internally, I look up and paste on a fake smile for the sexy bartender. Why can't a guy call me sexy, or even slutty? Nope. *Cutie.*

"Margarita, please. Keep them comin'."

"See your ID?"

Fuck. Off.

Fishing through my purse, I toss my driver's license onto the bar and watch him pick it up and study the details. "You're twenty-seven."

"Mmhmm." *No, I'm not twelve.*

"You and me, we're the same age." He passes my license back. "Like, exactly the same. If our mamas were in the same hospital, they would've high-fived in the hallway."

"Well, that's a fun visual. Can I get that drink?"

He flashes a pretty smile, then turns away and starts mixing and bopping his ass to the loud music around us.

Two hours later, I'm snorting as Edgar – that's legitimately his name, or at least he swears it is – mixes my next drink, but does a sweet bottle flip and almost drops the tequila bottle.

"I swear Ed, you're funnier than I gave you credit for."

"That's okay, Tink," – I told him my nickname somewhere around my fourth drink – "you're hotter than I gave you credit for. I thought you were a prissy chick ready to nickel and dime me on tips, or worse yet, an eighth grader who snuck outta her parents' suite."

I slam my empty glass down on the bar and snort at the loud boom.

"Not me. I graduated eighth grade, like..." I try to count on my fingers, but I'm drunk and have no fucking idea.

"That's okay, girl, I gotcha. We graduated eighth grade the same year, remember? We're cool."

"You know what we should do?" My eyes flare wide as I think up the best idea I've ever had. Ed's lip twitches in a cute *'I'm a hipster with lots of facial jewelry'* kind of way.

Leaning on the bar, he rests on his forearms and brings his face close to mine. "No. What should we do?"

"We should have a joint birthday party!"

He's amused by me. "Where do you live, Tink?"

"Not here!"

Edgar laughs and waves at a waiting customer. "That's what I thought. Will we party here, or at yours?"

"You should come to my town. I have a whole gym full of people that'll get mad if I don't include them..." Another thought crosses my mind. "Hey, Ed?"

His lips twitch with amusement. "Yes, darlin'?"

"Are you paid to flirt with the customers?"

He flashes a dirty grin and begins pouring a beer. "Are you?" He knows my job. I told him somewhere between the fourth and fifth drink.

"Well, it's not in the contract or anything, but the tips are usually better if I do."

He taps the bar in front of me. "Exactly."

I pout. "Am I a pity flirt, though? Do you flirt with the crotchety old Mrs. Burns, too, or do you think I'm a teensy bit hot?" I hold my fingers up to measure out a 'teensy' amount. "I don't want to be pitied."

"You're definitely hot, Tink. I'd do you in a heartbeat."

I flutter my lashes under his praise. "You would?"

"Definitely." He flicks his lip ring in a sexy, flirty way. "But not right now, sorry. I gotta go serve Mrs. Burns." He nods toward an old lady with too much lipstick, and I laugh so hard, I almost cry.

"Alright, Edgar. Go serve her, but come home to me, baby."

He laughs and walks away, and he definitely deserves to lose his job, because he left that sexy tequila bottle right near my lips.

Don't mind if I do.

I smell him before I see him, but I smile anyway, when the big sexy fighter sits in the stool beside mine.

I ain't mad. I love him.

"Want a drinking buddy?"

Turning in my seat, my legs slide into his and my eyes latch onto his sexy lips. "Hey, Leo. I missed you so fuckin' much."

His eyes scream a million words that I'm too drunk to understand. "I missed you, too, Sunshine. Wanna get drunk?"

"I'm *so* drunk already, but if you wanna catch up…" I push the bottle of tequila toward him.

JON

OOPS

*S*he's hammered.

Not quite *sleeping-on-the-floor-curled-up-beneath-a-stool* hammered, but hammered enough that she'd sleep *with* me on the floor if I asked.

Fuck, I'm tempted to ask.

I'm tempted to get down on my knees and beg.

Anything. I'll give her anything she wants, if she'd just always look me in the eyes the way she is right now.

She hasn't looked at me in weeks, *literally*, but right now, she stares into my eyes like she truly misses me and wants nothing more than to get lost inside me.

I wish.

"Want a drinking buddy?"

She smiles her pretty smile and my heart jumps in my chest. "Hey, Leo. I missed you so fuckin' much."

I love you, Casey! I love you with everything inside me. I love you so much that it literally hurts to breathe without you.

The game has changed since she walked away. There are no lines I wouldn't cross to get her back. No moral code. No history. Nothing. "I missed you, too, Sunshine." *I want you back!* "Wanna get drunk?"

She laughs and sways in her seat. "I'm *so* drunk already, but if you wanna catch up…" She pushes a three-quarters full bottle of tequila across the bar.

Nodding, I lean in close and take a deep breath of the cinnamon fragrance I've missed so much. Grabbing the tequila, I skip the first few glasses and simply bring the bottle to my lips. I'm catching up, and maybe the tequila will heal my heart the way it seems to have done for her.

"Oooh," she taunts playfully as I guzzle the burning liquid. "You're gonna be sick tomorrow, Jon Hart."

I smile bitterly when the liquid rolls down my throat. I'd rather a beer, but I'll ride this wave. "Not as sick as you, Sunshine."

"Bet I could drink more than you and not get sick."

She's about a hundred and ten pounds when soaking wet, and I'm more than twice that. "I'll take your bet." *Then I'll carry you to bed.*

"Hey, *Eddddgarrrrr.*" Cupping her mouth, she sing-songs across the bar and has a Scotch-lookalike turning toward us.

He looks at her – and laughs.

He looks at me – and swaggers toward us in challenge.

With suspicious eyes, he looks me up and down and wipes his hand on a dishrag looped through his belt. Stopping in front of Casey, he leans against the bar and brings his nose to almost touch hers. "Yes, darlin'?"

"Darlin'?" Standing from the stool, I imagine how good it would feel to tear his piercings out one by one. "You two know each other?"

Not stepping down from the challenge, Edgar stands tall and expands his chest the way Bobby does when his feathers are ruffled by someone he doesn't like. "Yeah. We know each other." His light eyes flicker. "Tink and I go way back."

Relief cleanses my body the way a heavy rain cleanses dirty streets. "You call her Tink?" He doesn't call her Casey. That means she didn't let him in.

He nods arrogantly. "She and I go way back. We're planning a joint birthday party and everything."

Casey snorts and sways dangerously to the side. Shooting an automatic arm out, I grab onto her shoulder and pull her back before she face plants on the floor.

"Yeah, *way back* to two hours ago and a d-and-m."

The dude leans close and whispers, "What's a d-and-m, darlin'? I'm not usually into those kinda clubs, but, well, you're awfully pretty…"

"Deep and meaningful…" She rolls her eyes. "Duh!"

Dismissing me like I'm not readying to rip his face off, he gets closer.

This is like Scotch and Club 188 again, but we're in a different state tonight, and these casinos are crawling with security and cops.

I'm not getting arrested today.

I'm not leaving her side.

"Casey, darlin'?"

She flicks her lashes and has me imagining slamming his ugly face against the bar. It would be so easy, just a simple tap to the back of his head. A quick slam would result in a shattered nose for him, and satisfaction… for me.

"Yes, Edgar?"

Edgar flicks his eyes toward me, then back to her. "Is he a rando dude? Do you need help, or do you know him? I can get security in for the meathead?" He pauses for a beat. "Blink once for *help*, blink twice if you're fine."

She snorts and sways on her seat. "Meathead!" She turns and throws her arm around my waist. I don't know if she's hugging me, or using me to stay vertical, but either way, her hands are on me and not fuckface-bling-boy. "He called you a meathead, Leo."

Edgar's eyes narrow. "Your name's Leo?"

I don't answer, I just let out a grunt in acknowledgement. I can be the 'meathead' caveman.

"He's okay, Ed. He's my *best* friend in the whole wide world." Brazenly, she presses a kiss to my ribs. "Except Kit!" She swings back to the bar. "I love her, too. But Leo, he's my best friend with a ding-dong. He's fly."

I bite my tongue to stop the laughter bubbling up. She thinks she's got swag.

She's a tiny fairy.

A tiny *white* fairy.

But she called me her best friend, and her hands are on me, so I can afford to cool my shit. "Yeah, *Ed*, I'm her best friend. I'm fly." I let my gaze track down the bar. "And you have thirsty customers, you may go."

He doesn't bother following my gaze. His eyes are for Casey only. "I'll be around. Shout if you need anything."

"It's alright Eddie. He won't hurt me." She sways and has me smiling prematurely. "I mean, like, he won't punch me in the face or anything. He breaks my heart a lot. It's like, a hobby of his."

Smile. Gone.

Ed glares for a moment longer, but his thirsty customers get impatient. He taps the bar and covers Casey's hand with his. "I'll be around."

She lets out a dramatic sigh and watches fuckface walk away, and her whimsical sigh has my molars grinding together. Is she watching him because she finds him attractive? Is she into *that* look? Because sure as shit, that's not what I look like.

Ed and that other fuckface, Scotch, have this trendy hipster thing going for them. But I'm just a *meathead* fighter whose creative ability begins and ends with thinking up new ways to choke someone out.

"So, Leo…"

Sitting back on my stool and holding her close, I look down into rainforest green eyes. I know she's drunk, but there's nothing I wouldn't do now. "How've you been, Case? I've missed you."

"Aww, Leo. I've missed you, too. You have no clue." She rubs her face on my chest the way a cat might their owner. "You make me so sad that you love Sonia more than you love me."

The pain in her slurred words has my heart squeezing. "Sunshine. That's not what you think it is. Sonia's not–"

"No, Leo. It's okay. I'm trying to be a grown-up about it. Plus," her lips move into a dramatic pout, "I really don't want to talk about her. She gets you and I don't. That ain't fair." She leans heavier against me. "Wanna do shots? I wanna get drunk."

"I think you are drunk, Case. Do you want me to take you back to your room? Just to rest, I promise."

Sitting up straighter, she stubbornly moves off me. "Nope. Not ready for sleep. My dreams always suck. I wanna get drunk."

Frowning, I bring her sad eyes back to mine with a finger under her chin. We're so close, her breath tickles my lips. "What do you dream about?"

"Mostly you."

"Yeah?" I move closer and luxuriate in the way her eyes stare into mine. "Good dreams, or bad dreams?"

"Mostly bad," she sighs. "Mostly about a sad little-boy-Leo."

Fuck!

I know what she's got in her head. I never wanted that for her! I never wanted that for anyone, which is why I never told a soul.

Not even Bobby knows.

"Sunshine. Can you look at me for a sec?" With that hand still under her chin, I bring her eyes back up. "Are you too drunk to listen?"

"Nope." She almost slides off her chair in her haste to act sober.

"Shit, okay, you're hammered. I wanna tell you something, okay? I want you to remember it, but don't worry, because I'll remind you tomorrow if I have to."

"You gonna tell me a secret, Leo? Like how best friends know secrets."

"Yeah, Sunshine. I'm gonna tell you a secret. Sonia and me—"

"No!" She smacks me on the chest. "Not Sonia! I don't wanna talk about the leggy blonde."

"Leggy blonde?" *Sonia's a sixty-three-year-old woman whose legs I've never seen.*

"She's probably beautiful, huh? And tall." Casey's eyes water. "Taller than me, anyway. Big tall guy like you deserves someone beautiful and tall like Sonia."

"Someone like Sonia?"

"Yeah," she slurs. "In my head, she looks like Tina. Sometimes I hate Tina for looking the way she does. Everyone's so tall and hot. Then there's me making the photos wonky and weird." She shrugs and sways. "But I love Tina, so I don't get mad for long." Her brows pull in. "I don't love Sonia, though. Nuh-uh."

"Sunshine, Sonia's my therapist. I've been seeing her for—"

"Since you've always known me?" Her tears finally spill over. "I was never enough, not even in the early chocolate-shit-Chewbacca-cake phase? I worked so hard on that cake, Leo."

"Can you stop talking for a sec?"

"No. You're making me sadder, Leo. You always make me sad."

"I'm not trying to, Case! I'm trying to explain that Sonia's my *therapist.* I want *more* with you. I've wanted more with you since the start, so I found a therapist that would help me offload some of my shit. My baggage used to only hurt me, so I carried it. But now it hurts you, so I'm trying to do better. I know I had a couple backslides recently—"

"Backslides?" She scoffs and sways dangerously. "You mean that time you thought I might be pregnant, so you told Bobby he could have it."

Fuccckkkk. "I'm sorry you heard that, Sunshine. I swear, I didn't mean it. I was just so scared." I pick up the tequila and chug a third of the bottle. I was supposed to be catching up, instead, I'm still sober, and she's getting sadder. "I didn't mean it, okay? I swear, I didn't mean it. I was scared, and I was being an asshole. It's my natural state, and I had a relapse." I take Casey's hand in mine. "Sonia, my ugly-elderly-not-tall therapist, has been trying to help me. I thought I was doing okay, but then you might've been pregnant, so I panicked. I was scared, but I was sorry as soon as I said it. Then I found you at the club, then that other shit happened... Then you were gone."

Finally, the tequila slides through my blood and softens the ache in my chest.

She's on to something here.

"I've been working with Sonia, Case. She's helping me understand. I don't *have* to perpetuate the cycle. I can have babies, and they can be perfect and beautiful and innocent, just like you. Bean's not like them, which means it's possible. If *you* make them with me, then it'll be okay."

"I can't, Jon." Big fat tears slide along pale cheeks. "I can't have babies, remember? Not only am I short and not blonde like Tina and Sonia, but my vagina doesn't work right. I'm all broken inside." Leaning across me, she snags the bottle and takes a hefty swig. "I need to be drunk to say this, mmkay? I love you, Jon. Like, the real, deep in my bones kinda love, so now that you know you're not a piece of shit, you can have all that stuff. You can make a family, you can be happy. The real kinda happy. Please don't marry Tina or Sonia."

Sitting up straight, she taps a fist to her chest and releases an inelegant burp. "And not Belle, either, since we're throwing out names from our shit-lists. Then there's this bitch, Melissa," she waves it off, "but don't worry about her. You don't even know her. *Godddd,* I hate her. And Tina's married, so she's not available to you, anyway. Can you believe she's married? Oh-emm-geee! Aiden Kincaid's married! Did you know he has booby rings?" Half excited, half green, her face turns sad. "I wish I was getting married by Elvis." She pouts. "Let's just get drunk, Jon. Give me one more night of Leo and Sunshine, then I'll help you plan the wedding of your dreams. I'll try to refrain from throwing a tin of paint at the whore's wedding dress. If she's lucky, I might not take the lid off, then I'll just swing and knock the bitch out."

I lean across the bar and snatch up shot glasses. "Are you sure, Case? You're already drunk as fuck. I'm not sure you can handle this."

"Line 'em up, Leo. I'm not sleeping tonight. Gonna squeeze every last second out of this while you're still mine."

"You want us? You want everything I can give you, tonight?"

"Uh-huh. I'm soaking this shit up before you leave me again."

"Can we be friends again tomorrow? Back to Leo and Sunshine?"

She shakes her head and has my stomach dropping. "I don't think so. Sunshine won't like your bimbo wife. Plus, I'm moving away soon."

My heart stops in my throat. "You're moving away? Where will you go?"

"I applied for a job in the city." She picks up a shot and tosses it back. Determined to keep up, I pour my own. "The city's not too far from Kit and Bean and the others, but far enough that I could fake car trouble when you invite me to your wife's baby shower."

"Have you heard back from this job?" She can't leave. I believe her; she'd only be an hour drive away, but she'd make it so I never saw her again.

"Not yet. I applied for three jobs. Two rejected me straight away. You'd think I'd be used to that now, huh?" She hits my arm like we aren't discussing her fragile heart. "But the other guys sent an email back and said they'd call me soon for an interview."

"But what about the rest of us? What about me?"

"I'll still see the girls. They'll visit me, and I'll visit them. Actually no," she mumbles. "I won't visit them, since you all live in each other's assholes. You'll be there, and it always hurts when I see you. But maybe I can visit the club. We can have girl's nights or something. So I'll see them, I just won't see *you*. And you'll be okay, because you'll have Melissa." She stops swaying and sneers. "Please don't marry Melissa."

I have no clue who Melissa is, but she's not the girl I'm marrying.

I eye off the remaining tequila and grin as the liquid sloshes in my belly.

She's swaying, and like dominoes, every time she leans into me, I lean a little too far into open airspace. My buzz feels pretty damn nice, which has me legitimately unsure if my heart feels better, or if the tequila's lying...

"Keep drinking, Leo. It helps, I promise."

"Casey?" I wait for her desperate eyes to meet mine. "What if I wanted to marry you? What if I wanted to make babies with you?"

"Aww, Leo." She brings her hand up to stroke beneath my eye. "You're just saying that 'cause you're drunk. Did you already forget my poon's broken?" She gasps dramatically. "Did you already forget about Sonia and Melissa? 'Cause, I ain't gonna lie, that makes me feel good."

"Are we good down here?"

My eyes snap up at the intrusion that has Casey's hand slipping away from my face. "Fuck off, Freddie."

"Oh, don't mind the cranky pants, Ed. He's got sand in his vagina, and he hasn't quite figured out how to live with the chafe yet. Can we get more tequila?" She pinches the bottle between three fingers and lets it dangle listlessly. "Ours musta leaked all over the floor or somethin'."

His light eyes narrow. "Jesus, Tink. Did you drink that whole thing? That's a lot of booze for a small chick."

"Ugh! I know I'm small, okay? I know I'm *'fun-sized'* and *'pocket-sized'* and all the other lame jokes tall people have meetings about. But no, *Edgar*, I didn't drink it all. Leo had about half, but he's a fighter and has better balance than me." Swaying dangerously, she demonstrates just how unbalanced she can be. "We just need another bottle, mmkay, thanks."

"Nuh-uh. Sorry, girl. I won't be responsible for you dying tonight. They'll probably already have to pump your stomach."

She turns on her pouty eyes. "But we have money."

He shakes his head. "Sorry. My parakeet died just this week. I can't take more grief so soon."

She turns on her smoldering eyes and flutters her lashes. "Pretty please, Edgar? We'll toast to your bird. She won't have died in vain."

I never realized how much she resembled an epileptic porcupine when flirting.

Biting back his smile, Ed side-eyes me, then looks back to Case. "No means no. Sorry, darlin'."

Whipping out a hand scarily fast, she snatches up the final three full shot glasses, downs two of them instantly, and slides the third across the bar until it rests against my hand. "It's on me, Leo. 'Cause I love you with all of my heart except the little bit that Kit owns. You suckers can stay here and talk girls, I'm going to dance."

Slipping off the stool, she stumbles toward the dance floor and has me standing to catch up.

"Hey, Leo?" Ed's hand comes down on my arm. "She really your best friend?"

I shrug and turn back to him. "She used to be."

"She mean something to you?"

"She means everything to me."

Tapping his knuckles against the bar, he shakes his head. "Right, well get her drunk ass off my bar and put her to bed before she's arrested."

I snap my gaze to the left; she's literally dancing *on* the bar and has dollar notes hanging in her skirt belt. "Fuck." Pushing away at Ed's laugh,

I stumble approximately seventeen steps too far to the left and come to the blaring realization that my half of the tequila bottle is laughing at me.

Pushing through the crowd of perverts, I grab her around the knees and throw her over my shoulder. Bringing my left hand up to shield her ass, I carry her out of the bar and toward the elevators.

She needs to go to bed before she does something she'll regret.

"Hey, Leo." She slaps my ass and has me coughing out a laugh. "Did you know Darth Vader can marry couples here, too? Just like Korean Elvis."

"No, Sunshine." I slap her ass, too, because it's right there and I've missed it. "I didn't know that." Like I was a child in Bobby's backyard again, like we've been spinning, and spinning, and spinning, I step three steps to the side, one forward, three more to the left, one more forward.

We'll get to the room in the next hour or three.

It'll be okay.

25

CASEY

WALK AND TALK

I dangle over Jon's shoulder and slap his jean covered butt. "Hey, Leo. Follow me!"

"Follow you?" he laughs. "Where? You're on my shoulder and facing backwards. You want me to turn around?"

He spins so fast, I have to swallow down – *swallow up?* – the impending tequila regurgitation. "Yeah." I concentrate on not vomiting. "Turn around. I wanna show you something."

"I think we should go to bed. You're *drunnnnk.*"

"I think you should put me down, I'm *siiiiick.*"

He laughs wildly, a carefree barking laugh that reminds me of good times we've had over the last two years.

Even covering my mouth to stop the sick, I smile.

Pulling me back over his shoulder, he slides my body down the front of his. I know the sneaky devil did it that way on purpose. He slid me over his thick thigh with the sole purpose to get a reaction from me, but I'm too damn drunk to lie to myself.

It felt *goooood.*

He throws a beefy arm over my shoulder and has my drunk knees momentarily buckling before I straighten out and carry his heavy ass.

"Come this way." I know I saw a sign a minute ago. I was upside down and turned around, but I bet if we walk on our hands and went backwards, we'd find it.

"Where you taking me, Sunshine?"

"We're gonna see Darth Vader."

He pulls me tight against his side. "That movie's not in the cinemas for *aaaages,* dummy. You think they got an early showing?"

"No!" I drunkenly roll my eyes and push him so we veer right. "Just trust me. This'll be fun."

"You know..." Swaying dangerously to the side, he almost falls and squishes me. "You should *never* trust someone that says trust me. It's like the bat signal for 'I *definitely* can't be trusted.' In fact, it probably means *you* have a Great Dane, and *I* have a dastardly plan."

I stop us in the main walkway of the casino floor and force people to walk around us. I stare up into his big beautiful eyes. "You don't trust me?"

"You?" He sways at the same time I sway, and since we're both smashed, we fall against a giant statue of... something. I don't even know what it is, but he has the face of a dog, a leaf covering his junk, and his leaf is almost in my mouth. "No, Sunshine. I trust you *impletely."* Frowning, he traps a plump lip between his teeth. "Expressly? Implessly? Exprisitly. *Fuck!"* He throws his hands up in frustration. "I'm an educated scholar, Casey! I know words. Fuck the English for making English so Englishy."

Laughing, I fall against his broad chest – my former pillow – and hold back a brand-new bout of grief. They just don't sell pillows like this. I've looked. "You're not a scholar, you dummy. You're a fighter with a big head and a *super*-big stubborn streak."

His hand comes down to cup my chin. "Is that why you won't love me? 'Cause I'm a dummy? I can go back to school, if you want. I graduated high school with honors, but I'll go back and get a degree. I'll be anything you want me to be."

"I don't want you to be anything, 'cept happy."

"You make me happy." He presses his plump lips against mine and has me sighing.

I've missed those, too.

"C'mon." I take his hand. "You still didn't let me take you where we're going. It's just 'round the corner here somewhere." *Damn this place for having so many corners.* "Aha!" I thrust my arm toward the statue in the middle of the walkway. "I found him!"

"You found Darth Vader?" He frowns like a grumpy old bear. "You really do have a crush on Anakin, huh? I don't like this shit, Casey. I should belt the fucker."

"Shhh!!!" My shush is *really* loud and has people stopping to look at us. "Spoilers alert, Jon! Not everyone knows Ani is Vader!"

"Sunshine…" He picks me up and throws me over his shoulder. I land against his solid muscle with a *thwump*, and clamping my lips shut, I work on not puking everywhere. "I think the whole world knows who Darth Vader is."

"Not everyone's as obsessed as you, Leo. Please put me down, we've got somewhere to be."

"Tell me where to go and I'll take you."

"Okay, my big strong Leo." Drunkenly sliding my hand along his back, I reach down and cup his ass. "Follow my pointer fingers."

He spins, then he spins again. "I can't see your hands!"

"I know, dummy! Cause you put me up here. Just walk backwards. I'll tell you left and right."

He laughs, and it almost sounds like a giggle. A *giggle* from meathead Jon Hart has me giggling, too. "That sounds super-duper dangerous."

"Are you scared, Leo? Lions don't get scared."

He slaps my ass and elicits a surprised squeak. "I'm not scared of falling. I'm scared of squishing you when I fall."

"I trust you, big boy. Walk backwards. Go straight for eleven paces."

"Eleven?" He laughs and bounces me. "How do you know how many *paces* I need? Are we pirates?"

"Yarrrr! Walk the plank you scallywag. No seriously," I snort when he slaps my ass again. "Walk. We don't have all night."

"But we do, Sunshine. We have *all* night." He hip thrusts and smacks my face with his returning ass.

"No, you idiot!" I rub my forehead where the metal stud on his jeans smacked me on the head. "The sign said we have until midnight. And don't ever do that again. It's embarrassing."

"You don't want me to hump the air?"

"Not right now, Jon. We'll have all night for that later. Then you can go to town with the hip thrusting. It'll be like the final Leo and Sunshine show. Make the fireworks go off, Leo. 'Cause after that, the curtains are closing on us. But first, we gotta go see Darth Vader. Turn left now." He turns right and comes within a hair of smashing my face into the wall. "Left! I said left!"

"Oops." He laughs and changes directions. "We just saw Darth Vader. He was back there, dumbass."

"Nope, we're going to say hey to the other one, but first we gotta see the fat lady. Have you got ninety-three bucks?"

"I knew you'd send me broke one day, Sunshine. It's been a ploy all these years, hasn't it?"

"Yeah." I slide my hand along his muscly back and hum appreciatively as the muscles pop and move when he walks. "It's been a ploy, Jon. My two-year long-game was to get my sticky hands on your ninety-three dollars."

It takes *hours* for Jon to walk backwards through the giant casino and reach the offices that the sign pointed us to. We stop at the desk with the old lady I saw earlier, and she looks up and sneers at my upside-down face. "Can I help you?" Her voice is nasally, like she's got a chicken bone stuck in there and now she's trying not to breathe in the rancid, rotten poultry.

"Yes, please," I giggle. "We'd like–"

Jon spins excitedly and almost slams my head against the desk. "We wanna get married. I have the hundred bucks, you can keep the change."

Shaking her head, she rolls her eyes. I know, because I'm peeking past Jon's ribs and poking my head near his armpit. He doesn't even smell. "You can't get married if you're intoxicated."

The nasally voice hurts my brain.

Jon shakes his head, and the momentum has him dangerously swaying to the side. "We're not drunk, Miss Posey."

She looks at me. "You can't get married if she can't even stand on her own two feet."

"No! She can stand. She just bein' lazy. Up we go." He slaps my ass and flips me over his shoulder, and right here, right now, I get how Evie feels when the guys *insist* on tossing her around. "Stand up straight, Sunshine."

He pulls me close to slow my swaying. "Oh!" I smile and stand on my tiptoes. When I'm still not even close to his ear, I grab his collar and yank him in half. "You should talk British!"

With a goofy smile, he pulls back to look into my eyes. "Huh?"

"It'll make you sound sober!" I look to the suspicious lady, then back to Jon. "Talk like a geezer, she'll *never* question your drunk-ness. It's brilliant!"

"Drunk-*ness*?"

"Just do it!" Jumping, I spin at the *'meh-meh'* sound coming from behind us. "They got a goat, Jon!" I reach out to pat its nose. "She's got a tiara! Oh my gosh, Leo. We should get a goat!"

"You can't bring those in here," Nasally Lady drones. "They might start chewing things."

"Can we get married, please?" Jon's voice turns wonderfully British and has me cackling and leaning against him. He sounds like *whatshisface* from Mary Poppins. "My fiancé and I have been planning this for months, you see. Do you know how many cups of tea I had to endure for this? Do you know how many scones and jam – *jam!* – I had to suffer through?"

She rolls her eyes and slaps a piece of paper onto the desk. "Fill out the paperwork. Drop your cash. Show me your identification. Blow into the breathalyzer." She slams a pen down on top, then rushes from behind her desk when the goat knocks down a vase of dusty fake flowers.

"Says we need ID," Jon murmurs with his accent. Bringing one hand up to cover an eye, he leans back and gives himself a double chin to read. "And says we can't be drunk."

"We're not drunk. We're British."

He flips his right leg up behind us and kicks me in the butt. "We're *not* British, and you most certainly *are* drunk."

"Most certainly." I giggle. "See, you even sound British. Or maybe that's your scholarly education. Either way, fill that shit out before it turns midnight."

"Why? You gonna turn into a pumpkin?"

"No, dummy. This office closes at midnight."

"Oh!" He giggles like a fool and picks up the pen. Filling out the forms with a flourish, he drops his credit card and our ID on top. "Goodbye, ninety-three bucks. When I was eight and hungry, you'd have been like winning the fuckin' lottery." He drunkenly presses a hard kiss to my temple. "Now, I'm not hungry anymore, but you're gettin' me a bride. That's even better than food."

Wrapping my arms around his hips, I lean in and press a kiss to his ribs. I'm so sad that he was ever hungry.

That's not fair. No kid should be hungry.

Distracting the lady when she mumbles about getting the breathalyzer out, Jon and I collect our license, we collect our papers, and we stumble out of the office and run to the Darth Vader chapel.

Storm Troopers patrol the front of the chapel and have me belly snorting, then Chewbacca steps outside and lights up a cigarette.

Excitedly snapping my hand from Jon's, I run up and throw myself at the furry fucker. My legs go around his furry waist, and his furry hands go straight to my ass. "Well, hey there, pretty lady."

In an instant, Jon wraps his arms around my hips and pulls me off. "There's still a guy in that costume, Sunshine. And my wife doesn't have permission to hug him."

"No!" Chewy pushes his Chewy head back to reveal an epic porn-stache. "She's fine, come back to Chewy, baby."

Jon angrily shoves him back. "Fuck off, asshole, you ain't invited."

"C'mon, bro. She's not your bride yet."

"Don't make me shove a light saber up your ass, man. I'll do it. I'll desecrate this icon, I'll ruin my favorite movie of all time. Don't touch her again."

Smoke and lights flash and blind us as we enter the chapel. Kesha's 'Tik Tok' blasts through the sound system, and the *'shoom shoom'* noises of a light-saber fight compete to deafen us.

Jon walks down the aisle with me still tucked under his arm, and I giggle, because I kinda need to pee and my buzz feels really good.

Darth Vader in all his glory meets us at the top of the aisle, Jon produces our certificate, then he sets me on my feet and steals the veil off the bride who went before us.

She doesn't even notice, since she's busy making out with a guy in a Storm Trooper costume *and* her new husband.

Vader's breathy voice moves through his mask, and I bite down on my giggles. I feel like a little kid in a giant toy store with a promise of ten minutes to pick anything I want.

"Do you guys have rings?"

Aww, man! I forgot about rings.

Tipping his chin toward a jewelry case against the far wall, Jon shakes his head. "No, but I wanna see what you've got in that cabinet over there."

Solemnly and in perfect character, Vader nods his head. "Come this way, sir." Then he drops *Vader* and picks up *salesman*. "We take cash or credit card. We have rings that range from these seventy-three-dollar silver bands, right up to these themed rings at twelve-thousand each, but they come with real diamonds."

Finding the exact set he wants, Jon grins like a kid on Christmas morning. "We'll take those. Let's get this show on the road."

26

JON

CONSUMMATE

"*P*lease, watch your head."

Shouldering the driver back when he steps in to help Case into the hot-pink stretch limo, I take her hand in mine and help her slide in. I step in close to shield her creamy thighs as her skirt rides up, but her new wedding shirt is big enough it hides everything, anyway.

Our faces, drunk, and making out just after the *'I do's'* are printed onto her white shirt and stretched over her luscious boobs.

My trucker hat, pulled low over my eyes, has the same blurry picture.

Best fucking hat in the world.

We climb into the limo – *stumble in* – and we sit down – *fall down* – then the driver slams the door, enters the front, and starts the engine. "Where to, Mac?"

"Just lap, *Mac*. And close the partition." He rolls his eyes and flips the switch, but I don't give a shit if he's unhappy, because I'm drunk, *I'm* happy, and I'm hitched to the girl of my dreams. "You. Come here."

Lifting her from the seat, Casey giggles as I pull her into my lap and settle her over my cock. She throws her arms around my neck instantly, then presses her lips to mine like it's our first drink after a drought.

Her tongue darts out to play with mine, and my hands slide along her every curve. She's mine now. I'll make her happy. I swear, I'll never let her regret this. "I love you, Sunshine."

"Mmm." Her hands come up to cup my face. "I always loved you, Leo. Don't break my heart tonight, okay?"

"Never again." I pull her down onto my dick and groan when she grinds against me. "I'll never break your heart again, Sunshine. I promise. Never again."

"Can you make love to me tonight, Leo? I've missed you so much."

"Yeah." I lean forward and trap her bottom lip between mine. "I'll make love to you every night for the rest of our lives. We promised forever."

She purrs and comes down to nibble on my neck.

"Are you going to remember this tomorrow?"

Am I going to remember this tomorrow?

Nodding and biting my neck, she soothingly slides her tongue along the hurt. Casey; the soothing balm to my heart, to my body. The soothing balm to my soul.

"When we wake up tomorrow," I begin. She grinds her core down over my cock and derails my focus. Sliding my hands beneath her skirt, I almost weep at the bare skin. "When we wake up tomorrow," I try again. "I'm keeping you, okay? Forever and ever."

"Mmhmm." She brings her mouth back over mine and scrambles my brains. Biting my lip, she pulls back and looks into my eyes. "I've always been yours, Jon. I'll always be yours. Please be kind to my heart tonight." Latching her mouth to mine, she tears my hat off and tosses it to the floor, then her hands come down between us and works at my zipper. "Undo these."

A small niggle in the back of my brain *screams* that fucking in the back of a seedy limo isn't *making love.* This isn't good enough for our wedding night. She's better than that, she's worth so much more, but I'm still drunk, and she's sitting on me and undoing my pants.

"Help me, Jon." She moves onto her knees and fumbles with my pants. Lifting my hips, we work together to push my jeans over my hips.

The fresh night air hits my dick. I hiss.

I'm so close to being inside her again.

Standing over me so her head and neck are bent and restricted by the car ceiling, she reaches under her skirt and pulls down the most divine pair of white underwear I've ever seen.

"White for my wedding!" Giggling, she slides the lace over her ankles and catches them on her heels. Balancing her with one hand on her hip, I

222 | EMILIA FINN

take her panties in the other and help her get them off. Slumping back into my lap, I groan at her fiery hot skin touching mine.

"Kiss me, Casey."

"Yeah." Fusing her lips to mine, she grinds her core down over my solid length and has my hips lifting each time she does. Like a magnet, I follow her. I don't want to be separated.

Her hand comes down between us and has me groaning into her mouth as she wraps me in her palm.

"*Fuccckkkk,* Case. I've missed you."

"Mmm." Lifting her hips, she maneuvers me until the tip of my cock sits at her fiery opening. Her mouth leaves mine for a moment, and her bright green eyes lock onto mine. I could almost believe we were sober, with the steadiness of her movements, the intensity of her gaze, but then I'm rendered thoughtless when she slides down over me.

Like a long-awaited homecoming, we sigh and pause to enjoy the sweetness that only *she* has ever been able to provide for me.

I could take this moment to imagine my life is all fixed. I could stop and pretend this is the beginning of a sweet marriage that'll never hurt us again, but then she rests her hands on my shoulders, lifts to my very tip, then drops.

"Ah!" Like a starving man, I lean forward and take her neck between my teeth. My hands move to her top – the sparkly sexy tank that shows off her pretty tits, plus our new wedding shirt over top – and I pull them both up and off.

I'm greeted with lace that matches her panties, and grinning like a drunken fool, I tug the cups down and feast on her nipples. Pulling them between my teeth, she pants and moves at a feverish pace over top of me.

She rides me, uses me, slams down over me and hungrily swallows my cock in fast strokes. Lifting her up, slamming her down, I help set the pace until I'm ready to explode inside her.

"Casey."

"Yeah," she groans on the next downward slam. "Love me, Leo."

"I do love you, Sunshine. Forever."

We're let out in front of our hotel, and still riding that amazing buzz we've been on, especially since we found wine coolers in the mini fridge, Casey and I stumble up to my room on the thirty-third floor.

Thirty-third!

Now who's ballin', assholes?

Not a poor kid anymore!

The whole family is staying on this floor, so we work hard to tiptoe in silence as we pass their doors, but in reality, we're giggling fools as we trip on the carpet and hold each other up.

For such a tiny girl, she does a good job of not letting me fall on my face. My beautiful, sweet wife. She's never let me fall before.

I don't know why I was so fuckin' scared.

With her mouth latched on mine, and my hands holding her close, we stumble into my room and throw our clothes to the floor in seconds.

She climbs my now naked body like the most skilled Jane, and I walk us across the room until we fall to the softest bed I've ever lain on in my life.

I make love to my wife until the sunlight filters through the floor to ceiling windows, and when I finally let her sleep, I stumble out of bed like a wounded soldier.

I've just gone to war. For months, I've been in the trenches, but now I finally win. I finally have her back.

Stumbling to the desk across the room, I noisily dig through the drawers until I find hotel stationery.

I hum the tune I've dedicated just for my Sunshine, and I sit my ass down to write the most important letter I'll ever have to write.

I refuse to forget tonight.

I refuse to risk her.

"Dear, Jon. LOL!! Do you get it? Don't worry." I gleefully turn to look at my hot wife as she starfishes our marital bed. *"Your dick is still gansta, bruh! FYI, Asshole. Her name is Casey HART, now.* ~~*Your.*~~*"* Scratch that. *"You're happy about it! Don't fuck* ~~*ot*~~ *it up! Go make love to your wiffffe, and don't call it* _fucking_*! She's better then (than?) that! Giddyup! Make her happy. Catch ya later, muthafucker."*

Even as drunk and stupid as I am, I know this is the most important day of my life.

I have a track record for fucking this shit up and hurting her.

I won't make the same mistakes again. I'll be the man she swore her life to. She's wearing my ring, and I have a certificate that declares her last name will soon be replaced with mine.

The Hart name *won't* die out with me.

We're just getting started.

Stumbling back to my girl, I pull her over my chest and bury my face in her hair. For the first time in a month, I go to sleep with a smile on my face.

———

What feels like only three minutes later, I wake to a cold bed, a missing wife, and the phone blaring in my ear.

Sluggishly crawling across the bed and reaching for the phone, I frown when the familiar name flashes across the screen. "Hello?" I clear the sandpaper from my throat. "Mom?"

"Jon, honey. Good morning!"

Bringing my hand up, I press my palm to my eyes. "Hey." Bean and Evie flash through my mind and have me sitting up taller. "You okay? Are the girls okay?"

"We're okay, baby. But you need to get out of bed right now. Find Casey. Run!"

27

CASEY

RUN AWAY

*S*lipping out of Jon's suite as silently as I can, I tiptoe down the hall and hold my breath as I pass the guys' rooms.

I have to get out of here. Now.

I'm going to the airport, I'm flying to the closest lawyer's office, and I'm taking care of my life before Jon wakes up and breaks my heart all over again.

I can't take any more of his hurt.

I literally cannot be here when he wakes up and sees what we've done. He'll get mad. He'll get *pissed!*

I can't take it anymore.

I can't survive him shouting about how he refuses to be with me.

"Good morning."

I jump with a strangled squeak at the voice behind me. Squeezing my eyes shut, I turn to my sort-of mother-in-law and try not to die of mortification as she watches me do the walk of shame.

I even have the cliché shoes in my hands.

And let's not forget the missing panties.

"Um." I brush my hair behind my ear, then bend to put my shoes on. I can't stand in the hall without shoes. In front of *this* woman. The woman who is essentially my... *husband's* mother. "Good morning, Mrs. Kincaid."

"Mrs. Kincaid?" Arrogantly, she leans against the door jamb to her room and crosses her arms. Her door remains open, and the girls giggle and chatter from within the suite.

I already miss those boogers.

And I'm applying for jobs out of town.

"You know I want you to call me Nelly. You're going to marry my Jon someday."

I groan and pray she has no clue what actually went down last night. Instinctively, I fling my arms behind my back, and still half drunk, fumble to pry the damn ring from my fat finger.

I don't know how we got it on, but it refuses to move over my swollen knuckle.

Nausea rolls in my stomach for every second the ring won't budge. My eyes are gritty like I rubbed them in sand for fun, and my stomach sends loud warning signals that it's about to erupt like Mount Vesuvius. For every second I stand with Nelly, new pockets of memory unlock from last night.

Sex in a car.

Dancing on bars.

Scotch – the person, not the drink.

Tequila… definitely the drink.

I'm pretty fucking sure Chewbacca got down on his hands and knees and bleeped like a goat.

Jesus. Was I stoned?

"So…" Oblivious to my emotional breakdown, Nelly grins. "Where are you going, Tink?"

Fresh and far too chipper for the morning after a night in this city, I internally begrudge this woman her smiling eyes, her ironed pants, her lean shoulders and styled hair.

I want to scream at her smug questions.

I want to cry that she gets to be so fresh this morning, when I feel rotten *and* in need of a lawyer.

"I'm just going to my room."

"Oh?" She looks me up and down and leaves me as vulnerable as Jon does. "You're just getting in?"

I hate her guts. "Yeah. I, uh–"

"You stay in Jon's room?"

"Nelly," I groan. "Can we not?"

She laughs playfully. "He's handsome, huh?"

Goddddd. "Don't do this."

"I've known Jon since he was about six years old, did you know that? I know you're always at each other's throats, but I like it."

She pops her head into her room as Evie cackles and something goes *thump!* but no tears, means Nelly's eyes come back to mine.

"Jon doesn't get wound up often..." She smiles wistfully. "He was such a quiet kid. Always so watchful and wary. He didn't trust anyone, not even me or Bry. But when *you* are sending him crazy, because you need to be bailed out of jail, or carried out of a fight..." Her eyes soften. "Your fire makes him smile, sweetheart. You make my son smile, which makes you one of my favorite people in this world."

She's killing me. "Okay. Uh..." I turn and get ready to sprint. "I have to go for now, but I'll see you–"

"Are you going to be at breakfast?" She checks the gold watch on her petite wrist. "These girls won't last much longer, so we'll be heading down soon. We'll see you there, right? Evie's been asking after you."

Damn her for using Bug against me. "Yeah, I'll be down soon." That was probably a lie. I want to see Evie, but I can't face the family over coffee and eggs.

"Oh, and Casey?"

I let my head hang. *Just let me go already!* "Yes, Nelly?"

"Don't break his heart, okay? He's fragile."

God, she has no clue! It's not Jon's heart that's constantly breaking.

"Okay. I'll see you later."

"Alright, honey. I have to make a call, anyway."

As soon as she closes herself back in her suite, I sprint toward my door twenty feet down the hall. Swiping my access card, I run inside and slam the door.

What the hell have I done?

I run to my bathroom and stop in front of the mirror. "Oh my God!" It's bad. Really bad!

My hair points in six billion directions. My mascara's smudged so bad, I look like a rabid raccoon. And the hand holding my face *still* has that Star Wars ring!

Motherfuck!

I pump soap into my hands and spin the silver. More soap. More spinning. It keeps catching on my knuckle.

What the fuck!

Did he have the ring made *around* me?

"Come on. Come on. Come on." I pump more soap and run my hands under the water to create more suds. "Come on, you little bitch. Come on! Fuck!"

The ring *refuses* to move over my knuckle, and every time I try to force it, causes my knuckle to redden and swell.

Slamming the tap off and bracing my hands on the edge of the counter, I concentrate on my breathing before I kill myself with a panic attack.

Somehow, I've gone from heartbroken and wanting more, to now being married.

Married!

He's going to wake up soon, and he's gonna be pissed.

He doesn't even have to speak; just one single look, one single glare, and he'll break me.

Did he get blackout drunk, too?

Maybe he doesn't remember.

If I never tell him, maybe he'll never have to know.

I can keep the secret and work out how to divorce quietly. Or better yet, since signing those divorce papers will for sure alert him that something's up, maybe I'll just pretend it never happened, too.

I won't ever try to get married again, and he screams every chance he gets that he's never marrying. So maybe I can just pretend nothing happened.

He can find out in my will, and by then, it won't matter.

Fuck!

Rushing out of my bathroom and toward my suitcase on my still-made bed, I groan. *I should've slept in this bed last night. Not Jon's!*

"Sunshine!"

I jump at Jon's angry voice and his thumping on my door.

He's angry. He knows! He already knows!

Silent as a dead mouse, the only sound I make is the thundering of my heart as I stare at the door and wait for him to go away.

"Sunshine! I know you're in there. I can *feel* you freaking out."

Fuck him.

"Dammit, Jon! Why're you bitching this early? Some of us are trying to enjoy a baby free sleep in!"

Fuck off, Jim!

"Casey's in her room," Jon answers casually. "She won't let me in."

"Tink!" *Thump-thump-thump.* "Open the damn door and let him. I want another hour with my wife!"

"Can y'all shut up out here? Jesus. It's the weekend."

"Tina!" Jon's voice escalates. "Get her out here. Use your girl powers and get her ass out here."

"Tink! Do you wanna come out?"

Nope. Definitely not.

"She's not even answering, dummy! How do you even know she's in there?"

"She's in there," he murmurs against the door. The deep vibration of his voice rumbles inside *my* chest.

Stepping away from my bags, I tiptoe to the door and press my cheek against the timber. Closing my eyes, I can almost imagine it's his chest I'm resting against.

"Open the door for me, Sunshine." His voice slides over me like a tender hug. He's only tender because he doesn't know. He's just coming off a night of a fuck-marathon. That always cheers him the hell up, but once he remembers... once those pockets of memories unlock...

"What the hell are you idiots doing out here?"

Could this get any worse? No, it probably couldn't.

"B! She locked me out!"

"Well, what did you do to piss her off?"

"Nothing! I swear."

"Alright, you bunch of idiots." Nelly's voice moves down the hall, then Evie's peel of laughter has my stomach dropping. *Yes. It could get worse.* "Go back to your rooms. Jon, take your business out of the hallway."

"I can't, Momma! She won't let me in."

"So maybe she's not there. Or maybe she's pooping." *Oh. My. God.* "Either way, be quiet. You're waking everyone up."

My phone vibrates in my hand and has me jumping a foot into the air.

Kit's name flashes and demands I answer.

She knows I'm hiding.

She's not as dumb as the hallway people...

If I answer, I can't lie to her anymore. I've been lying for years; my way of protecting her. I couldn't unload my shit on her when her life was going to shit. When her dad was dying, when her brother was a prick, when she was being hospitalized, on her wedding day... It was never the right time to tell her, and now here we are, with a mountain of untruths between us.

I need my best friend back.

I need to unload.

I need to share the weight.

Sliding my hand across the green icon, I bring the cell to my ear. "Hello?"

"Tink, you okay?"

"Yeah." I barely whisper, because Jon's only half a foot from me, and I'm not ready for him to know I'm not pooping.

She laughs softly. "Are you hiding from Jon?"

I nod and stare at my left hand. "Uh-huh."

"Did you sleep with him last night?"

I groan. "I'm actually not sure. But I think so. It's probably best to say yes."

"Damn," she laughs. "How much did you drink?"

"I honestly don't remember. I think I saw a Star Wars movie last night." *And I got married.*

"You're so strange." She laughs lazily. It almost sounds like she's lying back on her bed. "Why are you hiding?"

"Is Bobby with you?"

"No. He's still in the hall with his idiot brothers."

God, I love her. "I have... *stuff* to tell you."

She squeaks and, no doubt, shoots up in bed. She thinks this is exciting. "Tell me!"

"Can you get rid of Jon, then bring Iz and Tina, too? May as well do this in one shot."

"Holy shit. What did you do?"

"Just come. And bring orange juice. I think my liver's legitimately dead."

"Alright, we'll be there in five."

"You need to get rid of Jon. And don't bring Nelly!"

"Don't worry, I'll take care of it. I'll get Bobby to clear the hall."

"Don't tell him anything, just tell him to get rid of Jon."

She laughs. "What's there to tell? I don't even know what you did! Don't sweat it. I'll be there in five."

"Alright. I'll see you soo–"

"Hey, baby?" Kit turns on her flirt. "Wanna see my boobs?"

"Fuck yeah!"

Laughing, she comes back to the phone. "See you in a few, Case."

Hanging up and shaking my head, I press my forehead to the door and wait.

"Sunshine! Fuck off, B! Casey, open the door for me."

I knew this was coming.

I knew he wouldn't go easily.

"Jon, let's get breakfast." Bobby and Jon scuffle in the hall, and tears spring to the surface and blind me.

"No!" He hits Bobby. I can literally hear the exact thump his fist makes when it connects with Bobby's chest. "Casey, open the fucking door!"

"Jon!" Aiden's voice booms down the hall. "You've got nieces listening to your potty mouth. Pull your head out and get away from her door. Take a hint; she doesn't wanna see you."

My tears slide free as a brand-new coat of guilt layers over my heart.

"Tink, it's us. Open up."

"Is Jon there?"

"I'm here, Sunshine! Open the damn door."

"Jon!" Kit snaps viciously. "Bobby, take him to breakfast, please."

"I got it, baby. We'll see you in twenty."

Silently, I open the door and peek out, but when my eyes lock with his, Jon jumps from Bobby's arms and races right for me.

I step back in and fist the door handle to swing it closed, but Jim steps in Jon's way, and like two boulders clashing, they meet with a boom and Jon fights to move past him.

This is a mess.

He doesn't even know what the hell happened, but it's already a mess.

Tina and Kit squeeze through the gap in my door, then Izzy walks in next with Bean already suckling at her breast.

"Sit." Kit takes my hand and drags me across the room. "Talk right now. I thought this was gonna be cute and fun." She points toward the hall. "*That* wasn't cute or fun."

I sigh, but instead of sitting, I take my toiletries bag and start unpacking in front of the mirror. I need to work on my makeup. I need to clean myself up, then I need to run away.

"Actually, no," she snaps. "Who the hell is Sunshine?"

I wipe away raccoon makeup and spilled tears in one swipe. "I'm Sunshine."

"Jon calls you Sunshine?"

I nod. "He does. He's called me his Sunshine since... well, forever."

"True." Stroking Bean's face, Iz sits on the corner of my bed. "I already knew that. He's said it a billion times."

Kit turns to Iz. "Why didn't you tell me?"

She shrugs. "I didn't know it was a secret. It's just a name I've heard a million times."

"So he calls you Sunshine." Kit turns back and meets my eyes in the mirror. "That feels weird. I didn't even know you guys had a pet-names type of relationship."

Letting my head fall back, I groan and breathe through my nose. "There's a lot you don't know, Kit. We have a lot of stuff to cover." *Before I disappear and go into WITSEC.*

Her eyes narrow. "What don't I know?"

I turn away and lean against the counter. I watch Kit watch me with suspicious eyes, then I turn to a silent Tina, then finally Izzy.

She was the sister that I essentially lived with for months. She knows Jon and I had *something.*

Gathering my bravery, I finally bring my eyes back to Kit. "There's... a lot. I don't even know where to start."

Her brow lifts dangerously. "How about you start at the start."

She's already angry. It doesn't even matter *what* she doesn't know. Just the fact that there are any secrets at all hurts her. "Alright. Um... Jon's been my *other* best friend since the Hernandez fight."

"Okay...?"

"Like, *best friend* best friend. Actual, real friends."

She watches me warily. "I thought you guys were just..." She shrugs. "You know... Sex."

I shake my head. "We didn't even have sex until after your attack."

"My attack...?" Her eyes widen. "In December?"

I nod.

"That was, like, six months after the Hernandez fight."

"Uh-huh."

"But you were all over each other!" She frowns in thought. "I actually kinda assumed you'd hooked up that first night. Maybe even that night at 188. I saw you talking to him at the bar."

Great impression I've left on my best friend. *Talking to a guy at the bar, in her mind, means we hooked up.* "Yeah, well, we didn't. But we did go on a date." I smile at our ten-minute date, which to this day, is still my best date. "He and I were just friends...." I prepare myself for one of the doozies I'm unloading today. "Somewhere in that first six months, I fell in love."

As expected, Kit chokes and looks at me with new eyes. "Love? Like, how I love Jimmy and Aiden, or *love* love, like how I love Bobby?"

"Love love, the kind that tears your heart out when the other person doesn't love you back."

Iz's eyes narrow. "But he *did* love you! I heard him say it a hundred times."

Kit turns on the bed. "He did? Jon Hart?" She points at the hall. *"He said he loves her?"*

I cross my ankles and look at the floor. "He's been telling me he loves me since... well," I shrug. "Possibly even before you and Bobby told each other the same thing. But he said he loves me like he loves B."

"But you love him more?"

I nod. "I've loved him for a long time. But he doesn't want me. Not the way I need to be wanted."

Iz shakes her head. "No, that's not–"

I shake my head and cut her off. "So when you said I was settling for Jon's scraps that time–"

Kit's eyes turn sad. "I'm sorry I said that."

I shrug easily. "It was true, though. You hit the nail on the head, which is why I was such a bitch about it. I was definitely settling." Shrugging, I carefully choose my next words, the next step of my story. "Um, anyway, reverse a little. Iz knows this bit... I was basically living with Jon for the longest time. It was never official, but I was at Iz and Jon's house pretty much every night for a full six months."

Iz nods. "Truth. We shared hair straighteners more than once."

"What?" Kit snaps. "This is big news! Why didn't you tell me?"

Iz shrugs. "I honestly didn't give it much thought. Like the name thing, I didn't think it was a secret." She turns to me with sad eyes. "You were there, then you weren't. After Kit's attack, you ditched and never came back."

I brace for the next part. "Yeah. I have a giant secret."

"Oh, God." Kit's eyes turn sad. "This isn't a good secret. This is bad. This is a really bad secret."

I swipe away a tear for my baby.

"What happened?"

"We had sex late in December. For the first time."

Kit nods. "Okay."

"Early February, I was really sick."

Now it's Iz's turn to nod. "I remember that. You looked awful. You were vomiting a lot. Then you disappeared."

Kit's hand comes up to cover her mouth. "Casey."

I nod. "I was pregnant with Jon's baby."

"No!" Iz snaps. She looks around the room like I've been hiding an infant this whole time.

"There's no baby here now," Tina murmurs sadly. "This isn't a fun announcement."

Tears slide over Kit's cheeks.

I draw in a shaky breath. "There's no baby anymore." I look down at my feet, because the pain is still as fresh today as it was back when it happened. "My pregnancy was ectopic. That day I went to the doctor because I was sick, he made me pee in a cup, just in case. I was pregnant, but it wasn't viable." I swallow down a choking sob. "I was terrified to tell Jon."

"Why were you terrified?" Kit asks. "He would've taken care of you."

I laugh humorlessly.

"I mean," she amends. "I know what he said after the alleyway thing, but—"

"Oh, God." Izzy looks up with tears in her eyes. "You never told him, did you?"

"About the ectopic?" I shake my head. "No, I didn't tell him… Not at first, anyway. He found out eventually, but there's more before we get there."

Kit rubs soothing circles on the tiny bump that's only just starting to form. She probably doesn't even realize she's doing it, but the lance across my heart still burns, because I'll never have that.

I'll never carry a baby.

"The baby was ectopic." I take a deep breath. "They took it out that day, but they also took my tube. I only have one left, and it's pretty badly scarred."

"What's that mean for you?" Iz asks.

"It means… I'm probably never having babies in the future."

Kit's eyes fire with hurt. "You had a miscarriage, you had surgery, and you didn't tell us? You didn't ask for help?"

"Well, not a miscarriage—"

She frowns and has me swallowing my words. "You *lost* your baby, Case. Don't split hairs over this shit."

I sigh and go back to watching my feet. "Yes, I lost my baby. I lost Jon's baby. I didn't tell you, because you had *literally* just come out of the hospital. You were weak and sick. I didn't want to unload on you."

"You're an asshole!" she snaps. "You should've told me!"

The hurt bubbles in my stomach. "Yeah, well I couldn't, okay? My heart was broken, like literally, I swear I could feel it being torn open and emptied out. I couldn't talk about it."

"Jon went missing that week, too," Iz murmurs. "He said he was with you…"

I nod. "Yup. I tried to run away, but he followed. I tried to hide, he found me. I hated him, Iz." A lone tear slides along my cheek. "He wouldn't leave me alone. I was grieving, and I had to make up a bullshit story about fibroids just to get through."

"He looked after you after you lost your baby. *His* baby!" Tina emphasizes. "And he didn't even know?"

"Nope. He didn't know. I was so scared to tell him. I tried to. I tried a bunch of times, but it was never the right time. I was so deep in my own grief, I couldn't see the light… until I could. Then you happened, Iz. Bean happened."

"Oh my God."

"He was so fucking mad. He was mad that you could be so *irresponsible*." Her eyes spill over. "Don't worry about it, he's over it now. He adores his niece. But back then, he wouldn't fucking shut up about it." I clutch at the countertop behind me. "Every time I considered telling him, he practically took out a skywriter and reminded me how he'd *never* have kids. How he'd *never* marry."

I sigh. "So then I had choices to make. I was unable to have babies. I'd never be that woman again, but I still loved Jon. My Leo," I whisper to myself. *My lion.* "I still loved him. I always loved him. So I put on my brave face and pretended everything was fine." I take a deep breath. "He was learning to love Bean. He was doing his best to support her, but every day was the same; in his left hand, was his love for Bean, and his right hand, his hatred for the thought of having his own family someday."

"So you spent the better part of two years sleeping with the man you're in love with," Kit asks, "but he thinks you're just a casual thing?"

Iz shakes her head. "No–"

"Yes."

"No!" she snaps. "You were *never* casual to him, Tink. Yes, he's a stubborn ass, and yes, he yammers on about never marrying or having kids, but you were never casual to him. He *loves* you."

I nod. "Yeah, he loves me. He told me a million times. He loves me like he loves the rest of you guys. I'm his friend. Hell, I'm his *best* friend. But he doesn't love me the way I need him to."

Unlatching Bean, Iz cuts me down with a glare. "I wouldn't bet on that."

I shrug. "I spent the year sleeping with Jon sometimes, and running home to cry when he spent the night with someone else."

"No!" Iz snaps again. "I don't believe he hooked up with other women. I know you said he does, but I don't believe you. And I don't believe you've hooked up with others, either. You said you did, but I think you're full of shit. A woman in love doesn't do that."

I smile at the floor. "Well, I can't speak for Jon, but no, I haven't hooked up with anyone else. I lied when I said that."

"Mmhmm." Iz does her smug *'I told you so'* eyes.

I roll mine. "So anyway, I've been cheating on you, Kit. I've had a different best friend for two years, and I never told you."

"I still can't see it," she murmurs. "I mean, of course *something* was going on. Anyone with eyes could see you're into each other. We see the way you touch, or the way you *didn't* touch when you were mad at each other. We all *knew*, but we left it alone for the most part." Her eyes narrow. "*Best* friends? Like, does he know you the way I know you?"

I nod. "Pretty much. Our first six months was literally just hanging out over takeout and movies. That's a lot of time to talk."

"Does he know about Todd?"

"Who the hell is Todd?" Iz snaps angrily.

I want to smile. *She's her brother's proxy in his absence.*

"Todd's my ex. He was a piece of shit, but yes, Jon knows about Todd. Actually, I told him about Todd the first night we met."

"Really?" Kit smiles. "That's surprising."

"Yeah, I dunno." I shrug and think about the Jon and Casey from that first night. "Somehow, he always got me to talk... except the baby thing."

"Yeah." Her smile disappears. "Except the baby thing." She frowns. "Are you okay, Case? I mean, that's not a small deal."

"Honestly?" A hot tear slides from the corner of my eye. "No, I'm not okay. I'm a damn mess. I can't have the man I want, and I can't have the babies I want. I'm just me, with a heart that's been stomped on so many times, I'm not sure I'll ever be okay again." I take a deep breath. "People can heal from a broken heart, most people. But I don't think I can. I think there's just too much damage."

"You could have IVF," Tina provides softly. "Your tube issue... There are specialty doctors for that sort of stuff."

"Yeah, but Jon doesn't want kids, anyway. He doesn't want kids or marriage–" I stop on a groan and throw my head back. My hungover brain totally forgot about the whole point of this meeting. "There's more."

"What more?" Izzy demands.

"What more, Casey?" Kit's eyes narrow dangerously. "What's the rest?"

"Umm." I finger the folded certificate behind my back. "Something happened last night. Something big."

"You and Jon hooked up again." Tina rolls her eyes. "We know. The whole damn city knows. You were stumbling down the hall about three a.m. You weren't quiet."

The blood drains from my face. "Really?"

"Uh-huh. I heard you." She nods knowingly. "And I don't just mean the stumbling thing."

"No!"

She flashes a filthy grin. "Yes."

"Oh, please!" Iz smacks Tina's leg. "There's a reason you were awake and listening to her. I heard *you* still celebrating your nuptials, Little Miss Southern Charm. Did Aiden visit the South last night, Mrs. Kincaid?"

"No!"

Kit cackles. "Um, yes. I was awake at three, too, you bunch of horn-bags. You're gross."

I honestly don't know if I heard anything, but Izzy's serious eyes drag me back in an instant. "What happened? What's the *more?*"

Attempting one last time to rip my ring off – even at the expense of my finger, Kit's eyes flip to my arms... then they pop wide. "Oh my God. What do you have behind your back?"

"Nothing?"

"Don't you lie to me. You're standing in front of a mirror, dumbass! Oh my God!" Jumping up quickly, she snatches my arm and takes my left hand in hers. "What did you do?"

Bending to the floor, Iz picks up the dropped certificate and unfolds it in shaking hands. "You got married?"

"You got married!" Kit shouts.

I slap my hand over her mouth and turn to the door. "Jesus! Can you shut up?"

"You got married?" Her eyes are a million times louder than her words. "What did you do?"

Letting my arm drop to the side, I groan. "I don't know! I just woke up like this."

"This is a marriage certificate, Tink!" Izzy waves the paper like I don't know what she has. "It says your name. Jon's name. Your signatures!"

"Thank you, Captain Obvious." I snatch the paper away. "Now I have to figure out how to get a divorce before Jon finds out."

"What do you mean *before* he finds out?" Iz snaps. "He signed the damn certificate. I'm pretty sure he knows."

"Well, I mean, I legitimately don't remember it actually happening." Nope. I definitely don't remember the goats, the British accents. Darth Vader. *Oh God.* "I was hoping maybe he has a similar black spot on his brain."

"He's twice your size! He'd have needed gallons of alcohol before he forgets."

"Just roll with it, okay! You need to get me out of here. I need a lawyer. Yesterday."

"No." Tina grins. "You need breakfast."

"You've lost your damn mind, woman!"

"No," she laughs. "I'm not joking. You're probably right. He doesn't remember. If he did, he would've already said something in the hall. We're rolling with the blackout theory. Breakfast will be fine, then when we get home, we'll fix this. Don't run out right now; Evie told me how she wants to eat pancakes with you. If you ditch, one: it'll raise suspicion, and two: you'll upset my daughter. Then I'll be forced to punch you in the face."

I groan. "Why's everyone using Evie against me?"

"Because it works. Come on." She takes my hand. "Breakfast time. I promise not to spill the beans to your *husband.*"

I groan. *Why is this my life?*

28

JON

BEANS. SPILLED.

*B*obby shoves me into the elevator so hard, I bounce off the wall and come right back at him.

As soon as the doors close, he turns and snarls. "What the hell is going on?"

Breathe in.

Breathe out.

Don't panic.

She ran from me. She's hiding from me. *This is bad.*

Smugly, Jim leans against the mirrored wall and grins. "What did you do to her, Fart? I think this is a new record; you've got all the girls sneaking around and hiding from you. You got morning breath or something?"

"Shut the fuck up."

"No, seriously." Grinning, he lifts to the balls of his feet, then drops back onto the heels. "I wanna know. You're really good at pissing her off. I wanna know what *not* to do, you know, so I can have a long and happy marriage. You could write a book on this shit. I'd buy it."

"Jim—"

"Jim," Aiden grumbles. "Shut up. Jon, you good?"

"No! I'm not good! I need to go back up." *I need to know why my wife ran.* I mean, I get it. She's a runner. *But, fuck!* I'm not letting history repeat itself. This is it, this is our chance. "I need to go back up."

"Nope." Shaking his head, Bobby mirrors his brother and folds his arms. "Kit said Tink wanted to talk to *her*. You're not invited."

I rush forward and slam him against the wall. "Like fuck I'm not invited. She's mine!"

"Yours?" He laughs. "She's your one-night-stand that you just happen to keep revisiting. You have no rights to her."

"Like fuck I don't!" *She's my wife!*

"You need to cool your shit." Aiden's hand comes down on my shoulder. "Shouting like a spoiled brat ain't gonna get you anywhere."

"Spoiled brat, my ass!"

The elevator doors ding open and an elderly couple step in warily. My hands are pinning Bobby to the mirrored wall. Aiden's hand is holding me down because I'm a *spoiled brat*. And Jimmy's still fuckin' grinning. Because he's an asshole.

Letting Bobby go with a huff, I step back and shrug Aiden's hand off.

Breathe in.

Breathe out.

Don't get into a *Roller* brand brawl in the elevator and take out the old people.

"Where's Jack?"

"With Mom," Bobby answers. "Helping her with Bug."

"Where's Bean?"

He grins. "She's with Iz. Relax."

The elevator goes right to the lobby floor, and the old folks don't dare look over their shoulder at the four two-hundred-pound assholes with adrenaline zinging through their bodies.

Well. Three of them.

Jim's cool as a fuckin' cucumber.

He pulls me toward the buffet as soon as we flood from the elevator. "Have some breakfast, Jon. Tell Uncle Jim your troubles."

"Fuck you, asshole."

"Damn," Bobby laughs. "Jon Fart is salty today!"

"Fuck you, too, Peacock. I'll kick your ass if you want."

"Maybe tomorrow. Lemme enjoy today in the big city, then tomorrow we roll. Let's see how well you do with your exploded liver slowing you down."

"Bobby," Aiden snaps. "Stop teasing him. Jon, it's your fault I'm not with my wife right now, so shut your pie hole."

"*My* fault?"

His incredulous eyes come back to me. "She's with Tink right now, because *you're* a stupid ass and pissed her off. Now the girls have gone into lockdown. They're probably upstairs on a man-hating bitching rampage. If I cop shit from this, *I'm* gonna kick your ass."

"I didn't do anything wrong." *Except marry her.*

"Whether you did something or not, she's hiding. Now *all* the girls are incommunicado and our buffet breakfast has become sausage only. Which makes *you* the asshole."

"Here comes Mom and Jack," Jim murmurs. "Bottle it up, or Mom will smack us for swearing."

"Fuck."

"Dude!" Bobby's grumble comes half a second before the stinging slap on the back of my head.

"Don't cuss like that. Evie heard you, dummy."

"Dummy." Evie giggles and jumps from Jack's arms to Aiden's. "Hey, Biggie. I missed you."

"I missed you too, baby." Nuzzling her neck, Aiden leads the way to our reserved table. "Did you have fun with Gramma?"

"Yeah!" Her tight curls bounce with her excitement. "And Bean, too. And Unca Jack. Where's Mommy?"

Aiden's eyes shoot to mine. "She's with Aunty Tink, cause dummy over here made her mad."

"Jon," she giggles sweetly. "You're so silly."

"Jon?" Pretending to be mad, I glare at the beautiful toddler and press my fist to her shoulder. "That's *Uncle* Jon to you, young lady. Tomorrow, we roll."

She falls back and giggles like I'm the funniest fucker on Earth.

"The girls were good for you, Mom?" Jim pulls out a chair when Nell sits with a cup of tea. "They slept?"

"They were fine. They both slept perfect. Hardly heard a peep."

"I heard plenty of peeps," Jack grumbles teasingly. "Swear, a circus moved through the halls last night."

Shaking her head, Mom lightly slaps his muscular arm. "Don't be rude, Jack. Be tactful and they may return the favor one day."

"Tactful?" He laughs. "I don't think your sons have a single tactful bone in their bodies. Combined!"

She grins behind her mug. "I tried, baby. I really did. But be that as it may, we don't bring up the fact we could hear drunk couples stumbling down the hall last night. It's rude."

242 | EMILIA FINN

My heart thunders in my chest. "What are you talking about?"

She looks up with a wicked grin. "Nothing, dear. Oh look, here comes your bride."

"What?" Almost snapping my neck in my haste, I turn to find the girls walking toward us.

Case is with them, in her *regular weekend relaxation clothes*; as in, tight jeans, sexy top, tall heels, and beautifully made up eyes.

Though none of it can hide her ghostly white face.

"Aiden, honey." Nell's mischievous eyes leave me and land on her son. "Your bride is so beautiful. How does it feel to be a married man?"

"It's so good, Momma." Standing with Evie in his arms, he strides across the room and takes Tina against his chest. Even with his daughter clutched between them, he bends Tina back and kisses her stupid.

Most everyone else in this dining room watches the newlyweds, but I can't take my eyes off Casey.

She watches me watch her.

She's terrified.

Maybe I should've made her write herself a letter last night, too. I didn't end up needing mine, I remember every single minute from the bar to bed, but if she'd written one for herself, maybe she wouldn't look so terrified this morning.

I watch the girls approach. I watch Kit walk to Bobby, with her tiny baby bump poking out of her tight tank, then I watch Jimmy take Bean from Iz. He kisses the baby on the head, drops her in Nell's lap, then I watch him bend my baby sister upside down and swallow her tongue.

I want to kill the fucker.

I swear he does it to piss me off.

Asshole.

"Good morning, ladies." Nell settles Bean comfortably and goes back to sipping her tea. "Feeling rested?"

Kit sits in Bobby's lap. "Uh-huh. I'm fresh as a daisy."

Jim grabs my sister around the waist and pulls her into his lap. "I'm fresh, too," she laughs. "Perks to being pregnant; I didn't get drunk and make decisions I might regret this morning."

Tina sits in the chair beside Aiden's; because he's not quite the show pony that his brothers are. But he pulls her chair close and throws his arm over her shoulders.

"I'm a little fuzzy," Tina admits. Rubbing a thumb to her temple, she picks up a glass of water and chugs the whole thing in one go. "I definitely made decisions I regret last night. I think I need some juice."

"I got it." Jumping up and bumping the table with her jeaned thighs, Casey refuses to look me in the eye. "I'll get the juice. You guys relax."

As a group, we watch her practically sprint across the room toward the juice bar. Then as a group, we come back and everyone's eyes stop on me.

Fuck... "What?"

Kit's lips twitch with secrets. "Have a good night, Jon?"

I look from Kit's knowing eyes to Iz's, then to Tina's.

Then I look at the guys.

They're clueless, but the girls...

"Uh-huh." I try to stop the triumphant smile, but it tears across my face anyway. "I really did."

Sissy watches me warily. "You got a spotty memory like Tink, or are you good?"

"Case doesn't remember her night?"

Kit shrugs. "She's spotty. What about you?"

My smile remains. "I remember everything."

"And yet you're smiling."

I meet Kit's glaring challenge and nod. "I am."

Turning back toward the juice bar in search, I'm up and out of my chair before my brain catches up with my actions.

I'm her Leo.

I'll never stop being her Leo, and right now, a hipster looking fucker stands and blocks her movements as she tries to make coffee.

What's with her attracting all the artsy dudes? I'm nothing like them. I bet none of them have work roughened hands like I do.

"So, are you staying in this hotel?"

Fuckface brings his hand up, and daringly, despite her shaking head, he strokes from the ball of her shoulder to her collarbone.

Snapping my hand down over his, I tear it away and spin the guy around. "I'll thank you to take your hand off my wife!"

Casey jumps back like I electrocuted her.

"Did he just Jamie Fraser her?"

I spin to find my family – my *whole* fucking family – barely three feet away.

Izzy grins like a fool. "You did! You totally just Jamie Fraser'ed her."

"Who the fuck is Jamie Fraser?"

"No, Leo, stop–"

244 | EMILIA FINN

I spin back to Casey. "Who. Is. Jamie. Fraser?"

Kit snickers and leans into Bobby's chest. Her ability to find humor in this has my blood boiling. "Jamie Fraser's a strapping young Scotsman, Jon. He might even be taller than you. He rides horses. And he fights. Hell, he might even be the whole package."

Frowning, Bobby pushes Kit back until their eyes meet. "How do you know that dude? Where does he fight?"

Tina's laughter bubbles out. "He has really nice hair, too. All long and grabbable."

My eyes flick to Aiden's. He shrugs and pulls Tina under his arm. "I know who Jamie Fraser is. We're okay."

"This doesn't bother you?"

Aiden grins. "No. Like I said, we're okay."

"Wait, wait, wait, wait!" Jimmy steps closer with narrowed eyes. "Did you tell that guy to get his hands off your *wife?*" He looks between me and Case. "Is that, like, a new term of endearment? Is this like *yolo* or *fleek?* Just a trend."

"Jon." Casey takes my arm. Shaking her head, she looks up at me with watery eyes. "Don't do this. I'm begging you."

I look at everyone; at the guys with the confused faces, and the girls with the smug grins. Then I turn my back and block them out. "Why not?"

A tear slides free. "Don't."

"Do you remember?"

"We can't do this." She shakes. Her entire body shakes. "Just relax. I'll fix it."

Fix it? "Do you remember?"

"I'm..." She nods. "Yes. I remember."

"So, you remember your promises. You remember your vows."

"Oh my God!" Like a girl, Jimmy breaks into silly giggles. "Oh my God! It's not a trend. They really got hitched!"

"Casey." I pull her chin up so our eyes meet. "Do you remember?" When a lone tear spills over her left cheek, I bring my hand up to catch it with my thumb. "Answer me, Sunshine."

She shakes her head no, but answers, "Yes, Jon. I remember."

"You made a promise to me."

"We were drunk! *You* were drunk. I won't hold you to it."

My heart thrashes painfully at her rejection. "You won't hold me to it?"

Another tear falls. "No."

Fuck this. "Well I'm holding you to it!"

"Jon–"

I throw my arm over her shoulders and spin us around. Smiling like everything is right in the world, I squeeze her close and refuse to let her go. "Guys. Mom. Sissy. We have a very special announcement."

"Oh my God!" Jimmy giggles ridiculously. He slaps his thigh and buckles my sister's back as he leans on her.

Bobby stares at me. Floundering, his mouth opens. Closes. Opens. Closes. "Jon Fart." He looks between me and Case. "What did you do?"

I pull her closer as she fights against my hold. "Bobby." I take a deep breath. "I got married last night. She's legit your sister now."

"Jon... And Tink..." His eyes flick from mine to hers. "You got married?" Apart from Casey, Bobby's probably the only person on this planet that knows what this truly means. "Are you happy?"

Casey shakes her head *no.*

I nod. "Yeah, B. I'm happy."

She twitches in my arms. *"You're happy?!"*

Turning my back on my family, I bring her eyes up with a hand under her chin. "I'm so fucking happy, Sunshine. I'm in it this time. I'm not gonna fuck this up. I promise."

A tear slides along her cheek. "But it's already fucked up, Jon."

"No, Sunshine! It's not. It only just started."

"You got married while you were drunk! I'm not holding you to that. I know your thoughts on this–"

"No." I bring my hands up to cup her face. She's in runner mode. She's going to split as soon as I look away. "You *knew* my thoughts. But I've grown, Sunshine. I've changed. I want different things now."

"But–"

"I want *you.* Please believe me."

"Jon." Stepping forward, she wraps her arms around my hips and presses her ear to my heart. She must hear the rapid *thump-thump-thump.* It beats for her. It's always beat for her.

It feels like it's been a lifetime since we last held each other like this. This is what I need in my life; I just need *her.* I need her arms wrapped around me. I need her to hold me. It doesn't matter that she's the smaller half of our team. She's the strongest. She's the one who holds me at night. She's the one who holds me together.

"Jon." She doesn't step back. In fact, she squeezes me tighter. "This isn't a marriage I can continue. We were drunk, and I'm not convinced you're totally sober right now. I can't in good conscience continue this. I won't force you into a decision you made while drunk. I'm sorry."

"Sunshine. No—"

Now she steps back. "I'm sorry this happened, okay? I'll fix it. I'll fix it right away. Then you can go back to your life. I won't interfere anymore."

"Sunshine—"

"My name's Casey." She draws in a ragged breath. "It's Casey. Sunshine doesn't exist anymore."

She's tearing my fucking heart out. "Well, *Casey*, you told me last night that you loved me." Anger replaces the galloping heart. Rage fuels me, instead of hurt. We've danced this dance too long. "You told me you'd love me forever."

Devastatingly, she nods. "I didn't lie." She steps forward and pulls my shirt down to deliver the final blows. Pressing a gentle kiss to my cheek, she snaps the elastic in my heart. "I didn't lie, Jon. I *do* love you. I love you so much, I *know* this isn't what you want. It would be terribly selfish of me to trap you in a marriage you didn't mean to enter. I'll organize the lawyer. I'll forward the paperwork as soon as it's done."

Like blow after blow, she lands every single jab. "Paperwork?"

Nodding, she catches my pinky finger with hers. "You don't have to worry about anything, okay?" With wobbling lips, she *tries* to smile. *"Trust me.* I'll get the divorce started right away. You go back to breakfast. Pretend none of this happened."

Releasing my hand and stealing my chance to argue, she bolts. Side-stepping Evie's reaching arms, she runs without a single backwards glance. Through the large dining area, through the bi-fold timber doors. She sprints to the elevators, and she doesn't reappear minutes later like this was all a big joke.

She doesn't come back down to breakfast.

She's not in her room when I go up to check.

She simply leaves the city, the state, and she doesn't come back to me.

———

Sitting on my couch with a pen in my hand and paper on the coffee table in front of me, I make notes. More notes. The most important notes I'll ever have to write.

I have shit to do.

Plans to make.

I have one chance to get her back, then it's all over. There's no room for fucking this up again.

Looking up at the knock on my door, I glance toward my silent phone. The gates weren't opened, which means it's just the guys.

I don't bother getting up.

The door's unlocked, and even if it wasn't, they all have keys.

Slipping my tattered and overused copy of the King's Courtney under my couch cushion, I flip my notepad over and sit back to wait for the guys.

It's not just one or two, but all of them.

I sigh. All of them, plus the fucking dog. And they're out for my blood.

Swaggering into my living room, Bobby stops with his signature peacock smirk, but it's not real. The fire in his eyes... that's real.

Aiden steps in next, then Jim.

Jack closes the door, and Annie flounces in with her dopey tongue hanging out and her ears flopped over her forehead.

I had no clue bears had floppy ears.

Throwing my pen down, I arrogantly kick my legs up and get comfortable. They're here to tear me apart.

I don't have much of anything left to give.

"Morning. Just let yourselves in, huh? I didn't realize you lived here."

Bobby knocks my feet to the floor and sits on the coffee table. "Talk."

Denial. "About what, Peacock?"

"Don't be a dumbass. My pregnant wife's crying because *her* best friend is hurting. Tink is Kit's best friend, which makes her *my* best friend. *You're* hurting my best friend, asshole."

The jabs just keep coming. "Casey's your best friend. Kit's your best friend. What about me, asshole? Two decades of friendship, a pretty girl walks in, and now I don't mean shit to you?"

"Let me ask you something," he murmurs seriously. "Tink... She your best friend?"

"Depends."

Aiden's brows furrow. "On what?"

I bring my eyes back to Bobby. The others are here, but this is between me and him. "On what you know."

He nods. "I think I know most everything now, except your side of the story. Which, by the way, if I meant shit to *you*, you'd have already talked to me. A pretty girl walks in," he mocks, "and I don't mean shit to you?" He shakes his head. "But that's another chat for another day. Right now, I wanna know if Casey's your best friend."

I nod. There's no point lying anymore. "Yeah, she's my best friend."

"Right. So even though you love me, even though you're my best friend, even though we're brothers and have been for two decades, it's different, right? Tink being your best friend; that's different to me being your best friend."

I nod again. "It's different."

"Exactly. So when you hurt Tink, you hurt Kit. That's my wife, Jon. That's different to me and you. I never wanna have to choose, it would kill me, but if I had to, Kit would win. In a fuckin' heartbeat."

I know he's right. I get it. But the words still sting. "Right."

"So you're hurting my best friend, asshole. Talk to me."

Jimmy steps forward and perches on the arm of the long couch. "How the fuck did Tink go from being your one-night-stand, to being your *'oops! I'm married.'*?"

His cheap words roil in my stomach. "I meant my vows."

Bobby slams his fist against my thigh. "I have no doubt, dumbass! Even drunk, you're not an idiot. You had to stand in line to get the license. Then you had to haul your asses to a chapel. You walked down an aisle, and you bought ugly ass wedding bands. You did all that, so even drunk, I know you meant your words. Excuse us for being a little slow on this, but *what the fuck,* Jon? I didn't even know you guys were actual *talk-during-the-sunlight-hours* friends."

"She's been my best friend since the day you met Kit at 188."

Discounting my words straight off the bat, Bobby scoffs, but when I don't back down, he clears his throat and nods. "You're not kidding?"

"I'm not kidding. We hung out at the club, but I thought you were gonna mess around with the hot blonde and mess things up for me and Case. We didn't hook up, we just hung out. You walked Kit out of the club and I said goodbye to the beautiful pixie. I wasn't even mad, seeing as I owe you a lifetime of thanks."

His brows pull in tight. *"A lifetime of thanks.* For what?"

I roll my eyes. "Don't be dumb, B. You know exactly what."

"No." He shakes his head. "I really don't. What grand favor did I do for you that would excuse fucking you and Tink up?"

"Well, there's nothing good enough *now.*" Annie pushes her snout under my hand and has me thinking of Scooter. And Casey. "She's my true best friend now, but *back then,* she was just the sassy-pants hot chick from the club. I wouldn't have been mad at you. I owed you for saving my life."

His jaw drops. "Saving your life? What the fuck are you talking about?" When I don't elaborate, he taps my knee. "I'm not kidding. I have no clue what you're talking about."

Everything's finally coming to a head for me.

I spilled my guts to Casey in a dark parking lot.

I've spilled my guts to a therapist for years.

It's time I told my best friend. He lived it with me, and he doesn't even know.

He deserves to know.

Scratching the dog's ears, I pull her in for a hug and breathe her in. It helps more than I expected it would. "I have something I gotta tell you, B."

Looking up, I study each of the guys. Jim and Aiden were there, too. They saw me turn up with the split lips and black eyes. They fed Sissy just as much as Bobby fed me.

Jack wasn't there. He doesn't know my shit. He's still a kid, and I don't want to put my stuff in his head. But he's not *just* a kid. He's older than his years. He's one of us.

He deserves the same respect that I give the others.

"Bobby was the only reason I ate most days. Legit." I meet his eyes. "You patched me up. You gave me a safe space to land. I had absolutely nowhere else to go, I had nowhere that I could rest and close my eyes and feel safe. I trusted no one else, *especially* with Sissy, but I trusted Jim to take her to his room, to feed her, to let her rest while I was unconscious. Aiden had my back." I turn to Aiden. "You were younger, but you were formidable. I know you had my back." Looking at my shoes, I shake my head. "There's not much you guys could do that I wouldn't forgive. You saved my life. More than once."

"You were our friend," Bobby says. "You came over to play and eat, it wasn't a big deal."

"It was a huge deal to me. I was starving, B. Literally fucking starving. I could feel my spine through my gut half the time. I'll never forget the family that took us in when they didn't have to. Your folks had no clue they were harboring a couple abused and hungry kids. They just fed us, because they're good people. I was a starving boy with a kid to feed, but your folks asked no questions. Your mom just put a couple extra plates on the table, and when I looked up and said thanks, she let me pretend I didn't have black eyes."

Bobby taps his knuckles against my knee. "Kit told me some stuff last night. Some stuff about you and Tink."

That could be any of a million things. "It's probably true. Whatever she told you, it's probably true. I've spent two years fucking Case over."

"She told me Tink was pregnant with your baby."

My heart hammers at the reminder.

I never wanted kids. I never wanted to do that to her. But now that it's happened, I'm mourning the baby I'll never know. I'm mourning the child that would've been half Sunshine.

I've been so focused on *my* half, on *my* blood, I completely disregarded the most important half.

Her half.

I nod and run a hand through my hair. "Yeah. Around the time Kit was hurt. She lost the baby a little after that."

"Why didn't you say something?"

I shrug.

I won't throw her under the bus. I won't admit that I didn't know. It's my fault she was too scared to tell me. That rests squarely on my shoulders. "It was never the right time. I didn't wanna upset you."

"So you bottled that poison up?"

No. Worse. Casey did.

"You held it all yourself and didn't share?"

No. I lived obliviously, and Casey shouldered the load.

Bobby drops his palm on my head and drags my gaze up. "Are you okay?"

I shrug. "I will be."

"Yeah." Jim lets out a sigh. "It takes time. Trust me, I know what it's like, but time will pass and it'll start to feel better."

My eyes snap up. "*Time?* Time will make it better?"

He nods.

"Did *time* help you forget Sissy?"

"No, it didn't. Nothing could've healed that ache, but–"

"Exactly. Time doesn't do shit. So shut up."

"You gotta let it go," he says. "The hurt'll eat you up inside. You've gotta move on. She has."

"Move on? I'm not moving on!"

Jack steps forward angrily. He grew up with Casey. He's her brother. "You can't hurt her anymore, Jon. I won't let you. It's time to let her go."

"Fuck no. It's time to get her back."

"When was the last time you saw her, dumbass? When did you last speak to her?"

"Weeks." I blow out a gusty breath. "It's been weeks since she left the hotel. It's been that long since I spoke to her."

Bobby nods. "Exactly. She moved on, Fart. It's over."

"No." I smile. "It's just beginning. I have a plan."

29

CASEY

THE FINALE

*I*t would be three full weeks after Aiden and Tina's wedding – after my own wedding – before I saw Jon again.

It takes two weeks to get divorce papers drawn up, and another week to gather my courage for the final showdown.

I'm here to set him free.

I'm doing the right thing. It just sucks that the right thing hurts so much.

I enter the gate codes; zero-seven-zero-four-one-five – one of the best and worst dates of my life – then I roll along the driveway I've been so notably absent from for weeks.

The girls come to my apartment most days, but I haven't come here.

For obvious reasons.

Jon hasn't called, nor has he knocked on my door once. He hasn't been into the club, and funnily, my tips have surged. I guess my Leo was keeping the high paying men away.

I haven't asked once, but every time the girls have been over, I've silently screamed, *how is he? What's he doing? Does he miss me? Is he angry?*

But I don't say it out loud.

Nor do they answer.

I knew what I was doing the day I walked away. I knew I was essentially killing everything we ever had. It's like I left my limbs in another city. I can't function properly without them, but I can't have them back, either.

I'm doomed to live a half-life, though the hurt feels pretty fucking full.

I was finally successful in cutting the cord.

He's never left me alone before. No matter how much I bitched at him, no matter how much I begged for time out. Even during our worst fights, he was still blowing up my phone, or in the club watching.

But I did it. I've finally slipped away, and he really has moved on.

It hurts. It hurts so much, but it's the right thing. He deserves more. He deserves happiness.

He deserves *freedom.*

No doubt, everyone already knows I'm here. The gates are secure, meaning if so much as a stray cat passes the sensors, texts fly around the estate in warning.

They know I'm here, so I don't even bother trying to hide.

No doubt every soul on this estate have their noses in their phones. They see me on the security feed, and they're more than likely tripping over each other to be the first to press their noses to their windows.

It takes everything I have not to flip off the cameras.

Nosy jerks.

It took three days, a functioning liver, and several gallons of water before I was able to pry the ring off my finger.

I haven't put it back on, but I'm not giving it back, either.

It's my security blanket.

It's all I have.

Pulling up in Jon's driveway, I check my mirror and study my tired eyes. I'm so tired. So unbelievably tired.

This is it.

Like a showdown in the wild west, it all goes down today.

After this, I can rest.

Slapping my cheeks to bring a little color to my pale skin, I grab the paperwork and climb out of my car. This'll take twenty minutes at the most, then I need to force my ass back into this car.

Then I need to leave.

For good.

Walking along Jon's stone pathway, I force myself not to look back at the eyes I *know* are watching me. I can feel their beady stares. Their nosiness tickles the very tip of my spine.

Don't look, Casey. Don't you dare look.

Before my nerves get the best of me, I press my finger to Jon's doorbell and step back to wait.

I don't use the key I have. I don't dare cross that line.

It takes a few minutes to hear any movement, long enough to wonder if he's even home, but eventually, the locks click and the door swings open.

My eyes snap from the six and a half feet I expected, and pop down to the three feet that is Evelyn 'Bug' Soon-to-be-Kincaid as she clings to her stuffed puppy. "Evie?"

I look past her in search of Tina, or Jon, or hell, anybody. Squatting, I frown. "Whatcha doin', Bug?"

"Evie's getting cousins soon!"

My frown turns to a smile. "I know, baby. Exciting, huh? Where's Mommy and Biggie? Are they here?"

"Mommy's with Biggie."

"Yeah, but *where* are they?"

Smiling, she shrugs and drops puppy from in front of her chest. Skittering back, I almost fall on my ass as my own drunken smile printed on her shirt taunts me. "Evelyn! Where'd you get that shirt?"

She drops her chin to her chest and points at my pink drunk-girl eyes. "It's Aunty Tink! You're so pretty."

"I know it's me, baby. Where'd you get it? Who dressed you today?" *It's such an awful photo!* Of course I was a hot mess in my wedding photos.

"Evie dressed myself." She pulls the fabric away from her chest. "It's so pretty."

I bend over her. "You got anything on under that?" *No.* I answer my own question as I pull the collar back. Nothing else, so I can't even steal her shirt and burn it. "Bug, where's Mommy and Biggie? Are you here alone?"

I jump at Jon's scoff, then his cocky smirk as he rounds the corner. I resist the urge to scratch my own eyes out.

He's just as beautiful as I remember.

The beautiful asshole wears a shirt identical to Evie's, he's *twinning* with the toddler, but it gets worse. So much worse, as I focus on the hat pulled low over his twinkling eyes. "Of course she's not here alone, Sunshine. I can be a responsible adult."

"Jon." I stand tall and rest my hand in Evie's hair as she hugs my thigh. Swallowing down my tears and nerves and heartbreak, I order myself not to reach out.

He's so close, but I'm not allowed to touch.

"Hey, Sunshine." He flashes a truly happy smile. "I've missed your beautiful face."

I hungrily study his. "What happened to yours? Where'd you get the black eye?"

His hand comes up to slide along the also bruised jaw. "This? Jack hit me for hurting his sister."

"What did you do to Kit?"

Chuckling, he leans against the wall. "Not Kit. You." He looks me up and down appreciatively. "I missed you, Case. I missed you so much. I haven't slept in three weeks."

He looks fine and rested to me. "We can't keep doing this, Jon. You can't say that stuff anymore."

He shrugs and bites his bottom lip playfully. "I dunno. I think I'm gonna enjoy the ride this time."

"Jon–"

"Leo," he inserts with a smile. "I'm Leo. You're Sunshine."

"No! We can't– We're not those people anymore!"

The muscles on his shoulders ripple dangerously. "No, we're not. We're older and smarter now. I think we're even aging really well. I mean, I'm not conceited, not like The Peacock, but I'm pretty sure I'm hotter now than I was two years ago. And I *know* you are."

I hold back my groan. He's just playing games. "Fine. Listen." I extend the forms between us. "I spoke to my lawyer and I had these drawn up. She–"

"She?" He maintains his smug smile. "Daniels is a cool dude, but I don't think he'd like you calling him a she."

"Daniels?" I shake my head. "No, I spoke to Penny; she specializes–"

"But Daniels is our family lawyer. He's on retainer."

"Whose family?"

"*Ours.* Yours and mine." He grins arrogantly. "We're married now; what's mine is yours."

"Jon." I want to cry. I want to scream. I want to tug my hair out. But I do none of those things. *Get in, get it done, get out.* Like a Band-Aid. "I had divorce papers drawn up. They just need your signature, then they're good to–"

He casually rearranges his feet and crosses his ankles. I thought I'd shielded myself from his brand of heartache, but his aloofness right now fucking stings. "Why no annulment, Sunshine?"

"Annul– What?"

"Why no annulment? Why'd you choose divorce over annulment?"

My heart pounds painfully in my chest. Every careless word he throws at me slashes my heart. "Jon. Why are you trying to hurt me?"

His smugness wavers. "I'm not trying to hurt you, Case. I swear to God, I'll never hurt you again. I just want to know why you chose one over the other."

"Because... because we consummated it. Because–"

"Because we made love?"

I swallow the lump in my throat. "Yes."

"But for you to know that, then you must remember, right? You must remember the night."

"Yes." *I remember everything. Every single painful moment.* "Yes. I remember."

"So you remember making love to me. You remember the promises we made?"

"Yes Jon, but I also remember you being drunk. We were both drunk. I also remember taunting you. I knew what I was doing when I lined your shots up. I knew you wouldn't turn me down."

"You knew that about me; so my reactions were entirely in character. Maybe *all* of my decisions that night were in character. Maybe every decision I made was what I *wanted*."

"Jon, I can't. I can't do this. Here." I thrust the paperwork toward him. "Just sign. I'm begging you, just sign and let me file them." I look down at Evie as she traces circles in my thigh. "I have some other stuff for you, too."

"You got me a gift, Sunshine?" Smiling, he takes the folder and opens the cover. Instantly, his smile turns to a frown. "What th–"

"You don't have to do anything with it if you don't want to, but I wanted you to know there's precedent. You can do something about..." I stroke Evie's hair. "You can go to the police and talk about what happened to you. It's not too late to do something about it."

Murmuring, he flips the pages. "How do you know this?"

Because I took research on like it was a full-time job. I can't be with Jon – the adult – but I can help the boy. Ten years later, I can be the adult he wished he knew. I can help him. "I made an appointment with a lawyer... not Penny–"

"Not Daniels, either?" He smirks.

I smile. "No. Not Daniels, either. I spoke to someone who specializes in... these cases. He said he can help you. It's up to you whether you call him. But it's your decision, Jon. I won't push you into it. I won't chase and nag. I just wanted you to know that they won't get away with what they did. And I want you to know that little boy, the hurt boy inside you... I wish I knew him. And I wish I could've hugged him."

He frowns. "Why'd you do this, Sunshine?"

Because I love you. "Because you're my best friend. And because the little boy deserves justice. Trust me, if the law wasn't a viable option for this, I was already drawing up a plan B."

His lips twitch. "Yeah? What were you gonna do?"

"Itchy powder and keyed cars wouldn't cut the cheese this time. Mostly, my plan was to run them down with my car. Well, actually, yours, since your truck's big and would hurt more."

"What if you got caught?"

Just the thought of hurting them makes me smile. "I'd happily serve my time for you."

"You would?" His satisfied smile grows and stretches his face. "What's the average sentence for something like that?"

I frown. "I don't know. Premeditated probably changes things." I shrug. "Maybe thirty years for each of the jerks I run down."

"Thirty years..." He rubs a long finger across his jaw. "You'd serve thirty years for me?"

"For every single one of them. Yes. Happily."

"Sunshine. If you'll serve a life sentence *for* me, why not live a life sentence *with* me? My house isn't nearly as gross as prison. The sex will be mostly consensual, and I won't make you cook if you don't wanna. Though I'd really love more poo-brown cake every year. That was my best birthday ever."

"Jon. No–"

Sighing dramatically, he throws his head back. "Why not?"

"I can't stay in this marriage! You were tricked into it."

"You can't stay in *this* marriage? This one right now, because I wasn't sober when I entered it?"

"Right."

He stands from his slouch against the wall. "You got a pen?"

I hold back the sound of metal on metal as my heart seizes in my chest.

Reaching into my bag for the pen I made sure to bring, I try to control the shaking in my hand. "Here you go."

"Where do I sign?" *Damn, this hurts.* He's going to sign, just like that.

I step forward, and though I have to speak, to point out each required signature, I do my best to not breathe.

I don't want to smell him. I don't want to feel him.

He takes the documents and presses them against the wall. One flourishing signature. Zero hesitation. Two. Three. "Is that all?"

I'm dead inside. "Yeah, that's it."

"Are we officially divorced yet?"

"No." I hold back my tears. "I'll file, which will make it official. But yeah, as far as you're concerned, you're free."

"I'm *free?*"

I nod.

"I'm free to do what I want? To make my own decisions? To marry whomever I please?"

Please don't marry Sonia.

"Do I look sober right now? Of sound mind?

I nod. It's barely ten a.m. "Yeah, you look sober to me."

"Right. Let's go." Swinging Evie onto his hip, he takes my arm and turns toward the door.

"Where're we going?"

"To get married."

Digging my heels into the floor, I force him to stop or rip my arm from the socket. "Jon! No, we're not."

"Why not? I'm sober *and* I love you. It's perfect."

"He wuvs you, Aunty Tink."

Arrogantly, he nods. "It's true. You're not engaged to anyone else, are you? Because I'll duel or whatever that idiot Fraser does to win the chick. Who do I have to fight? And where the hell do they sell swords these days?"

"You're being an idiot."

"I'm actually completely serious. Will you marry me, Casey?" Dropping to his knee, he places Evie on her feet and takes my hand in his. "I'll love you for the rest of my life."

"Jon. Stop."

With a deep chuckle, he pops back to his feet. "That's what I thought you'd say. I didn't even get a ring yet, because I knew you'd reject me."

"Is this just a joke to you?"

"Not even a little bit. Wait here a sec, okay?"

He doesn't wait for my answer, he simply takes off inside and leaves Evie and I on the porch.

"Unca Jon is funny."

"Uncle Jon's a pain in my damn ass, Bug. Boys are stupid."

"I heard that, Sunshine! And so did Bug. Tina'll kick your ass if she hears you."

I mumble that he just said ass, but I don't have time to dwell as he returns to the front door with a tattered novel in his hand and a smaller version of his hat that he drops on Evie's head. Picking her up and plopping her on his hip, Jon drops a silly kiss on her nose and leaves her giggling.

Turning to me, he winks and turns my knees weak. "Let's go!"

"Jon." I struggle to tug my hand loose. "I need to go home."

"Soon, Sunshine. You need to come with me first."

"Where are we going?"

"Just shush and wait."

"Unca Jon!" Evie scolds. *"Shush* is rude. Use your manners."

His smile doesn't dim a single degree. "Sorry Bug. Sunshine, darling, can you please shut the focaccia up and follow me?"

He leads us – *tugs* us – across the lawn and onto Aiden and Tina's front porch. "What are we doing here?"

Condescendingly, he looks down at me. "Don't make me shush you, woman."

Taking a deep breath, he knocks on the door, sending my heart skittering with nerves. The locks roll, then the door opens wide.

Tina's big smile greets us... as does my face... on her shirt. "Seriously? Was there a special on at Shirts'R'Us?"

"Mommy!" Evie jumps from Jon's arms to Tina's, but then Aiden comes to the door and she jumps ship. "Biggie!"

"Hey, Smalls. I missed you, baby."

"Missed you, too." She plants a juicy kiss on his cheek. "I wuv you."

"Did you do your job?"

"Yes! Aunty Tink's funny. She said a swear."

Tina's glacial eyes meet mine. "Really, Aunty Tink? You couldn't keep your potty mouth quiet?"

"Why was she even there? It's not my fault!"

"You guys organized over here?"

"Yeah," Aiden answers cryptically. He turns to me, and uncharacteristically, winks, then points at his matching shirt.

"Are you people serious? What's with the shirts?"

"Come on, Case." Jon tugs me along. "You said you'd serve a life sentence for me. I want something else. Just as permanent, but less traumatic."

"Aww." Tina grins like a fool. "She already admitted to the life sentence?"

"Yeah. That was surprisingly easy. But she's playing hardball on the marriage thing. For now."

"You already asked?" Aiden questions. "Jesus, Fart. That was quick."

"I asked, but she said no."

"Tink!" Tina scolds. "That's rude."

"What are you people talking about?"

Jon ignores me. "Ian's here?"

"Yeah." Aiden nods toward the living room. "He's all set up and ready to go. We're just waiting on you guys."

Ian? "Ian who?"

"Inkalot Ian." Jon tugs me through Tina and Aiden's front hall. I trip in my heels, but he doesn't dare let me fall. Stepping into the living room, I stare wide-eyed at the temporary tattoo parlor.

The genuine chair he uses in the parlor stands in the center of the room, already wrapped in plastic. A small table holds the gun-thingy, pots of ink, wipes, cleansers. He brought everything. "What are we–"

"I want you to get the ink, Case. The ink we planned, but never got. You say you'll serve a life sentence for me, well, get the best friend ink you promised me. I already got mine." He pulls his shirt up before I get the chance to prepare or look away. Instantly, my eyes zero in on the Rebel Alliance symbol on his chest. A lot of his body is already covered in tattoos, but this one isn't lost in the crowd. It takes place of pride over his heart, then below the symbol is my name and our wedding date in beautiful calligraphy script.

"Ha!" Ian barks out a fast laugh from across the room. "No need, bro. I didn't realize this was the virgin skin you wanted. She's a virgin no more."

Jon's eyes snap to Ian's. "Come again?"

I shake my head. *No, no, no, no. Don't tell him.*

"I already took her virginity," he chuckles, but he pulls his shit up super quick when Jon steps forward. "Ah, that is, she came in last week. I already did it. But I can do something else for you today. I don't mind."

Jon turns to me. "What did you do?"

"Nothing."

I turn to run, but Jon grabs me. "What'd she get done?"

"I got nothing!"

"Ian, I love you, bro. You're my ink man, and you're good at what you do. But I'll kick your ass and go elsewhere if you don't tell me."

"She got the Rebel Alliance and some script."

"I did not!"

Jon turns to me with a wicked grin. "You already got our ink?" He leans in close to my ear. "Show me?"

"No."

Pulling back, he stares into my eyes arrogantly. "Ian, where'd she get it?"

"I got it on my ass," I snap. "Ian got to stare for hours. Then we went back to his place and hooked up."

Jon laughs. "Your pants are on fire, Casey."

"She got it on her ribs," Ian inserts. "Just below her–"

"You see my wife's breasts, Ian?"

"Your wife?" he sputters. "No! I didn't see– She was wearing a bra!"

"You saw my wife's bra, Ian?"

His voice turns anxious. "I was just doing my job, bro. We didn't hook up, I swear."

"Were you wearing a lacy bra, Sunshine?" Jon's gravelly voice drags across my sensitized skin. "Did you show him my favorite set?" He slides his tongue along my neck. "Show me your ink."

"This is my cue to leave." Aiden turns with Evie in his arms, but Tina snags his hand.

"No way! I'm not leaving. I wanna see, too."

"Peaches. I can't see. It's against bro code."

"So turn around, Kincaid! I ain't leaving."

"Show me, Sunshine." Jon drags his nose along the path his tongue took a moment ago. "Show me now."

"I don't wanna."

Ignoring me, he slides my top along my ribs and bunches the soft material in his fist. I don't bother stopping him. He's stronger than me, and he's on a mission. His breath comes out in a soft gravelly growl when he reveals the top of my ribs. I know what he's looking at; the exact same Rebel Alliance symbol that he has, but with the words *'we are encouraged to love'* scrawled below.

Ironically, Anakin and Padme married in secret, too.

"You can go, Ian."

"Jon—"

"Don't worry, you can keep the money. I transferred last week. It should already be in your account."

Leaning down and folding his giant body in half, Jon places a gentle kiss just above my tattoo. My eyes close without my permission; it's too much. He's in front of me again. His lips are on my skin again.

"Please stop, Leo."

He stands tall and meets my gaze. "Leo." He smiles brilliantly. "Yeah, I'm your Leo. Hey, Sunshine?"

"Yeah?"

"Will you marry me?"

A lone tear slides along my cheek. "No."

"Dammit!" he laughs. "I thought I had you that time. It's okay, I still didn't get you a ring. Let's go. We have another stop."

Tucking his books, the folder I gave him, and the divorce paperwork under his arm, he straightens my top and lowers the fabric. Taking my hand, he leads me back toward the front door.

"Jon, where are we—"

Looking around us warily, he makes sure Evie's not nearby, then he turns back to me with a wicked grin. "Shush."

"Don't shush me, Jon Hart! It's rude."

Laughing, he drags me across the street toward Jim and Iz's house. Stepping onto the front porch, he knocks, and like Jim was *conveniently* expecting us, the door swings open instantly.

Jim grins like an idiot, then he looks down at his shirt. He drew a moustache on my face.

Awesome.

"Hey there, beautiful people. Did you marry him yet?"

"She said no," Jon answers. "Twice!"

"Damn," Jim laughs and closes the door when we pass. "She's being stubborn today. That's alright, we'll crack this nut."

I look around the room, at Bean and Izzy sitting on the single recliner wearing my face, but I don't dwell, because I stop and study the strange older lady in a power suit.

About fifty or sixty years old, she's attractive in her sharp suit and low-bun hair. Wisps of gray weave through the dark browns, and her shoes, though professional, scream she knows fashion.

Standing with a kind smile, she offers a perfectly manicured hand. "Hi, Casey. I'm Sonia."

Fuck. Me. Sideways.

"Please forgive me," she continues. "I know more about you than you know about me. I don't mean to have that advantage, but Jon wanted us to meet. I'm here to answer any questions you might have for me."

I look to a watchful Izzy, then back to Jon.

He understands what I'm thinking instantly. "You can ask anything, Sunshine. Anything at all. Sissy and me... we talked. I was so caught up in my own shit for so long, I never stopped to notice she's a grown up. She's a mom, and I needed to trust her with the stuff that I kept from her for so long."

My eyes fill with emotion. "She knows everything?"

Nodding, he clears his throat. "*Everything*. She was also in the *steal-Jon's-truck* camp. She was willing to do life... We discussed it."

"We're all on stand-by," Jim murmurs angrily. "Give us the go-ahead, and we're all jumping into the truck." Pulling Izzy into his side, he drops a kiss on the side of her head. "We knew home was shitty for Jon. We knew... stuff. But we didn't know it all. I'm sorry we didn't protect you better, Jon."

Jon shrugs. "Doesn't matter anymore. Can't change it. But," he nods at Sonia, "she's here for you, Case. Any question, anything you wanna know, have at it. She's here to talk to you."

"About what?"

"I want her to tell you about the me from when I first started seeing her, to the me of now. I want her to convince you I've grown, and though I might sometimes say stupid shit, I've still grown. I've changed. I can be a family man, Sunshine. I can be a daddy. I would. I want a family with you."

"Leo." I swipe a hand across my cheek. "You keep forgetting, even if I believed that, I can't give you babies."

"Even if you *believed?* You don't believe me?"

"No." I'm starting to. Just like he pounded his anti-marriage message so much over the years, he's now pounding in the opposite message.

It's not so much that I don't believe him, mostly that I'm scared to.

"Sonia, do you think I've changed?"

I look up at the older woman and watch the way she watches him with a maternal pride. "I think you're the same Jon as always–"

"Sonia! You're killing me!"

264 | EMILIA FINN

She laughs. "Calm down. You want me to speak, let me speak. I think you're the exact same Jon as always, but I think you're not as scared anymore. Or more accurately, you're *more* scared of losing Casey, than you are of your past. You were always this good man, Jon. You were always a family man. You just couldn't say the words out loud. I think you might be the most loyal, the most hardworking, the kindest and most self-less man I've ever met, and considering where you came from, you and Izzy are beautiful flowers that grew from weeds. You were so scared to be a dad, but you don't acknowledge that you were Izzy's protector and provider since you were seven years old.

"I think Izzy's baby helped show you that blood isn't everything." Sonia points at Bean. "She's the epitome of your greatest fears, but you love her. She's perfect, and now you see you can have that, too."

"So, really," Iz adds with a goofy smirk. "I did you a favor when I got knocked up. I'll be accepting gifts and thank you cards all year."

Jon turns and glares at his sister. "Yeah, you really fell on your sword, Sissy. I appreciate your dedication." He nods at her swollen tummy. "You can stop after that one. You shouldn't even be having sex."

"Ha!" Jimmy laughs and pulls Izzy against his chest. "I love you, Jon. I've always loved your sense of humor."

Closing his eyes, Jon takes a deep breath and turns back to me. "Sonia's on retainer, too. She'll take your call, Sunshine. Any time, any day."

Sonia nods and offers a business card. "Precisely. Any time, any day. Any question. I have permission to answer anything, and you don't need Jon's permission to call. He doesn't have to know we spoke."

I stare down at the black and white card with her number and all the letters after her name. This woman has more than one degree. "Okay." I nod. "Thank you."

Jumping up, Jon claps his hands together. "Good job, Sonia!" He steps forward and high fives her. Literally. Then he turns to me. "Casey. Sunshine." He drops to one knee and holds my hand between his. "Will you marry me yet?"

I smile this time. He's playing with my heart, but it doesn't hurt so much anymore. "No."

"Ahhh!" He releases my hand and stands. "I knew you'd say that. I still don't have a ring, anyway. Let's go. We have another stop." Picking me up, he throws me over his shoulder and slaps my ass.

I laugh at the nostalgia, then I blush at the sight of Aiden, Tina, and

Evie standing at the living room entrance. He turns and has me facing Sonia, Jim, Izzy, and Bean as the blush burns hot.

Jesus, I was never a blusher before Jon.

Carrying me past a giggling Evie, Tina slaps my ass and has Jon's chest bouncing with soft laughter. Walking out the front door, down the steps, and across the lawn, he moves up Bobby and Kit's front stairs.

The process is repeated, the deep *thump-thump-thump* of Jon's broad fist on the solid timber, then laughter as Bobby opens the door. "Did she agree yet?"

"Three rejections so far, B. She's being stubborn."

"Damn, Tink. Is it shark week or somethin'?"

"Bobby!"

Kit slams her fist against her husband's shoulder. "Don't be so crass. Jesus, Kincaid. And get out of his way. He's trying to propose to my best friend."

"Hey! I thought I was your best friend?"

Ignoring him, Kit steps around Jon's body and stops in front of my dangling head. I groan at her shirt, at my face stretched across her adorable baby-swelled belly. Bringing her hands to cup my cheeks, she leans forward and places a soft kiss on my lips. "Make him work for it, Case. But don't shut him out completely. He loves you, so, so much."

I roll my eyes; my only shield against crying. "He can hear you."

She nods. "He should know what I think. You're my sister, Casey. You've always been my sister. I love you so much, and I want you to be happy. Whatever that choice means for you, I want you to be happy. If it's not with him, then I'll support that, but I hope it is, because he loves you so much. I don't think there's a man on this planet who'll love you more."

Even without seeing his face, I can *feel* Jon's smile. "True story, Sunshine." He slaps my ass, though it's mostly caress and no sting. "Let's go. We have more people to talk to."

Kit's hands fall from my face as he steps forward, then we pass Bobby – who also wears a ridiculous shirt.

Stopping in the middle of the living room, Jon bounces me off his shoulder with a grunt. "Have you been emotional eating, Sunshine? You're heavy."

I punch his shoulder as hard as I can. "You're an asshole, Jon!"

He laughs and rubs his arm. "I'm kidding! Jesus, if I didn't know you so well, *I'd* wonder if it was shark week."

I stop and frown. "You know my cycle?"

He shrugs shyly. "Mostly. You're a bit all over the place with your endo, but I know it mostly. And I *definitely* know it a day out. The whole damn town feels that storm brewing over our heads. That time you blew up at the gas station guy," he laughs. "That day's gone down in history, Sunshine. Our great-great-grandchildren will know the story about how grandma nearly made the dude piss his pants."

I shake my head. "You're seriously the biggest asshole I know."

"Yes, but I'm yours." He leans forward and presses a soft kiss to my lips. "Forever and ever."

"Ms. Irvine."

I spin at the new voice. More power suits. Two more professionally dressed women. One in her mid-forties. The other, easily a decade older.

But they both watch us with kind smiles.

"*Mrs.* Hart." Jon corrects the younger woman.

She meets his eyes with a playful smile. "Of course. *Mrs.* Hart, I'm Catherine Parker." She reaches forward and takes my hand. "I run the fertility clinic across town. Mr. Hart contacted me. He said you're having a little trouble with natural conception. He believes I might be able to help."

Bringing my hand back, I press it to my chest.

"I didn't tell her what happened, Sunshine. I didn't want to violate your privacy. But I Googled a bunch of stuff, and I think Doctor Parker can help us. I know you have your own doctor, but I figure Doctor Parker's a specialist, so maybe she can collaborate with yours or something."

"That's correct," she agrees. "I can meet with your regular doctor and we can discuss your case. I can provide you options for whatever your specific case entails. Whether that be IVF, a round of clomid to help bring on ovulation, whatever we need. Then if that doesn't work, we can discuss surrogacy–"

"I'll carry your baby."

Kit's soft voice has me spinning and tears flooding my eyes.

"Me, too." Izzy takes Kit's hand in hers. "I'll carry your baby."

"Or me," Tina adds. "I'll carry your baby if you want."

"And if that doesn't work," the older woman speaks for the first time. "My name is June Henderson. I represent the Department of Child Worldwide Adoptions. I can help you find the perfect child that needs what you need; a family. We can set up an appointment at your earliest convenience and we can get the ball rolling. I already have proof of your marriage, financial solvency, and career stability. You and Jon make wonderful, stable candidates, and I'd love to help you."

"Jon."

He pulls me against his chest. "My name's Leo, Sunshine. You keep messing it up."

"You want babies with me? *Really*, really?"

He nods and thumbs away my tears. "Really, really. I want you, Case. I want our family. And I want to start today. I've already wasted so much time." Watching me for a moment, his lips pull up into a shy smile.

"Am I breaking you down yet? Because I have a cake baking workshop set up in Jack's place. We have the premiere tickets for the new Star Wars movie in my pocket. Bobby can have Lila Royale here in an hour. Maybe. Probably not, but maybe you can call and say hey to each other."

The silly giggle rolls through my chest. "Jon–"

"I love you, Case. I love you more than anything in the entire world. Even more than I love Sissy."

"Hey!"

He chuckles. "*Way* more than I love her."

"But, Jon–"

Sighing, he shakes his head. *"Leo.* My name is Leo."

"Leo! You really hurt me."

"I know. I know I hurt you, but I'll spend the rest of my life making it up to you. There's no one in this world that makes me happy like you do. I love *you*, Casey. I want *you*."

"But why?"

Shocked, his head snaps back. *"Why?"* He takes my hands in his. "I love you, because you can't sing for shit."

"Hey!" Tina snaps. "Potty mouth!"

He grins. "I'm sorry. But, it's true. I love you because you can't sing, though you try so damn hard. You're like a walking encyclopedia for musical lyrics. Completely useless information, but you retain the hell out of it. I love you because you remind me of a feisty cartoon character, now every time I watch cartoons, I *have* to come looking for you. I love you because we both have outie belly buttons, and because you're a psycho who wouldn't hesitate to lace my cereal if I pi–" He pauses and grins. "If I *peed* you off. I love you because, when you smile, I smile."

My eyes narrow. "Did you just quote Justin Bieber?"

"See!" He laughs. "A walking encyclopedia. But Case, whatever I said, whatever I did, I didn't mean it."

"That's Take That!"

He snickers. "Yeah, it is. I'm on a roll. But Sunshine, you're the closest to heaven that I'll ever be."

I roll my eyes. "That's the Goo Goo Dolls."

He runs his thumb beneath my eyes. "You have my heart, Case. I'm not joking anymore. I can't live without you, not because I have a stupid little boy dependency thing going on, but because you're my other half. You're my soul mate. I know I hurt you. I know I did. But I'll spend the rest of my life fixing it. I know it's not that easy, I know I did damage, but I'd rather spend every single day of the rest of my life arguing with you, than a single day without you."

"Jon." I sigh. "Leo… you told me a million times; you love me like you love Bobby."

"Dude! That's gay as f–"

"I lied, Sunshine. I mean, Bobby's a cool dude, but I love you different. So different, and so much *more*. I love you like I've loved no one else." His hands cup my face. "If you say no again, I won't be moving on. I won't be having babies with anyone else. I'll always want *you*. I'll watch and wait for you to let your walls down, then I'll pounce. Every single time you waver, I'll be there asking again. You're it for me, Case. I've never been so scared of anything in my entire life." His eyes bore into mine meaningfully. "Nothing has ever scared me as much as your rejection does. I can't live without you."

"Leo."

"Do you still love me, Sunshine?"

Weeks, months, *years* of building up those walls, every loving word he tosses out tears them down, brick by brick. I thought I was coming here with a solid foundation, a solid plan to get in and out, but he's cutting me off at every turn.

I've always loved him. I never had a choice.

"But you signed the papers."

Taking the folded documents from his back pocket, he holds them up between us. "These papers?" He rips them to shreds without a second thought. "I signed them to shut you up. I was a hell of a lot more in control of my faculties than you give me credit for, Sunshine. But now, these don't exist. I have no clue what papers you're talking about."

Moving slowly, his fingertips caress the sensitive skin over my collarbone. Hooking the silver chain around his finger, he tugs it from beneath my shirt. "May I?"

Unclasping the chain that's held my wedding band since I got it off, he unthreads the ring and holds it in his palm. Digging his spare hand in his pocket, he reunites his C-3PO with my R2-D2.

I'm not sure we could've picked an uglier set if we tried.

Squeezing his palm closed, I almost wonder if he's trying to forge them together. Taking a deep breath, he drops to his knee. "Casey, I love you. I'll *never* stop loving you. Will you *please* stay married to me? I'll make you happy for the rest of your life, I promise."

He pinches my ring between his fingers and holds it at the tip of my finger. "I can get Darth Vader here if you need? I might even consider Chewy, if you insist."

Tears and laughter roll through my chest. "Are you always going to be this dumb?"

"I'll be anything you want, Casey. Just say yes."

Just like a million times before, he breaks me. My heart is no match for his. "I don't want you to change, Leo. I fell in love with *you*."

"I need your yes, Case. I need your promise. Real best friends make promises, then they keep them. No exceptions."

"What about Bobby?"

"Who?"

I laugh and swipe my free hand over my eyes. "Yes, Leo. I promise. You had me the first time you fell asleep with your head in my lap."

Pushing his ring back into place, he stands and has me arching my neck back to keep him in sight. "You'll marry me?"

I shrug. "Well, I already did. So, I guess now I'll just move the rest of my crap in."

"I've still got your hair straightener in my bathroom."

I laugh and press my forehead to his chest. "I know, Jon. I never expected you'd throw it away."

"I considered strangling you with the cord a few times."

I laugh. "I'm so happy you tore those papers up."

EPILOGUE

*I*t would take a little over three years before we get arrested again, but it's totally worth it.

I've been happily married to my Sunshine for three years, four months, three weeks, and a handful of hours – since we don't know the *exact* time we said I do... the first time.

We still fight. All. The. Damn. Time.

She's just as sassy as ever, maybe even more so, and her cooking might actually be getting worse. But she makes up for it in a million other ways.

I'm still seeing Sonia, though not nearly as often as I used to. And half the time I do go, Casey's right there with me.

I'm not done with Sonia yet. The little boy inside me still needs help talking it out, but it's not a poison inside me anymore. Just a story I'm compelled to tell once a month in an air-conditioned office.

My tattered copy of The King's Courtney... that novel I carried around like it was my bible; I started writing names as soon as I was old enough to copy words.

Almost every single page has notes written in the margins. Names. License numbers. Addresses. Every last detail an illiterate kid could copy from an ID card went into that book, then after Bobby taught me how to read and write, I wrote a hell of a lot more. I wrote descriptions, snaggle teeth, tattoos, receding hairlines. I wrote the things they said to me. The things they did to me.

Even when I was that kid, that hungry, tired, a-little-bit-dead-inside, kid; with Izzy sleeping on my chest, I knew I'd make them pay.

I might've been a scared little boy, but I was wily as shit. It's hardly difficult for a desperate kid to swipe a wallet.

For twenty years, those men went unchecked. They had no clue I was coming for them, but in the months after Casey finally agreed to marry me, *again,* we took everything to the cops, and not only were my parents arrested and sentenced to many, *many* years of prison, but so were a lot of other people.

The punishment felt a little too tame for the crime. Frankly, I was into the running-them-down ideas floating around our dinner table, but the law was the best way. That way, I get to stay on this side of the bars. That way, I get to stay with my bride.

After two full years of unsuccessful fertility treatments, we turned to the adoption process. Our home and hearts are open to any possibility, though adoption isn't overnight, either.

We're on a waiting list, and in the meantime, we'll just live our lives.

In February, the year after my first – *and second* – weddings, Sissy gave birth to a giant baby boy. Over ten pounds of fighter baby muscle.

She was *pissed* at Jim.

Her birth went perfect. No hemorrhaging. No emergency. No NICU. My perfect nephew, James the second, *Jamie,* was born.

He's a boy, he's half Hart, and he's perfect.

I'm in love.

The very next month, Kit gave birth to her own giant boy. Bobby, being the competitive peacock that he is, just *had* to saddle that poor girl with over eleven pounds of big-headed baby.

A month after Jamie was born, a brand-new Bryan Kincaid entered this world. He looks just like the first Bryan. And just like the daddy I kind of adopted, little Bry came out swinging.

After trying for so long, he was the perfect addition to their family.

Unfortunately for Kit, no one told her about that sneaky super-fertility period soon after birth. *Oops!* Ten months after Bry arrived, a little baby girl named Brooklyn came out to introduce herself.

Kit swore she was done after that. In fact, she swore she was getting a divorce. There would be no more babies for her. No more sex, if that's what it took.

Her third baby's due in a couple short months.

Over the following two years, Jim and Bobby *both* went back to the octagon. They won. Because they're show offs. Jimmy *finally* reclaimed that belt that he lost, and the year after that, he defended and kept it.

Bobby defended his title for three straight years, even with a perpetually pregnant wife, and severely broken sleep.

There was no stopping our train.

A year after their wedding, Tina and Aiden conceived their own baby. Tina didn't even have to birth in secret or in a corn field. She had freedom, *and* health insurance that covered obstetrics.

She was finally living the good life.

In July the following year, Evie became the proud big sister to Alexandra Kincaid, then a year after that, to baby Sarah.

Eighteen months after the paperwork was filed, Evie's adoption was settled, she legally became Aiden's daughter, *he* cried like a girl, and *she* got a brand-new last name.

God help him in a few years, because she's getting sassier each and every birthday. Evie's our first Rollin baby, and she's paving the way. Leaving a fiery trail for her sisters and cousins to walk.

In true Kincaid style, she's going *hard*.

Jack turned eighteen, then nineteen, then twenty.

He turns twenty-one in just a few months from now, he already has a manager – his sister – and he's fielding sponsorship deals daily.

Jack *'The Jackhammer'* Reilly is the face of several high-end sports brands, a men's cologne, a sports drink, and much to our disgust, a men's underwear line. Now we get to see his underwear covered junk on busses and bus stops everywhere we go.

His nieces and nephews think it's hilarious – except Evie. She's old enough now to think it's embarrassing.

Jack's been fighting professionally since he turned eighteen.

He was given his first shot at the belt at nineteen, and though he lost *spectacularly*, his first loss ever, he rallied, he trained harder, then he came back this year and brought the belt home.

His girlfriend, Steph, a linguistics major at a college only an hour from home, has been by his side every moment that she could. She's riding the fame train *with* him, and her shyness and quiet nature has kept our boy grounded. Without her, he might be swept away by the flash and glamor, but instead, he's the model sportsman, family man, and role model.

Kit and Bobby did an amazing job helping him grow into the man we always knew he could be.

I'm so proud of my family. Each and every one of them.

No matter what happened to me as a boy, no matter who hurt me, and in turn, who I then hurt in an attempt to keep them away, it was all leading us here; to the alleyway beside the drug store, at eleven o'clock on a Thursday night, halfway through my wife's shift at the club.

Casey was offered that job in the city. Of course she was. She's amazing. But she turned them down with a *thanks, but no thanks.*

Thank God.

She never quit working at the club, but in one of those crazy life cycles, way back when the club was bought out by *some city tycoon* and given the financial boost only a drug syndicate could afford, that tycoon would turn out to be none other than Sean *I-like-to-beat-my-wife-and-daughter* Frankston.

Word on the street, or more accurately, word passed on from the FBI agent that arrested the prick, is that Sean's getting awfully talented at giving head in Supermax.

He nearly killed my sister. The girl I worked so fucking hard to keep safe. She was simply collateral damage in his plan to hurt Tina. But he's not an issue for us anymore, and better yet, he's not an issue for Tina anymore. She's free.

And after the investigation was complete and assets were returned, she was also rich as fuck.

She was scraping peanut butter once upon a time, and now she's sitting pretty.

Karma will always win.

Setting up women's shelters all across the country, Tina funnels every cent the clubs make back into those homes. Like a game of Monopoly, she has her little houses set up all over the board, including a cute cottage on Gordon Street.

She's making a difference.

Laughing, I watch Casey peek around the dark alleyway like she's expecting the cops to jump out at any moment. "Let's just go back into the club, Jon. This is gross."

"No, Sunshine. This is tradition. It *has* to be done this way."

"But it smells out here. The trash is overflowing." She pouts. "I'm pretty sure there's dog poop."

I act as though I'm writing notes. "Enhanced sense of smell. Check. Are your boobs tender?"

"Shut up, Leo! You're annoying me."

"Enhanced moodiness. Check."

Her eyes flash to mine, and I work to keep my smile under control. She might actually kill me today.

Just like I've always known when my girl's period's on the way, I also know she's pregnant right now.

I can *feel* it.

Don't ask me how I know, but I know. Her period's not even due yet, she's not late, but I'll bet my life that it's our turn.

For the first eighteen months of trying, every month, we'd buy out the entire store of pee sticks, we'd hang around our bathroom with shaking hands, and our hearts would tremble with pain every time the test came back negative.

My wife went through eight rounds of IVF, but nothing would stick. Eventually, we stopped testing, and the months her period was late, we even stopped *hoping*.

Her body was fucking with us, and the second we'd smile and maybe just *wonder*, her period would arrive the next day and laugh in our faces.

It's been twelve months since she last tested, but I woke up yesterday with this feeling deep in my stomach.

This is it.

This is our time.

"Just pee, Sunshine. Pretty please? Do it for me."

"I don't wanna do *anything* for you. You annoy me."

I smile. She's not wrong. "Come on. One pee, one stick, then I'll buy you an ice-cream."

Huffing, she snatches a test from my hands and walks to the wall. "I think this is really dumb, Leo. *Stupid, stupid, stupid, stupid.*"

"Shut up, focaccia face, and pee."

"Anyone'd think you have a wee fetish," she grumbles. Lowering and leaning against the dirty brick wall, she moves into a ninety-degree squat and hitches her skirt up.

I don't even pretend like it doesn't turn me on.

"Are you ready for this, Sunshine? This is the first day of the rest of our lives."

"Shut the hell up, Leo! I'm peeing."

Studying her face, I smile when she relaxes into her squat. I bite my lip when she closes her eyes, and I pray I'm not wrong. She's not mad at me. She's scared of the negative. I don't want her to be scared. I don't want to be wrong.

"Ahhh..." Smiling, she lets go and widens her stance when urine slides along the concrete ground.

'Whoop-whoop'.

Jumping at the screaming sirens, I spin as blue and red lights flood the alley and illuminate my wife's lean legs. She springs straight and fixes her skirt, but the sound of heavy boots precedes the blinding flashlight. "Don't run, Hart. Swear to God, I'll chase you down and let my dog rip your dick off."

I groan. "Why're you such an asshole, Turner?"

"Let's go."

"We were just hanging out." Casey slaps my arm as she passes me. "I swear, Alex. We were being good."

"Too bad, Tink. This ain't your first offense."

"Goddamit, Jon! You asshole."

I laugh as Alex Turner cuffs me and my wife, then as he purposely slams my head against the roof of his cruiser. As soon as he's in the car and driving toward the station, I lean toward Casey's pissed off face. "I love you."

"Up yours, Jon."

I laugh and look to the front seat. "Turner. What's the test say?"

"It says shut the fuck up."

"No, seriously. Positive or negative?"

"It says Jon Hart's a pussy bitch who deserves some time in lockup."

I scoff. "Why do you have such a hard on for me? Is it jealousy? Is it because I'm already taken? I have friends who fuck dudes. In prison. I could hook you up."

His jaw grinds back and forth. "Shut it, Hart."

"Is it because I kicked your little brother's ass that time? I mean, seriously, who names their kid Scotch?"

"Alex?" Casey turns on her sex kitten voice and leans forward. *Checkmate.* "Honey, please tell me the result. I want to know, so I can punch my husband in his stupid face."

Alex's eyes meet mine in the rearview mirror, then they flick to Casey's. "Dunno why you settled for this asshole, Tink. My brother's a good man."

She laughs. "Your brother and I were *never* together." She turns to me with scared eyes. "Alex, please tell me what the test says. I need to know."

Sighing, he leans across the passenger seat and picks up the plastic baggie. Despite her outward sass, the nerves pour off my wife. Leaning forward, I place my forehead against hers. "It'll be okay, Sunshine. I promise."

"You promise? *Real* best friends don't break promises."

I press a kiss to her nose. "I promise."

"Well, hey. Lookie here." Alex smiles in the mirror. "I'm no doctor, but looks to me like you got a positive, Tink."

I catch her tears with a kiss. "Told you."

We would find out a few weeks later there are *two* heartbeats in there. My girl carried my twins until thirty-six weeks. That's full term for twins. Despite her size, she carried over twelve pounds of baby Hart in her tiny stomach.

My sunshine gave me my Luke and Leia.

Kidding.

It was two boys, and we named them Luke – of course – and since Bryan was already taken, we named the other Bobby.

Because he's my *other* best friend.

Plus, he bailed us out that night after Alex dropped us in the drunk tank for peeing in the alleyway.

The Rollin On Series continues with Jack's story in **Finding Hope**.

ALSO BY EMILIA FINN

(in reading order)

The Rollin On Series

Finding Home

Finding Victory

Finding Forever

Finding Peace

Finding Redemption

Finding Hope

The Survivor Series

Because of You

Surviving You

Without You

Rewriting You

Always You

Take A Chance On Me

The Checkmate Series

Pawns In The Bishop's Game

Till The Sun Dies

Castling The Rook

Playing For Keeps

Rise Of The King

Sacrifice The Knight

Winner Takes All

Checkmate

Stacked Deck - Rollin On Next Gen

Wildcard

Reshuffle

Game of Hearts

Full House

No Limits

Bluff

Seven Card Stud

Crazy Eights

Eleusis

Dynamite

Busted

Gilded Knights (Rosa Brothers)

Redeeming The Rose

Chasing Fire

Animal Instincts

Inamorata

The Fiera Princess

The Fiera Ruins

The Fiera Reign

Rollin On Novellas

(Do not read before finishing the Rollin On Series)

Begin Again – A Short Story

Written in the Stars – A Short Story

Full Circle – A Short Story

Worth Fighting For – A Bobby & Kit Novella

LOOKING TO CONNECT?

Website
Facebook
Newsletter
Email
The Crew

Did you know you can get a FREE book? Go to emiliafinn.com/signup to get your free copy sent direct to your inbox.

Printed in Great Britain
by Amazon

25341775R00169